The Family

by:

Willie Cordell

iUniverse, Inc.
New York Bloomington

The Family

iUniverse books may be ordered through booksellers or by contacting:

iUniverse
1663 Liberty Drive
Bloomington, IN 47403
www.iuniverse.com
1-800-Authors (1-800-288-4677)

ISBN: 978-1-4401-2174-6 (pbk)
ISBN: 978-1-4401-2176-0 (cloth)
ISBN: 978-1-4401-2175-3 (ebk)

Printed in the United States of America

iUniverse rev. date: 03/02/2009

THE FAMILY

The Family is a fiction story centered on a true family. Circa 1867 1994, the big family begins in Ireland soon after the great potato famine. Reason Marlow the patriot of the family beats himself out a life from an early age. Reason was, forced to leave Ireland with his wife and two daughters. His leaving brought shame and disgrace upon him but he refused to think about it again. His struggles were great while attempting to get his family to America and a new beginning. Little Eliza was two years old when her parent Reason and Louisa Marlow brought her to the new country. Tragedy hits the family while living near a small town in North Florida and Reason lost his beloved Louisa, his only son and seven of his daughters. Only Martha, Eliza, and Ellen, his only living children now left to bury Reason many years later. They overheard their father praying the night he died. A prayer for forgiveness from something terrible he had done. Reason had always been an honorable and Godly man. What could he have done that had forced him on his knees in prayer while he was dying?

The story follows the three sisters, Martha, Eliza, and Ellen and the twisting, turning, unusual, and unforgettable lives that they lived.

The Family: is a fiction, filled with the devastation of real events that real people went through while living through the early years, two world wars, and a depression. With our country coming closer to a likely depression and two wars going on, we may relive many of these times again in our own lifetime. Walk with them through the tragedies, hopes, dreams, and losses that they faced and see how they survived them all.

Willie Burgess Cordell is the author of two previous books: The Long Desperate Road and Caring for your sick at home. Willie spent her adult life working as a Licensed Practical Nurse. She always wanted to write but raising three children and working full time prevented it. Willie survived her name, Willie, and beat the odds in many other ways. She now happily lives with her husband whom she brought home with her from Saudi Arabia in 1985. They live happily together in their own little paradise on the water with its tropical gardens, in central Florida. They have two yorkies named, Haley and Harley. They are both retired and do pretty much what they want to do.

Special Mention

I especially like the link of history (political, economic, and historical) to the themes of the story. And, by introducing inventions, the reader has a perspective of historical time. Another important aspect of this book is reminding us that not everyone had information about culture, history, news, etc, and that the individuals living in this area may have a different worldview than a family living in the north. Nice touch!Primary Editor for First Editing, Jo.

I would like to thank my wonderful husband for always being there for me and encouraging my writing. I love you, Bill. I dedicate this book to my five grandchildren. The proceeds from this book will go toward my grandchildren's education. I love you, Josh, Ben, Lou, Sydney, and Katelyn Parker

Chapter One

Leaving Ireland

As the deck hands slowly lowered the ship's mast, Reason Marlow stood on the deck of the big black ship. Thick fog hung in the early morning air. The smell of salt water and fish permeated Marlow's nostrils. He saw the outline of many buildings on the horizon, both short and tall.

What will this new future bring for me? Will it be a chance to start over again? Maybe I am being too optimistic. Will this country one day be as anxious to get rid of me as my own Ireland had been? Ireland's reason for removing him would always remain his secret. He would never tell anyone. Not even his wife. It would remain buried deep inside him until God called him home.

Ma, Pa and their two daughters had come into Castle Clinton on the ship they had boarded in Ireland. They were coming to the new country and the land of opportunity. Reason Marlow was able to find free passage for the four of them. Reason Marlow were happy to leave Ireland. The country was so poverty stricken that after little Eliza was born, Ma and Pa had had problems just trying to keep her alive. Ma was not getting enough food to eat and her milk dried up. Finding and affording milk for Eliza had proven to be almost impossible. When the country offered free passage to the new country, Pa grabbed for it, or, that is the way Ma saw it.

Ma had collected everything that she could bring with her from their little shanty back in Ireland. She loaded her belongings on to the big boat as they boarded it. She hung old sheets over the wire she had found on the ship and she placed the wire line from wall to wall in one corner of the boat. She threw a throw rug on the floor to protect her family from the dirty floor. It made a perfect little triangle room providing them with a little privacy during their six weeks on the ship. Ma had managed to bring her old rocker along too. She needed it to rock Eliza to sleep each night.

They ate pone bread and buttermilk most of the six weeks on the trip to America. It was not much but it was more than we had in Ireland to eat. Most everyone on the ship had a little money, but Reason Marlow. He had none, not one cent. He knew when he arrived at Castle Clinton he would need some money. However, searching his brain, he still could not figure out where he would get it.

On their second night at sea, Eliza became ill. Ma sat up with her all night rocking her and holding the palm of her warm hand to little Eliza's ear. However, Eliza continued to pull at her left ear while she wailed loudly in pain. Finally, Reason could not stand the painful cries any longer. He arose from the pallet on the floor, reached for his hat hanging on the nail above his head. Reason placed the hat on his head, pulled the corner of the make shift curtain back and walked out of the little private palace.

Reason walked about the ship in the dark with only candle light flickering from the lighted candles along the walls of the ship. He spotted a young widow with two small children in the corner at the far end of the ship. Reason noticed that the young widow was wide-awake while her two young children slept at her side. As he walked the length of the boat, he saw people, young and old, male and female. They were all sleeping on the floors along the walls and in rows throughout the large steerage room of the ship. Everyone was going to the promise land. Most of them were so excited about going to a better place that they paid no attention to the big rats and bugs that crawled along the floor and right over them as they lay sleeping. When Reason Marlow reached the widow with the two small children, she looked up at him with fear showing in her eyes. "I won't harm you. Do you hear the baby at the far end of the ship crying?"

"Yes," the lady said. "Well that's my baby and I'm trying to get away from the crying. She has an ear ache and her painful crying is getting on my nerves." The lady looked down toward the other end of the boat where the sheets hung over the wire. "Is the private little room down there yours?" she asked.

"Yes, my wife is rocking our baby until the pain goes away."

"Can you fix me a private room like yours?" the woman asked. "I have the money and I'll pay you whatever you want," she said. "I have not slept since we boarded this ship," she told Reason.

"Why can't you sleep?" Reason asked.

"My husband died only one week ago. I haven't gotten accustomed to being alone yet and sleeping out in the open like this makes it even harder to sleep."

Hannah did not tell him about the living conditions she had walked out of to get on this dirty ship without decent living conditions. None of that mattered to Hannah any more. All she had wanted was to get away--get close to her mother. Jake was gone and nothing could bring him back. She had given away all of her property to the starving Irish before leaving. Things could not bring Jake back to her. It meant nothing to her without him.

"Do you have a sheet?" Reason asked her.

"Yes," she said as she handed him a sparkling white sheet. Reason knew where the remainder of the wire was that Louisa did not need after she had hung their curtain. He returned to the opposite end of the big open steerage and retrieved the wire. Within a few minutes, Reason had made the widow a privacy area like the one Louisa had prepared for them. The widow was so grateful. She handed him a pound paper piece. "I can't take this. It's too much…I did not do that much," Reason said to her as he handed the pound piece back to her. As much as he needed, the money Reason still could not make himself take it.

"Will you take ten pence?" she asked.

"Yes I'll take ten pence, but I really didn't mind doing it for you, for no pay," he said to her. The widow handed him the ten pence. Reason reached out and took the money from her as he thanked her. Reason turned and started back in the direction of his little, make shift house. The woman yelled at him. Reason turned around and she said to him, "tell your wife to pee in a cup and pour the warm pee into your baby's ear and it will ease the pain."

He stood stunned for a minute. *Is this woman for real*, he thought. "Ok", I'll tell her," Reason said as he walked away.

When Reason arrived at the make shift room he noted that poor Eliza had cried so long that she was very tired. Her cries had changed to long moans as she lay with her little eyes closed. He told Louisa what the widow had said. "I'll try anything," she said as she walked to the edge of the hanging sheet and wrapped it around her. Soon she emerged holding an old enamel cup in her hand. Within minutes, after Louisa had put a few drops of the urine in Eliza's ear, the baby was fast asleep and the moaning was gone.

Little Eliza was still sleeping when Reason, Louisa and Martha awoke the next morning. Everyone moved about very quietly so as not to disturb little Eliza. The cart soon came by with the corn pones and buttermilk. The Marlow family would take their portion with thankfulness. As the little man handed the food to Reason, he told him that it looked like bad weather was coming their way. This concerned Reason. He had his whole family on this

3

ship. Reason appreciated his immediate family more than any one would ever know. He could not think about something terrible happening to any one of them. He quickly ate his corn pone bread and said as he took a drink of his buttermilk, "I'm going on deck to look at the clouds. Louisa, this buttermilk has turned to clabber but it's still good," he added.

When Reason took one look at the clouds, his heart sank. "Captain, what do you think the weather's going to do?"

"Bad son; It's going to do bad things, I'm afraid," the captain said. "Mighty bad, I'm afraid." Reason watched as the big black clouds moved in. The wind was blowing and sprays of salt water were showering the deck of the ship. It sprayed into Reason's mouth and eyes as he stood talking to the captain of the big ship. The captain was a big man. He looked older than his years. He had operated this boat for the last thirty years and had seen more hard times than good times on this ocean. Mr. O'Brien had four wives in his 58 years of life, but he had not been able to hold onto any of them. Within his first year of marriage, his wives had already begun talking about how lonely they had become. They all had wanted him to give up his job as ship captain and get a job that allowed him to be home sometime. However, the sea was in his blood. The only time he felt whole was when he was out to sea and at the helm of his big ship. He loved the old ship. It reminded him of the one Noah had gathered his family and pairs of animals to prepare for the flood. Like Noah's boat, Mr. O'Brien's boat was made of wood but was not nearly as large as Noah's boat probably had been. Mr. O'Brien did not actually own the boat. The Irish government owned the big boat. However, he had always treated it as if it were his own. Reason stood on the deck at long intervals all day watching the weather. The wind continued to blow wickedly and the dark clouds only became darker. By night, Reason was more worried than ever. Now it was dark and he would not be able to see the clouds any longer. God only knew what would happen through the night.

Reason went to the make shift room after darkness fell. "Louisa, I won't be sleeping much tonight. The weather still looks really bad and I will need to stay awake for the safety of all of you." Reason was not an educated man. He had never gone to school. He had never learned to read and write. Louisa herself had no education but she admired her husband's ability to think forward and make plans for an emergency when one might be at hand. None of them had ever starved and that was only because of Reason's wits when push came to shove. Louisa could tell by the tone in Reason's voice that this storm was going to be serious. She got the children down onto their pallets for the night and sat down in the rocker.

Reason was already out of the little room and had gone back onto the deck. Mr. O'Brien stood wrestling at the helm as the waves began cresting over the ship's bow. Reason enjoyed talking to the old man. He was an educated intelligent man and had a university degree in common sense. Nevertheless, Reason knew now was not the time to talk to him. He watched as Mr. O'Brien put his all into controlling the ship's wheel. As the waves became larger and larger and Mr. O'Brien struggled more and more with the wheel, Reason found himself drawn to the old man's side. He grabbed the wheel at one side and began helping with the struggle. As the two men wrestled with the big boat and worried about the safety of all those aboard, the boat was swept almost totally on its side and immediately popped upright again. The sad thing was that they could not see the huge waves approaching until they were almost directly upon them. Suddenly a flash of lightening lit up the entire night sky just above their heads. When the deafening clash of thunder that followed was over, both men had been jolted from the bow to the stern of the boat. They had escaped tossing from the boat and into the churning waters below by only inches. As they pulled themselves up while holding on to the rails to maintain their footing, Reason saw something terrible on the upper deck just behind where they had been standing. A large hole had appeared on the floor and water was flooding into the steerage and onto the passengers packed inside. Smoke was coming from the edges of the large hole. Another large wave swept aboard pouring more water down the big hole and into the deck below. The wood immediately stopped smoking. Mr. O'Brien grabbed the helm and held on tightly to stabilize the ship while swirling aimlessly in the endless siege of waves. Reason ran to the large hole where the ladder once stood, leading to the steerage.

Reason caught the edge of the ragged flooring and swung himself down into the hole. He could not believe his own eyes when he fell into the water below. The curtain in the corner that had served as his family's little cabin was no longer there. Water reached to his waist as he waded across the big open steerage area where he saw people everywhere fighting for their life. Reason saw bodies floating on the surface of the water. Clothes and debris also floated about. However, where was his family? A small child floated by face down. It appeared to be that of a little girl about the age of Eliza. Reason reached out for her but the waves from his moving feet caused the little body to quickly float away. Reason tried again to catch the little body but his feet became tangled in something in the water and he lost his footing and fell head first into the water. When he was able to pull the debris off his feet, he pulled it out of the water and realized he was holding the sheet with the wire that had made their makeshift cabin. Now the little body had floated far away into the darkened deck and he had no clue in which direction it had floated. "Was it Eliza?" he said loudly to himself. In his panic, he began to call for Louisa. His calls for her got louder and louder but Louisa did not respond. The lightning and enormous thunder was still crashing about the water and near the upper deck of the ship. Reason waded through the deep water the full length of the steerage deck as he called for Louisa with every step he made. He heard moaning and groaning about the large room and would occasionally bump into someone who tried to hold onto his legs. There was no way out except the large hole that the lightening had blown out on the upper deck. Finally, Reason would need to give up on finding his family and try to help the others who were still alive. However, he could not find a way out of the four feet of water. He began to take the hands of those reaching for him and led them to the large hole. He would help them up so that they could get a grasp of the open flooring above. The first ones to escape began pulling people through the large hole.

Suddenly Reason saw the widow and her two children for whom he had made the make shift privacy curtain. As he helped her and the children up and through the hole, he asked if she had seen his wife. "No, I am sorry but I haven't seen them." Reason collected and pushed people through the hole for what seemed to be hours, but they were not his family. He knew his family was lying somewhere under the filthy water on the floor of the steerage deck and they were dead. His heart ached and tears flooded his eyes. He had loved his family so much and now they were gone. Now he would have no one at all. When the last living person left the lower deck, Reason went back down into the hole. He started at the end of the large deck and as he felt a body under the water he pulled it up, dragged it to the open hole where there was a little light from the candle's burning near the helm so that the captain could read the maps.

Each time the wind and water put the candles out the captain would light them again. It was imperative that he see what little he could. Now Reason would use the dim light too with the hopes that he would identify his family. For hours, Reason dragged the bodies of children, men and women to the large hole, one at a time, and examined their faces. Now he was down to the last two bodies. None, so far, had been a member of his family. One at the time, Reason pulled the last two bodies to the dim light. They too were not his family. What could have happened to them? I must have missed them somehow. They are under the dirty water somewhere. Reason would talk to the captain and see if he would assign a crew to clean out the lower deck. With shaking hands and weak knees, Reason climbed through the hole and onto the upper deck. The storm was beginning to let up and he could see the sun on the horizon peaking from the dark clouds. The rain was only at a drizzle now. Reason approached the captain to ask for the help. The captain's face showed worry and strain. Reason could tell that he was very tired. Reason walked away and sat down on the quarterdeck where some of the others were sitting. Suddenly it hit him how very tired he was also. Now is not the right time to talk to the captain about cleaning the lower deck. I will wait until the storm is over. I cannot do anything for my family anymore except care for their dead bodies and that can wait. With tears, streaming down his face Reason laid on his side with his feet still on the floor and fell asleep.

When Reason awoke, he realized he had been sleeping for hours. Apparently, the captain had assigned a work crew to clean the deck below. Reason rubbed his tired eyes and looked about. A large crew was inside the cabin with buckets, dippers, and mops. Another crew was rebuilding the ladder and closing the large ragged hole in the floor where the lightening had hit.

Reason thought about his lost family. He pushed a man aside and jumped down the hole to the lower deck where the work crew was busy with the floors and ridding it of the dirty water it still held. Reason did not want this horrifying job. However, even though it hurt he had to find his family. He should have been with them during the storm. He had done an evil thing when he left them to watch the weather. It was his fault that they were all dead now. If he had been there, he knew he would have saved them. Frantically Reason began to dip water. Now that it was day light, he could see the faces better. As Reason and the crew pulled up each dead body, they lifted it through the large hole above and threw the body over board. They had no way to preserve the bodies for another three weeks that it would take to reach New York and they could not keep them on the ship. Reason prayed each time a body was lifted it would not be that of his family. He did not think he could bear seeing his wife and children thrown overboard and into the big ocean where their bodies may be, consumed by sharks or ocean animals.

At last, the removal of the bodies was completed and the floors were free of water. The only thing left standing on the floors was Louisa's rocking chair that she had brought with her from Ireland. Only now, she would not sit in it again. She was gone as well as Martha and baby Eliza. They were gone forever. The heavy waters had probably sucked them through the hole and washed them away during the storm? Reason could not find their bodies in the murky waters. Reason would never know exactly what had happened to them and how they had died. Reason's spirit was gone. How was he going to live without his family? He did not want to go to New York and the New World. He did not want to start another life without his family.

The old man came again pushing his cart with pone bread from the galley. He handed Reason his pone bread and held the jar containing the buttermilk.

"You'll need to get you another cup if you want some buttermilk. There are extra ones in the galley," he said to Reason.

"I don't want any food or drink. All of my family is gone now and I have nothing to live for," Reason said to the old man as he sat on the floor at the place where their little hideaway had once been. His clothes were still wet and he felt cold, lonely, and miserable. No, he did not want any food or drink ever again. He only wanted to sit in the place they had once lived happily and fade away into the depths of emptiness. He had collected Louisa's rocking chair and place it back into the corner. He thought about getting off the floor and sitting in the chair but his misery would not allow him to make a move. In his mind's eye, he could see his two daughters and his wife running happily through a field of wild flowers. This would have been his property in America if things had not gone so dreadfully wrong. They would run to a little cabin where twelve-year-old Martha would knock on the door. He was the only one inside and he would open the door for his family. Only the knocking did not stop. He opened the door again in his mind and no one was there but when he closed it, the tapping began again. The tapping continued for some time. Suddenly it occurred to Reason that he was daydreaming about what might have been. He would need to pull himself out of this state, or his mind might start playing tricks on him. He wanted to die but he did not want to go crazy.

The tapping continued. Reason realized that the tapping was not in his mind. He was hearing an actual tapping. It was a light tapping but where was it coming from? Reason was devastated about his family and could not stir up enough interest in the tapping to try to look into it any more. As he sat on the bare floor that had once held Louisa's throw rug he began to doze off. Before he realized that he had fallen asleep, he was falling sideways and onto the floor. His head fell on to a metal plate about two feet by two feet on the floor. He tried to lift it but it would not move. He had never seen the plate before since the rug had covered it. He left his head there. The tapping was louder. He lifted his left ear off the metal plate and the tapping became faint again. As soon as he laid his head back on the metal plate, the tapping became louder. Reason sat up and began trying to get the metal plate off the floor. He broke all his fingernails off trying to pry them under the tight-fitting plate. He remembered the nail on the wall above his head that he had used to hang his hat before the storm. Reason stood up and began to work the nail until he had finally gotten it loose enough that he could pull it from the wall. He took the nail and tried to jab it under the metal plate with no luck. He tried again. It was impossible. He could not do it. The tapping became louder and more frantic. Reason was determined to get the metal plate out of the floor.

What was making the noise underneath it? He had to find out. He pushed the nail down as close to the edge of the metal as he could, then he took his shoe and gave it a heavy push into the wood flooring. The nail was now under the metal. He took his foot and gave a hard push downward on the nail at the head end. The metal popped up at that spot. Reason grabbed it with his fingers. He was determined not to let it go. He began pushing his fingers under the metal plate. The pain was excruciating as the sharp edge of the metal dug into his fingers. Blood oozed from between each finger but Reason held on. Soon he was able to get his left hand under the metal plate and begin to lift the plate up. It was very heavy and difficult to handle. The heavy plate hinged at the other end. Reason knew he would need to get it high enough so that he could swing it back and onto the floor at that end. The tapping had turned to knocking, but it was dark down below and his eyes needed time to adjust before he could see anything inside the hull. Suddenly a large wood box came into focus. He could reach the box if he placed his whole arm inside the open hatch. It sounds as if the knocking is coming from the box. Reason put his feet into the hole and then allowed himself to drop onto the wood box.

"Reason…Reason, is that you?" he heard his wife call out to him. His heart leapt with joy. "Yes, Louisa it's me!" he said. "Please get us out of here," she said to him. Reason began pulling at the covering on the large wood box. He pulled as hard as he could but it was no use. He could not budge the heavy wood cover. Reason climbed back through the hole and grabbed the first large male he saw. "Please come and help me," he said to him as he dragged the man by the arm and to the opening in the floor. He almost pushed the frightened man through the hole. When Reason followed him and they both stood on the big wood box the man said, "What is this all about? I never had anyone push, pull and shove me the way you have. I hope this is something important."

"It is sir," Reason said to the man. "Please help me get this heavy cover off this big box. I think my family is waiting for me there." It made no sense to the confused man but he began to help Reason with the cover. Together they were finally able to remove the heavy cover from the box. Reason thought he was seeing angels. His wife and two daughters were nestled in layers and layers of soft white fabric. None of them had one drop of water on their clothes. "What are you doing in this box and how did you get here?" Reason said to his wife. The confused helper was standing there waiting for the answer to that question too.

"Reason, did you know that this boat almost turned over?" Louisa said to him.

"Yes I know it turned on its side but then it popped right back up again."

"Yes, you're right; the ship did pop right back up again but not before a metal door opened in the floor above and threw us through the hole and into this box. Then when it popped up again, the lids closed and we were unable to get out. What have you been doing for so long? We thought you would never rescue us," Louisa said.

Louisa was not aware of the horrible things that had happened during the storm. In fact, she probably never even knew there had been a serious storm. Reason was so thankful that his family had not witnessed the awful disaster and all the lives that were lost.

After the two men helped them out of the big box, they examined the soft white material in the big box. "Looks to me like sails for a boat," the man said to Reason.

"Well, whatever it is it provided a soft cushion for my family to fall?" They carefully replaced the heavy wood cover on the box. Finally Reason had his family back together again and they were all healthy and happy. He gave his wife a long kiss while he held her in his arms and thanked God for sparing his family. He kissed his two daughters and told them how worried he had been about them. However, he did not tell them all that had happened while they were in the box.

Reason thanked the man completely from his heart for helping him to retrieve his family.

"I didn't mind at all. I was only concerned about where you were taking me, or shall I say, pushing me." The two men laughed, and then the man said, "We are having a gentlemen's card game tonight. I would be delighted if you would join us." Reason did not want to tell him that his religion did not believe in playing poker; but he gave it a second thought and decided that the man had been too helpful to him for him to decline the invitation. However, he could not play anyway since he had never played poker before and did not know how. Moreover, he had no money to play with anyway. It was too embarrassing to tell him about not knowing how to play so he would just tell him he had no money. That too was embarrassing but he would have to tell him. Reason slipped his hands in his still wet pockets to muster up enough courage to tell him that he was broke and could not play with them when suddenly his fingers hit something cold and hard. He started to pull it out of his pocket when it occurred to him. He still had the ten pence that the widow woman had given him. Reason opened his mouth and it just came out. "Thank you, I would love to join you and your friends tonight."

The man shook hands with him then walked away. "Why did I tell him that I'd play? I don't know how to play cards and certainly can't play poker."

"I don't know why, but you did it. You told him you would play with them tonight. I think you'll need to keep your promise," Louisa said to him. Louisa did not believe in gambling either. She was shocked that Reason would agree to do something as evil as gambling. She made a mental note to pray for Reason that God would forgive him for his future sin.

Reason sat with his family while they talked about the long hours they had spent in the box. He had much more than that to tell, but he would not. He would never let them know the horrors they had escaped.

The bread cart came around and the little man handed the Marlow family their portion of pone bread and clabbered buttermilk. They ate together and afterward Reason thought it was time for him to find the gamblers with who he had promised to play. "I only have the one ten pence. It won't last long since I have no idea what I'm doing and when it's gone I'll be back."
Reason walked around the steerage in search of a group of men huddled together in a card game. He knew one must use cards to play poker and that was the extent of his knowledge on poker. He had deliberately waited so that he would be late arriving at the card game. That way he would be able to watch the game before he actually had to play. Reason searched throughout the lower steerage deck for the card players, but finding them was futile. He decided to climb the ladder to the upper deck and look. Reason quietly walked up on the four men huddled around a make shift table made from crates on the quarterdeck. No one saw him arrive. It gave Reason the perfect opportunity to watch as they played the game. He watched as the man dealt two down cards and one card up, to each player. Then the men put in their bets starting with the man who had the lowest up card. Reason watched as the man dealt three more cards to each player. Each card, dealt face up with bets placed between each card.
I think I have it now, Reason thought to himself. *It will not take me long to lose my ten pence.* He walked closer to the men. The man who had helped him retrieve his family stood up. "Welcome, Welcome Mr...." "Marlow, the name's Reason Marlow", Reason said as he sat down on the floor at the make shift table. One of the men looked at him and said, "It's seven-card stud; that's our game tonight." The man handed Reason the deck of card. "You're our honored guest and you'll be the first dealer." Reason's heart sank to his stomach. Wheels were turning rapidly in his head. He could not allow the men to find that he knew nothing about poker. He reached out and took the deck of cards and under his breath he said, "Lord, I know you don't agree with what I am about to do but please don't let me lose face in front of these men." Suddenly Reason began shuffling the deck of cards and the controlled way the cards moved about in his hands without his dropping one of the cards gave Reason the confidence he needed. He began repeating what he had seen as he approached the men. When it came to raising the bet, Reason did not rightly know what they were talking about so when it became his turn he raised it and threw his ten pence out. When the hand was finished, Reason won all the money on the table.

"How'd that happen?" Reason thought. He did not know but he would repeat the same procedure again, and again he raked all the money from the table and piled it into a pile in front of him on the table at the end of each hand. Reason found himself enjoying playing poker. The five men played until well into the night. Reason announced it was time for him to check on his family. The men decided they would all end the card game and turn in for the night. "We'll play again next week," all the men agreed and all the players left for their sleeping areas. Reason arrived at his family's corner of the steerage with each of his trouser pockets filled with money. He had no idea how much money he had. He had not counted it yet. Louisa had a candle burning in their corner of their little room when Reason arrived. The large grin on his face reached from ear to ear. Louisa looked at him with a questioning look on her face. "What, Reason? Tell me what's on your mind."

"It's not what's on my mind Louisa; rather, it is what's in my pockets," Reason said to her as he began to empty out his pockets and place the large handfuls of money in his wife's lap as she sat in the rocking chair. When he was finished empting, his pockets the pence and pound notes were beginning to fall from Louisa's lap. "I'm telling you Louisa, I think it was the Lord who helped me."

"I don't know Reason; you know how Father Mallory feels about gambling."

"Well, I don't know how Father Mallory feels, but I'm telling you I believe the Lord was on my side all night."

Captain O'Brien knew he was behind in schedule. He would move the ship to full flank for the next few days to try to catch up with his schedule. Reason had noted that the boat was moving at extra speed lately. He hoped it was not bad weather again. *Was the captain trying to outrun the weather again?* Reason climbed the ladder to the upper deck and walked the deck to the helm where Captain O'Brien was handling the wheel. The scene was much different from that of the night of the storm. The worried, uneasy look was gone from the captain's face. He was handling the helm with total ease. Reason walked to the captain's side and before he could speak, the captain said, "I'm glad you came. I need you to do something for me if you will, please."

"Sure, I will do it if I can," Reason answered. "I need you to go back down the ladder to the steerage. In the far corner at this end of the boat, you will find a metal plate in the floor. I need you to get a crew of men to help you to open the metal plate and drop through to the hull floor below. There is a big wood box at the opening and it holds the sails that used to fly from this ship. Several years ago before the ship converted to a steam powered ship, I had the sails stored in the box in the hull so that if I should ever need them again, I would have them. I need you to bring me the sails. I have picked up full speed to make up for lost time and if the steam engine fails, I want to have the sails ready to put up immediately. The wind is right and the sails will carry us on into the New York harbor with no trouble if we need them."

Reason never told the captain that he knew all about the metal plate and the big wood box. He just responded, "Yes sir," turned and climbed back down the ladder. Reason got the same man who had helped him the first time. Reason had stuck the nail he had used back into the wall. He reached up and plucked the nail out of the wall. The two men tried with all their strength but could not budge the metal plate. They had to collect two more strong men for the job that only two of them had done before. "But we were doing it under great stress," The man said to Reason as both men had a good laugh.

Every few nights the men met for the poker games. By now, Reason was well adapted to the game and always did well. Sometimes Reason felt that he had his own angel sitting on his shoulder. It was as if he could do nothing wrong. Every hand included more good cards more than bad ones. The money kept mounting up and by now Reason had enough money to pay for about anything he needed when they reached New York. While the men sat at their make shift table on the quarterdeck with the poker game in full force, John complained that he smelled burning rubber. After the other four men began to smell it as well, the five of them put the game on hold and began walking around the ship deck. Reason asked Mr. O'Brien if he smelled the burning odor that they had smelled.

"No, sorry, but I don't smell it," he said. The smell continued and it befuddled the men that they could not discover the source of the burning smell. Suddenly the ship gave an enormous lunge forward and then began to slow. Then, it continued lunging dangerously and then the speed began to slow. The card game was over with the cards strewn about the floor of the deck. Reason had already picked up the money that he had won. Finally, the source of the smoke was obvious. Large puffs of black smoke began jetting out from under the bow of the boat. Two men from the boiler room came running to the captain.

"Sir, the boiler room is on fire and we can't get the fire out!" The five men overheard the distraught boiler room worker and started at a trot to the boiler room. All the men worked transporting buckets of water—most of them with two buckets at a time. They threw the water on the blazing equipment until the fire was out. Now the boat was at a standstill in the water. "Now hear this, all men on deck," the captain yelled. All the men did as the captain ordered. As they stood before the captain he said, "I need all these sails strung. We'll go back to a sail boat while the men work on the broken engine." The sails lay in many layers, just as they were at the boats christened in 1837. Captain O'Brien enjoyed sailing the boat. It had never been the same since the steam power had taken place of the sails. However, the powered engine was much faster than the sails, especially when the winds were blowing against him. Now the winds were blowing just right and it was a pleasure for the captain to sail the ship on to New York .With the wind cooperating, Captain O'Brien felt that the ship would arrive on schedule into New York Harbor.

Food was getting scarce on the ship and the water was stale with not much remaining in the vat. It had rained only three times since they had left Ireland except for the storm. There was no hope of collecting water that night. Everything was in total chaos and catching water was the last thing on anyone's mind at the time. Louisa tried to give her girls the whey off the clabber for water. She hated not having available clean water for her girls.

The ship would be arriving at Castle Clinton in two days. Everyone was getting anxious. Louisa was especially grateful. She longed to breathe clean fresh air. After the flood, the steerage was even dirtier and the odor was almost unbearable. Mold and mildew was growing on the walls and ceiling. Little Eliza had developed a cough and Louisa felt sure the cause was from the environment they were living in. She had climbed the ladder a few times and carried Eliza on deck for some fresh air but it was truly improper for her since no other women went on deck where the men hung out and played cards. Since the flood, there were more men on the ship than there were women. Most of the women and children had died in the flood.

As the sun went down and darkness closed in around them, the men standing on the upper deck could see harbor lights in the far distance. They were small and faint but it was definitely signs of land. Reason made two steps down the ladder and jumped the rest of the way to the floor below, "Louisa, Louisa we can see land," he yelled before he arrived at their little corner.

"By God; land lays ahead. It is in sight. We will be departing this ship tomorrow. We'll put foot on the promise land; finally." Louisa felt the excitement in her husband's voice. "How do you know?" she asked as she jumped from the rocking chair to her feet." "I can see the harbor lights already," Reason answered. Reason and Louisa came together in a long hug in celebration of their good fortune. It looks like they were going to make it after all.

The next day just before lunch, the big boat pulled into Castle Clinton at the battery in New York. They were not able to sail into dock so the captain anchored the ship near the shore and small boats came from shore to collect them from the sail ship. No one was happier to depart the dirty smelly ship than Martha was. She decided upon departure that she would never get on another boat in all her life.

As Reason and his family were walking down the gangplank, someone ran into Reason's back. He looked behind him and saw the widow running down the gangplank and reaching for her little boy who had lost his footing and had run into Reason. "I'm sorry," she said as she grabbed her son's hand and pulled him back.

"No problem," Reason said. "It's good to see you. Louisa this is the lady who healed Eliza's ear ache that night."

"It's good to meet you," Louisa said. "And the treatment worked well on my baby's ear ache." Everyone hurried on down the gangplank.

As they reached ground, Reason yelled over his shoulder to the widow. "If we can help you in any way, please let us know."

"OK," Hannah yelled back at him. "Thank you."

Reason and Louisa had no idea where they would live in the United States. They did not even know what the names of the states were or where they were located. It really did not matter to them, just as long as they would be Americans from now on. They waited in the holding area until their names was called. The widow and her two children waited there too. Reason noticed that she was apparently reading the papers dotted about the walls. He wished he or Louisa could read. Perhaps some of the signs told about places in America to live. "Pardon me, but are you reading the notices on the walls?" Reason asked her.

"Yes, would you like me to read them to you?" Hannah knew that Reason could not read or write but she was surprised that his wife could not read or write either. Most boys got very little schooling in Ireland, since boys had to work on the farm to help earn a living but the girls usually learned to read and write from their mothers. She would be happy to help them. She knew that they were embarrassed about it but she knew how to handle it to make them feel better.

Hannah began reading aloud. Reason and Eliza came to her side and stood quietly beside her as she read the posters on the walls.

"Live in Florida where it is warm all the time. Florida is deeding land and a mule to those who choose to live there and farm the land deeded to them," Hannah read. "Go to the court house in any county in Florida and apply for your sixty acres." Hannah went on reading. There were more posters for free land in other states but none attracted Reason and Louisa as much as the one about Florida. The map drawn on the poster showed they would need to go directly south and a little west and they would arrive in Florida. The poster said it would take about 20 days by horse pulled wagons to arrive in Florida. "That's where we'll live," Reason Marlow said. "We'll live in Florida."

"But where in Florida, will we live?" Louisa asked.

"That, I don't know." Reason said.

Florida was the oldest part of the United States. People first reached Florida about 12,000 years ago. Of course, the landscape was much different then. Florida was twice its size. Through thousands of years of the Atlantic

Ocean and the Gulf of Mexico rising from melting glaciers Florida gradually decreased in size. Spanish explorer Juan Ponce de Leon started keeping written records of the peninsula in 1513. However, long before Ponce de Leon's arrival to the peninsula of Florida, native societies developed cultivated agriculture and traded with other groups in what is now southeastern United States. Spain finally ceded Florida to the United States in 1821. At that time Florida was a wilderness sparsely dotted with settlements of native Indian people, (Seminoles), African Americans and Spaniards. The African American had fled slavery in other states and had come to Florida. Florida offered a safe place for runaway slaves as well as the ones who chose Florida to live after slavery ended. By 1840, white Floridians were concentrating on developing the territory and gaining statehood and by 1845; Florida became the twenty-seventh state. Florida was a Republican state and had fought for freedom from slavery since its beginning.

One of the posters Hannah read to them mentioned Madison County Florida. It read, "Farming is great in Madison County and the land is fertile for growing cotton, vegetables and tobacco." This appealed to Reason. He looked on the map to find where Madison County was. Hannah pointed it out for him. Reason placed an X on Madison County.

When the immigration clerk called the Marlow family, they all went to the table pointed out to them. After all the paper work was completed, Reason and Louisa placed their X on the line pointed out to them. Now they were full-fledged Americans. What a good feeling to know they were now citizens of the most prosperous country in the world.

One of the workers at the table told Reason about a place nearby where he may be able to purchase a covered wagon and two horses to make the trip to Madison County, Florida. It was a wonderful feeling for Reason to be able to go to the livery stable and make his purchase without worrying about the cost. However, he would be careful with his money since he would need money to get started with his homestead when he arrived in Madison County.

As the merchant was harnessing the horses to the wagon Reason had bought he said to him. "Are you riding with the wagon train that is due to leave in the morning for Florida?"

"I don't know anything about a wagon train that is leaving," Reason said.

"Well you'll need to get with them for traveling that distance because it's better to travel in a group," he said to Reason.

"Why's that?" Reason asked. There are renegade Indians every now and then that you may run into, and there are always carpet baggers."

"How will I find the wagon master for the trip?" Reason asked. "I have one of his horses over there by the gate. He needs new shoes."

"When do you expect him back for his horse?"

"I told him he'd be shoed by late this afternoon."

"I'll come back a little later then." Reason told him as he motioned for his family to follow him. "We'll need to find a hotel for tonight, Louisa." This excited Louisa and Martha. They had never been in a hotel before. In fact, none of them had ever been in a hotel before. Louisa could not believe their good fortune. Not only did they have money but also they had enough that they would not need to sit in the processing room all night on their first night in America and instead would be staying in a nice clean comfortable hotel.

However after Reason had gotten them a room in the Westminster Hotel and had carried his family inside their room. Louisa was not happy about what she saw. The walls and ceilings looked like the boat they had arrived in New York harbor, on. Mold and mildew was everywhere including the floors. The cot size beds sunk in the center as if they were oblong bowls. The linens and pillows were so dirty Louisa was sure they had never been in a washtub and had been in use for at least six to eight months. Oh well they are better that what we had on the ship, Louisa thought. The Marlow family was so tired and sleepy.

They ate the cheese and bread that Reason had gone out and purchased from a local market. After they had washed it down with water from the hotel, they were ready for their sunken cots. Everyone except Reason went to bed. Reason went back to the livery stable in hopes of finding the wagon master who would direct their covered wagon to Madison County Florida.

When Reason arrived at the livery stable, he found the wagon master talking to the owner of the livery stable about his horse. "So Charlie, now that you've changed all my horses' shoes, you suppose they will make it to Florida with no trouble?"

"I can promise you that you'll have no hoof problems with any of your horses." The merchant said. Reason stepped up to the man and said, "now that you have your horse problem solved, may I present you with another one?"

"Well I'm not anxious to collect myself a problem but if I can be of any help to you I'll try."

"I understand that you'll be leading a group of wagons and immigrants to the new state of Florida," Reason said.

"You understand right—we will be leaving at first light tomorrow morning. If you want to join us, be here promptly at first light and get in line." Reason reached out and shook hands with the new wagon master.

"My family and I will be here before day break." On his way back to the hotel, it hit him how very tired he was. No matter what the bed looked like it would feel good to him, he was sure.

Reason was counting his many blessings when he arrived at the hotel. There were only candles glowing on the front porch and no light was showing from inside the hotel. It appeared quiet and peaceful. Just what Reason needed? However, when he opened the door and walked into the hallway he heard a hell of a fight going on at the end of the hotel. "What is going on there," Reason said to himself. "I will never get any sleep if that is going to be happening all night." Reason decided he needed to check it out before going into his room for the night. As he got closer to the end of the hall, the noise got louder. When he arrived at the end of the hall, he realized the noise was coming from a cellar. He followed the steps down into the cellar. Four drunken men were sitting around a table with playing cards on the table.

One of them looked up as he entered the room and in slurred speech he said, "Howdy mister, we're playing seven-card stud and these fellows don't know how to play the game. Can you come and settle this argument?" Reason started to tell the men that he did not know anything about seven-card stud, but he felt it would be a sin since he had learned it in an emergency and with God's help had learned it well.

"What do you want to know?"

One of the men started trying to tell him where they were having the misunderstanding but he kept getting confused. Finally, the man said, "Here, you take the cards and play with us and when we get to the place they don't understand I'll tell you." Playing poker was the last thing Reason wanted to do tonight.

"Sorry fellows but I have to turn in. I'm leaving for Florida tomorrow," Reason told them.

"Ah, come on, play with us. We've got plenty of money and if you win you take the money." Then the other three chimed in. They all begged like little boys for Reason to play with them. Finally, Reason agreed to play a few hands. Reason took the cards and dealt two cards to each player downward then he dealt one card to each one upward.

Suddenly one of the men yelled, "That's it, that's what I told them to do but they said it was one card down and two up." The other men were not interested in pursuing the argument. They were happy with the cards they had just received and they wanted to get on with the game.

Every game Reason raked the money off the table and into his pockets. Reason kept telling the men that they should wait until they were sober to play poker.

"No, let's play another hand; I'm getting better at this," one of them said. Reason learned that they were railroad workers and were putting down new train tracks in New York before they moved on to some place else. "We want to learn this game well so that we can beat the others when we play with them," one of them said to Reason.

"I think you are paying a big price just to learn the game," Reason told them.

"Mister, we don't have nothing else to spend our money on and we want to learn this game. We'd rather pay an honest man to teach us than to play with a crook and not know when he's cheating us." That made sense to Reason.

Just before daybreak, Reason went to the hotel room with thousands of dollars in his pockets. Louisa was worried and angry. "Where have you been?" she asked him. Reason told her about the drunken men and the card games. Then he showed her the big pile of money he had won.

She was not impressed. "By midday today you'll wish you could trade all that money for just an hour's rest," Louisa told him as she got out of bed. Louisa trotted down the hall to the shared bathroom. The water was pumped by a hydraulic ram and using the pressure of running water from a flowing stream behind the hotel. The water was stored in cisterns in the attic. Louisa loved the tepid water shower while she stood in a large round galvanized tub used for catching the used bath water. When she was finished, she picked up the thick homespun towel lying across the arm of a chair. She did not remember ever feeling this clean before. She hoped she would one day have a shower bath in her house like this one.

Now, if Louisa just had clean clothes to wear. However, there was no hope of that since she had none and there was no time to wash clothes. She made herself feel better by thinking how dirty the trip to Florida would be with the long line of covered wagons. She supposed somewhere along the way they would find a river or lake where they might get a bath. She hoped so.

When the Marlow family arrived at the livery stable with all their belongings, everyone appeared to be there. A simple dressed woman approached Louisa. She told Louisa, "My name is Lunell Green. My family and I will be traveling with the wagon train also. We decided to go to Florida too."

That was good news to Louisa. She knew there would be at least one other woman on the trail with her. "I'm happy you'll be going. Do you know where you'll be settling in Florida?" Louisa asked.

"No, not yet and it's not written in stone that I'll live in Florida. If we go through a place that I think I might like I'll stop there."

The wagon master stood on his wagon and called loudly for everyone's attention, "We are going to be late leaving this morning. When I went to the general store this morning to get the last of the supplies for the chuck wagon, the merchant said his flour would not be arriving until 10:30 this morning. We will need to wait for the flour to arrive before we can leave since the cook will need it almost every meal. If you have not paid your travel fee, you need to see me within the next 30 minutes. The others can go about your business until 10:30 but you are to be here promptly at 10:30." Reason was never so happy to hear good news. He had already paid his fees and he knew immediately how he would spend the next four hours. "Louisa, I am going to hire a coach to carry you to a store where they sell dresses and you and the girls can gather you some new clothes while you wait."

Louisa loved the idea. Maybe she would wear clean clothes after all. Reason took a hand full of dollar bills from his pocket and handed it to her. He walked away and within minutes, he returned with the hired coach. He helped the girls inside the buggy and told the driver where they wanted to go. The driver gave a quick movement of his reins and they were on their way. Reason watched them pull away from the livery stable. When they were out of sight, he sprinted to the covered wagon he had bought for the trip. The two horses were harnessed and ready to go but Reason said whoa, whoa to the horses as he climbed up the front wheel and scooted into the covered wagon. He took his hat off and used it for a pillow. Just before his eyes closed in a most peaceful sleep, he looked up at the roof of the wagon and said, "Thank You Lord, for giving me this wonderful chance". Then he was asleep.

The coach driver took the girls to a big general store. "Yes, we have some ready-made dresses but we have many bolts of good material if you prefer to make your own," The store merchant said to Louisa.

"No thanks, we're not in a position to make our own now." Louisa found some full-skirted ankle length cotton dresses for herself and Martha. Then she shopped for Eliza. Eliza, only two years old did not want to shop for dresses. She was too busy looking at other things in the big store. However, her mother collected her several little dresses as well as pantaloons and petticoats for all of them. When they were finished shopping, they found the driver waiting in front of the mercantile store, for them. The four hours had passed so fast and the girls enjoyed every minute of it. They had never been shopping before now. Louisa hoped the clerk was honest since she knew nothing about American currency and she did not know how to count either. She had handed him all of the money that Reason had given her. The clerk had taken what she owed him and handed the rest of the money back to her. It seemed that he did not take very much at all. However, she trusted that he took all that was due him.

When the women returned to the livery stable with their bundles of goods, the trail master was loading flour onto a covered wagon. The wagon had two number two tubs attached to the back. Louisa learned this would be the cook's wagon where all their food would be prepared. Louisa found Reason still in the covered wagon asleep. He awoke when the women arrived with their packages rolled up in brown paper and held together with tan twine. Little Eliza began telling her Pa about her new dresses. She wanted to try them on. "Eliza why do you want to put the new clothes on now when I could not get you to try them on in the store before we bought them. I hope they fit. But no, you can't try them on now; we're about to leave with the wagon train." Eliza begged but Louisa held firm and refused to allow Eliza to try her new frocks

"Ma, I wane put them on now...now...now." Eliza begged but Louisa held firm and refused to allow Eliza to try on her new dresses.

Soon everyone was loaded into his own covered wagon and with the master; in front the twelve wagons were on their way to Florida. Second in line was the chuck wagon and third was the Marlow family. Almost everyone was an immigrant. Some had come from England and some from Scotland, but all of them were from Great Brittan. The Marlow's and the Green's with their two children were the only ones from Ireland.

Chapter Two

America

Reason and Louisa had watched as a beautiful carriage with a uniformed driver and a pretty woman in the coach pulled up to the battery. They had waved as their good friend Hannah and her children climbed into the carriage, while the woman inside the coach squealed with glee as each of them entered the carriage. Hannah fell into her mother's arms as she wept allowing all the grief, fear, and relief flow from her.

After they arrived at Molly's beautiful large apartment in downtown New York City, Molly showed each to their room and then she and Hannah sat down for a long talk and reminisced about the past, and the many years that had gone by.

Hannah was a beautiful girl with long blond curls. Her big blue eyes sparkled with tears as she told her mother about the fire and the night Jake and his mother had died.

Jake's father had been a wealthy man. He had owned the only tavern in the little village they lived in. Work was slow and hard to find and all the village men gathered at the pub to discuss the hard times and where they may be hiring this week. They sat there all day and drank since there was nothing else to do. Finally, they would find enough work to get them through another week and the routine repeated itself all over again. It was like three steps forward and two steps back but it was enough to make Jake's family a good living.

One morning Nate got out of bed. He had been concerned that Arlie was drinking too much. While Arlie still slept, Nate decided to search the house for brandy that she may have stashed away. To his dismay, he found bottles everywhere, behind all the cabinets, behind the furniture, buried in the ground just outside the front and back doors. His worst nightmare had come true. Arlie was indeed a dreaded alcoholic. Their only child, Jake, was twelve years old but she could no longer be responsible for raising him.

When Nate approached Arlie with her problem and what he intended to do about it she became infuriated. "You're not taking my son to work with you every day. I need him here to help me," she yelled at Nate.
"You have a maid to help you Arlie; you don't need Jake." Arlie continued to yell abusive words at Nate while he paid her no attention. He was busy pouring out the brandy.

She grabbed Jake by the arm and pulled at him. "Tell him you're not going with him, Jake." Jake began to weep. "You're no boy; you're just a wimpy little girl," she said to Jake. "You'll never be a man, go on, and go with your dad. I don't want you here anyway."

Jake's mother went into her bedroom and slammed the door. In tears, Jake collected the only thing he owned that meant anything to him. He grabbed his little wooden box that his granddad had made for him before he died. Jake had placed his granddad's pocket watch inside the box alongside his pocketknife. His granddad had given Jake the watch and knife just before he died. The box also contained some of his favorite marbles. Jake left with his father for work that morning carrying his box and nothing else. Day after day Jake went with his father to work. He could never understand what difference it made if he watched his drunken mother all day or a bunch of drunken men all day. He felt his having to go to the pub everyday was more his dad's way of punishing his mom than to protect him from drunkenness. Jake kept his small wood box close to him most of the time. Remembering his granddad brought him comfort.

Jake and his dad started staying later and later at the pub. It was obvious that Nate did not like going home any longer nor did he want Jake to go home either. Jake watched as his dad's health declined. His clothes were usually dirty and he never took baths anymore. If only Jake could help him, but he did not know what to do. Jake missed his mother too. Even though she drank to heavily and was sometimes mean to him, he still loved her and wanted to see her. Tonight, when his dad finally went to sleep on his cot at the rear of the pub, Jake planned to ease out of his cot and sneak to the house just to see if his mother was all right. He would hurry and return before his dad ever knew he had gone to visit his mother. He knew it would not be all right with his father for him to visit his mother. He could not understand why but he knew his father would be against it.

Jake quietly climbed out of his cot and without putting his shoes on; he quietly opened the back door and crept outside. His father did not move so he was sure he did not awake him. After he was outside and at the front of the pub, he sat on a bench that his father had placed there many years ago. He slipped his shoes on then tied them securely. He ran all the way to his mother's home. His attempts to enter the house through the door were unsuccessful. His mother had locked the door. He pushed on the parlor window. It slowly opened. He quietly climbed into the house through the window.

He quietly and slowly went to his mother's bedroom. She appeared sleeping. Now he was satisfied. His mother was all right. He had seen for himself and that is all he wanted. As he turned to walk out of her bedroom Jake's mother abruptly sat up in bed and began yelling foul, mean, and threatening things to him. "You little brat, you thought you could just walk right into my house and I'd never catch you. I heard you when you climbed in the window. I should have gotten my shotgun and blown you all the way back to the tavern. You walked out on me just as your old daddy did. Well you can stay gone. Don't come snooping around here again or I will have the shot gun waiting for you when you get here." As Jake was backing out the bedroom door with tears rolling down his face, his mother started yelling, "I hate you, I hate you." Jake ran back to the tavern as fast as he could but he could still hear his mother yelling, "I hate you," long after he reached the tavern.

Jake was too upset to take his shoes off before entering the back door again where his dad lay sleeping. He would be as quiet as he could. When Jake entered the back door light flooded over him as it came from inside the bedroom. *"That's strange. Dad must have awakened and now he knows I had left the tavern,"* Jake thought to himself. Jake turned around and started to run back out the door. He could not take anymore-verbal abuse tonight. As he hurried back out the door, he stopped dead in his tracks. "Why is dad not yelling at me? Surly he knows I came in the door. Jake turned around and slowly crept into the back door again. He looked at his dad's cot and his dad was not there. Now Jake was confused. Where was his father? Had he awakened and found him gone and had gone to look for him? On the other hand, had he been awake and followed him to his mother's house. Did he hear the awful things his mother had said to him? Jake hoped he had not.

After a thorough search of the bedroom, he knew his dad was not there. He lit a candle and went into the tavern. Something white came into view but he was too far away with the candle to tell what it was. As Jake got closer to the swinging object, he realized it was his dad hanging by the neck. He was dressed only in his union suit. The color of his face matched that of his white union suit. Suddenly Jake realized what he was seeing. His father hanged himself. His father was hanging from the rafter by a rope and he was dead. "Oh my God!" Jake yelled as he started pulling at his father's legs. "Please God, don't let him be dead," Jake pleaded as he looked for a chair to climb up to the rope. Jake felt for a nearby chair. He felt a need to keep one hand on his father's leg to protect him. His fingertips felt a chair but it was too far away to get a grip on it. Still holding to his dad's leg, he reached out with his left leg. He hooked the chair leg around his foot and pulled the chair to him. In a flash, Jake was standing in the chair when he realized he had nothing to cut the rope. He pulled at the knot. Big tears streamed down his face as he realized he would need to turn his dad's leg loose, get off the chair, and get a knife. As he jumped from the chair, his right foot landed on something hard and he almost lost his balance. Jake reached down, picked it up, and looked at it. He realized that he should use this knife to cut down his father. With the knife clinched tightly in his right hand he jumped back up on the chair. As Jake moved the knife to the rope, he saw something dark on the knife. As he touched it, he found it was wet.

Jake held his father's body up as best as he could while he cut the rope. He did not want his father to fall to the floor. Maybe he was still alive and Jake did not want to hurt him by allowing him to fall. As the tears almost blinded him Jake slowly, lay his father onto the tavern floor. Nate's body felt stiff and cold to Jake. His eyes were open and staring at Jake with a sole crushing look of sadness. Jake picked his father's head and chest up and placed him in his arms while he pleaded with him, "please come back to me." Jake sat on the floor rocking his father back and forth while he held him tight and told him how much he loved him.

However, Nate did not come back. When Jake finally let Nate go, he saw the dark wet liquid on his dad's chest and on his own chest. Jake sat there with his dad until daybreak and the light began to pour into the windows. He realized the dark liquid was blood. He opened his dad's union suit at the chest area and there he found a stab wound in the center of his chest. Jake knew that his dad was determined to die since he had readied himself for the hanging and then had stabbed himself before he let himself drop.

Why did he want to die? Jake thought his dad might have awakened and knew that Jake had gone to visit his mother and that is what caused him to do it. Maybe he was tired of him and just wanted to get away from him. Jake was still sitting on the floor beside his dad while the tears ran freely down his face as he tried to figure out why his dad would want to do something so horrific to himself. He felt sure; somehow, it was his own fault. He wished he had never been born. He had caused so much trouble for both his parents in his short lifetime that each of them had given up on life.

Jake was still sitting on the floor with his father when the first customer came to the tavern for a drink. The customer knocked on the door since it was not open for business as usual. He gave it a push but the door still would not open. Jack did not realize someone was knocking on the door. Jake filled with sorrow, could not believe that the whole world had not stopped too. The old man could see Jake and Nate through the window on the floor of the tavern. He could not tell what they were doing but something looked strange about the way they appeared on the floor. He went to the side door and walked inside the opened door. "What's going on mates?" the old man said. Jake was so engrossed with his own thoughts that he still did not hear the customer.

Suddenly the customer realized Nate was dead. He saw the rope still tied around Nate's neck and the other half hanging from the rafter above. However, the blood was a mystery. How could someone hang himself and stab himself at the same time. Something was strange about that picture. The old man never said another word. He quietly walked out the side door at the rear of the building.

"I'm telling you sheriff, there's foul play there somehow. Nate could not have hanged himself and stabbed himself at the same time. I think that son has just lost his mind and went and done something crazy. You need to go now and check this out. The boy is just sitting on the floor beside Nate and staring into space. I was all over the room and I'm telling you sheriff, he never even knew I was there."

"That's my job Luther, that's what I'm hired to do. I'll go and check it out."

Sheriff Buford preferred to do his investigations alone but it was obvious that Luther would be overseeing everything the sheriff did today. The sheriff had already started his day and was sitting at his desk having a cup of coffee when Luther rushed in. He stood up from his desk, reached for his gun belt with his gun in the attached holster, and fastened it around his waist. He put his full-brimmed hat on and with his cup of coffee in his hand; he left his office with Luther right behind him.

The sheriff walked to the backside door with Luther at his side and together they walked in. Jake was still sitting on the floor beside his dead father. He was covering his face with his hands and the two men could hear the blood curdling cries coming from Jake, "I killed you, dad. I am so sorry but I had to do it. I killed you; I killed you. It's my own fault." The sheriff took out a pad and wrote something then attempted to get Jake to his feet. Jake kept on crying and repeating those words over, and over. Together the two men finally got Jake to his feet. Sheriff Buford hand cuffed Jake and carried him away to jail. Jake never resisted. Jake did not realize the sheriff was taking him away nor did he know where he was taking him. He did not care. Right now, he did not care about anything but his dead father. If only he had not gone to the house. He should have known it would be too much for his father at a time when he was so frail. If his father he had not awakened and found him gone. He knew where he had gone. It was the last place his dad would have wanted him to go.

"I knew that. Why did I go?" Jake kept asking himself that question over, and over. He had killed Nate as certainly, as if he had slashed his throat and then hung him with the rope—just as if he had physically done it himself. It still had not registered with him that he was sitting in jail and had been booked with murder.

The next morning when Jake awoke, he found himself lying on a hard wood bench where he had been lead like a lamb going to slaughter the day before. Reality slowly set in. *Where am I? Why am I here? How did I get here? Who is at the tavern? Are customers waiting?*

Suddenly it all came flooding back. Somehow, he already knew his dad was dead and he had been the cause of his death. However, he could not remember exactly how he was responsible. He remembered quietly leaving the tavern and visiting his mother. He remembered very well all the hateful things she had said to him.

Someone showed up at the closed metal bars, which now served as his cell, with a tray of food. "Where am I and why did they bring me here?" Jake asked the food server.

"Buddy you're in jail. The sheriff brought you here yesterday because you murdered your father."

It took a minute for the man's words to sink in for Jake. "I didn't kill my father," he said. The man said nothing. He placed the tray of food on the wood bench and turned to walk out the open door made of metal bars. Jake jumped up and grabbed the man's arm. "Did you hear me? I didn't kill my dad," Jake said anxiously.

"Yeah, yeah, yeah, that's what they all say the day after," the police officer said to Jake.

"You've got to listen to me. I didn't kill my father," Jake said.

"Well you'll probably need to tell that to the jury who judges you," the officer said as he walked out the big heavy door and slammed it behind him.

"Send the sheriff in here, please," Jake yelled to him. The man kept on walking as if he had not heard a word Jake had said. Jake stood at the closed door waiting and watching for the sheriff. After an hour of waiting, Jake sat down on the bench. The cold food tray was still sitting on the bench. He looked at the food. There was a boiled egg, some fried fatback, and some grits with lumps. Jake sat the tray on the floor without touching the food. Even if he was hungry, he could not eat this food.

"Why do they think I killed him?" Jake said quietly to himself. "I need to get this straightened out." Jake did not want anyone accusing him of killing his own dad. It eluded him that they could even think such a thing. Jake lay on the bench trying to figure it out. He could barely remember coming here yesterday. He was trying to remember the man who had brought him here when suddenly the man showed up at the metal door.

"Well," the big man at the doorway said, "Are you ready to talk now?" he said to Jake.

"Talk about what sir?" Jake said. "Are you ready to tell me why you killed your father?" the sheriff said.

"I didn't kill my father. How can you even think that I killed my father?" Jake said.

"Because you said you did and I believed you."

"I have never said I killed my father. I love my father. He killed himself. I don't know why he did it but he did," Jake told the sheriff. "So...You're changing your story now--for what reason?"

"I'm not changing my story. I did not kill him," Jake said.

"Then, son," the sheriff said, "you've got a lot of explaining to do." The sheriff walked away.

"Come back sheriff. I swear to you I did not kill my dad."

Days rolled into weeks and Jake still sat in jail. He could not find out what had happened to his dad or what was happening to the tavern. No one would tell him anything.

Chapter Three

Jake's Awakening

Soon after taking Jake his awful tray of food at lunchtime the deputy returned to his cell. "You have a visitor. Do you want to see him now or do you want to finish your food first?" he said to Jake.

"I'll see him now," Jake said. He could not imagine who was visiting him. *Maybe he is one of the customers from the tavern,* Jake thought. Jake was shocked when the jailer opened the door and a well-dressed successful looking young man was allowed to enter his cell.

The stranger reached out his hand and introduced himself as Louis Parker. "I have been appointed your attorney. I will try to untangle this mess that you've gotten yourself into and get you out of here."
Jake reached for his hand and gave it a thankful shake. "I don't know who sent you but I'm grateful to them for doing it," Jake said.
"The state appointed me. I just do not know how we are going to get you out of the web you have spun for yourself. Oh what a tangled web we weave when once we practice to deceive," Louis said. I will be back tomorrow afternoon just after high noon and I will spend the rest of the day talking with you. I will be asking you questions and I want the truth and nothing but the truth," he raised his voice and said in harsh tones. "Do you hear me boy? I want the truth and nothing but the truth."

"Yes," Jake said, "I hear you and I have nothing to lie about." Louis banged on the cell door and the jailer entered. As Louis was leaving, he turned around and said, "I don't understand why you had to hang him too." Before Jake could say a word, he was gone.

"I didn't hang him." Jake knew Louis could not hear it but he had the need to say it anyway.

Jake could remember, so well, everything that happened that night by now. There was no tangled web. He went to visit his mother and when he returned, he found his dad dead. He had not done it, and no one else had either. His dad had done it to himself and he did it all by himself.

When Jake fell asleep on the bench that night he dreamed it was very dark, but far down the street he could see a mob of people all carrying guns, big sticks and clubs. They were all yelling and running toward him. They were very angry and Jake knew if they caught him, they would surely kill him. He was running as fast as he could possibly run. The people were getting closer and closer. While he looked back at them, he ran into a hitching post beside the street. As he tumbled and the mob stood over him, he awoke with a jump so hard he fell off the bench and onto the concrete floor. As he lay there on the cold stone floor and thought about his nightmare with his heart racing at two hundred beats a minute he felt frozen. He was so frightened. He had never felt so hated in his life. Even his mother had not made him feel as hated as he felt at this moment.

Jake climbed back onto the wood board but he did not go back to sleep. He was afraid to. He was afraid he might pick up where the dream left off. He stayed awake the rest of the night, thinking.

When tomorrow finally came and it was time for Mr. Parker's visit with him, Jake felt like his heart would beat out of his body. For some reason since the dream last night, Jake felt scared. Suppose they found a way to ascertain that, he had killed his dad. He did not see how they could but he knew nothing about the study of law.

When Mr. Parker entered Jake's cell he briefly shook hands with Jake and reminded him of the rule about "nothing but the truth."

"I understand and I will tell only the truth," Jake said. "First I have some questions to ask you and I want a direct answer to all my questions. Why did you stab your father and then hang him on the noose from the ceiling rafters?" Louis said to Jake.

"I didn't stab my dad and I didn't hang him from the rafters," Jake said.

"Then how do you explain the following problems if it wasn't you who killed Nate Gooding?" "Why was your name sprawled out on the ceiling above your dad's head in his blood?" Why did we find your fingerprints on the knife used to stab your father? Why did you go to Mr. Anderson's hardware store the day before his murder and buy the very rope used to hang him? In addition, how do you explain the sharpening stone used to sharpen the knife that stabbed your father in the chest with your fingerprints all over it? And most important of all, how do you explain the removal of all the money from the safe and later found in your wood box with your belongings buried under the oak tree behind the tavern?"

Jake sat stone faced as he listened to the accusations against him. Tears filled his eyes. "You have to believe me. I didn't do any of those things," Jake said.

"No I don't have to believe you. You have to prove to me that you are innocent of all those things," Louis said to Jake. Let's start at the beginning and you tell me all about what you were doing every minute on the night that your father died."

"On the night that my father died I was sleeping in a cot near his cot in back of the tavern. Only that night I did not go to sleep. We both went to bed and I lay in my cot quietly until I heard my father snoring. When I was sure he was asleep, I crept out of bed, took my shoes and quietly went out the door. I put my shoes on while I sat on the bench in front of the tavern. Then I ran to visit my mother at our house about a half mile from the Tavern. Then I came back to the tavern and when I walked inside I found my father like that."

"Like what?"

"He was hanging from the rafter with the rope around his neck."

"And that's all?"

"Yes that's the way it happened."

"And you expect me to believe that?"

"Yes, I'm telling you the truth."

"How old are you boy?"

"I'll be fifteen next month."

"If you had a home and a bed why were you sleeping on a cot in a tavern?"

"My dad wanted it that way."

"What way?"

"He moved out of our house and he wanted me to come with him?"

"When you visited your mother that night did you talk to her and did she talk to you?"

"Yes," Jake said. He would never tell him how mean his mother had been to him that night.

"Why did you and your dad move out of the house?"

Jake told Mr. Parker the entire story about his mother and her drinking and his dad wanted to get away from her. His dad made him go live at the tavern also. Mr. Parker drilled Jake over, and over about what he had just said. Finally, he said he had another appointment and had to leave; but he would be back tomorrow. Jake was so glad when he finally left. He felt very much drained.

Jake slept like a log all night. He got the best night's sleep he had gotten since he had been there. He could not understand why he slept so well when he was more worried now than he had been before. It seemed to Jake that Mr. Parker was against him, instead of being there to help him. If Mr. Parker was supposed to help him, he dreaded meeting the lawyer who would be against him. Mr. Parker had told him an attorney from the government would plea his dad's case.

The next day soon after first light, Mr. Parker was lead to Jake's jail cell. "Buddy you've got lots of explaining to do. Do you remember what I told you about telling the truth?"

"Yes sir," Jake said.

"Why did you tell me that lie about visiting your mother that night?"

"I did visit my mother that night."

"I talked with your mother when I left here yesterday and she told me she had not seen you in weeks."

"What's going on here? Why was your mother never told about the death of your father?"

"I don't know why she told you she hasn't seen me in weeks because that's not true. I never had a chance to tell her about my father since everything went blank to me when I found my father like that and all I remember after that was you bringing me here."

"Why don't you just plea a black out on memory for the whole night and save me lots of work?"

"I know what was going on, up until I cut my dad down that night."

"How did you cut him down?"

"With the knife that he used to stab himself with I guess. I found it lying on the floor below where he was hanging."

"Well that'll explain why your prints were all over that knife. Why did you lie to me about talking to your mother that night?" Jake knew his back was against the wall. He had to tell Louis about how his mother hated him. When he was finished telling Louis about how she had yelled the horrible "I hate you" over many times as he left that night, tears rolled down his face. Louis said, "Why are you crying?"

"Because she's my mother and I love her. No matter what she has said to me I still love her," Jake said while the tears continued to roll down his face.

Louis felt a tinge of pity for the boy. *If he loves a mother that much after she has treated him so badly, he surely must love his father too. Why would he have killed someone that he loved so much?* Louis searched his brain. *What would he have had to gain by killing him?*

"Jake, why were you repeating over and over, when the sheriff picked you up that night, that you had killed your father?"

"I think my father woke up and found me gone. He probably knew that I had gone to see my mother. He did not want me to go there and I think it upset him so much that he killed himself because of it."

"Why do you think he did not want you to visit your mother?" Mr. Parker asked.

"He never told me that he didn't want me to visit her. I just sort of felt like, he didn't want me to."

"And you think you're visiting your mother would have angered him enough that he would have killed himself?"

"No, I don't think it would have but why else would he have done it?" Jake said to Mr. Parker.

"Maybe he didn't do it. Maybe it was someone else," Mr. Parker said.

"Who would have wanted to kill my father?" Jake said.

"Now that's questions I should be asking you. Did your father have any enemies other than your mother?"

"No, everyone liked my dad and I don't think my mother hated him that much, even if she had been able to do it," Jake said.

"I think we can rule out your mother. She is neither physically or mentally able to do it."

"No, I don't think it could have been her, but why else would he have done it?" Jake said to Mr. Parker.

Maybe he didn't do it. Maybe it was someone else, Mr. Parker thought.

"Who would have wanted to kill my father?" Jake said.

"Now those are questions I should be asking you. Did your father have any enemies other than your mother?"

"No, everyone liked my dad and I don't think my mother hated him that much even if she had been able to do it," Jake said.

"I think we can rule out your mother. She is neither physically or mentally able to do it."

"I guess you've used the knife sharpener many times since you have lived at the tavern."

"Yes sir."

"So that rules that out," Louis handed Jake a pencil and a sheet of paper. "I want you to write your name here on this paper."

"I'm sorry but I can't write," Jake said.

"I only want you to write your name, Jake, just Jake, that's all," Louis said.

Jake took the pencil and paper and began trying to write his name. When he was finished, the J was backward, the A was an O, the K looked more like an

R and the E was backward. "My mom taught me to write my name when I was three but that was all she ever taught me since she got sick soon after that. This is the first time I have written my name since then, but I still remember it. My dad always told me not to worry about going to school since I would take over the tavern from him when I grew up. He always said he couldn't read or write and it had never hurt him," Jake told Mr. Parker.

"How did your dad sign his name?" Mr. Parker asked.

"He always just signed his name with an X since he never learned the letters for it." Louis was more confused now. *Whoever had killed Nate could write distinguishable letters. Much better that Jake and certainly better that Nate. Someone else had killed Nate. It was not Jake or Nate himself, but someone else. However, who and why, that was the question.* Louis realized his work was just beginning and it was going to be hard work to find what he had to find, which would be the truth

Louis went by the tavern every day just to be sure everything was all right. He wanted Jake to have something to come back to if he was fortunate enough to find and then provide the truth behind his dad's death. Louis started canvassing the neighborhood. It seemed that everyone loved Nate and no one could provide a single ray of light on the mystery surrounding his death. Every day Louis worked from day light until dark researching Nate's case. Time was running out. There were already rumors of a lynching for poor Jake since the community knew he was the one who had done it. Louis had talked to the sheriff about watching out for Jake since the mob might someday barge the jail and attempt to pull him out. They desperately wanted to hang him from a noose. Louis would need to work fast.

Jake never had any visitors except Mr. Parker. He came occasionally just to see him and sometimes he would bring him a snack. Jake had always thought the customers at the tavern had liked him. He knew they all loved his father. He had always been nice to them but it seemed that no one even knew he was there. Jake did not know at that very moment there was a meeting going on at the hotel on the other end of town.

"I'm for going into the jail right now and breaking down his cell door if we have to. We can pull him out of there right now. I'm holding the rope that we can throw over that old oak out back of the tavern of his daddy's place and let him hang until he's dead like he did to Nate," Perry O'Brien said as he twisted the rope in his hands.

Jake had sat down on his bench. He was beginning to feel sorry for himself when the jailer appeared at his cell. "You have a visitor," he said as he was pulling a chair up to his cell. Walking right behind the jailer was a lovely woman. The woman was well dressed and she was wearing light rouge.

Warmth seemed to glow from her. She sat in the chair that the jailer had left for her.

"Jake, I know you don't know who I am so I'm going to tell you right off, since we don't have much time left. My name is Molly and my husband killed your father. We need to tell the sheriff now. We have to get you out of here. I think they're coming to get you soon and they'll hang you Jake if they get their hands on you," Molly said to Jake as tears spilled down her face. She stood up and with both hands on the rails of Jake's cell door; she started telling Jake about that fatal night.

Suddenly there was a loud bang at the front door of the jail and then a fight started. There was yelling and cursing.

"Get out, all of you. You are not getting your hands on my prisoner," Jake and Molly heard the sheriff yell, "Oh My God, they're here for you now. You stand right behind me Jake. Don't move."

Molly stood with her back to the cell and her hands locked onto the bars. The sheriff and jailer having been pushed to the floor and were held there by the unruly intruders. The crowd rushed into the cellblock. Perry O'Brien was leading the pack. As soon as he saw Molly, he stopped still in his tracks and gasp.

"You take one more step Perry and I'll tell the whole bunch all about it." The other men pushed on, determined to get to Jake but O'Brian stopped them. "Wait mates, we don't need to do it this way. We can think of another way that will be much worse that just hanging him." O'Brian began to back up with his arms out stretched pushing the others back also.

One of them yelled, "Let's do it now. Let's hang this killer." They all began to push O'Brian aside and get closer to the cell when suddenly there was a loud yell.

"Everyone back up. Do not say a word and do not look back. We have enough ammunition to blow every one of you through that cell at one time if you don't do as I say. Drop your guns on the floor, now."

Jake looked beyond the bunch of men and there was Mr. Parker, the sheriff and the jailer all holding long shot guns in each hand. The men began to back up. "We'll have a trial and then you can decide if Jake is guilty, but there won't be any lynching until we had found the guilty party."

Molly spoke up and said, "There's no need for a trial. I can tell you now who killed Nate. It was my husband Perry O'Brian. He killed Nate because I loved him. He tried to nail it on Jake so that no one would suspect him and he hates Jake too just because he's Nate's son."

She turned toward Jake and said, "someday I'll tell you all about it Jake but not now. I just wanted to save your life and I see no need for a trial since I can clear it all up without that," Molly was saying to Jake as the sheriff was placing handcuffs on her husband. Jake walked out of the cell and O'Brian walked into the cell.

As Molly, Lou Parker and Jake walked out the door of the jail together; Louis asked Mrs. O'Brian if she would meet with Jake and him tomorrow at the tavern. Molly agreed to meet with them. Louise walked with Jake to the tavern. Lewis unlocked the door and they both walked inside. Someone had cleaned up the tavern since that horrible night. Everything looked fresh and clean, with no signs of ropes or blood or any other reminders. Lou handed Jake the money that O'Brian had buried in his box behind the tavern. O'Brian had been the one spreading the rumor that Jake was seen in the hardware store buying rope when if fact it had been himself who had bought the rope there.

Jake spent the night getting everything back in order in the tavern. He checked the ale and liquor supply and found that none of it had been disturbed in the seven months that he was away. He dusted off all the bottles and shelves. He thought a lot about his father and what a prosperous man he had been. With no education, he had established a good business from the ground up. He had been a very clever man and Jake loved him so much. Jake took his father's cot down and put it away. He hoped that after tomorrow that he might be able to take his down also. He would visit his mother as soon as his meeting was over with Molly and Mr. Parker. He hoped this time would be different since now they only had each other.

When Molly and Mr. Parker showed up the next day, Mr. Parker was carrying a large brief case. He opened it up and it had papers inside. He took out a note pad and said to Molly, "Mrs. O'Brian—I want you to start at the beginning and explain to Jake and me how this horrible tragedy could have happened."

"When Nate and I were very little our families lived very close and we went to the same church. We played together every day but Nate's father refused to allow him to go to school. He made him start working on the farm when he was barely six years old. In addition, he really had to work. He was expected to take a row of potatoes just like every other worker and he was responsible for chopping all the weeds out of the potato plants as well as all the other workers who were grown up. Sometimes, I would take a hoe to the field and help him even though I was no older than he was. I felt so sorry for him having to do a man's work. We grew up being very close and we were best friends. When we became teens Jake ask me out on a date one night and my father refused to allow me to date Jake. We had been together all our lives, we loved each other so much, and that was all right with my dad. But Jake wasn't good enough for me to fall in love with and marry someday," Molly said with tears stinging her eyes. "I asked my Pa why I couldn't continue just to see him. Jake was the only person I want to be with."

"Molly, we have brought you up a proper lady and we want you to marry someone some day that can provide for you the way we have provided for you. That someone will never be Nate. He cannot even read and write. How will he ever make a girl a living?" "Sorry Molly, but you can't see Nate again."

"My heart was shattered; I begged and begged. I cried for days. However, nothing worked. Pa held steadfast to his rule. Finally, when Nate and I could not bear our separation any longer we started sneaking around and meeting each other. Oh what wonderful days those were. They were rare and far apart but when we were able to get snippets of time together, we valued them greatly. Then one day my dad caught us at the soda shop in town sharing a soda and laughing together. He took my arm and he threw me out of the soda shop and kicked me in the backside while everybody watched and sent me home running. Nate wanted so bad to go after him but I had warned Nate against a confrontation."

"Nate, if you ever do that it's for sure we'll never see each other again. When my dad and I got home, he told me to start packing my clothes. He sent me to live with an aunt and I had to attend school there. I hated it there but I could do nothing about it. Every time I came home on a visit, Jake and I always managed to see each other. We both lived for these moments. After my living away for three years, my dad found a suitor for me. I did not want a suitor and I told his so. Nevertheless, all the pleading, praying, crying, and refusing got me nowhere. The wedding day was set and I was now obligated to Perry O'Brian. His family was not wealthy but they owned property and that would satisfy my father. My mother never once stood up for me. She was never on my side. Perry was much older than I was and there was nothing gentle about him. He knew I did not love him and longed for Nate but that seemed to make his life more exciting. He had something that someone else wanted and would never have."

Chapter Four

Nate Takes a Wife

One day a new family moved into the community. They were gypsies and very poor. There must have been ten of those children. However, most of them were grown up and had families of their own still living in the circle with the mother and father. One of the girls was large and had big bones. She had ratty stringy hair. The father had been unable to marry her off to anyone. One day he was having a drink in the tavern and he asked your dad if he would take her.

"She's a hard worker and never complains. She will do your housework and treat you like a king. Nate did not want anyone but me, but now he knew that would never be, so, he married her.

Her father was right. Nate and his father owned a farm that they had been trying to run but it was never prosperous, because of the tavern. Your mother jumped right in and started doing all the farm work allowing Nate's father to expand on the farm. Nate took over the tavern. He spent most of his time there. Your mother was up at dawn and worked harder than any hired hand or her father-in-law. She was a dream come true for Nate's father and he threatened Nate if he ever did anything to mess it up. Nate stayed at the Tavern at long hours. He knew Arlie was a fine woman and he wished he could love her but it just was not there. After Nate and Arlie had been, married about six months and Jake still had done nothing kind for her or even said much to her. He decided he would take home a bottle of wine.

38

He could just take home the cheapest bottle since she would never know the difference anyway. As far as he knew she had never drank alcohol of any kind. When Nate's mother placed the dinner on the table that night, Nate whipped out the bottle of wine. He held it up to Arlie and said, "This wine is just for you."

"What is wine?" poor Arlie asked.

"It is a very good drink and it also makes you feel good."

"Ok, she said as she tried to pull the cork out of the bottle. When it would not come out, she put her teeth around the cork and pulled it, right out.

"I was going to get you a cork screw," Nate said to her.

"What's that?"

"Never mind Nate, you already have it out now," Jake said to her as he thought how different the woman he loved was from the woman he lived with. Molly would never do a thing as she had just done. Nate reached up to the cupboard to get a wine glass but before he could hand it to her, she had turned the bottle up and had it half drank.

She took the bottle away from her mouth long enough to say, "You're right Nate, this is mighty good stuff." Sooner than her words were out, she put the bottle back up to her mouth; this time she took it down, it was empty. Before dinner was finished, Arlie made a funny remark. No one heard what it was but they all laughed with her since she rarely ever laughed or showed emotion of any kind.

They had their dinner, got their baths, and went right to bed as they did every night. Jake and Arlie shared the same bedroom but not the same bed. Nate was so tired. It had been extra busy at the tavern today. However, Arlie wanted to talk. She talked and talked and then she giggled. Before Nate could realize what was happening to him she was under his covers on his bed head and all.

What is God's name is she doing? Nate thought. However, it was too late when Nate realized what she was up to and that was the night of Jakes conception.

Later when Nate realized he would soon be a father he was excited. He would see to it that his child always had everything he needed. He would always be allowed to make his own decisions and never forced to do things he did not want to do.

When Jake was born, Arlie came alive. She had born this family's namesake. Everyone in the family was so thankful. The family fussed over Arlie and made her queen of the home. She did not have to work any longer but she chose to do so anyway.

Nate's parents were getting old. Nate hired servants to limit their workload. Arlie worked all day in the fields and with the livestock with Jake right by her side. When the day was finished, she enjoyed getting her bath and relaxing with a bottle of her favorite wine. One bottle turned into two then three. She knew that she could have anything she wanted but not the thing she wanted most. Nate was always kind to Arlie and saw that she never needed a thing that she did not get. However, he could not give his heart to her because Molly had always held that part of him. Jake thought about Molly every day. Sometimes he would talk to her as if she were beside him. He knew she would never be but he could make believe.

Before anyone realized what was happening Arlie had a drinking problem. It did not really matter since there were farm laborers to do all the work. Arlie chose to manage the farm from the house and allow the hired help do the work. Her drinking became worse.

Nate's parents died within two months of each other. Nate's father found his wife dead in bed one morning upon arising. She had not been ill and had never been to a doctor. She always stayed busy. She was the best cook in all of Ireland. Her family was always well fed. Nate's father grieved every day after his wife's death. His health began to decline and when winter came and the flu started spreading, he was so weak he was first to catch it. Within three days, he was dead.

Nate knew his family's future was now totally in his hands. He had run the tavern since he was a boy and his knowledge had grown each day in the business. He never went to school and never learned to read and write but that never stood in his way. Arlie was still running the farm. However, she was not as efficient as she once had been. Her drinking had really become a problem now that Nate's mom and dad were no longer there. It angered Nate so much to come home every day from work and find her drunk. She would send a hired hand to pick up her wine now that Nate refused to bring it home to her.

Molly graduated from school abroad. She had married Perry O'Brian and they had a three-year-old daughter. Perry was the son of a prominent family in town. He had never worked but Molly's parents knew he would inherit the banking empire that his family owned someday. Molly did not love him. In fact, Molly did not even like him. She still loved Nate but she knew by now that would never be. She had always hoped, somehow, things might work out for her and Nate after all. However, all that had been so long ago. Molly wondered if Nate still remembered her.

Molly recently moved back home with her husband and daughter. She had always been interested in decorating her own hats. She decided she would open her own millenary business and make hats for herself and other people. She found a small empty cottage and bought the property. After sprucing it up inside and outside and filling it with pretty hats that she had designed and made, Molly had a little hatter and she was very proud of it.

There was a planned business meeting for all business owners of the town that night at the local hotel dining room in town. They would be discussing paving the downtown streets. Nate had no knowledge of Molly's hat business since she had opened less than a month ago.

Nate walked down the street that night, dodging mud holes and headed toward the hotel. He thought about the wet sloppy streets. It had rained that morning. Nate thought to himself, *four-year-old Jake would never have to dodge these mud holes. By the time, he is old enough to take over the tavern; all these streets will be paved streets.* He lived for Jake. His world was so miserable now with Arlie's drunkenness and his mom and dad gone. Jake was his only ray of sunshine. He loved him so much.

As Nate walked into the hotel dining room with his dirty shoes, he spotted a beautiful woman sitting at the far end of the table. He had been to every meeting in the last several years and the same people were always there. He never remembered seeing this beautiful woman. As he got closer to her Jake's knees became weak and a weak feeling overwhelmed him. It was Molly. It was his beautiful wonderful Molly. Nate found a chair next to her and sat down. Oh how he wanted to gather her in his arms and hug her tight enough to make up for all the lost years.

When Molly saw Nate, her heart flipped over. She was so glad she was sitting. Had she been standing she would surely have fainted. He was as handsome as he had been all those years they had been together while growing up. She knew in her heart she had not lost one ounce of the love she had always had for him. She so wanted to reach for him and give him that big hug she had dreamed about all these years.

The tablecloth draped off the table and onto their laps. No one in the room suspected anything since no one knew anything about their childhood years and no one in the room remembered Molly. She was an adult and different now. Molly and Jake had only looked at each other. The two of them never spoke a word. Suddenly Jake lowered his right hand under the tablecloth and over to Molly's lap. He took her hand in his. Molly's hand gave his a tight squeeze.

The meeting went on. Molly and Jake never heard a thing said in the important meeting. Their hands said it all. They were so grateful to be together again that the roads could go unpaved all of their lives and that was all right. Right now, nothing mattered except them. They were together again.

After that night, Molly and Nate saw each other as often as they possibly could. They just picked up where they left off. Their love for each other now seemed deeper and more precious than it had ever been. They spent hours discretely sitting by the bay talking and reminiscing. The years rolled on. They were as happy as they had been when they were children together. Only now, they had to be very careful about where they met and who was around when they were together.

Sometimes Nate would complain to Molly about Arlie's drinking. Sometimes it really got on his nerves. She always allowed him to talk and vent his feelings even though she knew there was nothing she could do about it. Molly was surprised when Nate took Jake and started living in the tavern. Somehow, she felt sorry for Arlie. Soon after Nate started living at the tavern, Molly told him that they needed to see less of each other for a while. She suspected that Perry was on to something. Nate was not willing to see less of Molly but she knew his life might depend on it. The less they saw of each other the more depressed Nate seemed to get. It was like going back to their teen years when they were forbidden to see each other at all to him and he couldn't except that again.

The love between them could have moved mountains but it could not prevent Perry O'Brian from finding out about their illicit affair, as he called it. He still did not have a job but he stayed busy stirring up trouble. Now he had caught his wife in an affair and he was never so insulted. How would he look if the town found out about his wife two timing him? He was a man. A mans' man. He could hold his woman against any man in this town. What would they think if they found she had chosen the bartender above him? He would figure out a way to fix that. Moreover, he did.

"Jake, please don't blame your mother for any of this. Not even her drinking. None of it was her fault alone. Nate and I are probably the cause of her drinking problem. She never deserved the hand she was dealt. Go to her. Try to return home to live with her and tell her that you love her. I know there is nothing she would rather hear. She did not mean anything she said that night. She was hurting. I am sure she missed you and Nate and neither of you ever came back until you returned that night. Tell her you're sorry and try to make her know that you still love her," Molly said to Jake. Tears streamed down Jake's face as he listened intently to each work Molly said to him.

Jake and Molly would still spend time together at a trial to put her husband away forever. He was luckier than Jake would have been if Molly had not been at the jail that faithful day. He would spend the rest of his life in prison but Jake would have hung from a tree.

Jake did go back home. At the beginning, Arlie still had her defenses up. Jake kept up his desire to get through to his mother. Soon Arlie started drinking less and less. If she asked Jake to bring her a bottle of wine when he came home from work he brought her the wine. He never complained about her drinking. He only showed her the love that he felt for her and showed her how proud he was of her and it did not matter to him if she drank too much or not. Within three months after the death of his father, Jakes mother had totally given up drinking alcohol.

It was summer and Jake was at work. He had enlarged the tavern and remodeled so that the tavern was much nicer now. His father had left him more money than he and his mother could ever spend. Now Jake was quickly adding to that money since the business was growing everyday. Jake had hired an employee to help him behind the counter. Jake was in his office located behind the counter when he heard a voice that he recognized but he could not remember who it was. He heard the employee say, "He's in his office. I'll get him." Jake got up from his desk and walked to the door. He stuck his head out and saw Molly standing there. She had a beautiful girl with her who resembled Molly. Jake knew immediately, she must be Molly's daughter. Jake imagined she must look like the girl his father had fallen in love with so long ago. She looked so like Molly, only younger.

"I had a free day today from the Millenary Shop and Hannah and I decided to come to the drug store for a soda. Since we were so close, I thought it would be nice to bring Hannah by to meet you. Silly me, I should have introduced you a long time ago but it never occurred to me that you two have never met."

"Hannah this is Jake, Jake, Hannah, my daughter." Hannah and Jake shook hands. Hannah told Jake that she had just returned from her four years away at school. She said she was home for good now and would really like to meet other young people.

"It's a little boring around here if you don't have any friends. All of my friends have moved away or are still in school somewhere."

Jake made a date with Hannah to show her around and let her see for herself how things had changed since she lived at home.

Hannah was surprise to see so much poverty in her hometown. She knew that Ireland had still not recovered from the great famine. Ireland had seen the last of the famine in late 1851 and it was now 1860. Hannah thought by now there would be no need for soup kitchens. They still dotted the village.

"Maybe some people still haven't recovered," she had said to Jake. "It isn't some people, Hannah. Most people still have not recovered since the great famine. People are still starving and dying of diseases related to starvation. I give freely to the cause and I am politically involved with attempts to help our country recover."

Hannah knew she would make this her mission also.

Arlie was so happy for her son. She had never seen him as radiant and joyful as he had been since he had met Hannah. Jake had brought Hannah to the house to meet his mother. Arlie really liked Hannah. Later she said to Jake, "Son, she'd make a good daughter-in-law."

"Not so fast, Ma, we're just dating now." Jake said to her with a laugh.

However, Jake and Hannah did get married. It was the wedding of the year in their small Irish village. Jake wished Nate could have been there to enjoy the occasion with them.

Jake had Hannah's dream home built just as she wanted it. He allowed for lots of room since they planned to start a family soon after they were married.

Within two years, Jake and Hannah had their first child. He was a handsome fellow and looked so much like his dad. Jake valued his son with so much pride and joy.

Two years later their baby girl was born. Now they were a perfect family. Jake was a wonderful father and Hannah was an excellent mother. They put their all into raising their children. Sometimes Jake felt a little guilty. Most of Ireland was poverty ridden and many people were still going hungry, but he and his family had more money than they knew what to do with. Of course, they shared their good fortune. Now both of them fought to make things better for their country.

It occurred to Jake that he had been, so consumed in his family that he had devoted very little time to his own mom. He made a mental note to start spending more time with her as soon as they returned from the vacation they were on in France. "After all, she only lives about a half mile away. Surely I can take enough time to visit her," Jake said to himself.

However, a day rolled on then several days then several weeks that turned into several months and Jake still did not find time to visit with his mom. Every time he thought about it, he felt guiltier. There was work, the kids, his wife, social functions and it was hard to squeeze in time for something else.

Jake was walking home after closing the tavern that night. It was fall and the air was brisk. Jake got a whiff of smoke in the air. It was not cold enough for fire in the fireplace. It was unusual to smell smoke this early in the season.

Suddenly his eyes rested on a big ball of smoke in the distance. When he arrived at his house, he kept on walking. He had to rest his curiosity about the big plumb of smoke in the distance. He would walk until he was close enough to figure out where it was coming from.

As Jake got closer to the smoke, he realized it was coming from the area of his mom's house. He picked up his pace. As he neared the house, his pace changed to a fast sprint. In horror, Jake realized it was his mom's house on fire. Jake ran up the front steps and to the front door. He found the door closed and locked. He looked for something to break in the door but was unsuccessful. He ran to a window and broke it open with his bare fists. He jumped through the broken window and into the house. Jake ran through the house calling loudly, "Mom, Mom, Mom." Smoke was thick inside the house. It would be impossible to see his mother. "Mom, where are you?" Jake yelled. "I'm here, I'm in my bedroom." Arlie called out to her son. Jake ran in the direction of his mom's voice and felt until he found his mother. He grabbed her up in his arms and ran for the door. When he arrived at the door, he realized he had turned the wrong direction. Jake still holding tightly to his mother turned and ran to the opposite side of the room but before he reached the door, he heard a crashing sound. Jake and Arlie never knew what had hit them. The roof crashed in on them with the force of a fatal blow. They would die there together holding to each other.

They did not burn to death nor did they suffocate. These words brought comfort to Hannah at a time when comforting words would mean the most to her. Hannah had no shoulder for weeping. Molly had previously closed her Millinery Shop and moved to America. Hannah needed her. She could not remember ever needing her mother so much. Hannah sent Molly a telegram. *Mom; I need you Stop; Jake died. I feel that I am dying also Stop.* When Molly got the telegram, she sent an answer back immediately. *Hannah I am so sorry Stop; You and the children come immediately to New York Stop I will be waiting for you Stop.*

It was 1867 and Molly was so grateful for the invention of the overseas telegraph. The cable had been lain across the Atlantic just last year. If it had not been for the telegraph, her poor baby would need to wait for weeks before their messages exchanged. Molly found it hard to believe that Jake was dead. She could not imagine how her daughter would live without him. They had grown so close. She would be at the battery waiting for her daughter and grandchildren when they arrived from Ireland. Molly hoped that Hannah would soon feel the same as she. Molly had no desire to return to Ireland to live. She was American now and she would remain so the rest of her life.

The wagon train started out early on Thursday morning. The wagon master was in the first wagon. He was a serious old man with his suspenders always in place holding his britches up and part way over his potbelly. He appeared to enjoy his role as wagon master more than his necessity for the job. Mr. Brown did not know how much longer his job would be available. The railroad soon would be finished from New York to Florida. There were already courier ships going from New York to Florida. Many small ships left over from the Civil War now transported travelers. The Marlow's had thought about taking a boat to Florida but then they would need to get from seaside to inner Florida. Reason felt it best to buy his wagon and the horse and go in a wagon train. He would take the top off his wagon when he arrived in Madison County Florida and the wagon would still be their only means of transportation. He could use the horse around the farm in many ways from hauling to riding. He would be getting a mule free with his land. He would need a mule for plowing his crops.

As the wagon train chugged on, day turned to night. By about sundown every evening, the wagon master stopped at a clearing. The chuck wagon entered the center of the clearing and all the covered wagons arranged a large circle around the chuck wagon. They built a big campfire and every one carried chairs from their wagons and sat around the campfire while the cook prepared the meal on the campfire. Martha enjoyed watching him prepare the food. By the time, he was finished and the meal was ready to eat, everyone was very hungry.

"Reason, I don't believe I've ever eaten better food," Louisa said as she finished the last of her stew with thick pieces of tender beef, potatoes, carrots, and onions.

"I agree, its good food but I think your Irish stew is better." Louisa did not know if Reason's reply was serious or just because he was a gentle man and always showered her with kindness.

As the wagon train slowly pulled through Washington, DC, Reason realized this was the capital to his new country. He knew all the laws that governed America were made right there in that big white building. America seventeenth president was in office at this time. Mr. Andrew Johnson, Vice President, had moved into the president's position after Mr. Lincoln's death. Mr. Lincoln was attending an opera at the Ford Theatre when an actor who worked there shot him. John Wilkes Booth thought he was doing the South a favor if he annihilated the president who had brought about emancipation. Reason would never know that President Johnson was the one responsible for his free land. He had made a bill that all poor people in the country would receive free land for farming. It was a hard bill to pass since both houses in the congress were mainly Republican. However, he finally pushed the bill through. Poverty swept the nation in the first years after the Civil War was over—more so in the South than the North. Andrew Johnson was from North Carolina and it tore at his soul to see his people struggling for a living.

Camping tonight would be fun for all the children and for the adults who wanted a bath. They would camp near a river. The children spent every minute they could in the water. Louisa and Martha finally got the bath that they had hoped they would get. Even Reason took his bar of lye soap and entered the water. After their baths, the family took turns playing with little Eliza in the water. No one enjoyed the water as much as Eliza did.

Dinner tonight consisted of slabs of beef steaks cooked on an open fire, roasted potatoes, and canned green beans. The cook had grown, picked, prepared, and canned the whole green beans in jars. Louisa thought he had gone through lots of hard work with the beans to serve them to a bunch of strangers. The wagon master told them he canned food every year just for the wagon trains they would escort that year. There were always plenty of sour dough rolls with butter and lots of jams and jellies.

Breakfast very early every morning was a meal to remember also. The cook made biscuits like none Louisa had ever seen. Biscuits in her native Ireland were little flat thin cake-like sweets. These biscuits were big and fluffy. The biscuits were crusty outside, soft and moist inside and they were not sweet. Some of the breakfast diners ate syrup with the biscuits and some ate butter and jam or jelly. The biscuits were always delicious no matter how you ate them. Reason enjoyed placing his slice of country ham inside the biscuit and eating them together. Martha learned to enjoy the grits. She had never heard of grits before but she enjoyed eating them with her eggs cooked soft and mixed with the grits.

In the middle of breakfast the next morning little Eliza needed to go to the toilet. Louisa took her by the hand and led her out into the brush. As Eliza squatted there doing her business and playing with a small hard-shelled bug with a small stick she had found, Louisa heard something in the bushes. She looked toward the tall bushes. The bushes were moving ever so slightly. Louisa knew someone was there. She wished she had not walked so far away from the others. Louisa could hear the others back at the camp laughing and talking. She knew they probably would not hear her if she yelled. "Who's there?" Louisa waited for an answer. There was none. She asked again, "Who's there?" When there was still no answer, Louisa knew this was not good. She reached for Eliza. As she was pulling Eliza to her, someone grabbed her right arm. Then before she could yell as she had intended to do, his other arm came around her face and a big hand clamped over her mouth. He began attempting to pull Louisa away. Eliza saw what was happening to her mother and she put out a blood-curdling scream "Mommy, Mommy, Mommy," she yelled as she ran after her mother while Louisa struggled in attempts to free herself. The invader tried to kick the little girl away but she kept on coming. He was running backward and pulling Louisa with her back to him and his hand still covered her mouth to prevent her from screaming. Louisa was attempting to pull his hand away from her mouth. She had not seen Eliza when she ran behind them. Suddenly the man fell backward onto his back. He was still struggling to hold onto Louisa but Louisa was able to get away. She grabbed Eliza up into her arms from where she lay under the man's legs and in a flash; she was running through the brush back to the camp. After they arrived at the campsite, Louisa realized that little Eliza still had her underwear down. As she put her down and was getting her clothes back in place Reason came running to her. "What happened to you? You look like you've seen a ghost."

47

"He wasn't a ghost and I didn't see him but he sure tried to drag me away," Louisa told him.

"What happened out there?" Before Louisa could began telling him about her near certain death the wagon master and some of the other families came to her also. When she had told them about the intruder and was telling them about him falling backward and that was all that saved her, she stopped mid way the sentence.

"What?" Reason Marlow said.

"Why did he fall backwards?" Louisa said as she looked at her two-year-old daughter. Her little dress was all muddy. Suddenly it hit Louisa. Her baby daughter had gone to the thug's back. She had gotten on her hands and knees so that the thug would fall over her and let her mother go. Louisa picked her baby up and gave her a big hug. "You saved our lives Eliza. Thank you." Eliza looked at her mother with big brown shinny eyes and a little giggle escaped. It was obvious that Eliza knew exactly what she had done.

A posse was organized and the men from the wagon train went looking for the thug. "I'm sure he is a carpet bagger. He's probably homeless and has no morals or standards," the wagon master told them. They searched for the man for two hours but when his tracts ran out in the watery mud they lost his trail and was not able to pick it up again. Louisa was secretly glad they did not find him. She was sure they would have hanged him if they had caught him. Since no one was hurt, she is glad she would not have to live with that on her conscious. After that incident, Louisa was careful never to get too far from the others when she carried her children to the toilet or needed to go herself.

When the wagon train arrived in Georgia, they had their first encounter with Indians. The wagon master said that they were Cherokee. They were watching the Wagon train from a distance off to the side of the trail. The Indians sat so stately on their horses with their straight backs and bronze bodies. They wore feathered headbands and bright paint on their faces and chest. Martha and little Eliza thought they were watching a make believe story that was just for them. The wagon train moved on. About every two miles, the Indians would appear over the horizon again. They sat quietly on their horses and watched the wagon train but never attempted to come toward it.

That night around the campfire, the wagon master told them how the white man forced the Indians off their own land, and forced them to walk to Oklahoma, where they would live out their days on a reservation. He told them about how the Indians had resisted the displacement and desired to keep their land, but they chased them down and forced them to go anyway. Reason voiced his dislike for such treatment to the people who had inhabited this land for centuries before other countries arrived. The wagon master agreed with him that it was cruel but he said, "You're right, they lived on

48

this land for hundreds of years before we ever got here and they did nothing to develop this country. They did nothing but hunt for their food and have wars with other tribes so that they could either steal their horses or appear superior to that tribe. If we had joined, their world instead of taking it over, Americans would still be living in tee pees and scrounging for food. Would you rather live in a country that is developed or one that still doesn't even have a government and its people die almost at the same rate that they are born?" Reason thought for a few minutes. Then he said, "Yes, I guess you're right. The Europeans really had no choice."

It was fall and the wagon train was approaching Florida. It seemed that the closer to Florida they had been, the hotter the weather had begun. By the time they were well into Florida, beads of sweat were showing on Louisa's face.

"Reason, I don't know if I can take this heat.

"Love, you might need to get use to it since you'll be living in it about ten months out of twelve from now on.

They were well into Florida now. Everything was going along smoothly. Eliza was getting a mid-morning nap. The Marlow's new home was not far away. Reason and Louisa was sitting in the bench seat while Reason drove the horse. "Reason, look at that dark cloud over there. I don't think I have ever seen such a dark cloud as that before."

Reason took one look and it seemed that his heart flipped over. He had never seen a cloud like that one either but he knew enough about clouds that he thought they were going to have very bad weather. Suddenly it was as if the bottom of the sky fell out. Rain and hail was beating down so hard that Reason could no longer see to drive the horse. Then a bright streak of lightning lit up the whole sky. The bolt of thunder that followed was so loud that it took all that Reason could do to hold the horse and prevent him from bolting. The hail beat the cover off the back of the wagon and Eliza was wet and screaming in fear. Louisa was trying to reach her when suddenly she was whisk up and carried away with a fierce heavy wind. Then Eliza was whisk away also. Martha held on to the wagon post for dear life. Reason was still attempting to keep the horse quiet while he screamed loudly for his wife and baby. He could not see through the weather to find them. The wagon master showed at the wagon. "Try to drive your horse over to that tree and tie him up and unhook him from the wagon."

Reason could barely see the tree the wagon master was talking about but he began trying to get his horse to go in that direction. The horse continued to buck and scream in terror. Just before he got him to the tree, another strong gale of wind came. It swept the wagon up in the air and slammed it down on its side. "Martha, are you alright?" Reason yelled. "Yes, papa, I'm fine." By now, she was out of the overturned wagon and holding onto the tree. Reason finally got the wagon disconnected from the horse and the horse tied to the tree. The horse was still frantic and wanting to get away. The rain and hail beat down on them. Martha sat down just inside the overturned wagon to get out of the rain and hail. Reason began to walk the area calling loudly for his wife. It was impossible to see more than a foot from his face but that did not stop Reason Marlow. He had to find his family.

The rain and hail continued to fall in massive amounts. Lightening was flashing all about near their feet. The weather continued for another fifteen minutes and then it was over as abruptly as it had started. Reason set out for the second time in so many months to try to find his wife. He heard a moan about thirty feet beyond the tree. He ran to the moaning as fast as he could go. He found Louisa there almost unconscious but holding tight to Eliza. When Reason attempted to take her arm and pull her from the many branches and debris lying on top of her, she moaned again and began to stir. Suddenly Reason saw what appeared to him to be blood. It was blood. If fact, Reason had never seen so much blood, in one place, in all his life. He picked little Eliza up. She had blood on her too but Reason could not tell where it was coming from. Eliza seemed to be fine. The blood was coming from his wife. Reason fell to his knees beside Louisa. She was bleeding profusely. He scooped her up into his arm and began to run to a wagon still standing. Few were still standing. Most of the wagons in the train no longer stood upright. When he reached the wagon, Charlie's wife was waiting. She led Reason to a dry place in the wagon. When Reason laid Louisa down, he too was bloody. "I am so sorry sir," the woman said to Reason.

"What; what do you mean, is she going to die?" Reason said while his voice trembled. "I hope not. She is having a miscarriage. We will need to get the bleeding stopped. She needs to see a doctor." Reason left his wife with the woman while he ran to find the wagon master. Charlie's wife placed Louisa's head down and her hips high above her head. The bleeding seemed to slow a bit. Soon Reason and the wagon master were standing by the wagon.

"Can we take her to the doctor in your wagon? It appears the only one that came out of this tornado still standing. The wagon master said to Charlie. "Yes, we will take her. Where will we find a doctor?" Charlie asked.
"The last town we came through back there was Valdosta. We will take her back there. Surely, they have a doctor there. It's the last town of any size before we reach Madison."

The ride back to Valdosta was rough for poor Louisa. She continued to bleed each time the wagon went over a bump on the narrow dirt road. Martha and Eliza had stayed back at the battered wagon train with the others. The wagon master sat in the wagon seat with Charlie and Reason stayed with his wife as Charlie's wife cared for her. Reason could not understand why his wife could not wake up. She would moan each time the wagon hit a bump but other than that, she appeared to sleep. Reason was so worried about her.

The ten miles back to Valdosta seemed to take forever. Reason kept looking out the cover of the wagon watching and waiting for signs of a town. Finally, he saw some buildings clumped together in the distance. "Thank God, I see *Valdosta*." Reason said to Charlie's wife. He could see the relief on her face too.

Upon arriving in Valdosta, the wagon master saw a building with a post office sign above it just as they entered the city. "Charlie, stop at this post office. I'll go inside and ask where the doctor may be." Charlie pulled up at the post office and stilled the horse. The wagon master jumped from the wagon and disappeared into the post office.

James Goldwire ran the post office. He was faithful to his government job. If he was, suppose to be at the post office he was at the post office and he did his job with pride and joy. Mr. Goldwire was happy to give the wagon master directions to one of the doctors. "Actually, you have three doctors to choose from." He said to the wagon master as he walked out and into the street. "You're standing at the corner of *East Central and Patterson Street* now. You'll need to go over one block to *Patterson* and you'll find Dr. John Walker and Dr. Ashley's office facing Patterson street between Hill Avenue and Central. Now if you need medicine you will need to go to Dr. Ellis's drug store. He's over there with the other doctors."

The wagon master thanked Mr. Goldwire and hurried back to the wagon. He directed Charlie to the building that James Goldwire had directed him. He helped James and Charlie get Mrs. Marlow into the doctor's office then he would wait outside.

The nurse helped Louisa into a wheel chair. The nurse rolled her to the back. The nurse told Charlie's wife to follow her but directed Reason and Charlie to have a seat in the waiting room. She told Reason that the doctor seeing his wife would be Dr. Ashley and he would come out and talk with him as soon as he was finished with the patient.

As the wagon master waited out on the dirt street, he remembered seeing a general store on the corner of *Patterson Street and Hill Avenue* as they had rode past it. He had needed a pack of chewing tobacco since before the storm hit. While he waited, he would walk down to the store and purchase some. It was a short walk to Tom Griffin's general store. The doors were open and he walked in. "Do you have a pack of Prince Albert chewing tobacco?" he asked Mr. Griffin.

"I sure do," Mr. Griffin said as he reached behind the counter for the chewing tobacco.

"This is a fine town. Not many towns this size have a choice of three medical doctors. I'm impressed," the wagon master said.

"Well thank you, sir," Mr. Griffin said to him. "Did you know that our little town is only three years old?"

"Now that would be hard to believe," the wagon master said.

"Yep, it's just three years old. It was down the road to the northwest of here. The town's name there was Troupeville. Troupeville was a bigger town there than it is here. But we had to move it here," Mr. Griffin told him.

"Why did you move your town?" the wagon master asked.

"Because we found out that the rail road is not going to come through Troupeville and we would have to move here if we wanted the train to stop in our town. The train route will bring the train from the north to Jacksonville, Florida and from there to Tallahassee. If we had stayed at Troupeville, the train would have bypassed us. However, now that we're here, the train will stop here too and that'll help our city to grow even more."

The wagon master admired Lowndes counties desire to grow with the times. While he slowly walked back to the doctor's office, he took his pocketknife from his pocket. He cut himself a plug of tobacco and slipped it in his back jaw.

"Mr. Marlow, your wife has lost a lot of blood. I have done a dilation and curettage and that should slowly stop the bleeding. Your wife has lost so much blood that her hemoglobin is only five and that is why she is so weak. She will slowly recover. However, you will need to see that she drinks many fluids to build her blood volume back fast; and she will need to eat lots of red meats and liver to build her hemoglobin back. Do you think you can manage that?" the doctor asked Reason.

"Yes, I will see that she gets all the care that she needs," Reason said.

"I have checked her over good and I don't think she got any other injuries in the storm. I guess you are very lucky. She probably escaped a serious injury. Strange, but that tornado did not come through here. It rained some but that was all."

The nurse appeared in the doorway pushing Louisa in the wheel chair. She seemed to be a little more alert now but Reason could tell that she was very weak. He paid the doctor and helped his wife out of the chair and out the door where the three men lifted her onto the wagon. Charlie's wife again sat beside her in the wagon. Reason sat on the opposite side and held his wife's hand. He watched, as she seemed to doze off. She appeared comfortable. Louisa slept almost half way back to the wagon train. Suddenly she opened her eyes and looked at her husband. Big tears welded in her big brown eyes.

"I'm so sorry, Reason. I should have told you but I wanted to wait until we arrived at our property before I told you."

Reason allowed his wife to weep for the loss of their baby. He only told her how much he loved her. He reassured her and tried to give her encouragement. Louisa wept as long as she felt the need. Reason just blotted her face with a damp cloth that Charlie's wife had given him and held her hand. He knew that she needed this time. He would never tell her how disappointed he was that she lost the baby. He would never tell her how the men on the wagon train had teased him about starting a new homestead and a farm with no boys in his family to help. They had told him he would need many helpers on the farm and would need to supply his own help.

"There's no available help except what you can supply for yourself. We suggest you get busy and have a whole herd of children if you want your farm to be a success," they had told him. He wanted nothing more than to make his farm work. Reason worried that Louisa might not able to produce more children after this miscarriage. He wanted to ask the doctor but could not pick up enough courage to do it with everyone standing around. If only he had known she was pregnant, maybe he could have protected her more. He would have to put that behind him. That was then and this is now.

When they arrived at the wagon train, the men were happily surprised. While they were gone, the men left at the camp had righted all the wagons and repaired them. They had the campfire going and the cook had dinner almost ready. The cook prepared a big bowl of beans with lots of meat cooked in them and a slice of beef liver for Louisa. Reason helped her to eat. Getting her to drink was no problem. Louisa had never felt as thirsty in her life as she was when she woke up. She ate all her dinner and continued to drink. She was already feeling better by bedtime. She felt well enough now, that all she wanted was to hold her daughters and say a prayer to God for keeping them safe through out the awful storm. She felt so fortunate.

Tomorrow they would arrive in Madison County, Florida. Today, however, it seems that between Valdosta and Madison they had seen nothing but wilderness. It was hard to comprehend that ahead was civilization again. Most of the way they had to make their own roads. They would travel through marshy swamplands at intervals and there they found alligators waiting to greet them. It was intriguing to the children but to the adults it was horrifying.

Only seven more miles down the narrow little trail they happened upon another little settlement. "Oh, I forgot about this little town. There might have been a doctor here in Quitman that we could have seen." However he didn't regret going back to Valdosta since they had his brand of chewing tobacco there and since this little town only had a scattered few buildings he doubted they would have had Prince Albert here.

Soon they had arrived in Madison County. The land lay in small rolling hills with plush green grass and foliage growing everywhere. There were tall long leaf pine trees and many majestic old oak trees. They were massive in size. It was obvious that this land could grow anything. The dirt was black and fertile. As Reason pulled his wagon over the land, he kept searching out the spot he would like to call home. He knew it would be on this end of Madison County. As he looked about, he saw wild rabbits, raccoons, and other small animals running about on the fertile soil.

"Whoa," Reason yelled at his horse. He yelled at the wagon master to hold up a minute. "I think this is the place I'd like to start my homestead and farm if it's available. I'll get off here and I'll go into town on my own after I've looked around some."

"OK, the town of Madison is only about nine miles down this road when you are ready to go into town," the wagon master told Reason. Reason thanked him for the good trip he had provided for his family and then they shook hands. Other families wished the Marlow's well, and then the rest of the wagons left on their way to the town of Madison while Reason and his family stayed behind.

Reason helped Louisa and the girls down from the wagon. Louisa was still weak but feeling much better. As they walked about the land a baby, rabbit hopped up to Eliza. She squatted and touched his back. The little rabbit did not move. He looked at her with his big brown eyes. Eliza was thrilled. "Can I have him, Ma? Can I please have him?"

"Tell you what Eliza, now that you're almost three and big enough to take care of him yourself and if we get this land, you can have him." Eliza squealed with glee. She followed him back to his nest. "Now I know where he lives and when we come back I'll get him," she said.

After Reason had looked about and had the land fixed in his mind they all loaded back onto the covered wagon and headed the nine more miles down the narrow dirt path to the city of Madison. When they arrived, Reason looked for a building that might be the courthouse but saw none. He saw an old man sitting on a bench in front of the general store. He stopped his wagon and yelled to the old man "Can you direct me to the court house?"

"Sure, you see that wood structure over there?" Reason looked in the direction the old man was pointing. "Do you mean that small wood building there?"

"Yes," the old man said. "It used to be the *Territorial Court* but now it's our court house." Reason thanked the old man and pulled his wagon the short distant to the courthouse. He parked and tied his horse up.

"Louisa, you and the girls stay with the wagon until I go in and check it out." Reason went inside the small wood frame building while the females waited on the wagon. Soon he appeared. "I have our land. We have forty acres in the area that we were standing in." Louisa said another little prayer of thanks to the Lord.

Reason returned the wagon to the general store and he, Louisa, and the girls went inside to gather supplies that they would need. They would camp from their covered wagon until they built their home. When they had loaded the wagon with sacks of flour, bags of sugar, cans of coffee, supplies for making lye soap, and other staples they would need they focused their attention on seeds. They found that the wonderful soil around Madison County would grow just about everything, they would be able to plant, and harvest year round, since freezing weather was rarely a serious problem. They bought green beans, corn, field peas, tomatoes, onions, and collard and turnip greens. Some of the seeds they bought Louisa had never heard of, but if it were an edible vegetable, she would figure out a way to cook it. Reason also bought cottonseeds, cane seed, and field corn seed. He bought bags of rye seed. He intended to raise livestock and feed them on hay and corn to fatten them for the market. Louisa bought herself some live hens and a rooster. She carried them home in a wood crate box supplied by the store.

When everything was loaded onto the wagon the family got on and Reason started the trip back to what was to be their paradise on earth. Eliza loved the chickens. She played with them all the way back. She had already picked out the bright red hen that was going to be her pet. Now she would have a rabbit and a hen to play with.

Pioneer life was starting for this family. Reason would find the local sawmill to split the logs. He would take the pines off his property for building his house. They found a church in the community where they would go. Concord Baptist Church was nearby and even though Louisa could not understand, why they did not try to find a Catholic church, she agreed that since the Baptist church was close they would attend services there. There they would meet other pioneers and settled people who could give them advice about planting and surviving on the land. They would find during the following years many barriers and setbacks. However, they were always able to get over this adversity with the help of their friends.

Finally, Reason told Louisa about what the men had told him about having many children to help run the farm. She obliged him and they immediately began having children. They were all healthy and each birth was easy and uncomplicated for Louisa. She would go on to have nine more children. All together, there were ten girls and one boy. Reason would teach his girls to do farm work just as if they were boys. He would need James, his only son, to grow up learning the workings of the farm and someday take over his role.

Everything in their lives was just as Reason had dreamed it would be when he reached the promise land. He would have a house and plenty of land for his crops. He would have many children to help him grow the crops and he would have a wife who loved and supported him. Now he had it all and everyone was happy.

They had found the perfect school for the children. Carrabelle School was only three miles from the homestead. The children walked to school if they were not working on the farm.

However, Reason's wonderful world would be short lived. Everyone in the family was always busy. The smaller children fed the livestock and chickens. The older ones helped with the planting and harvesting. Louisa was always busy caring for the house and cooking. She gathered her own vegetables from the garden. She prepared them and then she cooked them. She was an excellent cook. She had learned Southern cooking well. The women from the church had taught her. Her family thrived on her cooking. She served them meat every day. Some days she would ring a chicken's neck and when the chicken was finished flopping around on the ground she would pick it up and dip it in scalding water. Then she could almost slide the feathers off. The chicken would be cleaned dressed and in the pot within thirty minutes. Louisa learned to use her time wisely since she had so much to do for her family. She even placed nets over all her family's beds so that they could sleep at night without the mosquitoes biting them. Mosquitoes were always a problem since so much of this region was swampy. Louisa was always treating mosquito bites on the children. Left alone, the small bite would turn into massive sores sometimes. In addition, the sores were much more difficult to treat than the small mosquito bite.

Today, Louisa was sitting on the front porch shelling peas for canning. She always canned extra food when it was in for the season so that it would be available out of season too. Nothing was ever wasted. In the distance, she saw a wagon coming down the tiny dirt road. She watched as she shelled her peas. The wagon stopped in front of the house. Louisa set her peas aside and stood. As she walked to the edge of the porch, she noticed that it was a woman who had been driving the horse and wagon. When the woman approached Louisa, she had a desperate worried look on her face.

"Ma'm, do you have a drink of water that I can offer my husband. He is lying in the wagon and he's very ill," she said to Louisa.

"Yes, I'll get him a drink," Louisa told her. Louisa went into her kitchen and to the water bucket for the fresh water that she had drawn from the well that morning. Louisa poured a mason jar full of the cool fresh water and carried it through the house to the front porch. She handed the jar of water to the woman and then walked with her to the wagon.

She wanted to see for herself if the man was actually that sick. When she peered into the wagon, she felt faint. She could not believe her own eyes. The man was lying on his back and he was a bright yellow. There was blood appearing at his eyes and the corner's of his mouth. Louisa touched him and he was burning hot. The man was talking incoherently in low tones. Louisa could not make out what he was saying.

"He's talking out of his head," his wife said. "What he says doesn't make sense." She was trying to give him the water but it only seeped in one side of his mouth and out the other side. Louisa felt so sorry for him. Flies and mosquitoes were sitting on his face and arms. Louisa tried to shoo them away.

"I am trying to get him to Quitman where they have a doctor but I don't know if he'll make it or not. Louisa did not think he would but she did not want to scare her.

"Wouldn't it be closer to take him to Madison? There is a doctor there too," Louisa said.

"I don't know, for some reason I just thought Quitman is closer," she said to Louisa as she was attempting to get more water in her husband. This time he started to cough on the water and suddenly large amounts of blood came gushing from his mouth. The woman started shaking all over and began to cry. "He's been sick several days but I did not know he was this sick."

Louisa said, "Let me go to the field and get my husband and we'll help you to get him out of the wagon and into the house and my husband will go to town and bring the doctor back to see him here." Louisa backed toward the plowed field. Louisa ran as fast as she could until she reached Reason. She told Reason about the sick man at the house. "You need to come and help us get him out of the wagon and into the house on a bed. Then you can go and fetch the doctor." Reason agreed with Louisa.

Both of them rushed back to the house. They got the very sick patient out of the wagon and into the house. Louisa and his wife put him to bed. He continued to vomit the blood. Reason took the woman's wagon and horse since it was already hitched and ready to go, and in a fast trot, he drove the horse to Madison. Madison was about two miles closer than Quitman. Reason wished he could have taken just the horse. He could have traveled much faster. However, he would need the wagon to bring the doctor back.

Louisa and the woman worked with the sick man constantly for the many hours while Reason was gone. All the children came in from the field. They all stood watching the very sick man with so much sympathy in their hearts.

Before Reason returned, the old man was gone. His wife sat there with his head in her lap rocking back and forth while tears rolled down her face. "We have been married thirty years and now he is gone," she said with a trembling voice. By the time, that Reason arrived both women and all the children were weeping. Reason felt like weeping along with them but since he was unable to get a doctor and had worried all the way back he could breathe now that the old fellow no longer needed a doctor anyway.

Reason loaded the expired patient and his wife on the wagon and drove them to their own home. Then he went to find the Concord Baptist Church pastor. He would help the poor grieving woman with all the arrangements. The Marlow's would attend the funeral.

However, when the day of the funeral arrived the Marlow's would not attend. They had sick children in their home. Two of the daughters came down with diarrhea and vomiting. Louisa put them right to bed and made a pot of chicken soup. She would see that they had fluid in them. However, the girls did not get better. Louisa realized she was watching her sick little girls dying before her own eyes.

"Reason, you have to go as fast as you can and get the doctor for my babies," Louisa said as tears welded in her eyes. It had only been two weeks since Reason had gone to town to fetch the doctor. He did not know if he should go to Quitman or Madison. They had told him in Madison that the doctor would be back in a few days so he assumed he would be back by now.

Reason hitched the horse to the wagon and started out for Madison as fast as he could make the horse go. When he arrived at the doctor's office, he found that the doctor was at another house in the neighborhood that very moment treating a very sick child who had contracted yellow fever. "It seems that there is an out break of yellow fever here. This is the third patient my husband has seen in the last two days," The doctor's wife told Reason.
"Oh my Lord, I hope that isn't what my children have," Reason said to her.
"You said they have diarrhea and vomiting with low fever?" The doctor's wife asked Reason.
"Yes, and they are mighty sick."
"I pray not, but it sounds like the onset of yellow fever to me," Doctor Smith's wife said.

When the doctor returned Reason ran to the carriage before he had time to get down. "Dr. Smith you have to go with me to see my children. They are very sick and we need you to see them." "Ok, just let me go inside for a drink of water before I leave." The doctor disappeared into his home. Shortly he reappeared. "I'll follow you in my carriage so that you won't need to bring me back," the doctor said.

When they arrived at the house, the two little girls had raging fevers and they were vomiting blood. Two more of the daughters had also started with symptoms exactly like their sisters. Doctor Smith told Louisa to bring pans of cold water and bathing cloths.

"We have to cool the fever with a cold water bath. Put a little friction with the rubbing. I'll also help cool the fever," he said. He, Louisa, and Reason began sponging the little girls but it seemed to do no good. The fever has raged on and elevated at every hour.

Soon the first two little girls were gone. Louisa stood over her little girls with tears streaming.

"If only I hadn't brought the sick man into my house. I caused their deaths," she said as she paced the floor and rung her hands.

"Oh no!" Dr. Smith said. "Don't blame yourself. The girls died of yellow fever and you cannot catch yellow fever from another person. You can only get it from a mosquito that carries the germ and bites you. We have a large out break of yellow fever carrying mosquitoes. I do not know where they came from. They probably came in on a ship from Africa or South America. However, they seemed to have all settled here in our part of the country. You had nothing to do with them getting yellow fever. There is no way to get rid of the mosquitoes. The sick man that you told about helping into your home did not give your children the disease. They got it the same way he had gotten it. If you didn't already have yellow fever carrying mosquitoes around here, the man's wife could have started them here if a mosquito bit her husband while he was in the wagon out front of the house."

"But it wasn't your fault. If she did not start yellow fever carrying mosquitoes here when she brought her sick husband, they would have soon been here anyways. They are all over the county. I think we're starting in an epidemic," Louisa remembered trying to fan the mosquitoes and flies' off the dying man.

Soon the other two sick daughters died and following them, another three of the little girls in the family came down with yellow fever. They gave a hard fight for their life but in the end, they succumbed to the dreaded disease also. Louisa seemed to loose her spirit after losing seven of her daughters. She felt that she could not go on. "Louisa, I love you and the rest of the children love you and need you. Please do not get sick. It is not your fault that, our children died. You heard what the doctor said," Reason said to his wife.

What Reason did not know was his wife already had the yellow fever and he would lose her too. "Fight Louisa, please don't die. I need you. I love you. You can't leave me," Reason returned to the doctor. "You have to come with me and see my wife. I think she is going to die." "Mr. Marlow, I'll go if you want me to but there is nothing I can do. There is no cure for yellow fever. You can only treat the symptoms and try to make the patient comfortable but there is no cure." Reason returned home and watched his loving wife fade away. Now he had no reason to go on. He saw no life without his wonderful Louisa. He sat for long intervals with his head buried in his hands. He had wept so much that there were no tears left. Within two weeks, he had lost seven of his children and his wife. How could he go on?

Reason Marlow needed to think about the future for this family. It was now the year of 1876. He had built his homestead and started his farm in 1867. He had had almost ten good years here. This farm had brought him much happiness in these years. He and Louisa had had nine children in this house. They had been born close together but it was what Louisa wanted. She had felt like a failure when she had the miscarriage in the tornado and she was determined to make it right. She wanted many children. She loved each one of them as if that child was the only one she had. He still had his son and three daughters left. He loved them all but Eliza was always first in his mind. She had always been a daddy's girl. They need me. Reason thought to himself. They need me now worse than ever. If I give up on life what will happen to them. They cannot give up on life. They are children. They do not know how to give up. Reason decided he had no choice. He would live for his children. He would continue to provide them with a good home. Martha was older now. She was already over twenty years old. She could try to take her mother's place in the house. He would help her. When Reason laid his head down on his pillow that night, he felt that a heavy burden was lifted from his shoulders. He was not in limbo anymore. He knew he would go on.

Martha, Eliza and Ellen missed their mother and sisters but they would carry on the way they knew their mother would want them to. James was 12 years old. He had just begun helping his father out in major ways on the farm. His father depended on him now. Reason was able to do things that he could not do before. He would grow mostly sugar cane and less cotton. James was old enough to help him harvest the cane and grind it. He could also help Reason cook the cane juice until it became syrup or sugar. Either way it was a good moneymaker. Then he would sell the compressed stalks of cane to Puerto Rico. They always bought all the crushed cane stalks so that they could get to make their rum. Rum was their main cash income. There was no need to grow cotton in large amounts any longer now that he had no help to pick it.

Martha had proven to be a good housekeeper and mother to the other children. Sometimes she showed signs of dislike for her new role but Reason seemed to pay little attention. There was no need to talk to her about it since she had no choice. Eliza helped as much as she could in the house but her job was in the field if she was needed there, or helping with the cane harvest and cooking of the juice. James always tried to prevent his Pa from calling on Eliza when it was cane grinding and juice cooking time. She was always snapping at him for drinking too much cane juice. James loved cane juice and cane syrup. He also loved to eat the big crystal clusters of brown sugar that would finally develop at the end of the cane juice cooking.

"You are eating and drinking too much sweet stuff," she would always say to James. James wanted her to keep her opinion to herself since he had no intentions of letting up on his consumption of any of it. Besides, she was only saying it to make Pa yell at him.

The big high-bodied wagon pulled up beside the crushed cane stalks. The four horses pulling the big wagon were set free so that they could eat and drink. While the horses finished with their favorite part of the trip, all the crushed cane stalks were loaded onto the wagon. "Pa, are you sure we ground that much cane?" James asked his dad.
"We sure did son, where else would it have come from?" Reason said.

"It just seems like so much cane. Look it is hanging off that big wagon. The wagon men are going to need to tie it down or they might loose some of it," James said. Reason looked at his son. He was so smart for his twelve years. Reason reckoned James would grow up to be a brilliant man some day. He was so proud of him. He had received his ability of thinking ahead from his mother. James watched as the two men tied down the cane stalks, hooked up the horses, and drove away toward the coast where they would transfer the cane stalks to a waiting ship for transport to Puerto Rico.

"Martha, we made enough money from the cane stalks yesterday to allow us to go shopping. This coming Saturday I'll take you to town so that you can restock your kitchen supplies, if you want to." This pleased Martha since the flour and coffee had almost run out. It was the end of the cane season and Martha supposed there might not be any more money for six more months when the cotton would be ready to take to market. Of course, Pa had already sold much of the syrup and crystal sugar but he had more to sell if they should get in a tight spot.

Shopping day was always fun. Eliza and Ellen always got something special. This trip Eliza got a strand of beads and Ellen got a little sock doll. Pa asked James if he wanted something but he refused. He appeared not to feel well but he did not complain. All he wanted was a drink of water. He had brought a quart jar full of water when they had left home. By the time they arrived in town he had already drank the whole jar. The girls did not mind him drinking water. Constantly stopping the wagon for him to run behind a tree is the thing that bothered them. It seemed to take twice as long to get to town as it usually did.

When Martha had gathered up all the goods she needed and Pa had gathered the things he needed it was loaded onto the wagon and everyone hopped on with it. Eliza played with her beads and Ellen played with her doll all the way back. James slept, drank water and peed all the way back.

After all the supplies were unloaded from the wagon and placed where they belonged, it was near dark. "James, will you milk the cow for me while I cook our supper?" asked Martha. James was lying on a bench in the kitchen. James did not answer Martha. She waited a minute and repeated her request. "James, will you please milk the cow for me?" she asked again. James still did not move or answer. Finally, Martha walked over to him. He must have fallen asleep she said to herself. As she reached for his shoulder to give him a little shake, she realized that something was wrong. When she reached out and gave him a little shake, she realized something was dreadfully wrong. "Pa, come quick. Something's wrong with James." Pa came rushing into the kitchen immediately. Both girls followed him. Pa went to Martha and saw James lying on the bench with Martha shaking him and calling out for him. Pa grabbed his son and tried to sit him up on the bench but James's lifeless body did not respond.

Pa grabbed James and carried him back to the wagon. He hitched the horse back to the wagon again and yelled loudly, "Get Up, Get Up, to his horse. By this time, the girls were all loaded on the wagon too. Pa ran the horse at a gallop all the way back to town. Martha held James head in her lap while Eliza and Ellen prayed for James not to die. When they reached Madison, Reason pulled the wagon in front of Dr. Smith's house. He jumped off the wagon and ran to the doctor's door. "Doctor, please come quick. Something's wrong with my boy." Dr. Smith arrived at the wagon almost as soon as Reason did. He jumped up on the wagon and started feeling his wrist. Then he took a tube instrument with a metal disk from his coat pocket and placed it on James's chest. The doctor put the other ends in each of his ears. "Help me to get him into the house," the doctor said to Reason. They carried James into the doctor's house and laid him down on a narrow bed in the living room. The doctor put the instrument to James's chest again. "We need to carry him next door to the infirmary where we cared for the confederate soldiers. It has not been in use much since then but it is always there when we need it."

The doctor and Reason transferred James again. This time he would stay in the infirmary. His father saw that it was with love and care. "What is wrong with him Doc?" Reason asked.

"I'm not sure but his breath smells sweet and you said he's been drinking lots of water and urinating often?"

"Yes," Reason said. "It sounds to me like he may have that sugar disease."

"What can we do about it, if that's what he has?"

"Son, I'm sorry to say but there is nothing that can be done for that disease. If we had known long ago when he first got the disease, we could have treated it through his diet but if that is what he has, it's already in the last stages. I'll keep him here in the infirmary and watch over him and when he wakes up

I'll see that he gets no sugar; I'll try to get lots of water in him and maybe he'll be alright. But the most important thing right now is for him to come out of this coma."

The doctor put James to bed in the old infirmary. The doctor stayed right by his side but James never moved. Reason refused to leave him. He talked to his son as if he was fully awake. "Son we'll start chopping the cotton next week. Don't you think next week will be a good time to start chopping the cotton?" Reason wept a while then he prayed. "God please don't take my son." Martha, Eliza, and Ellen slept in the wagon and they prayed too.

By morning, it was evident that James was not going to wake up. He was going home to be with his mother and sisters. James's father and sisters along with his doctor was at his bedside when he sighed his last breath. Reason did not think he could bear the pain of loosing his son. He pleaded with James to wake up and not to leave him. Dr. Smith placed his arm around Reason and said to him, "Son, when the Lord gets ready for us he takes us. God is ready for James. He needs a special angel and James is the one he chose. Reason wept in the doctor's arms. Nothing could console him.

Life was never the same for Reason Marlow. His spirit was gone. He had lost the most important part of his life when Louisa died and now his only son was gone too. He seemed to go through each day like a ghost and not feeling anything. The year was 1885. If only it were not for the three girls left. If it was not for them, he could just lie down and die himself. Someone had to provide a living for Martha, Eliza, and Ellen. Since he was responsible for bringing them into the world, he would need to stay alive to take care of them. Martha could almost read her father's mind. She felt like such a burden. If only she had had a chance to go to school and get an education. If she had, she could make her own living but the farm needed her to much. Then, when her mom died, the house and children needed her too much for school. She did not see any hope for any of them to finding husbands since they were stuck far out into the country and never saw anyone except the people who went to Concord Baptist Church with them. There were no suitors in the church. It was all married folks, children or young women. However, there were never any young men. If only she could get rid of Eliza and Ellen, then she could focus all her attention on Pa and maybe he would see life differently. Martha felt sorry for her father. She could see defeat and dismay in his eyes every day.

Reason worked from daylight until dark every day. He went through his duties using only his hands. He did not use his mind any more. It hurt too much. He and the girls were in the backfield picking cotton. This was the last of the cotton for this season. Reason would load all his picked cotton and take it to the cotton gin in Quitman since they were offering a better price per pound than Madison was this year.

Reason looked at the loaded wagon. The cotton mounted high above the side bodies and it was not all loaded yet. He decided he would need to put the covering on the wagon again. It would be the first time the wagon had its cover since his house was finished. The covered wagon made a good home for them while they waited for their house—but that was then. Those were the happy times. He had his wife and children with him then. Now nearly all of them were dead. Reason placed the covering on the wagon and they continued to pile the cotton into the wagon. It was a good idea. Now Reason would be able to carry all the cotton at one time instead of making two trips to Quitman.

Reason would not allow the girls to stay at home when he knew he would be away for any length of time. Martha sat in the seat with her dad and the other two girls piled on top of the cotton and covering. They would need to hold on tight or there was a possibility they would fall off and into the first hole the wagon rolled over. Eliza and Ellen enjoyed riding high on the wagon. However, they had learned not to show signs of happiness or excitement since their brother had died. Pa did not like it. He wanted things kept solemn at all times. The girls supposed it was in respect for their deceased brother.

They finally arrived in Quitman and at the cotton gin. Reason slowed his horse and began pulling the wagon to the line where all the other wagons filled with cotton awaited their turn at the gin. He would fall in line with the others.

The wagon was moving at a slow pace when out of nowhere a little boy flew from the front of a wagon waiting on the left side of the line. He ran into the turning wheel of the Marlow's wagon. It was the front wheel and Eliza watched as the horrible accident unfolded. The little boy bounced away from the wheel and fell onto his back. Eliza was off the high pile of cotton and with one leap, she was at the boy's side. Eliza had always seemed to be more caring for the health of others. Eliza seemed to have a natural instinct to respond immediately to anyone in an emergency and she always seemed to know what to do. Reason immediately stopped the wagon and he too was at the boy's side. The little boy lay on his back and was unconscious. He had small amounts of blood coming from his left nostril. Eliza slipped her hand behind his back for support and pulled him up while she blew in his face. Almost immediately, the little boy began to cough and cry. Eliza kept reassuring him, "It's ok...you're going to be alright." Several people had seen the accident and had gathered to look on. Eliza heard a man's voice yelling "Eddie, Eddie. Is your name Eddie?" she asked the little boy. The boy shook his head yes. Eliza turned her head and spoke loudly. "He's over here." The desperate man appeared at the site. He stooped and carefully took his son from Eliza. "Are you alright, son?" he asked. "Yes sir," the little boy said. Eliza had torn off a piece of her petticoat and was dabbing at the blood on the little boy's nose. "I don't think he hurt his nose. I think he just broke the skin at the opening of his nose," Eliza told his father.

"Do you have pain anyplace else?" she asked the boy.

"No Ma'm, I feel fine."

Reason watched his daughter. He had never been so proud of her. She was in charge. She had a bad situation and she had handled it so perfectly. Reason stuck his hand out to the boy's father, "I'm Reason Marlow, and I'm so sorry. Your son ran from that parked wagon but instead of running in front of my wagon, he ran into my wagon wheel. I know he got hurt but I thank God that he ran into the wheel instead of in front of the wagon. The wheel would surely have run over him."

"I'm Robert Browning and I'm sorry he ran into your wagon and inconvenienced you so much. I work here and I try to keep an eye on them but sometimes it is hard to do. It's too dangerous for them to stay inside the cotton gin since they could get sucked into it."

Mr. Browning reached over and helped Eliza up. She would never know how grateful he was for her helping his little boy. He tried to thank her but she would not hear of it.

"I did nothing more than anyone else would have done."

"I have a lunch break in one hour. If you're still here, I would like to take you to the canteen and buy lunch for you." Eliza was twenty years old and she had never dated anyone. She had never even been in the presence of a male unless he was a relative. She knew Mr. Browning would not be calling this a date. He was only taking her out to show his gratefulness and besides he would have his children with him. Eliza looked at her father.

"It's fine with me, Eliza. You can go if you want to."

"OK, I'll go with you," she said.

Eliza could not get over her agreeing to have lunch with a stranger off her mind. She would not know what to say or how to act. What if he has a wife and she is visiting somewhere else. I am sure he does have a wife, besides he has not asked me on a date. This is just a thank you meal. She did not have to act in any kind of way. She just needed to be herself and let him thank her for helping his son. That is all he wanted. She ran to find her father. Maybe they would have his cotton off the wagon and they would be ready to go before lunchtime. She hoped so.

However, it was not to be. Her father still waited his turn at the cotton gin. Eliza spent the hour playing with Eddie and Sis, whose real name was Mittie. They were great kids and Eliza enjoyed being with them.

All too soon, Eliza found herself sitting at the canteen sipping tomato soup and munching homemade bread with the two children and their dad.

Little Eddie was much better now and seemed as though nothing had ever happened to him. He was five years old. His sister was almost two years older than he was. She was seven and she let Eddie know at frequent intervals that she was the oldest, biggest, and bravest. Eddie always argued with her and assured her that he would be the oldest, biggest, and bravest some day "just because he was a boy". Sis enjoyed rousing Eddie up about her superiority.

"Eddie, where were you going in such a hurry when you ran into the wagon wheel?" Eliza asked.

"I saw a lady across to road. She looked like my mommy and I wanted to see if it was her and if she had come back to us," Eddie said.

"Did you get to meet her?" Eliza said.

"No Ma'm, she was already gone when I got up."

Eliza's heart went out to the little boy. How sad it was. Eliza looked at Robert with tears in her eyes. "She died five months ago. I keep telling Eddie that she is in Heaven and won't be coming back here to see us. He knows that someday we'll go to see her there but she won't come back here."

"I'm so sorry; she must have died so young," Eliza said to Robert.

"Yes she did. Sometimes it's rough but we manage. I bring them to work with me since I have no one to care for them at home." Then Robert said something that made Eliza's knees turn to jelly. "Will you marry me so that they can have a mother?" Eliza sprung from her seat, ran out the canteen and to her father's wagon. Tears were streaming down her face as she reached the wagon. Martha and Ellen were waiting on the wagon seat.

"What is wrong with you?" Martha asked as she got off the wagon seat and went to her sister.

"He asked me to marry him," Eliza said through sobs.

"Why are you crying because he asked you to marry him?"

"Martha, he wants me to marry him so that he will have someone to take care of the children. His wife died and he has no one to care for them."

"Eliza, I don't think he would want to marry you unless he loves you," Martha said. Eliza sat by the wagon and wept. She was still weeping when Pa returned to the wagon. "It's our turn. I will pull the wagon into the gin. You girls will need to wait out here. Why are you crying Eliza?"

"Pa, Mr. Browning has asked me to marry him."

"Isn't it a little early to be thinking about something like that? You've just met him."

"I know Pa, but the children need a mother."

"I'll be back in a few minutes," he said as he pulled the wagon away and into the gin. Soon after Pa was gone, Robert showed up. Eliza was still weeping.

"Eliza I am sorry that I made you cry. It's just that my babies need someone like you more than you'll ever know."

"Mr. Browning, marriage is supposed to be about love, or so I always thought," Eliza told him.

"We can learn to love each other later."

Eliza cried louder.

"Why are you still crying, Eliza?" Martha asked.

"It's just that I would like to be a mother to the two children but I don't want a husband," Eliza said through sobs again.

"Well, I don't believe Pa's going to let you be a concubine." This made Eliza weep even louder. Poor Robert stood there with dangling arms. He did not know what to do. Eddie and Sis looked up at Eliza with pleading little faces. They already loved Eliza.

Pa returned with the empty wagon. He was whistling a song when he stopped the horse. It was easy to tell that Pa was happy with the amount of money his cotton had brought. However, when Pa arrived at the place where everyone stood he knew he was the only happy one there. "Why do you all look so sad?" Pa said.

No one said a word. "Come on girls, speak up," he said.

Robert was the one to speak. "Mr. Marlow, I would like to marry Eliza and take her home with me. I will take good care of her and I will treat her right. I know that she is younger than me but that makes me more able to take care of her."

No one said a word. Finally, Martha leaned toward Eliza. She whispered in her ear, "Eliza, you'd best not loose this chance. I am twenty-nine years old and no one has ever asked me to marry him. If they had I'd been gone a long time ago."

Pa finally looked at Robert and said, "Well now that's up to Eliza isn't it?"

"Pa... I do not know if I want to. I mean I love the children but I don't know about being married."

"Well Eliza, you can't have the children without being married to their father." Silence again.

Suddenly a big grin spread across Eliza's face and she looked at Robert Browning and said, "Alright, I'll marry you." The two children tore away from their father and were in Eliza's arms in an instant. They were squealing with delight. Robert said, "Thank you Eliza. I haven't seen them that happy since their mother died." He took out his handkerchief and dabbed at his eyes. Eliza knew he was crying.

Once Eliza accepted the fact that she would marry Robert, she never looked back. The more she thought about it the happier she became. Robert told her before she left the cotton gin with her father that he would come tomorrow and they would go to Madison and get a marriage license.

Eliza Takes A Husband

Eliza was ready and waiting when Robert and the children arrived the next morning. They went to Quitman to the courthouse and in 1888 applied for their marriage license. They would walk down the isle after church at the Concord Baptist Church this Sunday and the preacher would hear their vows.

Martha got up early that Sunday morning on March 25, 1888. She prepared a nice breakfast, since Robert and the children would be there in time for breakfast with the family. Then she helped Eliza pack her clothes and get dressed for her wedding. Eliza wore a light blue wool dress for her wedding. Robert was handsome in his suit. They looked a little strange together since Robert was six feet tall and Eliza was not quiet five tall and very petite. They would return to Quitman after the wedding where they would live at Robert's home.

It was a bittersweet day for Eliza. She was happy to be with the children and help them, but she was not happy about leaving home. She had never slept away from home before.

Eliza settled in with her husband and his two children. Robert slowly began to fall in love with Eliza and before he realized it, he was madly in love with her. Eliza felt that she had always loved Robert. Now she could not imagine living away from him. Mitty (Sis) and Ed (Eddie) were Robert's children by his deceased wife. They called Robert, Pa and Eliza, Ma, just as they had done before their mother had died.

Eliza learned that Robert and his brother Orval were very close. He and his wife, Christiana, lived next door with their six children. The two women enjoyed each other. Christiana taught Eliza many things about keeping house and cooking. Eliza had helped Martha for years but she had never had the total responsibility for preparing a full meal and keeping a house up all by herself.

The two brothers rented a farm in Brooks County, Georgia. They would tend the land, grow, and harvest the crop, and when the goods went to market; they gave up half of the money it made to the landowner. The landowner did nothing and still got half the money his land produced. Sometimes they would accept a job in town for a short time to supplement their income. Making a living was very difficult. Eliza and all the children helped when they were needed which was most of the time. Right away Eliza and Robert started having children of their own. First, there was Robert, who was born within a year of their wedding. Then they had Ellen who was born two years after Robert. By now and with another two children to care for, squeezing out a living really became very difficult. Eliza was missing Little Cat Road where she grew up and especially Concord Baptist Church. Eliza loves her family. She would never leave them. However, she longed to go back to her roots and live near where she grew up and near her sisters. Robert loved her so much and after talking it over he and Orval decided they would go to Florida and see if they could find some other land and see if they could make a better living where the soil seemed more fertile.

They were lucky. Both families found a house near each other and near Little Cat Road where Eliza grew up. Soon they had all their belongings moved into the sharecrop landowner's houses. The houses were simple wood frame houses with tin roofs but they did not leak and were safe to live in. Now they were Floridians. Struggling to find a way to make a living did not get better but everyone seemed happier. They enrolled the little children in Carrabelle School about three miles away.

Eliza and Christiana were in the garden gathering vegetables. Eddie was in the field working with his dad and Mittie was mending clothes in her room and caring for baby Russell and little Rittie. Ellen and Laura were at Carrabelle School. Robert Jr. had come home from the field to get fresh water for the field workers. He was in the kitchen looking for a big jar with a lid when someone knocked at the door. Robert Jr. went to the door. "Hello young man, my name is Bob and I am the census taker for this year, 1900. I'd like to come in and take your census."

"What is census?" Robert asked. "Every ten years we take a count of all the people in our country. That way we know who is here, how many people are here, and where they live."

"You can come in but I'm the only one home right now," Robert said. He did not know that Mittie was in her bedroom with the babies. The census taker stepped inside the door. "Can you start at the top and tell me who lives in this house with you and how old they are."

"Yes, my father lives here. His name is Robert and he is 48 years old. My mother is Eliza and she is thirty-five years old. My sister Mittie lives here. She is seventeen years old. I have a brother named Eddie and he is sixteen years old. My name is Robert Jr. and I am twelve years old. My sister Ellen is ten years old and she lives here. My sister Laura is eight years old and she lives here. Then there is Rittie who is three years old and Russell my baby brother who is one year old.

"Do you know where all of them were born?" the census taker asked.

"Yes sir, Mittie, Eddie, Ellen, and I were born in Georgia and Laura, Rittie and Russel was born here. Rittie had awakened from her nap and she came wandering into the living room where the census taker and Robert were. Suddenly Mittie came hurrying into the room also.

"Rittie I couldn't find you." She stopped abruptly when she saw the strange man and Robert standing there. Robert introduced Mittie to the census taker and said, "I gotta go. They're waiting for some fresh water." He hurried out the door with his jar. He would stop at the well and draw fresh water for the jar. "Your brother is one very smart boy to be only twelve years old," the census taker told Mittie. "I hope your neighbors are home. If I don't catch the residents at home I have to go back until I do."

"I think Milissa is home with James but all the others are in the field like my family. They are our cousins. The man is Orval Browning and he is my father's brother. They have six children. Willie and Minnie are twins. They are fourteen. Milissa is the oldest, she is nineteen, and then there in Joseph who is seventeen, then Ida, she is ten years old and little James is three years old like Rittie.

Bob was smitten with Mittie and he wanted to talk to her. "Robert said your name is Mittie. I guess I did not have to ask that. I have your name right here on my paper."

"Yes, my name is Mittie and I'm not interested in meeting someone for social reasons if that's why you ask."

"Why?" Bob asked. "I intend to live my life as an old maid," Mittie told him. "That's fine as long as you're OK with it," Bob said.

"I am thank you." Bob tipped his hat and was on his way. "She's a strange one." He said to himself as he walked down the steps. Mittie turned to return to the bedroom where baby Russell was still sleeping. "If you're the only man in these woods to spend my life with I'll be happy to spend the rest of it as an old maid." She said as she leaned over the crib to check on baby Russell. Bob was not good looking at all. In fact, he seemed a little whimpy to Mittie. If she could not have a real man, she did not want one at all. However, Mittie did not intend to spend the rest of her life alone. She was just waiting for the perfect man to enter her life. He would someday. She knew he would.

Ma came in from the large vegetable garden. She had a croaker sack over her shoulder filled with fresh black-eyed peas. She knew she would need to hurry. She would shell enough of the peas for their dinner; put them on to cook and then shell the rest of the peas for canning. Eliza could zip right down the pea and push the pea out as she unzipped in what seemed like a split second. She could have won any pea-shelling contest if she had had one to enter. Ma was putting the salt pork in the big pot to boil while she shelled the peas. Baby Russell and little Rittie saw their Ma as they came into the room. Russell was just beginning to walk and he wobbled his way to his Ma and held to her leg. Rittie had the other leg. Rittie wanted Ma's attention and Russell wanted his dinners that she had tucked under her clothes. Ma picked Rittie up and gave her a big hug. "Ma will hold you tonight after supper, I promise," Eliza told Rittie.

She picked Russell up and went back to her chair. Eliza balanced him on her left leg and took her breast out for him to feed. Little Russell held on tight. He was hungry and he did not intend to let that dinner get away. Eliza placed the pan of peas on her right leg and began to zip the peas out again.

Ma heard a wagon coming down Little Cat Road. She watched it until it got close enough that she could see who was in the wagon. It seemed to be in a hurry on the dusty narrow dirt road. It was the year 1900, the first year of the new century. Some people were driving automobiles now. There were 8,000 automobiles on the roads now but there were only 144 miles of paved roads in the USA at this time—Little Cat Road was not one of them.

Ma stood up to get a better look at the wagon since it seemed to be slowing down in front of her house. To her surprise, it was Martha. Martha pulled the wagon into the yard. She climbed down from the wagon. "Martha since when did you start driving the wagon by yourself."

"Eliza, Pa's dead," Martha said. Eliza started to cry.

"What happened? Has he been sick? Why did he die?"

"He got sick about a week ago but he kept on working in the field until three days ago. Then he got so that he was having trouble breathing. Ellen and I carried him to Dr. Smith in Madison and he said he had pneumonia. He said there was an epidemic going on in Madison County and we would need to take him home and put him right to bed with his head elevated. Said to get him to drink lots of water and encourage him to cough so that he could get the pneumonia out of his lungs. He gave him some cough tonic and that helped him to sleep some, but he got worse. When me and Ellen woke up this morning and went in to see about him, he was dead in his bed." Both girls wept while they held each other.

Eliza went back home with Martha. Eliza, Martha, and Ellen had long talks and reminisced at great lengths about growing up with their father. "He was a good man. I remember when we were coming from Ireland on that big ship and I remember all the things Pa did to take care of you, Mom and me, Eliza. Our getting to America seemed to take over Pa's world. It was the most important thing in his life. He was determined to get us here no matter what it took to do it."

"The strangest thing happened the night before he died, Eliza. Ellen and I heard Pa in his room talking. Pa talking out of his head was nothing unusual since he had started taking the cough syrup the doctor gave him, About an hour after he would take the cough syrup he would talk out of his head but this time his words were very clear. Ellen and I went into his room. We found him on his knees by the bed with his head bowed and his eyes closed."

"What was he saying?" Elisa asked. "He said, Lord I know I haven't been perfect and I regret what happened there in Ireland but I had to do it for my dear friend. I hope you will forgive me and let me meet my Louisa in Heaven. And then he said 'Amen' and climbed back into the bed."

"We wanted to ask him what had happened in Ireland but he was too sick. We thought he'd get better and then we would ask him, but he didn't."

Chapter Five

The Cross

When Reason climbed back into bed, his mind wandered back to that day. *I had to do it Lord. I could not let my best friend die trying to save his and his dead brother's family. After his death or he was locked up in prison, nine more people would have died because of it. They were already starving and he was killing himself trying to prevent it.*

Reason had grown up on a big farm in Ireland that his family had rented for three generations. His best friends lived just down the road on a farm not quite as big as the one Reason's family had but they too rented their farm and had lived there for several generations. Reason's best friends were twins whose names were Timmy and Tommy Mallory. They were the same age as Reason, lacking one month in Reason's favor. In the early years, they were all one big happy family. Both families went to St. Patrick's Cathedral to church in Dublin every Sunday. They would eat Sunday dinner that Reason's mother had prepared one Sunday and the next Sunday they would eat at the Mallory house. Sometimes they would go down to the meadow and have a big picnic and both families had prepared the food. They would swim in the river, play ball and do lots of foot racing. The girls had jump ropes, played hop scotch and jack stone.

They worked hard all week but Sundays were always fun time. Reason and the twins were inseparable almost every moment that they were not working on their farms. However, as with most situations, nothing last forever and a horrible thing happened to all of them when the three boys were only fourteen years old. A fungus spread over the entire potato crop on both farms. The blight was so severe that it killed every potato growing on both farms and left nothing but brown dried up stems and leaves behind. Not only were these two farms involved but also every potato field in the whole of Ireland had rotted with the fungus before it was ready to harvest. Since potatoes were the main crop grown in Ireland, this left the whole country penniless with no way to earn money for at least another year. The two families struggled on for a while, but finally in 1850, when the potatoes had failed again and people were starving on the streets, London made a new law. It stated that every landowner was compelled to provide food for the people living on his land. The landowner had no money either since his land could not produce potatoes. He got nothing out of his lands either. The only way he could get around this law was to throw the families out of their homes on his property. This was devastating to the families. At least, up until now, they had a roof over their heads. Now they would be homeless. Timmy and Tommy's parents refused to move out. The property owner burned their house down so they would have no choice but to leave the property.

"What in the name of Heaven is to become of us? What are we to do?" Timmy and Tommy's mother said to their dad. They had no cows or chickens like Reason's family, so now they were very destitute. The Marlow's took the Mallory's in. They would do the best they could. As long as Marlow paid their lease, they could stay in the house. In addition, they intended to do what ever they could to see that it was paid. Everyone worked hard with the chickens and cows so that they could produce to the best of their abilities.

The three teen-age boys decided it was time for them to get out on their own. Their leaving would mean three fewer mouths to feed. They took all their clothes, tied them in a bundle, attached them to the end of a stick, and went off down the road with their belongings on their shoulders. They walked along the soggy dirt roads not believing their eyes. They saw old men, old women, and little children walking as if in a daze. They were wandering along appearing to be going no place. Their faces tallow and gaunt. The little children had over sized bellies and most of them were whimpering as if they did not have enough energy left to cry. They were just walking along aimlessly with no place to go. They saw mud huts with people living in them with no roof over their heads. They saw people living in holes dug in the Irish bogs. They also saw many houses had become heaps of rubble as the proprietor destroyed them to prevent anyone from moving in. At one point, the three boys stopped, huddled together beside the road, and prayed to God to help these poor starving people.

When they arrived in Dublin, they began to look for work. After three days and what seemed like an impossible task, the boys finally found work. Timmy would work as a livery boy at a stable. People coming into Dublin on business left their horses there to be shod, fed, watered, and cared for while they were in town. Tommy found work as an apprentice at a black smith shop. He would be the errand and cleaning boy until he learned enough about the business to make horseshoes and other iron works. Reason found a job at a fish market cleaning fish. He hated the smell of fish but he would do anything until something better came along.

Sometimes Reason would go to St. Patrick's Cathedral and just sit on the benches in front of the church. Reason had a soft gentle heart and he missed his family terribly. He could find solace in the familiar place that had been such a great part of his childhood. He never saw his family anymore. They had lost the horses and wagons to the poverty-ridden times. All that his family had now for transportation was an ox and ox cart and only two or three could ride on the ox cart at one time. Dublin was too far away to walk. Being away from their family did not seem to bother Timmy and Tommy too much. Reason supposed it was that they had each other. Reason wished it did not bother him either but it did. He certainly did not want Timmy and Tommy to find out about his soft side though. Reason was not afraid they might tease him, but for some reason, the twins seemed to look up to Reason. He did not know why but he sure did not want to spoil it. Reason would sit in front of the church and reminisce about all the fun times they had had there together and with their families. He never told the twins about the story his Mother had told him long ago. She said that her grandfather from many, many generations ago had been born of royalty and when he was sixteen years, old pirates kidnapped him from his family, brought him to Ireland, and sold him as a slave. She said he converted to Catholicism while he was in captivity. She said he had to work for this family for six years. However, when he was older he ran away and went back home. He went to the finest schools and had the best education available. When he was finished with his education, was older, very wealthy and on his own, he had a desire to return to Ireland. She said he returned and stayed for most of the remainder of his life there. She told Reason that he loved St. Patrick's Cathedral so much that he placed a solid gold cross somewhere in the church as a replica for his love for the Church. She said he never told anyone where he had placed it and to this day, no one knew where it was. However, everyone knew it was there... somewhere.

One day after church and while the adults socialized, Reason wandered off alone. He wanted to look for the gold cross. It eluded him that day but the next time he had a chance to wander alone in the church he thought he found it. Reason knew that church members were not, allowed inside the Father's side of the confessional booth but he had looked everyplace else and knew there was no gold cross anywhere else in the church. He would pray for forgiveness later but right now while he had the chance, he had to look there. He looked around to be sure no one was there to see him do such a sinful thing. When he was sure, no one was watching he jerked the dark curtain open and jumped inside. He quickly closed the curtain back. He looked on the walls, nothing there. He looked under the bench, nothing there. Just as he was beginning to peek outside to see if the coast was clear, something caught his eye on the floor. It was just a tiny spot on the stone floor. It looked like a small shinny rock mixed with the stone and built into the floor. He tried to give it a good look but it was impossible since the tiny room was near dark and he would not dare open the curtain to let light in while he was there. There was nothing to do except leave and hope no one saw him. Maybe that was the gold cross, embedded in the floor and maybe it was not. He would never know.

One day the twins told Reason that they had met two sisters and had fallen in love with them and they were getting married. Reason knew they had been seeing the two girls. He did not get to spend as much time with them now as he had before but that was all right with Reason. When he saw the look of happiness in his best friend's eyes, he was so happy for them. He wished them luck and gave each of them a hug. Their wedding day was two days away and Reason had obligated himself to go out on the fishing boat for the next three days to help with the nets. The next time he would see his friends they would be married men. It seemed strange since it had always been the three of them. Now they were tuning into five.

Reason met Louisa one month after the twins wedding and had been seeing her ever since. The twins already had little homes. They were not much more than one room shacks but it would be home to them and they would make it into a happy home. Reason could not help but envy his best friends. One day he asked Louisa if she would marry him. "I'll have to ask my dad. He will probably say no, since we have only known each other for six months." To Louisa's happy surprise her father said, "Tell the boy to come and ask for your hand."

"You had better mind your manners when you ask my dad. Sometimes he get's upset at simple things and once he's said "no" he never changes his mind."

"I don't want him to say no," Louisa said. "Me neither and rest assured I'll be on my best behavior." Reason would go to Louisa's house for dinner this Saturday evening. He had gotten off the whole day since he knew it would take him the better part of the day to wash the fish smell off. He tried not to be early for dinner that night and he would have to try extra hard not to act over anxious in front of Louisa's dad. He was more nervous than he had ever been in his life. Partly because, if her dad said "yes" then he would be obligated to marry Louisa and if he said "no" he would surely loose the love of his life. Reason only hoped it was the right thing to do. He kept weighing one decision against the other and every time the "yes" came out on top. He decided to put it to rest and leave it in God's hands. If her father said "yes", God meant them to be together and if he said "no" God was not in favor of the marriage between them.

After a delicious dinner of Irish stew and corn bread that Saturday evening, Reason popped the question to Louisa's dad. "Sir, I love your daughter very much and I would like to marry her. Will you give me her hand in marriage please?" Louisa's father took a long draw on his pipe, leaned back in the upholstered chair, and slowly let the smoke escape his mouth. Then he said, "Only if you promise to take care of her."

"Oh yes sir, I'll take very good care of her, I promise you," Reason said.

"Alright, you have her hand in marriage if it's alright with her mother." Reason had not allowed for this answer. Now what was he suppose to do? Was he supposed to do it all over again for the mother? He looked at Louisa. Then he looked at her mother. She was smiling and shaking her head yes, while she never missed a stitch with her knitting.

"You have my blessings on a wonderful marriage son, one filled with lots of love and lots of children." Louisa heard the sigh of relief come from Reason. She knew he was the man for her. She was happy.

After their simple little wedding, Louisa and Reason moved into their own one room adobe shack with the thatched roof. It was small and not much to look at but it was home and had all the warmth and love of any home.

Louisa took in sewing to supplement their income. Ireland remained in a state of desperate poverty. Thousands of Irish people had died from starvation or related diseases since the 1845 potato famine began. It had lasted five years and the ravages from it lasted another ten years. Irish people continued to die on the streets in large numbers. Dysentery was the number one killer. It would begin in one household and quickly spread to every family member, leaving the entire family dead. Since no one was left to bury the bodies, and clean away the disease causing bacteria. The dead bodies remained in the roofless huts. When the rain fell, it washed fragments of the diseased bodies into the streets and other areas, contaminating everything it touched and killing more and more people and the cycle started all over again in a never-ending loop. Reason and Louisa felt themselves very fortunate. At least their shack had a roof. Timmy and Tommy felt the same. They were grateful for what little they had. They knew that they were better off than their own family who was still living in squalor with Reason's family in the country.

Soon babies were entering each household. Within a few short years, Timmy had four little ones and Tommy had three. Martha had arrived at the Marlow house. It would take another ten years before Eliza would arrive.

"Reason, next Thursday will be Eliza's second birthday and I want to have a party for her with all her little friends. Do you suppose you can be available to help me with it?" Louisa asked.

"Baby, I am so sorry but I promised the boss that I would go out with the crew next week for four days and help pull the nets. They are going to be short one hand if I don't go."

Reason occasionally went with the crew in the large fishing boat owned by the company. He would not turn down his chance at sea since he received more pay for every hour while he was at sea. In the fish market, his pay was only for the eight hours that he worked. It always gave a nice boost to the family's income.

"That's alright. I will get it done. I don't want you to loose the chance at the money since we certainly need it," Louisa said. Sometimes she did not think they could go on another day. Food was so short sometimes that she went for days without eating so that the food would last longer for her family.

After four days, at sea Reason was especially tired. Reason got very little sleep on the noisy ship while the men pulled the nets both day and night. He dreamed of a good long sleep after a nice warm bath when he returned home. However, that was not to be. Louisa had devastating news waiting when he returned.

When she told Reason, what had happened while he was gone he needed her to repeat it. It was too horrible for him to comprehend. "I said, Timmy was shoeing a horse when a fight broke out at the pub across the street. Someone started shooting. The horse Timmy was shoeing spooked and began kicking in attempts to run. His hoof caught Timmy right at the forehead and his kick lifted off Timmy's entire skull exposing his brain. The doctor said he had died immediately."

"Oh my God, Louisa, when did it happen?"

"It happened the day after you left on the fishing trip. They've already buried him," Louisa said. What about Katie and the children?"

"Katie seems lost and still in a daze. Her heart is totally broken. She keeps saying that she wants to join him. She doesn't want to live without him."

"I keep reminding her of the four children and how much they love and need her but she seems not to hear."

"She needs you Reason. She needs your wisdom. You need to go now to her."

Reason took his wife's advice and started walking toward his dear friend's home. He wept as he walked. He wept for the loss of his friend, for Timmy's family and for the end of a life that the three of them had shared together. He could not imagine the pain that Tommy must be feeling. "Poor Tommy," Reason said aloud to himself. He and his brother had always lived as one. Reason knew that Tommy felt that half of his self were gone now.

When Reason arrived at Timmy's house, he found Tommy there. He was sitting alone in a corner with more pain and sorrow showing on his face than he had ever seen on one person's face in his lifetime. Reason tried to comfort him but his hurt was too deep.

Reason found Katie wandering aimlessly about the house. Her face appeared without expression. Reason tried to talk to her but he soon realized his words only bounced off her face. She was not hearing a thing he said. The four little children were huddled in a corner looking as afraid and lost as their mother. Reason knew he would need to do something for the children. This was entirely too much trauma for children this young. It would scar them for life. Reason gathered the children and some clothes for them and told Tommy and Katie that he was taking the children to his house for a while. They never heard him. Reason walked out the door with the four children.

"Louisa, we need to do something for these children," Reason said to her as uncontrollable tears flowed down his face. Louisa took the four dirty children. She placed them at the dinner table where she fed them a hardy soup with vegetables and mutton. Tears filled her eyes as she watched the eager little eaters empty their bowls. Not only were they afraid and hurt but they were hungry too. When they had eaten their fill, Louisa carried them to the back where Reason had a tub of warm water waiting. Each of them got a bath and clean clothes. Louisa showed each of them mounds of love with lots of hugs and kisses throughout their baths. Louisa placed the children in clean warm beds where they slept the rest of the day and throughout the night.

Reason tried to think of a solution for the desolate mother and four little children. He knew the children needed to be with their mother if she was ever to get out of the state of mind she now suffered. They needed their mother completely again.

Reason decided to go back to visit Katie and Tommy. He would leave the children with Louisa. When he arrived, he found Tommy and his wife with Katie. Their three children were running and playing about the house. Suddenly it occurred to Reason. Katie and her children needed this extended family. This would be normal for them since they had lived most of their lives together. "

"Tommy, will you and Betsy take Katie and her children into your home if I can help you find a bigger home to live in?"

"Yes", Tommy said.

"Katie, will you and the children live with Betsy and Tommy if you have enough room for all of you to live together?"

Almost automatically, Katie answered "Yes". Reason felt this is something they would have done anyway if they were thinking with clear minds now. All they needed was someone to suggest it.

By nightfall Reason had Katie and her belongings moved into Tommy's little shack. The families were crammed in the little house but it would have to do until Reason could think of something else.

Reason felt that it was not safe for Katie to keep the kids alone in her state of mind and besides that, Timmy's rent was due weekly. There would be no money to pay rent for another week nor for any weeks after this since their breadwinner was gone. At least the problems were solved short term.

A week passed and Tommy had gathered his wits again but Katie still had a ways to go. Betsy just led her sister about and told her what to do and she did it. The children were safe now but they missed their father and the mother they once had.

Another week passed. Reason stopped by Tommy's house after work that afternoon. Tommy was not home.

"He had to take a night job since his job at the blacksmith didn't bring in enough money to feed all of us," Katie told him. Tommy was now working all day at the blacksmith shop and all night as a night watchman at a bank. Reason wondered how long Tommy would hold out. Besides that, he had promised to find them a larger place to live. Where would the money come from to pay for it even if he could find a larger place? If only they could come up with some cash, they could buy a farm cheap now since so many farms had been lost during and the years after the potato famine. There would be seven children to work on the farm and Tommy knew how to run a farm. Where could they come up with the money? Reason checked into a farm for sale and found, if they could come up with four thousand, three hundred and seventy five pounds, they could buy the perfect farm for Tommy and his large family. It had a big farmhouse already there. "Lord, please help us to find a way to get the money we need to buy the farm."

Reason told Tommy about his find. "Tommy it would be enough land that you can have a good living and the big house is already there. All of you would have plenty of room to live there."

"It sounds wonderful. I'll ask my boss if he'll loan me the money." Tommy looked so haggard and tired. It pulled at Reason's heart to see him looking that way.

Tommy was going to ask his boss while he was at work today. Reason prayed all day that his boss would loan him the money. "Sir, I need a bigger house for my family now that I have my brother's wife and children also. My friend has found a house large enough for all of us. Can you loan me the money to buy the house? I could pay you back with interest."

"Where is this house?" his boss asked. When Tommy told him where the house was his boss questioned the property. "I thought they were selling that place with the farm included."

"They are sir," Tommy answered. "You're asking me to finance a home for you and if I do I'm going to loose you to a business of your own?"

"I guess that's right sir," Tommy answered. "You don't suspect I have grown this black smith shop this big by doing stupid things like that, do you lad?"

"I guess not," Tommy said. He could feel the embarrassment and humiliation flow over him. However, he knew this would not be the last humiliation he would feel. He knew he would need to go on from here and try to find someone to loan him the money. When he went to the bank to work that night he picked his courage up and tried it again with this boss. The bank owner started laughing as he finished his request to him. The man with the big belly and fat jaws laughed and laughed and finally between laughs he said. "Son, I am holding on here by a thread. If this country did not have so many debtors in it and more people paid their bills and did not rob the ones who are not in great debt, I might have some money. However, just having to hire you to keep the destitute away at night is more than I can afford. Sorry but I can't help you."

Tommy did not know his boss felt that way. It was obvious that he begrudged having to hire him. Tommy knew his boss put him in the category with the other poor individuals who could not make a living wage. He wanted the farm more than any thing now. He did not want to work for the jeweler any longer. However, there was no way out now. There was no one else to ask for the money. He would have to tell Reason. He wished that Reason did not worry so much about his problems. Nevertheless, every night when he said his prayers he thanked God for a friend like Reason.

When Reason heard the dreaded news about the refusal from both bosses, he felt that it might be over for poor Tommy. If it was, he did not know what was to happen to that family. Katie's and Betsy's families were as poor as Tommy's. It was certain that they could not help them. Their mother had already died from marasmus. Reason knew that there was nothing left to do except ask his own boss for the loan. Reason dreaded discussing his friend's financial situation with his boss but there was nothing left. He would ask him as soon as he arrived at work tomorrow morning.

Reason rehearsed his plea for the loan to his boss until he fell asleep that night. "Mr. Lowery, I have never asked anything of you and I know this is a big thing to ask, but my good friend and his family's life depends on your answer."

No, I do not want to sound like I am begging. "Mr. Lowery do you have some money that you can loan my best friend. His brother died and now he has his brother's wife and children. They need a bigger house." *No, that did not sound convincing enough.* After thinking through the problem repeatedly in his head and missing half a night's sleep, he decided he would just wait until arriving at work the next morning and say whatever came out. However, he was still worried. It would be their last hope.

When he arrived at work the next morning Mr. Lowery was not there. Instead, a young lad appeared with a key to open the business for him. "Pa's laid up today. Ma says she's afraid he has consumption," the boy said.

"Will he be in later today?"

"No, Ma's making him stay in bed all day today." Reason hoped the lad did not see the disappointment showing on his face. "Tell your Pa when close this evening I'll come by with the receipts for the day," Reason said to the boy. He had to ask him today. He could not let another day go by without knowing what was to happen to Tommy and his family. It was a busy day. Everyone wanted one fish. He stayed busy all day since it had been a steady stream of costumers.

When evening came and it was time to close, he gathered his receipts and walked to his boss's house. Mr. Lowery was in bed and Mrs. Lowery appeared slightly agitated when he asked if he could talk to him. "Hold it down to only a minute. He's a sick man," she said. Reason walked into Mr. Lowery's bedroom. He reached out his hand. Mr. Lowery extended his hand in a weak looking manner."

Before Reason could say anything Mr. Lowery said, "Son, I think I'm mighty sick. I have known for sometime that something was wrong with my lungs and now I know there is since I am coughing up blood. I might have to give the business up and if I do, I would like to sell it to you. You could pay for it by the month according to how much money you made that month. That is if you would want the business." Reason was stunned. This was the chance of a lifetime. Anyone would want a deal like Mr. Lowery's offer.

"That would be the best thing that ever happened to me. There is nothing, I would want more than to own the fish market. I would always take care of it and see that it prospers and grows as it has done since you opened it twenty five years ago."

"Give me a day or two to see if I'm going to get better and I'll let you know something." He said to Reason. Reason was now, left in a dilemma. The reason he had come to Mr. Lowery's house was for one thing and that was to ask for the loan. How could he do it now after his offer? Reason stood there silent for a minute then it just came out as if he had no control over it. "Mr. Lowery, do you remember when my friend who was killed by the horse?" "Yes, lad I do." Well his twin brother is working two jobs now to make ends meet since he now has both his and Timmy's family to earn a living for and it's about to get the best of him." "I've found him a farm that he can buy for less than five thousand pounds. Tommy could run the farm, make far more money, and work half as much. However, he has no money. I was thinking if there was any way that you might loan it to him?" *There...now it was out.*

"Reason I'd give it to him in a minute if this hadn't happened to me but now I need to save what I have for medical bills and for my family if something should happen to me. I wish I could give your friend the money and I certainly would if I could. Tell him I hope him the very best and it's a noble thing that he is doing."

"Yes sir, I'll tell him," Reason said. He could not let his disappointment show especially after the offer he had given him. Now they were back to square one.

As Reason walked home, he thought about any other possibilities that might be available to them. It eluded him. They had gone through every option they had. Face it, there were no options left for them. Reason wanted to be happy about Mr. Lowery's offer for the business but now he was so worried about Tommy that he could not even think about it. When he reached home, he told Louisa everything. He had not told her about his finding a perfect place for Tommy and his family. Now he was telling her about that and the attempts they had made to get the money. He wanted to be happy about the possibility of owning the fish company one day but Tommy and his desperate situation kept him from even thinking about it.

"Reason you are a good man to put your friend and his family first and try to help them. Do not give up. Sooner or later something will fall in place for them."

Reason went to bed that night with a heavy heart. What could they do? It is for sure they had to do something or soon there would be no breadwinner in the family at all. Tommy was looking worse every day. The hard work and very little sleep were taking a horrible toll on his health. How much longer could he hold out? When Reason fell asleep he had a dream about the shinny little spot on the floor of the Father's side of the confessional at the St. Patrick's Cathedral. The little spot shined so bright that it almost blinded him in his dream.

The next day he could not get the dream off his mind. He thought about it all day even though he was busier than ever. Mr. Lowery was still at home in bed with his illness. Reason could handle the business alone, and he was determined to keep it clean and prosperous for Mr. Lowery. Mr. Lowery had told Reason that he could deliver the receipts once a week and unless he needed something, he would see him then. Reason felt proud that his boss trusted him that much.

A fishing boat had just entered the battery. He heard loud voices using profanity, coming from the boat as it was docking. Reason looked out the side window of the old fish market. He saw two men fall over the side of the big boat. Two other men came to the side of the boat and looked over at the fallen men. They stood watching for only a few minutes then walked away. Soon Reason saw the two men lumbering from the battery to the fish market. Reason wondered if the two men seen falling from the boat were actually thrown over by these two men. It was obvious that they were all pirates. Probably they were pirates from Spain. Each of them had the mossy Spanish beards like those worn by the old men of Spain. One of them had a stick for his left leg and the other one had a black round patch covering his right eye. Both of them smelled worse than the fish market had ever smelled even on its worse day. They had dirt and mud caked on each of them as if it they had purposefully smeared it there but Reason doubted that. They had dried food on their faces and in their beards.

All Reason could think was, "Lord don't let them cause any trouble." He did not want the store trashed. He could not face another major problem now. Reason had never been a fighter. He always believed in solving problems with talk. "Please don't spit on the floors." Reason said to the first man who was chewing a large plug of tobacco. Dark tobacco juice dripped from each corner of his mouth as he turned his head to the side and spit a large thick brown splatter on the fish market floor.

"Ah Lad, tan't none yo bousiness. Yo don own dis stablishment. Dat be Mr. Lowery. He be me mate. Wher hell be he dis day?"

"He's home sick today. I am in charge today. Can I help you?" Reason said.

"What hell he want me do tis stuff he want?" The man was holding out a medium size dirty sack that might have been white one day. "What is it?" Reason asked as he reached for the sack. When Reason opened the sack and peaked inside, he was completely surprised. He found himself looking at a beautiful gold angelic flower vase that weighed approximately four pounds and a beautiful cherub statue weighing approximately five pounds. "You brought this for Mr. Lowery?" Reason asked.

"Ya, I bing he wot he wans."

"Did he tell you to bring him this?"

"Ya, he collect pure gold."

"Do you mean both of these are pure gold?"

"Yah, Yah, twenty fo kart gold."

"Why does Mr. Lowery buy these?"

"Vestment lad, Vestment." "If you want to leave them I'll take them to him tonight and you can wait until tomorrow and I'll have the money for you before you leave."

"Nah, Nah, lad I take 'em to hem now. Ah know wher he live." He took the bag from Reason and the two men walked out the door. Reason assumed he knew where Mr. Lowery lived and they probably knew each other better than Reason suspected. Reason thought it strange that they were so familiar with Mr. Lowery. He had never seen the two men before and he has been working here for Mr. Lowery going on fifteen years now.

About an hour later, the two pirates returned to the Fish Market without the sack. "Me mate mighty sick. He says you come when you close business tonight."

"How long have you known Mr. Lowery?" Reason asked. "Ah, lad we ben mates goin' on twenty-five yers now." He guessed Mr. Lowery might be a very wealthy man. He had owned the Fish Market and he had been gathering gold from the pirates all these years.

Reason figured he knew what Mr. Lowery wanted with him tonight. He was probably much worse now and was ready to turn the business over to him. He would need to think of something fast so that he could help his friend before he took over the business. There may be no time to do it then.

Reason watched as the two pirates walked toward their boat. "Hey fellows," Reason yelled at the pirates. "When are you leaving?"

"Tis nite, mate, why yo ast? May I talk to you a minute?" Reason asked. "When yo want ta talk?" the man asked.

"I'll talk to you right now," Reason said. The two men turned and walked back to the market. The three men stood in the doorway of the Fish Market. Reason turned to one of the pirates. "How would you like to have a solid gold piece that weighs about forty pounds?"

"Gad amighty, wher yo git a piece o gold dat big?"

"It doesn't matter where I get it from if I can get it for you tonight--will you give me five thousand pounds for it?" it.?"

"I'll giv yo six thousand pounds for dat much gold lad." Wait for me on the boat. I should be back in about an hour," Reason said as he was closing the Fish Market door. Reason always hid the receipts for the business under a loose board on the floor. He knew no one would ever look there.

Reason ran as fast as he could. He knew he could find Tommy walking from the Black Smith Shop to the bank if he hurried. Before he reached him, Reason knew it was his life long friend from the distance. "Tommy!" he yelled.

"Hey Reason," Tommy said as he stopped to wait for his mate.

"Tommy I have to talk to you." Tommy looked at his old friend with a confused look. He did not remember ever seeing Reason looking this anxious. Tommy and Reason walked to a near by bench. They sat down together on the bench. "Tommy there is something I want to tell you."

Tommy's face lit up. "You found a loan for me?" Tommy asked.

"Sorry but no, that is not what I have to tell you," Reason said.

"Then what is it?" Tommy asked. "I think I have a way to get the money for the farm. But you'll have to agree to do something that you are not going to like if we get it."

"Something happened long ago. I never told you since it never seemed important before but now it does." Total confusion was showing on Tommy's face.

My mother had a relative several hundred years ago who lived in Scotland. He was from royalty and when he was sixteen years old he was kidnapped by pirates, brought here to Ireland and sold to a family here as a slave. He stayed here for six years before he ran away and back to his home. He went to the St. Patrick's Cathedral while he was here and since it was the first time he had ever known Christianity, it stole his heart away. After he was educated and very wealthy, he returned to Ireland to convert Druid's to Christianity for the church. When he grew old, he wanted to give the church a relic to show his love and devotion to the church forever. He had a cross-made of solid gold and implanted it in the floor of the church. I know exactly where the cross is and my mother told me the gold cross weighs about forty pounds. No one in the church knows where the cross is. They know it is embedded somewhere in the church but they do not know where. I finally found it one day when I was searching on my own. Tommy, I have a buyer for the gold cross if you will go into the church and dig it up."

"When will I have to do this Reason?" Tommy asked.

"You'll need to do it right now."

"Reason, I'm going to need time to pray about this. You know it's a sin to break into the church."

"Yes, I know it's a sin to break into the church and it's also a sin to steal the cross. But Tommy, that's our only hope of getting you into a bigger house and providing a living for your family without killing yourself."

"You're right Reason. Lets go, I'll do it." The two boys turned toward the church. Neither of them had committed such a sin in their life. They never said a word all the way to the church. When they reached the church, they stepped into the woods in front of the church.

"Tommy it is embedded in the floor on the Father's side of the confessional booth. Here, I brought this pick from the Fish Market for you to use. Just remember, what ever you do, please cover up the space when you're finished so no one will notice it."

Tommy took the pick and the boys quietly walked across the street and toward the back of the church. There was a small window. The boys pushed hard on the window and it finally opened. Reason watched for anyone walking in the area while Tommy slid through the window and with his pick went directly to the confessional. This had also been his church and he knew where everything was inside. While Reason watched, he found himself praying that it was the gold cross, buried in the booth floor. Suddenly he started to laugh quietly and said to himself, "I can't pray to the Lord for him to help me to rob him." He really felt bad about what they were doing. He knew he was going to start going back to church the next Sunday and he was never going to quit going again. He knew God would forgive him for this grave sin they were committing if he prayed hard enough afterwards.

It seemed to take forever while Reason waited at the window. Finally, Tommy came to the window in the dark but the cross was so heavy and shinny that Reason knew immediately it had been the gold cross, buried there. The shine from the cross was exactly as it had been in his dream. "Reason this cross weighs more that forty pounds, I believe."
"Well, whatever it weighs we're getting six thousand pounds for it." When they finally got the cross and Tommy out the window Reason could see that, it was truly a beautiful cross. The two boys ran while they were in dark areas all the way to the boat. They lugged the cross onto the boat hoping no one saw them. When the pirates saw the cross, they were extremely excited.

"Ah when yo say yo got a hunk o gole n a full piece you mean it, lad." The man with the stick for a left leg handed Reason six thousand pounds. The two boys counted the money a second time before they left the men to be sure they had it all. All of it was there. As the two boys walked toward the bank, they each had emotions they had never felt before. They were relieved to have enough money so that Tommy could be a free and healthier man soon. They were happy that instead of ten people attempting to live in a one-room shack now they would each have their own bedrooms and plenty of room for nine children to grow. They felt small and dirty for breaking into the church and stealing from it. The two boys felt guilty for disrupting something placed in the church so long ago by a man who loved the church so much.

"Reason, one thing that I forgot to tell you, I could not completely cover the hole up. We need to go back and get some more dirt and rocks to fill in the hole completely before Sunday."

"OK, I will go back and do it early in the morning before I go to work." Reason was so relieved now that Tommy no longer had a major problem. Tommy had never been happier in his life. He loved his friend now more than ever. He made a promise to himself that he would find someone in need and help him as Reason had helped him.

Early the next morning Reason left thirty minutes early to go to the church. He had his bucket filled with dirt and rocks. He did not think anyone in the church knew the cross was there. Even if they could tell that, the floor had been slightly disturbed they would not know why and so it would not be important. Reason squeezed through the same little window. He carried his dirt and rocks to the booth. Tommy was right. Removing the cross had left a small crater in the floor of the confessional. Reason put the dirt and rocks in the hole and began stomping it tightly. He had his back to the curtain while he filled in the hole and stomped it down good with his feet. As he turned around facing the curtain to pack that side of the filled in hole, he saw black shoes at the bottom of the curtain. The black well-polished shoes sticking inside under the curtain were not moving but Reason knew there were feet in these shoes. His heart started racing. Who was standing in those shoes? There was only one way out and it was through the curtain. Reason had not thought about anything like this happening to him. He did not have a clue what to do now but he knew he was in serious trouble. Finally, the curtain slowly opened and standing face to face was Reason and the Priest. "May I ask what you are doing in my confessional?"

"Father, the last time I was at church I noticed the floor here was wearing out and I came this morning to repair it."

"You saw the need to climb in the window to repair the floor in a room that you have never been in unless you sinfully did it." The Priest looked down at the floor.

"You got the cross, didn't you?" Reason was speechless. How did he know the cross was there? "I don't know what you're talking about Father." Reason said in a shaky voice. The Priest leaned over and touched the soft dirt and rocks. "Yes, that's what you did. You stole the golden cross." He looked Reason directly in the eyes. "Why did you do it my son?" "You have committed an atrocity that will admonish you to hell. What could have been so important to you that you are willing to spend eternity in hell for?" the Priest asked.

"Father all I can say is the lives of seven little children depended on that cross."

"Why did you not come to the church with your problem?"

Funny, Reason thought but he never even thought about the church helping Timmy. It was too late now so he would have to decide what to do next. It is for sure he could not get the cross back. Nor would he tell where the money from the cross was. Reason made his mind up in that few short minutes that he would prefer Tommy get the farm than go to heaven himself. Reason wanted to save the children but more than anything he loved his friend and wanted to save him from certain death if his quality of life was not soon changed.

"You need to come to my study. You are aware that I will need to send for the police," the Priest said to Reason. The Father walked away and Reason followed him. Reason knew his scheme to help Tommy has now, been exposed and he would have to pay the price. Reason waited in the Father's office while he left the room for a few minutes. The Priest returned and said, "How did you know where the gold cross was since no one in the church has ever known where it was imbedded?" Reason did not want to tell the Priest how he had found it.

"Father, you are in the church and you knew where it was." "Every Priest who has ever preached in the church knew where the cross was. They were told by the Priest before them and each of them took an oath that they would never tell where it was."

"And this, my son, is the reason no one was ever to know where it was." Suddenly two burly looking police officers walked in the door. They walked to Reason and said. "Is this the bloke who stole the gold, Father?"

"Yes, he is," the Father, answered. One of the officers grabbed one of Reason's arms while the other grabbed his other arm. They literally picked Reason up and started taking him to the door. "Wait, don't take him away. I need to talk to him," the old Priest said. "You said you did this for the lives of seven children. Is that true?" the Priest asked Reason.

"Yes, My Father that is why I did it."

"Are these seven children your own?"

"No Sir."

"Are they relatives of yours?"

"No Sir."

"Are you telling me that you committed this serious sin for people who are no blood to you?"

"Yes Father I did."

The Priest looked at the officers and said, "I do not wish to pursue this matter any further."

Then he looked at Reason and said, "I want to tell you that God is not pleased with what you did even though you had good reasons for doing it, I am not please with you for doing it and I'm sure no member in this church will be pleased with it. I will need to tell my parishes that the dear old cross is gone from its resting place. I will also tell them who took it. My advice to you is to leave the church and never return. I will destroy your letter. I will advise you never to enter another Catholic church in the name of our Lord and to repent of your sin and pray faithfully for the rest of your life to the Holy Father."

The Priest turned to the police officers and said, "That is all, I am finished with him."

"Father you need to file charges against him for theft," one of the officers said.

"No, let him go."

"Well it's not going to be that easy for him," the other officer said.

"I told you I will file no charges against him."

The two officers looked bewildered. The Priest stood and walked out of his office. One of the officers looked at Reason and said. "He's throwing you out of the church but that isn't enough punishment for the crime you committed. Therefore, we are throwing you out of the country. There is a free ship leaving tomorrow morning for the new country. We will be there when it leaves and if you are not on it, we are coming after you and the city will file charges against you. You will spend a long time in prison paying for this crime."

Reason thought of ways to tell Louisa this devastating news. There was no doubt that the Marlow family would be leaving tomorrow on the early morning ship headed for America. He needed to figure a way to tell her without telling the real reason they would be leaving so soon to a foreign country where they would stay forever. *How would he ever tell her? They had never discussed leaving Ireland – not ever. Maybe if he could tell her that it was a vacation she would accept it but this --- never.* Another problem Reason had was no money. He did not have a pound note to his name. It took all the money that he made each week just to feed them and even that was not enough. It would be difficult for Louisa to understand why he would want to leave for such a long trip with no money.

Reason did not go by the fish market when he left the church. He went to Mr. Lowery's house. "Sir, I am afraid I have bad news for you. My wife and I are leaving in the morning for America. I have enjoyed working for you all these years and I wish that I could stay but accounts beyond our control are forcing us to leave for America tomorrow morning. I hope you will forgive me for leaving you in such dire straits as now."

Mr. Lowery was so sick Reason wondered how much of what he had said to him had really sunk in.

"I am leaving all the receipts with your wife."

Mr. Lowery only nodded his head and said, "I'll miss you lad."

With that, Reason turned and walked out. He almost hated himself thinking of the potential he could have had if he had not committed the crime. When he thought about his reason for the crime it all went away. Nothing could have prevented him from helping his dear friend and his family.

Reason still did not go home to his family. Instead, he went to the Black Smith Shop.

"Tommy I went back to the church this morning to fill the hole with dirt and rocks. I was busy packing the hole when the Father showed up at the confession booth. He called the police. Father refused to file charges against me. However, he called the police and they were determine to punish me"

"Oh my God, Reason. I will go, right now, to the police and explain, it was I who took the gold cross. You cannot take the blame for this," Tommy said as he started walking away.

Reason caught him by the arm. "You will do nothing of the kind. No one knows you were involved and you will never tell. I have already received punishment for it and now the crime is behind us," Reason said.

"What kind of punishment, my dear friend?" Tommy asked.

Reason could see the anguish in his friends face. "My family and I will be leaving at first light on a ship headed for America," Reason told him.

"How long will you be gone?" Tommy asked.

"We will be gone forever, we will never return here."

Reason saw tears well up in Tommy's eyes and they began to flow down his face, as he asked, "Is that the punishment? Are they throwing you out of the country?

"Yes, Tommy, and it's a light punishment compared to what it might have been."

"I'll be fine; we will go to America and start a new life and I will never discuss this crime again. You have your money now. You can buy the farm and still have hundreds of pounds left for getting started. I hope that you will use your money wisely and make a wonderful home for your beautiful family. They are worth all that we have done. You, my friend, are deserving of so much more than was handed to you. You took in your brother's family and worked day and night to prevent them from the impending starvation that that was sure to follow, had you not done it. I wish you all the luck in the world."

Tommy grabbed Reason and gave him a long hug while tears streamed down both their faces.

"If you see my dad and mom tell them, I left for America in hopes of making a better life for my family," Reason said to his friend as he walked away and headed for his house to tell the most important person of all about their plight.

Louisa met Reason at the door when he arrived. Surprised, she said, "You left work early. It is not yet lunchtime. Are you sick?"

"No, Louisa, I am not sick. I have been thinking. We have been married almost fifteen years and I have worked hard to provide you and the children a good living. It seems to me that we are going nowhere. We are just spinning our wheels. With all the hard work I do and with all the sewing you take in by now we should be alright but instead we barely have enough to money to last from one week to the next."

Louisa backed away from Reason. Fear was showing in her face. She had tried to be a good wife and she thought she had been. What was her husband about to tell her? Was he about to tell her that he wanted out of their marriage? She loved him with all her heart and knew she could not live without him. She had tried to hide the desperately hard times from her husband. She had forced smiles and a happy face many times when she lay beside him at night so hungry that she was miserable. She had made excuses when her milk had dried up well before Eliza needed weaning. Louisa's legs suddenly felt weak as if they were going to fall from under her body. She backed to the rocking chair near by and sat down. Faintly, she heard Reason saying, "Louisa, are you alright?"

She just could not answer him. When she gathered her wits, she realized Reason was standing by her side holding to her shoulder. "Louisa, are you alright? Your face is as white as a bed sheet."

"Yes I am alright. What are you trying to tell me Reason?" She did not know if she really wanted him to tell her. She looked up and into his eyes. She did not think she could stand yet. "I was telling you about how hard it is to make a living here. I have been thinking. There is a big ship leaving in the morning from the battery and we can get free passage to America. We can go there and start a new life. One that will be so much better than the one we have now."

Louisa jumped to her feet, threw her arms around her husband and while she squeezed him tightly she said, "You mean all of us; like me and the girls too?" "I wouldn't think about leaving without you and our girls." Reason said.

Louisa hugged him again. "Oh, Reason, it will be the chance of a life time. We can make it there, I know we can."

Chapter Six

Without Reason

They had the wake in the house and the funeral was in the Concord Baptist Church before the burial. Out of a big family of thirteen, there were only three Marlow family members left. Many people got pneumonia that year and the survival of the fittest applied. No one survived except the strongest. There were funerals going on at cemeteries across Madison County almost every day for months. Life expectancy was only forty-seven years and most people did not live to be nearly that old. However, those who were brave enough could live a very carefree life if they wished, while they were living. Marijuana, heroin, and morphine were all available over the counter at the local drugstores. The pharmacist said that heroin clears the complexion, gives buoyancy to the mind, regulates the stomach and bowels, and is, in fact, a perfect guardian of health.

Now there were only Ellen and Louisa to live in the house that Pa had built when they first arrived from Ireland. It was getting old but it was still a good house. Eliza and Robert were married now and lived down the road about five miles away. They were sharecropping their land and raising their eight children. At least, Martha and Sarah owned the house they lived in but they were poor at farming. However, the farming had to go on and they would be the ones to have to do it. Eliza involved herself deep in raising her children and keeping food on the table for them as fast as Robert raised it. She found if she worked hard enough, she didn't think of Pa as much.

Life rolled on and things remained the same. Eliza and Robert's small children had their syrup buckets packed with their lunches consisting mostly of biscuits and syrup. They would take the same three-mile route to school every morning. They were scurried out the door before daylight so that they could make the trip to school by eight a.m. when school started.

This was the same schoolhouse Ma and her siblings went to when they were children. Eliza and her siblings called their parents Ma and Pa and now that Ma would be the only child in her family to grow up and have a family herself, her children also called her and Robert Ma and Pa. Some times Eliza thought about it and it made her sad to think of all the children her parents had given birth to she would be the only one to actually grow to adulthood and build a family of her own.

Most of the children had stolen snuff from Ma's snuffbox. They would dip the snuff on the way to and from school. The teacher did not allowed tobacco in the one room schoolhouse, so they would hide it in the woods and pick it up again on the way home. Some of them never learned to read or write. The ones who did learn to read and write told the others, "You're mind was on the snuff all day instead of your school work"..

The older children and Pa went to the field. Ma gathered vegetables for canning and prepared the meals every day. Mittie was stuck in the house caring for the babies. She was so tired of changing diapers until sometimes she felt like a diaper herself and a dirty one at that. The only thing interesting in her life was the mail and sometimes she would have to wait for up to two weeks before Pa went to the post office in Madison to pick it up. Mittie enjoyed staying in contact with her family on her mother's side. She especially loved her grandmother who lived in Berrien County Georgia. The mail had been arriving quicker now that the north-south line by the Augusta Southern Railroad had established a railroad line from Nashville, Georgia in Berrien County straight to Madison, Florida. In addition, just recently the rural free delivery service had started. Now Mittie could pick up the mail every day from the new mailbox Pa had placed out by the road. She was so thankful they lived on *Cat Creek Road*. If it was not a good road, the RFD was not required to deliver mail to your address. The farmers were happy about the Rural Free Delivery service since the government would now push for good roads all over rural America.

Mittie rocked Eppse on the front porch while she waited for the mail carrier. Eppse was only three months old and he loved the rocking chair. Mittie was expecting a letter from her cousin. They never had the opportunity to visit together but they could write letters to each other.

Finally, she saw the motor car coming down the road. She knew it was the mail carrier. Her heart raced as she waited to see if he would stop at her mailbox. Only the mail carrier owned one of the motorized vehicles. Unless you went into Madison, you never saw one except that of the mail carrier. He received an electric engine motor car from the government for delivering the mail to the people living in the county around Madison. It was the mail carrier's call, if the roads were fit for mail delivery or not.

The mail carrier did stop at Mittie's mailbox. When he pulled away, Mittie held the baby tight and sprinted to the mailbox. Mittie did not get the letter she was expecting from her cousin but she did get one from her grandmother. This was as exciting as getting the one she had expected. She returned to the front porch and clumsily opened the letter from her grandmother. Little Eppse's safety was more important than the letter even though she was so anxious to open it.

> *My Dear Mittie,*
>
> *It has been so long since I have seen you and little Eddie. I miss both of you terribly. If I send you and Eddie a train ticket to come to Nashville, will you please come and spend some time with me? I would love to see you. I still miss your mother. Sometimes I weep when I realize, all over again, that she is no longer with us. How are your dad and Eliza? I hope they are in good health and are taking good care of you and Eddie. Please answer my letter as soon as possible and let me know if I can send the train tickets. I will be so looking forward to hearing from you and spending some time with the two of you. Grandpa is doing quiet well right now. He has his good days and his bad days. Give my love to Eddie, your dad and Eliza.*
>
> *Love,*
> *Grandma*

Mittie would need to wait until Pa came home from the field to ask permission to go to grandmas. She hoped he would allow her and Eddie to go. She would love to see grandma and grandpa. She remembered Pa telling them that grandma got angry with him when Ma died. She wanted him to move to Berrien County so that she could take care of Eddie and her. However, Pa said he had already had a disaster with loosing Ma and he did not intend to make another one for himself. Mittie never knew what Pa meant by that. She had decided never to question him about it.

Mittie went inside to look at the clock. Two p.m. Mittie could not wait for Pa to come home to show him the letter. Pa might not be home until six thirty or seven o'clock tonight. Since it was summer, it would not be dark until eight thirty. Pa usually wanted everybody to continue working as long as it was day light. The minute it was sunset Pa usually stopped them all immediately. Last year Eddie had a strike from a Cottonmouth. He was leaning over with his hands in the large cotton plant pulling the bowls of cotton out when something touched his face. He back off quickly while giving a loud yell. Pa came running and he found the cottonmouth snake curled up in the middle of the cotton bush. Pa examined Eddie's face well and could find no sign of a bite.

Apparently, Eddie's face was just out of reach of the snake. If he had bitten Eddie he would have surly died before they could have gotten to a doctor and even if a doctor had been immediately available, he might not have been able to save Eddie's life since there was no medicine for snakebites except poultices that rarely ever worked. Now everyone knew to shake the cotton bush and look for snakes before they stuck their hands in when cotton-picking time came.

Mittie bundled little Eppse in his blanket and got Orval by the hand. She started walking to the field where she thought Pa would be with Eddie, Robert, Ellen, Laura and Rittie chopping cotton. Luke, Russel and General were all at school. Mittie had time to find Pa and still make it back before they came in from school, if she didn't waste time. It was difficult to keep Orval walking. He was four years old and he wanted to catch every butterfly and every bug he saw along the way.

When Mittie reached the field, just as she thought she found all of them in the middle of the cotton patch chopping as if their life depended on it. When they saw her coming, they all stopped chopping and leaned on their hoe as she approached. They knew this must be something serious. Mittie would not take the children away from home if it had not been.

Mittie walked up to Pa and handed him the letter. He took it, opened it up and said. "What is this?" "Can't you see Pa.? It is a letter from Grandma," Mittie told him. "Mittie, you know I can't read or write." Mittie had forgotten that he could not read or write. He knew numbers so well and worked with them so much that it was hard for her to remember that he only knew his numbers but could not read. She had never been able to understand how anyone, who could do numbers so well, but was unable to read or write. When she was in school learning her reading and writing was easy but she could never getthe number thing. She could barely count to one hundred now. She could not even imagine trying to do all the things that Pa could do with numbers.

Mittie took the letter from Pa's hand. By now, all the children had gathered to hear the letter. Mittie read aloud. Eddie let out a loud "Yea!", when she was finished reading. Pa did not say a word. All the children stood staring at him. To Mittie, his two-minute pauses seemed more like a two-hour pause. "Well that is not entirely up to me. You'll need to ask Eliza too." Mittie threw her arms around her sweaty Pa and gave him a big hug. She knew she would not have a problem with Ma. Ma had always encouraged her relationship with her grandparents.

That night, over the supper table, Ma and Pa discussed Mittie and Ed's visit with their grandparents. "We will need to do some adjustments while they're gone, you know," Pa said. "We'll need to let Ellen take Mittie's place here at the house with the two little ones. That means we're going to be two short in the field". Pa said while Ellen squealed with delight. "Maybe we can pull Laura out of school now that she's twelve and can already read and write." Ma said. Not a sound came from Laura. She did not like the idea at all. She loved school and was one of the family brightest children. However, she felt herself lucky since they had allowed her to attend school this long. Pa had pulled most of the others out by the time they reached ten.

Now, the decision on their trip is settled. Mittie and Eddie would be going to Grandma and Grandpa Becton's house in Nashville, Ga. Mittie answered her grandmother's letter that night. She placed her Grandma's address on the envelope and placed the two-cent stamp in the right upper corner. She would carry the letter to the mailbox now even though it was dark. She wanted to be sure; the mail carrier would pick her letter up tomorrow. Mittie was too excited to sleep very much that night. Even thinking about riding on the train was exciting to her. She had never ridden in anything but a buggy or wagon. In addition, a mule had pulled them.

Within days, Mrs. Becton received the letter from her granddaughter. She read the letter to Mr. Becton. His face lit up. "I can't believe they're really coming." He said. Mrs. Becton could tell that he was as anxious to see Mittie and Eddie as she was. "I need you to hitch the mule to the wagon and take me to the train station." She said. Mr. Becton had arthritis so bad it was hard for him to get around but he was still able to do some things without great difficulty. He got the mule hitched to the wagon and pulled the wagon up to the front porch for his wife. They rode over the dusty *Coffee Road* to Nashville and to the train depot. Mrs. Becton climbed down from the wagon and went into the train station. "I need two train tickets from Madison, Florida to Nashville, please. I am sending them to my grandchildren who are almost grown now and I haven't seen them since they were babies." She said to the stationmaster.

"Would you like round trip tickets?" he asked her.

"No, just one way, please," she answered.

"The tickets are cheaper if you buy the round trip rather than waiting until they are ready to return to Madison and buy them then," he said.

"You don't understand. I do not intend to send them back. I'm going to keep them here forever, I hope," Mrs. Becton said to the stationmaster.

"Oh, then you are right. They will only need a one way ticket." She paid the man for the tickets and had her husband take her straight to the post office. Mrs. Becton placed the tickets in an envelope and addressed it to her granddaughter. She handed the envelope to the postmaster and told him. "Please, hurry it along."

The tickets came from Grandma. Mittie would not need to do any packing. She had all her things packed days ago while she waited for the tickets.

"Eddie you had better pack your clothes. We are leaving for Grandma's early in the morning," Mittie told him. The closer it came to the time for leaving the more uncertain he was that he really wanted to go. After all, Grandma had only sent a one-way ticket. How was he supposed to get back here? He wondered if any of the others had thought about the one-way ticket. It seemed to him that Grandma was trying to tell them something but he did not know just what it was.

Eddie packed some of his clothes and purposely left the rest of them. Pa carried them to the train station early the next morning. As he was hugging them good-bye he asked, "When are y'all coming home?"

"Soon, very soon Pa," Eddie said.

"I don't really know Pa. Grandma did not write anything in her last letter. She only sent the tickets. But I will ask when we arrive and write you back with the answer," Mittie told her Pa.

"We'll miss you," Pa said to the two of them. Both children said simultaneously, "I will miss you too." Pa had the sincere feeling that Eddie really meant it. He noticed tears in Eddie's eyes as he boarded the train.

Robert watched the train until it was out of site. He wiped tears from his eyes as he wondered how long it would be before he saw them again.

The train master watched as the grandparents and their grandchildren came together. There were tears, laughter, and excitement as they hugged the children. It was hard to tell who was happier, the grandparents or the teenagers.

Mittie and Grandma talked none stop all the way home. Her grandparent's home was still the same as she had remembered when she was a little girl. It was a big house with a front porch reaching from one end on the house to the other end. The house was so pretty all painted white with pretty flowers growing in the yard. Mittie and Eddie had never lived in a painted house before.

Grandma showed them to their rooms. They would each have a bedroom of their own. This was too good to be true. They had always shared a bed with two or three others and there were two or three beds in each room. This would be akin to dying and going to Heaven to Mittie. *What would she do with all this room? She was use to the one tiny table in a corner of the room where she slept with two of her siblings.* Her bedroom had two more beds in it and six more of the children slept there. She sat on the corner of her bed to write letters on the little table. That little corner was her only privacy. She now had her own shift robe where she could hang her clothes and drawers to put them in too. Mittie could close her bedroom door and she had her on private little world. She was truly in Heaven now.

Robert Jr. was about to finish his row of cotton back in Madison County. This was the last of chopping cotton for this year. The field was finally finished. He was ahead of the others as they chopped on their last row. He had chopped at his row so fast his hoe look like a blur in movement. He was sixteen and faster than all the others, except Pa. Robert had made his plans at the beginning of the row. He would chop as fast as he could and finish long before the others. He would not double back on Laura's row as he usually did. He planned to jump in the creek that flowed just beyond the trees at the end of the cotton patch. He would swim and bathe in the water. He had brought a bar of lye soap from home this morning. Robert loved swimming. Sometimes on Sunday after church, he would gather with some of his friends and spend the rest of the day at Cherry Lake and the springs nearby. They had discovered caves under the water in the springs. They enjoyed exploring those caves. Of course, by church time Sunday night, Robert would be home, dressed and ready, to go with the family to church. He had always loved going to church and worshiping God.

Pa never scolded Robert Jr. for not helping Laura with her row. He saw him when he went into the woods and he knew where he was probably going. Let him have a little fun on the last day of chopping cotton. He is a good boy and most boys would have headed to the swimming hole at the end of each day, but he never did. He always turned back and helped the others. *Besides I do not know what I would do if I did not have him now that Eddie is gone.*

Robert missed his brother and sister. "Ma, have you heard from Mittie and Eddie yet?" he asked Eliza after supper one night.

"No son and I don't understand why. It's been three weeks since they left now," Ma said.

Cotton chopping was behind them but now it was time to gather tobacco. Normally, females left the cropping of the tobacco to the males but since the only males left in the family were Pa and Robert, the older girls had to help crop the tobacco. The old mule would pull the sled with high bodies up to the tobacco barn. Everyone helped to unload it and lay it on the big shelf with the stalk end facing toward the barn. The older girls working at the barn would string the three leaves of tobacco onto the tobacco stick as fast as the two handers could hand them to her. The handers were the youngest children in the family who could reach the tobacco. When each stick of tobacco was finished, a male, left at the barn for this job, would take the stick of tobacco and hang it on the rafters in the barn where it would cook. It would cook all night and someone would need to stay at the barn all night and continue to put the logs in the firing pit. This was a precise procedure. They would need to keep the tobacco going at a precise temperature all night and the temperature would depend on how they fed the wood onto the fire. If they put too much wood the tobacco would burn and if the did not put enough wood the tobacco would not cook and would get mold and mildew. The whole barn of tobacco could ruin by the next morning if the cooking was done incorrectly. This usually took the expertise of Pa. He did not trust any of the children yet to handle this major responsibility. A good crop of tobacco could bring in hundreds of dollars and he needed every dime of it but he would not get the full amount. The property owner of the farmland would get half of it.

One day when they got in from the tobacco barn Ma said. "Laura, we got a letter today. I imagine it's from Mittie and Eddie." Like Pa, Ma could not read or write. She went to school for a short while but never learned to read or write. Ma handed Laura the letter. Laura opened it and read it aloud to the family.

> *Dear Ma, Pa, and family,*
>
> *Sorry it took me so long to write you. I held off since I did not know what to tell you about when we will come home. I still do not know. Every time I ask Grandma, she just says, "We'll talk about it later." I do not think she wants us to go home.*
>
> *Eddie and I are doing fine. We each have a bedroom of our own. I help Grandma in the house and in the garden. Eddie goes out to the field's everyday just as he did at home. Grandpa has this big farm and he is getting old so that it is hard for him to walk past the back yard. Eddie is already making decisions about the crops as you always did Pa. I think Grandpa really needs Eddie.*

I helped Grandma put up twenty-two quarts jars of string beans yesterday. We are always canning something from the garden. Grandma has canned jars still left over from two years ago but she is still canning. I told her it seemed strange to see a jar of food that was two years old. All the canning we did every year at home was never enough to last until the next crop came in. I told Grandma by the middle of winter we never had any food left no matter how much we canned. However, there was so many of us. Is it better now with two less mouths to feed?

We always go to church every Sunday. Grandma has a good friend who also goes there. Her friend is Mrs. Edwards and she has a son who is a little older than me and a daughter who is a little younger than Eddie. We have all gone on Sunday afternoon picnics together. We enjoy being with them and we always have a good time.

I miss all of you but I do not know when we will come home. I like it here but I would love to see all of you.

Love to all of you,
Mittie

With tears in her eyes, Ma said. "I'll bet they are never coming back."

"Maybe they will," Pa said as he left the table and headed for the barn for the entire night. He would add wood to the burning fire that was cooking the barn of tobacco. He would watch the thermometer and if it began to rise above the desired temperature, he would remove some of the burning wood. He would put wood in and take wood out all night. Pa put the small load of wood logs that he had chopped himself to fit the fireplace attached just outside the wall of the tobacco barn. The flues inside the barn attached to the fireplace would take the heat evenly over the entire barn of tobacco where the sticks hanging on many rafters held the many, many layers of tobacco sticks filled with tobacco. The sticks of tobacco hung from the ceiling of the barn to six feet from the dirt floor. The distribution of the heat spread from the top of the barn, which was as tall as a two-story house to the bottom layer of tobacco.

Chapter Seven

Martha and Ellen

Martha was now forty-five years old. She grieved her fathers' death. Life would be aimless now. What would happen to her? She was getting older now and had no means of support. Eliza and Ellen tried to reassure her but it was hopeless. She had found Pa's wallet after his death and after she paid for his funeral, she had only seventy-five dollars left. She took the money, went to the church, and paid for her own funeral with it. Now she could die.

Revival started at Concord Baptist Church. It would last the full week. Concord Baptist Church had built an important name for its self. The church members who had been to the Baptist convention in Atlanta many years ago had come back and started the first Baptist convention for the state of Florida. Many Baptist churches had sprung up in Florida and most all of them had joined the Florida Baptist Convention started by the church. Any time the church had a special event it was always easy to get the best of speakers or singers in the state for the event. Everyone wanted to be a part of Concord Baptist Church in any way possible. Everyone had been looking forward to the revival. They would have good preaching by a visiting preacher. However, the song leader invited to assist with the revival was the one everyone was so excited to hear. He was famous throughout the state as he was one of the most sought out soprano singer in the south. He played a piano beautifully and his voice flowed with the words of the hymn in such a manner that there were no dry eyes in the church when the song was over.

"Martha, what will I wear to the revival tonight?" Ellen asked.

"Ellen, I can't make all your decisions for you. You will have to decide what you wear yourself."

"I do not have anything to wear," Ellen said.

"You always say that, but somehow you manage to dress yourself before time to leave and I am sure you will do it this time also." Martha was forty-five now and such things as frocking up was no longer interesting to her. Tonight she would wear her black dress with the mother-of-pearl broach pinned at the neck. She knew it looked drab but she felt it appropriate since only recently her dear dad had gone to his grave.

Sometimes Martha looked back over her life and wondered why she was born. Up until this point in her life, she had only been a caregiver for others. She had always gone with the flow, with no plans or hopes of a future of her own. Now that Pa was gone she would have to manage the farm. Oh, if she could only manage the farm, but that is not the way it would be. She would need to work along side of Ellen and do her half of the labor too. That meant that she and Ellen would now be doing all the things that the three of them use to do before Pa died. She wept in her hands and thought about the long hard road ahead for her.

Come on Martha, you cannot think about that now. You need to get dressed for church since the revival's first night will be starting in one hour, she thought to herself.

Martha hooked the old mule up to the wagon and the two girls climbed in the wagon. Martha was good at handling the reigns and directing the old mule. He was slow but he was faithful. He did not seem to have enough energy to pick up a trot. The old mule not only pulled the wagon but he pulled the plow while Martha plowed the fields.

The girls were surprised at the many people crowded in the church when they arrived. There no empty pews and chairs were down each side of the church and many more behind the pews. Martha and Ellen finally spotted two empty chairs on the left side of the church. Ellen bolted for the chairs. When Martha sat down beside her, she asked Ellen why she ran. "You don't see all those people still coming in the door. One of them was bound to get it if I had not hurried."

Martha realized the beautiful singing was coming from the church choir. She loved the song they were singing. It was one of the newer church hymns but it was in their church songbook. Concord Baptist Church always kept all their material updated. Although Martha could not carry a tune in a bucket, she loved good music and singing. Mr. Lewis Jones published this new song in 1899. Martha silently sang along with the choir. "*Would you be free from the burden of sin? There's pow'r in the blood; pow'r in the blood; would you o'er evil a victory win? There's wonderful power in the blood."*

When the choir finished singing, the Reverend Stephen Crockett, the church pastor, came to the podium. He welcomed everyone and introduced the guest song leader and the preacher for the week's revival. When the preacher sat down in one of the upholstered chairs on the platform behind the podium, the guest song leader came to the podium. He was a middle-aged looking man with beautiful premature white hair and black eye brows. His clothes told that he was a wealthy and probably, well educated man. He sang a song and as everyone had said, it was beautiful. Ellen and Martha could have sat there in their chairs and listened to him sing all night. Ben Parker not only sang beautifully but he also had a funny side. If he was not singing, he had the whole church rolling in laughter at his funny jokes and antidotes.

The visiting preacher preached on what would be the week's theme "Christians being revived and encouraged to still attain a higher plan of spiritual life." It was a good sermon and Martha and Ellen looked forward to tomorrow night.

The two girls shook the visiting preacher's and the church pastor's hand as they left the church. Martha took a few seconds to let them know how much she had enjoyed the service. As the girls walked out and down the steps, two women were waiting for them. "Martha, we are taking turns preparing a meal for the visiting preacher and song leader. Will you and Ellen take Wednesday night? We are preparing the meal before the nights service since its late when the service is over," one of the women asked Martha.

"Yes," Martha answered. "We will prepare a meal for them on Wednesday night." While Martha was answering the women she was wondering, what could she come up with to feed the guest? Times were hard and there was not much in her kitchen to cook, especially for company.

On the way home, Martha thought about what she could cook for Wednesday night. She had wanted to concentrate her attention on the song leader and his beautiful voice. Something about Ben Parker intrigued Martha. She would sure like to know him better but she was sure all women felt that way about Ben Parker. She imagined that he had a beautiful wife and at least five children. She had looked about the church tonight for strangers who might have fit the description she had imagined for his wife and family. However, the church was so over crowded that she could not see everyone.

"Ellen, did that woman say we would be feeding only the two men or did she say we would prepare for them and their families?"

"I did not hear her say anything about their families. I suppose it is only the two men," Ellen said. "We will ask her tomorrow night after the services," Martha said.

When they arrived home, Martha unhitched the old mule and put him away for the night. She put more water in the half drums that sat just over the fence for the mule and cows to drink. She went inside and headed straight for the kitchen. She opened the doors of the cupboards and stood staring inside at what she could have for her menu Wednesday night. She saw meal and flour. She had salt, black pepper, coffee and plenty of lard. She would need to rely on the yard, garden, and foods she had canned for the rest of her dinner. It was spring and nothing was in except green beans, yellow squash, and green onions.

"Ellen, don't forget we need to be in the back field by day light tomorrow morning. We need to finish plowing and get the field ready for the tobacco plants by the first of next week. We will spend the weekend pulling the plants from the tobacco beds. That way, we can start planting first thing on Monday morning."

Ellen yawned. She was already in her nightgown and ready for bed. "I know Martha; I'm going to bed now because I am tired."

When Martha went to bed, she wanted to concentrate on the dinner for her guest but again her mind kept going back to Ben Parker and his beautiful music. She could hear him singing in her mind. *He has no idea how good he is*, Martha sighed just as she fell asleep.

The girls were in the field at daybreak on Tuesday morning. They were not strong enough to push the plow into the ground deep enough for the furrows on each side of the row. If the furrows were not deep enough the rainwater could not run off properly and the tobacco would rot before it was ready for harvesting.

They took turns standing on the narrow little plow while the other one guided the mule. It was important that the rows remain very straight since jagged rows would be difficult to crop when it was time for harvesting. Standing on the plow to provide weight so that the plow would make a deeper furrow was a dangerous maneuver but it worked.

The girls had carried themselves some buttered biscuits and water. By eleven thirty, Ellen was complaining of hunger. "Alright Ellen, we will stop early and eat," Martha said. They were over half way through the field by now. They walked back through the plowed field to the old oak tree where they had set the syrup bucket with their biscuits and their jug of water, when they arrived at the field. They each took a biscuit from the bucket and sat down on a root of the tree. The weather was beautiful. It was nice and warm but not hot. There was a nice breeze blowing. The breeze stirred up the black dirt behind the plow making each girl look as though she suffered a black coal powder dusting. They were black from head to toe. They were enjoying the buttered biscuit and cool water when Ellen said, "Who is coming?" She was pointing in the direction of the house. Ellen climbed up on a big root of the old tree in hopes she could get a better look. She still could not see who it was.

"Who on earth would want to visit us in the field?" Martha asked.

"I bet it's that insurance man who came two weeks ago. He is wearing a suit." Ellen said. "Wait a minute; it looks like he has white hair. It can't be the young insurance man." Immediately, Martha thought about Ben Parker. He had white hair. Now the man was close enough to see well. Martha's heart dropped to her stomach. It was Ben Parker. Martha started wiping dirt from her face with the tail of her dress as she bent toward her knees. Mr. Parker boldly walked up to the two girls.

"Good morning ladies," he said.

"Good morning Mr. Parker, Martha said. "How did you find us back here and how can I help you, Mr. Parker?" Martha asked.

"Oh I don't need anything Martha. I just saw you last night in church and since then, I have thought about nothing but you. I tried to make my way to you last night after church but I did not make it before you were gone." The singer was holding something in tissue paper with a red bow tied it together.

He handed the package to Martha. Martha opened the red bow and almost lost her breath. The package contained one long stemmed red rose. Martha had always heard one long stem red rose silently said, "I love you." Martha was speechless. *What was this all about?* "Mr. Parker, do you always select a girl from the congregation when you attend every revival that you sing at?"

"Please call me Ben. In addition, no, I don't always pick out a girl. I have never done this before and I do not really know how to go about it. I dated a few girls when I was younger but that is about as far in the girl department that I have ever gone. I never married because I never found the right girl; finally I gave up on it and haven't even thought about it again until I saw you last night."

"Ellen and I will attend the revival again tonight. Couldn't you have waited until then?"

"I am so sorry if I have offended you, it's just that I was anxious to meet you and I was afraid I might never see you again."

"It's not that I'm offended Ben…it's just that I look a mess with all this dirt caked on me," Martha said.

"You are still beautiful to me," Ben told her.

Ellen had made herself scarce. She had walked to the opposite end of the rows. She was watching two doves on the branch of a tree. One of the little doves was apparently attempting to pick something off the other one's neck. It looked as though he was providing foreplay for his mate. Soon her eyes shifted to the trunk of the tree. There were two lizards playing around on the trunk. Suddenly one lizard stopped and Ellen watched as his beautiful red throat expanded almost to the size of a log roller marble. She knew he was attempting to entice his girlfriend into romance. "Is everyone, but me in love today?" she said aloud. She wanted to yell the words but decided against it since she knew it would frighten Martha.

Mr. Parker stayed the rest of the day and in his handsome suit of clothes, he pushed the plow for the girls and no one had to stand on it to make the furrows deep enough. Martha walked along beside Ben through the rest of the field as he plowed. Ellen wanted to go home but Martha refused her request.

By the time the last furrow was finished, Martha felt quiet comfortable with Ben. They all walked home together. After arriving at the house, Martha had a good laugh. "Look at you, Ben; you are covered in dirt. This is the first time I have ever seen someone in a suit and dirty from head to toe."

Ben laughed with her. He looked down at his clothes and said. "I think I would make a good hobo."

Martha got them a glass of fresh water and they sat in the rockers on the front porch while they drank. Ben told Martha about the difficulty he had trying to get her name. "I ask Reverend Stephen Crockett and I described what you were wearing and how you looked but he couldn't figure out who I was talking about. Finally, he suggested I go next door to Mrs. Miley and see if she would know. I did and as soon as I told her you were wearing a black dress with a pretty broach pinned at the neck she immediately knew it was you. I ask her lots of questions about you. She answered them and then she said she hoped you didn't get mad at her for doing it."

"What did you ask her?" Martha asked.

"Well the first thing I ask was if you were married. I had prayed so hard that you were not. She also told me that your father had died only a month ago. I am so sorry. I would have loved meeting him. I know he was a fine man."

"Yes he was," Martha said with tears sparkling in her eyes.

"You won't need to tell me anything about yourself. I think Mrs. Miley covered it all, and I need to say that I loved everything she said," Ben said.

"I have known Mrs. Miley since I was a little girl. She is a sweet woman but I have to say you could have never asked a more able person about my life. She always loved to gossip. I imagine by now, everybody in the church knows you are interested in me," Martha said.

"That's fine with me," Ben said as both of them began laughing again.

Now that you know my life you can tell me about yours," Martha said.

"I grew up in New York with wonderful parents who discovered music in my blood at an early age and encouraged me to develop my talent. I took music lessons throughout my childhood. I went away to college at age seventeen and of course, my major was music. While I was away at college, my parents came down with yellow fever. They refused my coming home. They were afraid I would get it too. Mom and dad only lived two weeks before succumbing to the disease. Loosing my parents was devastating for me. Their funeral was the worse part of my life. I thought I would never get over it. I was an only child, so I had no siblings to weep with me. When I graduated from college, I went on the road with my music. I was always a Christian but when I lost my parents, I became even closer to the Lord. He helped me through some tough times. One day it was as if an Angel spoke to me. *"You're mother and father is in a much better place now and someday you will join them."* It was as if my burden suddenly lifted and faded away. Now I can think about them and it brings joy." There was a long pause. Martha had stopped rocking and had listened intently to Ben.

"Ben, I'm so sorry about your parents. I just do not understand. You say you finished college and if Mrs. Miley told you the truth, you know that I only went to school long enough to learn to read and write. I grew up in a poor household with many siblings and I cannot carry a tune in a bucket. I just don't understand why you chose me above all the other girls in church last night," Martha said.

"I can only tell you that when I first saw you, my heart skipped a beat, and I knew immediately you are the girl God intended for me. I liked what I saw but I listened to my heart. I don't know what I would do if you were already taken."

All too soon, Martha and Ben agreed it was time they part so they could be at church on time tonight. Ben said good night to Martha on the front porch with just a handshake. As he rode his borrowed horse back to the preacher's house where he and the visiting preacher were staying for the week he couldn't get his mind off how much he had enjoyed the day. He could not remember the last time he was this happy. As he thought about it, he really could not remember ever being this happy. He lifted his head to the Heavens and said, "Thank You My Lord. I know you saved her just for me and that is why you sent me to this church."

Martha watched Ben until he was out of sight. As she walked in her house, she swooned and almost lost her balance. She thought she would faint. In this one day, her whole life had changed. How happy she was about it! Words could never describe just how she felt now. Suddenly it seemed that the whole world had just become alive and she wanted to live forever. She felt like running down the road, kicking up her heels and singing loudly but there was no time for that now. She and Ellen must get their baths in a hurry so that they could arrive at the church early tonight. She wanted to arrive early enough to get a seat near the front of the church so that she could be near Ben while he sang.

Martha and Ellen got their baths quickly in the washtubs on the back porch and got dressed for church. They grabbed another buttered biscuit and they placed black berry jam on it this time. They ate their dinner in the wagon on the way to church. They were fortunate enough to find two seats on the third pew from the pulpit. Martha floated through the welcome from the pastor as she watched Ben sitting in the upholstered chair and as handsome as ever. When Ben was up to sing her heart flipped over. His singing mesmerized her as well as everyone in the church. He sounds like an angel from heaven, and he is in love with me. Martha thought to herself. He had not told her he was in love with her yet but she was sure he would and when he told her, she had already made her mind up. She would tell him she loved him too. That strange feeling that she had felt when she first saw him--now she knew it was love. She too had fallen in love with him the first time she had seen him. She could not wait to find out more about this wonderful man. She listened in awe as he sang his songs. She could not take her eyes off him.

Ben watched Martha from the pulpit. "Please Lord—help me to remember the lyrics to this song," he silently prayed each time he sang his song. Normally, remembering his lyric would not be a problem but now his life long dream was sitting in the congregation watching him. He loved her so much and did not want to disappoint her. He knew his eyes were supposed to shift over his audience while he sang. He had learned that at the New England Conservatory of Music in Boston while he was in college there but now Martha sat there and he could not take his eyes off her. His heart tugged for her. He had to admit to himself that Martha is a beautiful woman but not the most beautiful one he's ever seen and not even as beautiful as so many of them who had thrown themselves at him over the years. However, she had a beauty unlike any girl he has ever seen. He wanted to spend the rest of his life with her.

When the visiting pastor had finished his sermon, Ben came back to the podium and led the congregation in the invitational hymn: *Just as I am Without One Plea, But That thy Blood Was Shed for Me.* Ben loved the old song and used it often for the invitational. He felt like this song had led many people to Christ. Even the one who wrote the song was lead to Christ by a few of the words in the song. In 1835, Charlotte Elliott was at a gathering with a few other people. An old man came to her and asked, if she were a Christian. She felt insulted and told him to mind his own business. However, after she left, she could not get the question off her mind. She went back to ask the man how to find Christ and he told her to "come just as you are." She did and later wrote the beautiful song.

As Ben held both of Martha's hands outside the church, she said to him, "Tomorrow evening you are having dinner at my house."

"Are you serious?" Ben asked. "I am serious. Mrs. Miley ask me Monday night after church, if Ellen and I would prepare the meal for Wednesday night for you and the preachers. I told her I would be happy to do it and now that I know you, I am happier than ever." Ben wanted to kiss Martha desperately. However, this was not the time or place.

"I will come to your house early tomorrow afternoon so that I can help you."

"Help me to do what?" Martha asked.

"Help you to prepare the meal, Martha," Ben said. "Since when did men know what to do in a kitchen?" Martha asked. "I have always known. My mom taught me how to cook while I was growing up. I always prepare my own meals." Cogs were turning in Martha's head. *How did I get so lucky? Not only, do I have a handsome man but he cooks too. Who could possibly be luckier?*

On Wednesday morning, Martha and Ellen got out of bed early. Martha wanted to have the gory stuff finished before Ben arrived. "Ellen we need to go out and catch one hen and two fryers for supper tonight. I will head them up and you grab them one at the time until we catch all three." Martha went to the kitchen and put a big pot of water on the wood burning stove. She got the fire going in the stove. "Come on Ellen, let's get the chickens."

Ellen came into the kitchen grumbling, "Why do we need three of them for one meal?"

"'Cause, I'm going to make chicken and dumplings with the hen and I'm sure we'll need more than one little chicken to fry for three men. You know how preachers eat."

They rounded the hen and two pullets up in no time and Martha rung each one's neck. When they stopped flopping around in the yard Martha brought the big pot of boiling water out to the back porch. She took the hen and quickly dipped her into the hot water. The hot water released the feathers and Martha quickly pulled them out. This hen was loaded with pinfeathers. She went inside and got a paper bag, brought it outside and set it on fire. She quickly passed the chicken over the burning paper and all the pinfeathers disappeared. She got one of the pullets and dipped it into the hot water. She was able to have the feathers off all three chickens within thirty minutes. She thought that might be a record. Now she would gut the chickens. These procedures are the things she did not want Ben to see since she wanted him to enjoy the Wednesday night chicken supper. Martha cut the chickens into pieces. The chicken was now ready to season and roll in the flour for frying or put in the pot for boiling.

Martha had learned well from her Ma. Louisa had learned to be a wonderful cook after she arrived in America and had good things to cook. She had been one of the women who pioneered Southern cooking. Martha had the hen in the pot and already boiling by noon. She thought Ben would probably arrive around two this after noon. Suddenly Ellen stuck her head in the kitchen door and said "Ben is coming. He is coming into the front yard, now."

Martha was both excited and disappointed. She had wanted him to wait until she was clean and dressed before he came but she was so ready to see him.

Ellen invited Ben in and led him to the kitchen where Martha was. "Hey, Sweetheart, how are you doing?" Ben said.

"I'm fine Ben but I wasn't expecting to see you until around two this afternoon," Martha said.

"Would you like me to leave and come back at two this afternoon?"

"No!" Martha was saying before he had his sentence finished. I guess you have seen me looking worse than I do now. The only thing is that you were dirty and grimy too. Now it's only me."

"You look wonderful to me," Ben said.

Soon Martha had Ben flouring chicken parts and placing them in the hot lard. "Be careful, the grease might pop on you." "Baby this is not the first time I have fried chicken. I use to go to my aunt's house and catch the chicken right off the yard. I'd ring his neck, dip him in hot water, remove all the feathers and then gut him and get him ready to cook." Ben said. "Do you mean that I got out of bed early this morning to prevent you from seeing the preparation of a chicken when you've done it yourself?" Martha asked. "'Afraid so if that's what you got up early for." Ben said. "Did your aunt cook the chicken or was it you?" Martha asked. "All by myself," Ben said. "I guess I can relax and just let you take care of the chicken frying and I'll get all the vegetables finished.

Martha made the dumplings in the big wood flour bowl. She mixed the dough to the perfect consistency. She rolled the big ball of dough out on the floured tabletop until it was almost as thin as paper. Then she cut it into short strips and placed them one at the time into the boiling chicken pot. She stirred the dumplings often to prevent them from sticking together or to the pot.

Martha had a pot of cream corn cooking, a pot of white acre peas with whole pods of fresh okra. She also had a pot of squash and onions, a pot of small new potatoes and a pot of white rice for eating with chicken gravy. She would make the gravy from the fried chicken drippings. After Martha had poured most of the lard off, she would add flour, mix it well and when the flour was brown and the roux was ready she would add water and make a beautiful light brown delicious smelling and tasty gravy. She had made a big bowl of banana pudding for desert and she would roll biscuits for the bread. She would allow them to wash it all down with cold glasses of ice tea, thanks to Ben. Ben had brought the ice with him. He had also gotten out of bed early this morning and rode his borrowed horse to Madison to pick the ice up from the icehouse there.

Ben was right by Martha's side until the dinner was almost finished. "Ben I think I need to wash up and get dressed in presentable clothes before the preachers gets here."

"Even though you are already beautiful I will finish this wonderful meal up and you are free to go."

Martha barely made it back to the kitchen before the preachers arrived. When she invited them in and they walked into the kitchen, together Ben had a beautiful table set and most of the food already on the table. Ben was not too proud to announce to the preachers that he had helped to prepare the meal. It was truly a beautiful and delicious looking meal. The preachers ate just as Martha knew they would. Ellen wondered if they were eating so much because they knew the meal had been prepared for them and there was so much of it or was it that they were that hungry. If they were that hungry the other two suppers they had been to this week must have been no good. They ate as if they had had nothing to eat the whole week. However, the meal was extra good. With both Martha and Ben, putting their touches in each dish the food was especially good.

"Martha you and Ben did a good job with this meal," Ellen said. Before she was finished, the two preachers joined in praising the two for a job well done. When everyone was finished eating all but Ellen moved to the front porch and sat down. Ellen started putting away the left over food and cleaning the kitchen.

When the two preachers finally left to go to the church Martha said, "Why didn't you talk while they were here Ben? I'll bet you didn't say a dozen words."

"Because I wanted them to leave so I could spend some time with you alone before church. I knew if I kept a conversation going, they would sit here until past church time while everyone at the church waited for them. They were full and happy and enjoyed the nice breeze on your front porch. I know preachers Martha. I've worked with them for years."

Ben took Martha's hands and pulled her from her chair. He led her to the swing and she sat down. Ben sat beside her. Martha was thanking him for helping her so much with the supper as Ben raised his arm and placed on around her shoulder. "It's because I love you Martha Marlow." Martha's heart flipped over. He had said it. He had said the love word.

Martha looked up at him as the sun was setting in the west and with a beautiful glow showing on her face she said, "I love you too, Ben." Ben took her in his arms and sealed their words with a long passionate kiss. Martha had never been so happy in her life. This was Martha's first kiss by a lover and it seemed so natural and wonderfully normal. She wanted the kiss to go on forever.

Nothing else mattered; Martha and Ben were in their own little world. They were totally, oblivious to anything or anyone else in their world. They clung to each other sharing one kiss after another. Suddenly Martha came to reality when she heard someone vaguely calling her name. She pulled her head away and looked and Ellen was there.

"I apologize for interrupting such a romantic scene but if we are going to church we need to get started. We barely have enough time to get there now. Ben took his pocket watch attached to the gold chain, from his pocket. "You are right Ellen; we have less than fifteen minutes to make a twenty minute ride." Ben hitched the mule to the wagon for Martha and Ellen. "I'll go back on the horse since it will faster." "I'll see you two in church," and Ben was gone.

Martha and Ellen were right behind him for a while but then Martha watched as he faded out of sight. Martha could not believe this was happening. She had never in a million years though she would be in love with some one and if she were that, the other person would really be in love with her too. This was the best that life gets.

Ellen was driving the mule while Martha sat on her right side of the wagon bench in her own dream world. Suddenly from the right side of the woods two rough looking men jumped out right in front of them. Both of them were holding guns and they had them aimed at the girls. One of the men grabbed Martha by the arm and jerked her off the wagon. Blood pored from her legs where they had hit the metal covering on the wagon wheel. The other man grabbed the mule reins and brought the wagon to a stop. Martha yelled, "What do you want?" "Never mind you what we want. You just do as we say." One of the men said. The other man climbed into the wagon. He pulled Ellen from the seat into the back of the wagon and began pulling at her clothes as she began trying to fight him off. Ellen fought as hard as she could but she was no match for the dirty, stinking man. Martha saw what was happening in the wagon and she made one big leap back into the wagon and on top of the man. She was on his back and beating him in the back with her fist and kicking him with her feet. By this time, the man had most of Ellen's clothes torn off. Both girls were yelling to the top of their lungs. The man still standing on the ground and holding the long gun yelled, "Not now fool, we need to get this wagon off the road before someone comes by."

The man got off Ellen while both girls continued to beat at him with their fist. "Hand me the rope," the man said while the two girls still struck at him with their fist. The other man jumped onto the wagon with the rope. He handed one rope to the molester and he began attempting to tie Ellen up. Martha pounced on him again. She was kicking, biting, and scratching the man on the back. She felt someone pulling at her from her back. She quickly turned and gave a heavy blow to the man who had come on the wagon with the ropes. She stunned him and he fell back shaking his head in attempts to get his wits back. Martha jumped from the wagon and started running down the road. If she could stay ahead of them, she could get help from the house just down the road. She had not understood why the people who lived there had not already come to rescue them. She knew they had heard their yells. Martha looked behind her and her wagon was coming at a fast pace behind her. She picked up her pace and ran as fast as she could possibly run. The wagon reached her just as she got to the house. There was no one home. Then she remembered the residence of this house was at church. *Church*, Martha thought. *I know Ben is waiting for us. If only he were here.* One of the men jumped from the wagon and almost effortless tied Martha up with a rope. Martha fought back as much as she could but she was so tired from the long run that she could provide little resistance. Her legs were still bleeding from the when she was pulled from the wagon.

With both girls tied up and lying in the floor of the wagon the two men ordered the mule to carry on. When they came to a lane leading into the woods they turned the wagon, went through the shallow ditch and into the woods.

Ben had barely made it to church on time. He had to rush to the pulpit. The preachers were, already seated. The piano player sat at the piano with an anxious look on her face as he entered the pulpit. She was relieved as he sat down in his chair. It was time for the opening song. Ben rose to the pulpit. His rendition of the *Old Rugged Cross* was breathtaking. He gave the song new meaning in the way that he sang it. Tears pooled in the eyes of everyone in the congregation who were forty years old and above. The song had meant so much to them over the years.

When Ben had finished the song, Martha and Ellen were not there. Ben had made his mind up that he would leave the podium and sit with Martha throughout the service. He would go back to the podium to lead the invitational. He had even planned to hold her hand throughout the service. If people wanted to talk, so let them. He loved her and he wanted to announce it to the world. However, when he was finished with the singing and it was time for the pastor to come to the pulpit Martha and Ellen still had not arrived. Ben was a little concerned. He knew they had left home right behind him. They must have forgotten something and went back home to collect it.

The preacher went on with the sermon. Ben wanted to wait for Martha and Ellen on the podium. He watched the front door. He would see them immediately when they walked in the door. He prayed they would sit pew with three available seats. He planned to leave the podium and sit with them even though they were late. The sermon was especially long tonight. Will he ever finish? Ben thought as he watched the front door for any sigh of Martha and Ellen. When it was time for Ben to lead the invitational hymn, the girls still had not appeared at the church door. Ben was extremely concerned now. As soon as the preacher said the closing prayer, Ben bolted out the side door. He jumped on his horse and went as fast as his horse would carry him to Martha's house. When he arrived, he saw that the mule and wagon was gone and no one was home. It was too dark to see if the wagon had left tracks.

Ben rode slowly back to the church looking into the wood on both sides of the road. Maybe something had happened to the wagon and they pulled off the road. He saw no sign of them or the wagon. By now, Ben was worried out of his mind. God, please help me to find them. He rode the horse to the pastor's house where he had been staying. He jumped off the horse and ran into the house. Both preachers sat in the living room carrying on a conversation. Ben broke into the conversation, "I'm sorry to interrupt but something has happened to Martha and Ellen."

Both preachers stopped and looked at Ben. "What do you mean?"

One of the preachers said. "I mean they are missing both of them."

"What happened?" the other preacher asked.

Pastor Crockett said, "I noticed they were not at church tonight. I thought it strange that they would not be there since earlier when we had supper with them they didn't say they were not coming."

"I left their house just before church time and they were right behind me on their way to church. I have just gotten back from their house and neither one of them are there and the wagon and mule is gone too," Ben said with a shaky voice.

"I'm worried about them. I know something has happened. "Maybe one of them became ill and they went to town to the doctor," Reverend Crockett said. Ben turned and started out of the house. "Where are you going, Ben?" he asked.

"I'm going to Madison and see if I can find them," he said to the two preachers as he ran out the door.

The preachers decided they could not sit there and do nothing. They went out, hitched the horse to the buggy, and started toward the girl's home. "Maybe they had shown up since Ben was there. They were there within twenty minutes but saw no signs of the girls. They walked around the house calling their names. They got no response.

Ben put the horse in a gallop on his way to Madison. All he could say was, "Lord please let them be safe." He kept saying the prayer repeatedly all the way to Madison. He wanted so much to run the horse at full speed but he knew the horse would probably not make the ten-mile trip if he did. Ben had never felt fear as horrible as he was feeling now. He tried to keep his hands from shaking but it was impossible. When he arrived in Madison, he went straight to Dr. David Yates house. Since he was the most popular doctor in town Ben decided Martha would have chosen to go directly to his house on Bunker Street. Ben used the knocker on the front door. He kept knocking until the doctor appeared at the door. Ben knew the doctor was already in bed but he had to find the girls. "Sir, pardon me for knocking on your door so late at night but I need to know if you have seen two women whose names are Martha and Ellen Marlow."

"Sorry, but I haven't seen them. Why do you ask?" the doctor asked.

"They are missing," Ben told him.

"How long have they been missing," The doctor asked.

"They have been missing since before dark this evening. I thought one of them might have gotten sick and they came here to see you," Ben said with a quiver in his voice.

"No, no one has come to me for treatment since lunch time today. And that was a little boy with a bad cough who was brought in by his parents."

Ben thanked the doctor and walked away. He felt that his world had just ended. *Would he ever see Martha again? Did she get afraid by his advances and leave home until it was time for him to leave Madison County?* Tears wailed in his eyes. He could hardly see as he mounted his horse for the long trip back to the church and the preacher's house. He held his face toward Heaven. "Where is she Lord? Please help me to find her. I love her more than anything in this world," Ben let the tears flow as he made the trip back.

When Ben arrived at the house, he found the two preachers walking down the road. "Were they at the doctors?" one of them asked Ben. "No, the doctor said he has not seen them. I didn't see the wagon any place around Madison."

"We went to their house and searched around the yards calling them, then we took turns walking from there to the church but we saw no sign of the girls."

Ben broke down in a flood of tears. "What has happened to them?" he asked. The preachers put their arms around him and allowed him to cry until it was all out of him.

"You go to bed now and we'll get up at day light in the morning and start searching again when we can see," Preacher Crocket said to Ben. Ben followed the men into the house but he was sure he would not sleep tonight. He went into his room and stood staring out the window.

The two dirty men directed the mule to pull the wagon deeper and deeper into the woods while the two tied up girls lying in the wagon tried to wiggle out of the ropes. Martha noticed that Ellen was not struggling any longer. She wiggled until she saw her face. Martha screamed for the men to stop. "Ellen can't breath." The old men never heard Martha. They had taken out a bottle of whisky and were celebrating "their find". They were singing disgusting songs, "*Me and my gal went huckleberry hunting. She fell down and I seen sumptin.*"

Ellen's face was very white. Martha discovered that the rope was around her throat and she was chocking. She knew that Ellen would surely die if she did not get the rope away from her throat. Martha scooted around until her back was facing Ellen. Martha's hands, restrained with the rope, and the rope was coming from her chest and arms. They had wrapped the rope around each girl from top to bottom, tying their feet tight together. The girls could not stand nor could they straighten out their bodies. The men had pulled the rope so tight that the girls lay in a curled position. Martha reached her fingers out until she felt Ellen. With her fingers, she felt until she found the rope around Ellen's neck and began to pull at it with her fingers. She could not see what she was doing and did not know if she was even making a difference. She pulled at the rope with her fingers until she heard Ellen cough and the rope seemed a little looser. She rolled herself over to face Ellen. Her face was getting its color back. Martha said a little prayer of thanks. "Ellen, are you alright?"

In a weak voice she said, "I am now. I couldn't breathe."

The old men were oblivious to what had almost happened to Ellen. "Hey, we didn't just get a wagon and old mule. We got two fillies with it." Now deep in the woods they decided to stop the wagon and "help our selves to these little fillies." They pulled the wagon into a small clearing and stopped. One of the men said, "I gotta go drop my drawers." The other one said. "Well hurry up 'n let's get this show on the road." Suddenly Martha thought, if I could use my fingers to get the rope off Ellen's throat, why can I not be able to untie her with them. She wiggled close to Ellen. She begins fingering for the ropes tied around her. She could not see so she would need to feel until she found the beginning or the ending of the rope. She soon found the beginning of the rope tied around Ellen's upper chest. She began pulling at it. The old man still sitting in the wagon seat turned around and gave them a good look. Martha lay very still. He turned back around and then jumped off the wagon. Martha started working on Ellen's rope at a rapid pace. When she had freed Ellen's arms and hands Ellen finished it by untying her feet. Martha heard water poring on the dried leaves on the ground. She assumed the old man was toileting himself.

"Stay in that position, but roll over and untie me," Martha whispered to Ellen. Ellen did as Martha had told her and shortly she had Martha's hands and arms freed. They knew they would not have time to escape right now since one of the men was standing by the wagon with the big gun at his side. The girls left the ropes on them so that they appeared to remain tied up. The water quieted and the girls heard the old man yell, "What ya doin out there? Git back here so as we can git down to bisness." The other man didn't answer. The old man took his gun and walked away from the wagon to the edge of the clearing.

"Hey, wher ya at?"

Martha knew now was the time to go for it. "Ellen quietly jump off this side of the wagon and start running in that direction opposite them, as fast as you can run. I'll be right behind you." Ellen jumped just as the old man yelled the second time

"Hey, are ya a comin' ?" He did not hear Ellen jump. Ellen ran as fast as she could toward the woods. Martha jumped from the wagon. The old man heard her feet hit the ground. "Who's at? Is at you, Luther?" He walked to the other side of the wagon and saw Martha just as she disappeared into the wood. He raised the gun and fired a shot at her while running in her direction. "Yo better stop, I'll git ya." He yelled at the girls. Now they heard the other man who had been in the woods. He had joined his friend and now they were both chasing the girls. Martha knew they could not out run them in the long run. "Ellen you climb the next big oak tree you come to." Within a few minutes, Ellen was scurrying up a tree and Martha was right behind her. They heard the men behind them but they could not see them. The girls climbed high into the tree. There was no way the men could see them in the dark. The girls watched as they ran past the tree with one of them carrying the long gun. They were mumbling something but the girls were too high to hear what it was. The girls watched as the men searched in the woods for them. Finally, they returned to the wagon and took the whisky bottle out again. Then they started arguing loudly about which one had allowed the girls to get away. "I hope Ben is looking for us." Martha whispered to Ellen.

The next morning by daybreak Ben was out on the road searching again for the love of his life and her sister. The two preachers came out and joined him. They decided they would walk the road that they would have come to the church on. As they walked along seeing nothing, suddenly Ben said, "What is this." The preachers looked where he was pointing. There in the middle of the road were tracks that appeared a wagon had stopped there and had dabbled about on the ground. There were mule hoof tracts that showed a mule has stood in that place as he moved about on the ground. There were shoe prints coming from the ditch and to the spot where a wagon had stopped. There were shoe prints around where a wagon would have sat. They found no tracks going back into the woods. They turned around and started walking back toward the church looking for wagon tracks that might have left the road. They carefully searched each little opening for wagon tracks but were unsuccessful. However, suddenly Ben saw it. He saw where a wagon had pulled off the road across the little ditch and into the woods. He saw no return tracks.

Martha and Ellen sat high in the tree. They watched as the men continued their party in the wagon. They switched the bottle of whisky from one to the other. They would laugh awhile then their laughter would change to fighting. They continued their ritual while the girls prayed they could wait the old men out on their tree branches. They knew when the sun came up and the light came through the trees the old men would probably see them there. The girls prayed all night for someone to come and rescue them before daybreak. Just before daybreak, the two old men seemed to have collapsed in the wagon. Martha could see them better than Ellen could. "What are they doing now Ellen whispered?"

"They're lying very still in the wagon." Martha was happy that it had been a full moon night. She had been able to keep her eye on them all night. "If they are passed out why can't we climb down now and make a run for it?"

"We can't chance it, Ellen. I think when they wake up they will probably never leave the wagon. I think they will just leave and take the mule and wagon with them. That is what their intentions were in the beginning. I think they wanted to steel a wagon and mule for transportation. We just happened to be the ones in it at the time," Martha whispered to Ellen. Both girls were so thirsty they did not know how much longer they could hold out.

Ben and the preachers followed the wagon wheels. The tracks seemed to go forever. There were no sigh of the wagon wheels stopping anywhere along the trail. They kept following the winding trail. It was thick with trees on each side. Suddenly they saw a small clearing ahead. Ben picks his walk up to a trot. Martha saw Ben as he entered the clearing. "Oh, my God! There is Ben and the preachers are coming behind him," Martha whispered to Ellen.

"Thank God!" Ellen said. "Not now, Ellen, if the old men wake up they will shoot them." Martha pulled a dead branch away from the tree and threw it at Ben. Ben never saw it. He rushed right up to the wagon to look inside. He knew the wagon and mule belonged to Martha and Ellen. As he peered into the wagon, he found the two sleeping men. Ben quietly turned around and motioned to the preachers to be quiet. The three men stood around the wagon. Ben reached in and carefully pulled the gun out of the wagon. He cocked the gun and aimed it at the old men. "Where are the two women who were in this wagon?" Ben yelled loudly. The two startled old men quickly jumped up and one of them started looking for his gun. "You do not need to look for your gun. I have it right here and I intend to use it on you right now if you don't tell me where the two women are that own this wagon." Martha and Ellen still sitting in the tree watched the whole scene. Martha was afraid to call out. She was afraid it might distract Ben and the old men would overtake him. "Get out of the wagon." Ben ordered. The two old men quickly climbed from the wagon. "I'm going to ask you one more time where those two women are and you will answer me this time or I will blow you apart with your own gun." The two preachers stood by silently praying. They knew Ben meant what he had said. "Where are the women who own this wagon?"

The two men started mumbling, "We ain't seen no women." Ben fired a shot at their feet. The two men danced around. Ben cocked the gun again.

"Are you going to tell me now? The next shot is going to your faces." Martha knew she had to do something. Instead of calling Ben's name, she called for Brother Crocket. "We're here in the tree." The two preachers looked up into the tree where they found Martha and Ellen clinging there like two monkeys. The preachers rushed to the tree. Ben continued to hold the cocked gun on the two criminals. Only God knew the relief Ben felt when he heard Martha call out. He did not know what these two old men had done to the girls but the most important thing was that they were alive. That was enough for Ben to go on another hour, another day, another week, another month, and another year for years as long as Martha would be with him.

The preachers helped the girls down from the tree. Ben continued to hold the cocked gun on the two men. Martha could not help herself. She ran as fast as she could to Ben. Ben handed the gun to one of the preachers who held it like it was a long sprig of poison ivy. Martha wrapped her arms around Ben and wept. Ben held her close until she was finished crying. He ordered the two men into the wagon. Then he told the other preacher to help him tie the criminals up with the ropes they had used to tie the girls up. The other preacher continued to hold the gun. Even though he had it aimed at the men, he did not intend to pull the trigger. Only they did not know that. When Ben had the criminals tied up and secured to the wagon he told Reverend Crocket to go with him to guard the criminals and he ask the other preacher to walk the girls' home. He left with the criminals in the back of the wagon on his way to town and the jail. On his way down the lane, Ben yelled, "Martha I'll be back soon and I will see you at your house."

120

Chapter Eight

Eliza and Robert

Eliza could not read the letter she had gotten from her stepdaughter but she sat on the front porch holding it. She missed Mittie more than she had imagined she would. Nevertheless, life goes on and so it must for the children too. They have found a better life in Berrien County Georgia. She would be the last to deny them of that life. Eliza could not remember leaving Ireland with her family but she remembered hearing her mother and Martha talk about it. They had made a big move and it had been a good one for them, or so Eliza thought it had. Anyway, she was glad they had come to America and North Florida. She would surely never have known Robert Browning if they had not. Slowly Eliza had learned to love Robert with all her heart. She had loved his children first and it took some time before there was a full place in her heart for her husband but he had found a wonderful and stable place in her heart. As she held the letter, no tears came. Eliza only felt joy for her stepchildren. She only hoped they were happy and safe now.

Eliza rarely saw her sisters any longer. Even though Martha and Ellen did not live that far away, Eliza was so busy most of the time. She had missed the revival. During that time, they had been busy unstringing the cooked tobacco, separating the good leaves, which would be number one grade from the rest and it. The less prefect leaves was graded, down as to its quality of tobacco and getting it ready for the market was a busy time. They would place the leaves in a circle, on a burlap sheet and when it was finished the sheet of tobacco would be about four feet high. Robert would carry the tobacco sheets filled with tobacco to the tobacco warehouse and place it on the big open floor with all the other sheets of tobacco placed there by other farmers. On auction day, the tobacco buyers would walk along the rows of tobacco with the auctioneer. Robert was so good at cooking the tobacco that they had very few leaves that were not number one grade.

When Laura came in from helping her dad and Robert Jr. deliver the tobacco to the warehouse in Madison Eliza ask her to read the new letter from Mittie. Laura looked at the address on the envelope before she opened the letter. "This is strange." She said, "This is a different address than before and her return address says Mittie Edwards.

> *Dear Ma, Pa, and family,*
>
> *So sorry it has been so long again since I have written to you. A lot has happened in my life since I last wrote you. I am now married and have a house of my own. I love married life and I love Bill with all my heart. We just had a quiet wedding after church one Sunday morning. The women of the church brought in big pretty plants and put extra flowers in the church. Bill and I walked down the aisle after the service was over. I think it was a pretty wedding.*
>
> *We live about a mile from Grandpa and Grandma's. I have a neat little house. It has two bedrooms, a living room and kitchen with a dining table. I love keeping my own house and you can now call me Mrs. Bill Edwards. It sounds so good to me when I hear it.*
>
> *Ed is still dating Bill's sister Nancy. I believe they will marry some day too. They seem to care a lot for each other. He is still working on Grandpa's farm. Grandpa is so proud of him and the way he has sorta taken over. He makes most all the decisions on the farm now. Grandpa is getting more disable eveyr day. Grandma worries about him all the time.*
>
> *Grandma helped me to get up three dozen mason jars for canning and I have already bought the caps and lids for them. The green beans and squash are looking good. I hope they do well and I can get several quarts of them canned. I plan to have some of everything canned by the end of the year.*
>
> *We have a smoke house out back and we killed three hogs back in the winter. We have hams, sausage, bacon and pork loin hanging out there and it sure is good. I cleaned up all the*

innards and Bill carried them to the packing plant in town where they store it until I need some of it. I made hog head sauce and it sure is good. I wish y'all were here to eat some of it.

    I promise I will not wait so long next time to write. Please answer back as soon as possible. I love all of you and miss you terribly.

Love Always,
Mittie

    Ma made Laura sit right down and write Mittie back to let her know they were all right. Ma told Mittie, congratulations, and she could not believe that she was now a mother-in-law. "But I will try to be a good one for Bill," she told Laura to write.

    "Your brother Robert Jr. has met a girl and spends every day that he is not working with her. He seems to care a lot for her. I look for them to get married anytime now, Ma told Mittie in her letter. Laura addressed the envelope, placed the stamp on it, and carried it to the mailbox.

    Ma was not going to the field now. She was almost full term with her eleventh child. She had done all right but it seemed that each pregnancy got longer and longer. Little Noah was born less than two years ago. It seemed that Ma's breast never got a rest. They were feeding one and getting ready for the other one at the same time. Noah had proven to be a hand full. He was always in to something. Yesterday he pulled a bucket of syrup off the washstand. The lid came off and Noah came running to Ma with a thick layer of syrup dripping from the top of his head to his feet. Ma put him in the washtub and had to scrub him for thirty minutes before she could get the thick syrup off him. One day last week, Noah caught a yellow jacket with his fingers. He was bringing the insect to Ma when the yellow jacket stung him. His little hand was still, somewhat swollen, from the bite. It seems that he will never learn to stay out of trouble.

    "Robbie, (Ma's favorite name for Robert Jr.) you need to eat your supper before you leave," Ma said to Robert Jr. as he was getting ready to walk out the door all dressed in his suit.

    "I will eat at Jo Ann's, Ma. She knows I am coming for supper. She's going to cook it all by herself." Rittie heard the conversation. "Well big deal. She is certainly old enough to be cooking all by herself. All of us were cooking all by ourselves way before we were her age." Some times Ma worried about Rittie. She had a touch of rebel in her. She never seemed to be the proper little girl that the others had always been. She loved spending the night with her girl friends. She seemed to love adventure, something that the other girls were not interested in at all. Ma did not understand why since she had raised them all the same way.

When Robert Jr. arrived at Jo Ann's house, she ran out the door to meet him. "I have your favorite for supper tonight."

"Yea, what is it?" Robert said. "I'm not going to tell you, I'm going to let it be a surprise." Robert did not care what it was. He would enjoy syrup and biscuits as long as he was having it with Jo Ann. He wanted to ask her how she felt about him. He just seemed not to be able to pick up enough nerve to ask. He knew he was in love with her. He went with her to church every Sunday and every Sunday afternoon they spent together. Sometimes they would go to the river and play in the water all afternoon. Sometimes they just sat on her front porch in the swing. No matter what they did it was always fun. Robert really wanted to marry her but as of yet he had not even told her he loved her.

Jo Ann led Robert into the dining room holding her hands over his eyes. He loved the touch of her hands. "Stop!" she said to Robert. Then she moved her hands from his eyes and Robert saw the beautiful table she had prepared for him. It had a big platter of mullet fish in the center of the table. She had truly picked his favorite food for supper.

"How did you know this is my favorite food?" Robert asked. "I knew because, you told me. Do you remember that day at the river? You tried to catch a fish with your hands and when he got away you said, "If he had been a mullet fish I would cry now. I knew then that you loved mullet fish." Robert gathered her in his arms and gave her a hug. However, he had to back away quickly. Jo Ann's mother and father walked into the dining room. They greeted Robert and welcomed him to supper. They really liked this boy. He seemed to have a level head on his shoulders and a big heart to go with it. They would be proud to have him for a son-in-law. He was a fine fellow.

After supper, Jo Ann and Robert cleaned up the dishes. Some men would not have worked in the kitchen. They would have chosen to sit and talk to the girl's father while she cleaned the kitchen by herself. Nevertheless, that was not Robert. Jo Ann deserved help with the kitchen and he wanted to be with her anyway. After the kitchen was clean and the dishes all put away they went to the front porch and sat in the swing. Robert eased his arm around her shoulders. He was so nervous. He was afraid she would pull away. However, instead of pulling away Jo Ann cuddled up to Robert. He was truly in Heaven. They sat without saying a word for almost an hour. Suddenly both of them saw the bright streak coming across the sky. "It is a fallen star." Jo Ann said. "Wasn't it beautiful?"

"Yes it was very beautiful. I wonder what it means," Robert said.

"Does it suppose to mean something?" Jo Ann asked. "Yes, I think it does. I have heard all my life that it is supposed to mean something every time you see one."

"Do you think it is true?" Jo Ann asked.

"Yes, I believe it is, especially if you make a wish when you see one. I made a wish when I saw one and it actually came true."

"What did you wish?" "I wished that cotton would go up to twenty cents a pound one year and when we carried our cotton to the market that year we got twenty cent for every pound we had."

"That does not sound very romantic to me," Jo Ann said.

"It wasn't supposed to be romantic—it was about the price of cotton."

"Well, I want us to make a wish on this fallen star that is romantic," Jo Ann said.

"We can do that," Robert said.

"OK, let's do it. You make your wish just in your head, do not say it aloud and I will do the same. Both of them were quiet for a few minutes while the swing swung back and forth. "I have my wish." Jo Ann said.

"I have my wish too." Robert said. They swung back and forth without saying a word. Five minutes later Jo Ann said. "I can't stand it any longer. What did you wish?"

"I thought the wish was supposed to be a kept secret," Robert said to her.

"I did not say that. I just told you not to say it aloud then."

"Oh," Robert said. "You tell me yours first."

"I don't know if I can say it." Jo Ann said. "What do you mean?" Robert asked. "I am afraid to say what I wished to you."

"Why," Robert asked.

"You might not like it." Jo Ann said.

"Say it and I promise I will like it or if I don't I won't tell you."

"Well that's no good. Now no matter what you say about my wish I will not know whether it is true or not. "Ok, I promise to tell the truth about how I feel about your wish. Now what was it?" Robert asked. Jo Ann was quiet again. Suddenly, she blatted it out. "I wished you would tell me you love me."

Robert's knees turned to jelly. He immediately grabbed her and giving her a big relieved hug, he said, "I love you Jo Ann." Jo Ann held on to Robert with sincere devotion in her heart. "I love you too, Robert." Robert never knew he could feel so much love for one person in his entire life. He was happier than he had ever been in his life. It was as if a new world had just opened for him. He knew what ever life held for him from here on he would be happy.

"Now, you tell me what you wished," Jo Ann said to Robert.

"You will never believe this but I wished that you would fall in love with me."

"I knew I was in love with you a long time ago. But I didn't think you loved me."

"Oh, Robbie, I have loved you for a long time too." Robert took her in his arms and gave her a long passionate kiss. "That kiss sealed our love for each other. Now we never have to wonder and doubt any more," Robert said.

Ma could not imagine what must have happened in her oldest son's life. He seemed happy all the time. He sang church hymns while he worked. He played with the little children and seemed to enjoy it. However, he had always been such a good boy that it seemed natural for him.

Cotton was the family's main crop. They still grew tobacco and sugar cane but cotton was their best moneymaker. Pa had tried another crop this year. He did not know how it would come out but other farmers had started growing peanuts. Pa decided he would try one crop and if it did not make money, he would not plant it again. When he told the family, they would be working with peanuts this year Ellen sighed, "Something else to hoe. I hate hoeing; can't you come up with something that does not need hoeing?"

"Ellen, we have to do anything that can keep a roof over our heads and food on the table." Rittie piped in, "You would think God could invent a crop that didn't have to be hoed. I'll bet he never even thinks about it."

"Pray about it Rittie," Robert said.

"Pa, praying about it ain't going to help either. God don't care if we get a back ache," Rittie said.

"Don't you back talk me?" Pa said. Rittie drifted away. She would not answer that one.

Pa had many cows and hogs now and Ma kept plenty of chickens. When they went to Madison for supplies, they only needed to buy flour, coffee, salt, and sugar. Ma always had a big garden and she grew corn, peas, beans, squash, onions, butter beans, okra, tomatoes, sweet potatoes, and new red potatoes. Sometimes she would buy rice at the general store. All the children loved rice and tomatoes. Every year she canned more tomatoes than any other vegetable.

Now she had the new baby. She was a darling little girl. Ma had named her Liza Mae. She was an especially good baby. Ma was thankful for that since Noah was not quite three years old yet and still mischievous. However, he was the life of the family. If it was mischief, Noah could think it up. He had gotten a dozen eggs from the egg basket in the kitchen. He threw them one at the time, so that he could see them splatter on the kitchen wall.

All the children loved Liza Mae. She loved cuddling and all the children loved to cuddle with her. Mae had a head full of beautiful dark hair and big brown eyes. Ma wished she had one of those new picture takers. She would love to get pictures of the babies when they were little. Ma might be partial but she thought all her babies had been extra pretty babies.

Ma was out of bed again even though Liza Mae was only one months old. Pa came in from the field. "Eliza those panthers are injuring the cows and I've found one pig that they slaughtered," Pa said.

"I know they are out there. I hear them screaming every night," Ma said.

"I don't know what to do. They are going to keep on until we won't have any hogs left and some of the cows they have injured may die too," Pa said.

Ma loved Pa so much and she could feel the hurt he was experiencing with his injured and dead livestock. "I know what we can do, Robert."

"What can we do?" Robert said. "Tonight I will hide out back and scream like the panther's scream. They will think it is another panther and maybe they will come out of the woods to investigate. As they come out of the woods you and Robbie can shoot them," Eliza said to Robert.

"It sounds like that plan may work, Eliza." That pleased Eliza since she saw a ray of hope on her husband's face.

Just before dark that evening Ma could hear the panthers screaming. She told all the children to stay inside the house except Robert. Pa and Robert got a gun out of the house. Ma stood on a stump at the edge of the woods. Tree branches and bushes hid her. She began screaming the same sounding scream that the panthers were screaming. Pa and Robert were on the ready with their guns raised. After a few screams by Eliza the panthers began to appear in the open. One by one, either Pa or Robert shot the panthers until, the others got wise and left or they were all dead. After that, Pa had no more problems with panthers.

Ma announced to the family that she was pregnant again. Of course, she did not say it exactly that way. "I am in the family way and that means you children are going to need to take over most of the garden work." It seemed that Ma was always pregnant. Liza Mae was only one year and two months old. She had only been walking two months. She was an independent little girl. She dappled about the house but never got into anything. Ma was glad since Noah had made up for all of them in mischief.

"Eliza, I have been thinking. If this baby were a girl would you be willing to give her the name of my first wife. She was such a good person and she did not deserve to die so young. I think she had a pretty name too," Pa said. "Her name was Mary Jane, wasn't it?" Ma said.

"Yes, will you name her Mary Jane?"

"Yes, I think that is a very pretty name too. I'll be happy to name her Mary Jane," Ma said.

It was almost time for the baby to come. Pa hoped it would be a girl so she could carry Mary Jane's name on.

Mary Jane was born on a cold night in February. The girls sat on the front porch and cringed as they heard the moans from Ma while she tried to deliver the baby. "I'll never have as many babies as Ma has had," Laura said.

"I'm never getting married," Ellen said.

Rittie was swinging in the swing. "Well I will get married but I will be the one to decide how many children I have. It won't be my husband."

"And how are you going to do that, may I ask?" Ellen said.

"Just trust me, I will figure it out." Rittie said.

Orval and his family still lived just down the road and the two women traded out when it came birthing time. They always went to the aid of the other. Between both of the women, one of them were having a baby every year and sometimes soon after a baby was born the new mother would be called to assist the other woman with her delivery. Both Eliza and Christina had become professionals at assisting with the delivery of a baby.

Pa came in from the cotton field the following summer and said to Eliza. "There is some kind of beetle in the cotton this year."

"What is it?" Eliza asked.

"I don't know, he has a hard back and looks like a horn coming out from his face," Robert said.

"Do you think he is poisonous?" Ma asked.

"I don't know but I am going to walk down to Orval's house and ask him if he has any in his cotton." Robert walked two miles to his brother's house.

"Orval I have some kind of bug all in my cotton. Have you seen any in your cotton?" Robert asked.

"Yes, I have and I hate to tell you this but, this bug is probably going to destroy our crop of cotton," Orval said.

"How do you know?" Robert asked. "Because he has migrated from Texas into Florida and they have destroyed crops from Texas to Florida. He is called a boll weevil and there is nothing that will kill them."

"My landlord came and told me about them. He said the best thing to do is try to pick them off and kill them."

"Are they poisonous?" Robert asked. "No, they don't even bite," Orval said.

When Robert got home and announced to the children the chore, they had before them there were loud groans. "Pa, do you expect us to really pull bugs off with our bare hands?" Rittie asked.

"Yes, that is what I am telling you," Pa said. This was a horror the girls could not imagine. All of them hated bugs. They cringed every year when they had to pick the tobacco worms off the tobacco. However, bugs...it was too horrible to think.

Early the next day everyone gathered in the cotton patch to pick bugs off the cotton. "When you pull him off squash him in the dirt. Be sure he is dead before you go to the next one," Pa told them. The girls grumbled as they started toward their row of cotton. There was a scream here and a scream there, from the girls as they did as Pa had told them. "That one bit me," Rittie screamed. No one looked up; they kept on with their job. They knew if one of the bugs had really bitten Rittie it was not going to end their job so they might as well make the best of it.

Pa and the children stayed in the cotton patch for a week picking the bugs off and smashing them. When Pa went over the cotton stalks they had finished there was as many boll weevils on them as there was before they picked them all off. This is doing no good. Pa said to himself. He paid another visit to his brother. "Orval picking the bugs off is not helping. They have covered the rows again that we have already picked off."

Tears weld in Orval's eyes. "I know; it's not helping our cotton either. Both men knew what that meant. They would stand by and watch their cotton eaten away by the little bug. The cotton was a total loss for the two farmers. They learned later, that it was not only, their fields, the boll weevil had invaded. The annoying little bug affected every farmer, in Madison County. Most all of them had lost their entire crop of cotton also.

Since cotton was the main moneymaker for the farm, many farmers folded that year. Robert was holding on by a thread. He tried to make up the difference with turnips, mustard, and collards that winter. However, with everyone in the same condition as the Browning family, it was hard to sell anything.

Ma told the family they were going to have another brother or sister in the family. She was in the family way again. Times were hard this year. It was 1913 and the world seemed to be unaffected, despite the problems the Browning family was having. America had elected Woodrow Wilson the twenty-eighth president of the United States. His vice president was Thomas Marshall. This gave Robert some hope since Mr. Wilson was a democrat and he knew he was farm friendly. Times were definitely changing and it seemed for the better everywhere except Madison County. Automobiles were everywhere now and if Robert had five hundred dollars, he could buy a brand new car. He could buy a house for $4,800.00 if he had it. Robert wished he had a job and could give up the farm. The average salary was one thousand, thirty-four dollars a year. That was about twice what he made on the farm. Everyone was excited about the opening of the Panama Canal. They said it made it possible to sell American goods over seas much faster than in the past. President Wilson had the Congress pass The Federal Farm Loan Act. It was easy for him to get his Democratic Congress to pass legislation. Robert did not know much about politics but he knew this man was going to make a difference. He just hoped some good from it would swing his way soon.

A new song had just come out. The girls had a battery radio and they loved listening to it. They listened to it every evening when they came home from work or school. When the song "Danny Boy" came on everyone in the house knew to be completely silent. They all huddled around the battery radio when Danny Boy was on. The boys would not admit it but they loved the song too.

Late that night Eliza woke Robert up and told him her water had broken. Robert jumped out of bed, got dressed, and ran out the door. He hitched the mule to the wagon and made the horse go in a gallop to Christina's house. "Eliza is ready to give birth." He said to Christina. She grabbed her robe, threw it over her shoulders, and was in the wagon with Robert. When they arrived, Christina found Eliza was already having contractions five minutes apart. She sat by Eliza's bedside and they talked until the pains got closer and closer.

"You'd think after as many as I have had, I'd be used to it by now," Eliza said to Christina between pains."

"Don't matter how many you have they still hurt just as much as the first one," Christina said.

"I think it's coming now," Eliza said between clinched teeth. Mary Jane entered the world in February 1913. She also was a beautiful baby and looked so much like Mae when she was born. Ma just hoped she would be as good as May had been.

When Mary Jane was only three months old Ma was pregnant again; this one would be number twelve not counting her two step-children who she considered her own children too. Eliza finally had an opportunity to go to church again. She saw her sisters there and enjoyed talking to them again. Martha told her about her friend. Eliza believed she was in love with him. She pressed Martha on a wedding day but Martha declined an answer. She had never seen her sister so happy. Martha told her that Ben would be coming again soon and when he arrived, she would take him to meet Eliza and her family.

Less work was required on the farm now that the boll weevils had wiped the cotton crop out. Even though Eliza could tell that Robert was worried, he still showed excitement about having another new baby. He loved all the children and was a very good father and husband. He saw that his family was well fed and had a solid roof over their heads. Madison now had doctors who cared for pregnant women and aided in their delivery. Pa took Ma to see one just to be sure she was all right since she had had so many babies and they had been so close together. This baby would be her thirteenth delivery. When the doctor finished checking her, he said, "Mrs. Browning you are one of the healthiest women I have ever had. It is hard to believe that you are pregnant with your thirteenth baby. You are barely five feet tall and yet you have healthy babies every time. I think you need to write a book on how you live, since it must be the perfect life for someone who wants many healthy children.

Ma rode back with Pa in the wagon. She was feeling good. Eliza looked up to the Heavens and said a special thank you pray for her good health. She only had one problem and that was her fingers. She had used them so much shelling peas, picking vegetables, cooking and attending babies that her fingers gnarled and, twisted, were always painful. She had seen a doctor about them one time and he had told her she had bone fellows. (bone fellows are known medically as an abcess on the bone usually caused by a thorn entering the skin and working it's way to the bone. But Eliza did not know that.) Someone had told her, if she slept with her painful finger down a live frog's throat that it would bring the bone fellom to a head and her finger would get better. She had slept many nights with a frog jumping around and her finger down his throat. However, she knew the doctor was right. She had never had a complicated pregnancy and all the children were extra healthy, both mentally and psysically. She sang songs and tried to cheer Robert up but it did not seem to help. She hoped his worry would not turn into depression.

When spring came, Pa again, needed to go fetch Christina in the middle of the night. It was another baby girl. They would name her Mattie Lee. Ma loved Mittie so much that she wanted a name similar to hers for this little baby.

Ellen called Ma from the front porch. "Aunt Martha is coming Ma, and Aunt Ellen and a man is with her." Ma knew immediately who the man was. *We, are going to meet Martha's new beau*, Ma thought, to herself. She came running to the front porch. The wagon pulled up in front of the house. Eliza ran down the steps to help her sisters off the wagon but by the time she got there, the handsome man had gotten down and was helping Martha from the wagon. Eliza helped Ellen out of the wagon and then gave her a big hug. She went around the wagon to greet Martha. Giving her a big hug Eliza said, "I am so happy that you came."

"I told you I would come when Ben came back." "Ben this is my sister Eliza Browning." She swept her hands across the yard and said, "And these are all her children." Ben shook hands with Eliza and told her he was happy to meet her. Then he went to each child and introduced himself, shook hands with each child and asked the child's name. From that moment, Ben never forgot any of the children's names. Everyone immediately loved Ben. Eliza could certainly see why Louisa loved him so much. Eliza could see that Ben loved Louisa and was very devoted to her. Eliza was so happy for her sister.

Ben announced to the family that he had a camera and he would like the family to gather for a photograph. This pleased Ma since she had always wanted a picture taken of her family. She shooed the children into the house to get dressed in their Sunday clothes for the picture. "Hurry up since he has to take the picture while it is still day light," Ma told them. She had heard that somewhere long time ago. Soon the children all came running out all dressed in their Sunday best including their Sunday hat but none of them had their shoes on. Mae refused to wear her hat. "No," she said as the hat went from her head to the floor. Ma started to shoo them back inside to get their shoes but Ben said it was all right if they did not wear shoes. Robert Jr. came out dressed in his Sunday suit and new felt hat and Pa put his Sunday jacket and his hat on too.

Ben and Louisa arranged the family for a good portrait. Cameras were Ben's hobby. He had always enjoyed taking pictures even before the automatic camera came out. Ben placed Pa in the back of the group and he held Mary Jane who was barely a year old. Ma stood to his right and she held tiny baby Mattie Lee. Ben was able to get all twelve children, Ma, and Pa in the photograph. "I will send you one when I get them developed," Ben promised Eliza.

Eliza, Louisa, and Ellen then went into the kitchen to prepare the evening meal. They talked continuously trying to catch up on everything that had happened in their lives since they had last seen each other long enough to talk. Louisa told Eliza about, the kidnapping of herself and Ellen, by the two dirty old men. She told how they had climbed the tree, where they spent the night, to get away from them, and how Ben and the preachers rescued them from the woods the next morning. Eliza was stunned at her sister's dilemma. "That is awful, Louisa. I would have lost my mind if I had known about it while it was happening. I hope they put these two men away forever."

Louisa wanted to know, in detail, how Eliza felt about Ben. "Do you remember what you said to me on the wagon that day after I had met Robert? You said, he is a good man and do not let him get away. You said you had lost your chance at a good husband and now you would probably die an old maid." "Well I think you have found the perfect man and if I were you I would not let him get away." Eliza said to Louisa.

At the supper table that night, Robert Jr. announced to the whole family that he was getting married. Ma gave him a big hug and Louisa wanted to know all about the girl he was marrying. Ma jumped in and told Louisa, "She is a good girl and comes from a good family. She is pretty and sweet too." "And her name is Jo Ann," Robert Jr. told her. "And I love her very much."

Laura said, "I think she loves you even more."

"No way," Robert said to her. Robert Jr. was happy now that his engagement was out. He and Jo Ann had planned their wedding already and she was getting ready for it. They would be married this coming summer. He was so looking forward to their wedding.

"Laura, go to the mailbox. The mail man stopped and put something in it," Ma said. Laura ran to the mailbox. It was a letter from Mittie. Laura had the letter torn open by the time she reached the front porch.

> *Dear Ma, Pa and all,*
>
> *Well Ed did it. He and Nancy got married. They are as happy as they can be. They had a nice little wedding at home. I think they will continue living at Grandpa and Grandma's since Grandpa needs Ed so bad. Grandpa is really getting feeble now and he cannot remember much. I do not think he will be with us much longer.*
>
> *It is so neat that Eddie and I are brother and sister and we married a brother and sister. I guess that makes Nancy my sister-in-law two times.*
>
> *Did I tell you that I am in the family way? Our new little one will be born in two more months. I will be glad when my time comes. I am so big and round I cannot even see my toes. I cannot imagine what I will look like in two more months. Bill is wishing for a boy but it does not matter to me. Just as long as he or she is healthy, I will be happy.*
>
> *I hope all of you are well and happy. We all are except for Grandpa. Please write me all the news from home. I love getting letters from y'all.*
>
> *Love Always,*
> *Mittie*

"We need to write her right back so we can tell her about Robert's engagement. She'll be happy about that," Ma said to Laura. "I don't have time this evening Ma, I am working on my Sunday school lesson for Sunday," Laura said. "Well as soon as you have a minute, we need to write her," Ma said. Laura went away whispering to herself "as if I can write a whole letter for you in a minute."

Chapter Nine

Robert Looses his Life

On Monday, Robert went to check the yellow neck squash. He had planted a large field since the boll weevils had taken oven the cotton for the second year. His turnip, mustard, and collard crop did not bring in much so he would try other vegetables. He had to do something. He had fourteen mouths to feed. He had also planted a large field of pole beans. Tomorrow he would put the prop sticks in the field so the running beans would have the support they needed to grow.

When Robert came in from the squash field, his face was pale and he was coughing. "What is wrong, Robert?" "I just don't feel good. I must be coming down with the flu."

"You need to go to the doctor now," Eliza said.

"I'll just get cleaned up and go to bed and maybe tomorrow I'll feel better," he said. When Eliza got the supper on the table that evening, she went into the bedroom to wake her husband up for his supper. She had difficulty waking him. She could hear a wheeze coming from his chest. When she finally got him awake, he refused supper.

"I don't want anything to eat. I'll just rest," he said to Eliza in a weak voice. Eliza was worried about him but she knew he needed the rest. He had seemed tired and listless for the last several weeks. Maybe if he gets lots of rest he will feel better. Eliza thought to herself. Ma told the children at supper they would need to stay quiet since Pa was sick and needed to rest.

Eliza got up during the night to feed baby Mattie Lee. Pa was sleeping sound with a snore. He really is tired, Ma thought, to be sleeping this hard. She was careful not to awake him. Robert was usually out of bed and out of the house before Eliza woke up. He always got up well before day light. He would work around the barn until breakfast was ready and then he would eat and go to the field with all the kids who were old enough to work.

Ma woke up just after daybreak and found her husband was still sleeping. She decided to wake him up just to check on him. Eliza could not wake Robert up. He was still breathing the loud breathing as he had done during the night. Frantically she called for Robert Jr. to come and help her. Eliza and Robbie, tried to sit him up. He opened his eyes part way. "Robert, are you alright?" Eliza asked him.

"Yes, I am alright," he said in a voice so weak they could barely hear.

"Go to Madison, Robie and get the doctor as fast as you can go." Robert Jr. got on his horse and raced to Madison. When he arrived at Dr. Yates house he told him about Pa. Dr. Yates grabbed his satchel and was out the door. He hopped in his motorized car and followed Robert. Robert ran the horse as fast as he could. When they arrived at home, Robert Jr. jumped off his horse and led the doctor to his dad. The doctor took out his stethoscope and placed it on Robert's chest. He listened for a while then he turned to Eliza and said, "Mrs. Browning your husband is gravely ill. He has contracted a germ called pneumococus. It causes pneumonia and there is no cure for it. He is in a coma now and probably will not wake up again. Eliza fell to her knees by his bedside. In a flood of tears she began calling her husband's name and willing him to wake up. However, Robert did not move. Eliza stayed by his bedside until he slipped away in his sleep. The funeral and cemetery services were a blur in Eliza's mind. She was so absorbed in the sudden loss of her husband that she could not live in the moment. Life would have to go by without her at this time.

It had been only one week and five days since Pa died. Things at the Browning house had not gotten back to normal since Pa's death. Everyone walked about in a daze. No one could believe he was truly gone. Robert Jr. came home from his visit with Jo Ann. "I was not expecting you home this early Robbie," ma said to him.

"I left early because I don't feel good." This really got Ma's attention. Robbie never complained. For him to say he did not feel good let Ma know he was sick? She placed her hand on his forehead and he was burning hot. "Come on Robert. We are going to take you to the doctor." Ma called for Laura and Rittie to get the mule hitched to the wagon and pick them up at the front door. Ma pulled a blanket off the bed to wrap around Robert. She helped him to the door. Laura and Rittie helped Ma get Robert into the wagon. Rittie ran back into the house and brought out a thick quilt and a pillow, for Robert to lie on in the wagon. The three women carried him to see Dr. Yates. Dr. Yates came out to the wagon when they arrived. He took one look at Robert Jr. and said "Mrs. Browning it pains me to have to tell you this but your son has the same thing that you husband had. By now, Robert was getting lethargic. Take him to the infirmary, Ellen, and I will stay with him and see what I can do. Ma was so relieved that the doctor was willing to try to help him. It was rare for him to admit someone since he could do no more for a patient than his or her own family could do at home. The doctor had done the same for Eliza's brother, James, when he died.

Laura and Rittie helped the doctor to make Robert Jr. comfortable in bed. Robert Jr. went into a spell of coughing and almost lost his breath. The doctor brought a bottle of medicine and the girls held their brother's head, while the doctor gave it to him. Robert had trouble swallowing. The doctor had to repeat swallow several time before Robert got it all down. After that, Robert went to sleep and slept peacefully. When midnight came, Robert was still peacefully sleeping. Ma told the doctor that she had a three month old at home and needed to go home to feed her. The doctor told her to go since Robert was sleeping and she could come back in the morning. Laura and Ma left but Rittie stayed by Robert's side with the doctor.

When Ma got home, she fed Mattie Lee but she did not go to bed. She stayed on her knees the rest of the night praying for her son. He could not die. Ma could not bear another loss. She was supposed to die before her children. She could think of a million reasons why Robert Jr. could not die. He was the one she was going to lean on since Robert died. Who would run the farm? Who knew how? She loved him too much to loose him. Nevertheless, she would. When she and Laura got to the infirmary the next morning Robbie had just slipped away. "He is gone. I did all I could but I could not save him." Dr. Yates had tears in his eyes as he told her. Eliza thanked the doctor and walked out with her daughters. Eliza's eyes were dry. She had been defeated. She was alone now with twelve children to raise, all on her own. She knew she could not run the farm alone. What would she do? Ma told Laura to stop at Jo Ann's house on the way home. Jo Ann came to the door as soon as they arrived at her house.

"Jo Ann, I have bad news for you," Ma said with pools of tears in her eyes. Robbie died this morning. "Jo Ann started screaming No, No, No, My Robert can not have died. Please tell me it is not true." She begged. It was true and he was to be buried the following Sunday which was to be their wedding day. The church pews were all full at Pa's funeral with friends and family but Robert's funeral was twice the size of Pa's funeral. Everyone loved Robert Jr. and everyone loved Jo Ann. She leaned over the coffin and pleaded to Robert to come back to her. No one in the church had ever been to a funeral where a loved one was so distraught. Her begging and pleading went on until her parents caught her just before she hit the floor in a faint. They assisted her out of the church but her screams still were, heard inside the church. There was not a dry eye in the church. Everyone wanted to help Jo Ann get through this nightmare but there was nothing, anyone could do. She was in her own world now and it was a world of torment. Only time would provide her with some healing. Everyone knew how much Jo Ann loved Robert and how she had looked so forward to their wedding day. The saddest part of all was when Jo Ann stood over the coffin, as it they lowered in the grave. She kept calling his name and begging him to come back to her. Her parents caught her just as she fainted again and they carried her from the gave site

One week after the Robert Jr. funeral, Eliza asked Laura to sit down and write a letter for her.

> *Dear Mittie,*
>
> *I do not know where to start. Our lives have been, turned up side down here. I am so worried I do not know what we will do.*
>
> *Your dad died two weeks ago with pneumonia and last Sunday we buried Robert Jr. with the same thing. Both of them are gone within two weeks. I need yours and Eddie's help. Can you please come as soon as possible and help me to decide what I need to do?*
>
> *You know your dad always made all the decisions and worked hard to make us a living. Now we do not have that any longer.*
>
> *I will wait to hear from you. I hope you and your brother can come.*
>
> *Love Always,*
> *Ma*

When Mittie got Ma's letter she sat down and had a good cry. Her dad and brother was gone forever they would never talk to her again. It seemed impossible. Poor Ma! Mittie knew she was worried out of her mind. She took the baby and went to the field where Bill was plowing. She told him about the letter through tears. "What can we do, Bill?" she ask him. "We will go to Madison and get them. They can move here where they will be closer," he said. Mittie went across the field to find Eddie in Grandpa's field. She told him what had happened. Eddie broke down and wept. "I wish I could have seen them before they died," he said. Mittie held to her brother and they cried together. They talked about what might be best for Ma and the children. Mittie told him what Bill had said. "There is enough room in the big house for them to stay until they get a place of their own. I will ask Grandma but I am sure she will not mind. When Mittie got back home, she sat down and wrote Ma back.

> *Dear Ma,*
>
> *I am so sorry to hear about Pa and Robbie. It still seems impossible that they are gone. We will come and get you in two weeks. I have talked with Eddie and he said we will come on the train and help you load up the wagon and we will pull the wagon back here. You and the children can stay with Eddie at Grandma and Grandpa's. There is plenty of room for all of you. We will help you to get started again. Try not to worry Ma, as that will only make you sick. Start packing up your things now. I love you and I will see you soon.*
>
> *Love Always,*
> *Mittie*

Eliza was so relieved when she got the letter from Mittie. She knew Mittie would find a way to help them. She had always been a very smart girl. Ma had never been so happy that she had named Mary Jane after Mittie's mother's namesake. She hoped that Mary Jane would turn out just like Mittie.

Martha and Ellen came to both funerals and they returned for a visit with their sister. "How are you doing?" Martha asked Eliza. Eliza told her she was just trying to get through one day at the time. She told her about the getting the letter from her stepdaughter. "Mittie and Eddie will be here next week to help us move to Nashville. We will stay at Mr. and Mrs. Becton's house until we can get settled and find somewhere to live." Martha was relieved that Eliza had figured out what to do. She was so worried about her since she had just lost both her breadwinners.

Martha brought one of the pictures of the family that Ben had taken while they visited. Eliza looked at the picture. Tears pooled in her eyes. "Thank God, I will always have a picture of my husband and son," she said as she clutched it close to her body. The children passed the picture around. Each one looked at a picture of his or her self. They had never seen a picture of themselves before. Later when Ma was studying the picture again she said, "Mae where is your hat?"

"Ma, I could not get her to keep the hat on her head long enough for the picture," Rittie said. Eliza Mae had been only four years old when the picture was made and she did not like anything on her head.

Martha told Eliza about the wedding that she and Ben were planning. "Ben is building us a nice home in Lakeland. That is where he wants to live. He said it is so pretty, there. I told him where we live do not matter to me as long as we are together. He had agreed for Ellen to live with us. We are looking so forward to it. We will get married as soon as the house is finished. Ben is coming next week and he is taking us to Lakeland to look at the house. He has bought one of those new motor cars. He can go and come so much easier now. Sometimes it is a little hard to get gasoline. When he is in our area, he always has the gasoline brought in by the train from Atlanta. Eliza was so happy for her sister. No matter what happened, she knew Ben would see that Martha and Ellen would be cared for as long as they needed help. Eddie and Mittie came and helped the family get their belongings packed in the wagon. Eliza was shocked at the many things she had collected over the years. They were unable to get everything on the wagon. Some things would need leaving behind. Maybe they could come back and get the rest of it. Eliza hoped so. Orval bought all the livestock from Eliza. The money would come in good when they got to Nashville.

Eddie wanted Luke to come with him on the wagon. All the others caught the train to Nashville. Eliza felt tears sting her eyes as they rode away in Orval's wagon. She took one last look. The place held so many memories for her. There were unfinished crops in the fields. Eliza had no idea who would eventually take the place over. Right now, the most important thing was getting her family to safety and that they would have food on the table. Eddie and Luke had a hard time getting the wagonload of household goods to Nashville. Not long after they left Madison County, a wheel ran of the wagon and broke into several pieces. Luke walked to Quitman to get another wheel. He had to roll the wheel back to the wagon since it was too heavy for him to carry. He and Eddie got the new wheel on the wagon and started their route again heading to Berrien County Ga. They had made it about twenty-five miles when the old mule showed signs of wearing out. They stopped at a farmhouse and Eddie talked the farmer into swapping mules with him. He sweetened the deal by throwing in a dollar and a half. The farmer did not want the old worn out mule but he needed the one and one half dollars so he made the deal.

The family arrived in Nashville long before Eddie and Luke got there with the wagon. Mittie had been right. There was plenty of room in the big house. Mrs. Becton welcomed them and was very gracious. Mr. Becton was very disabled. His wife introduced him to the family but he showed no signs of understanding what was going on.

Luke, now the oldest son, was seventeen years old. He would now be the family's leader. Russell was right behind him at sixteen years old. Russell enjoyed competing with Luke. He hated being the younger one. Since he and Luke had grown up together, they were very close and that forced Russell to be more advance for his age, so that he could stay ahead of his brother.

Every morning all the children got up, had their breakfast, and went to the field. Some went with Ed and some of them walked down to Mittie's and Bill's house where they worked with Bill on his farm. They came in for lunch and then right back to the field until dark.

Chapter Ten

Martha and Ellen

Mittie came to her grandparent's house to see Ma. "Ma, you have a letter from Aunt Martha. I do not know why she sent it to my house." Ma did not have the heart to tell her that her address is the one she had given Martha, since she could not remember what her grandparent's address was.

Martha had a difficult time trying to write the letter to her sister. How could she ever get over this horrible tragedy in her life? Ben had left her house only three days ago. He had come a week before. He was so excited. "Sweetheart, our house is almost finished. I need you and Ellen to go with me so that you can see it and you can decide the colors for the inside. He had a hotel room rented in Lakeland for herself and Ellen to stay while they were there.

Martha and Ellen packed a bag each and climbed into Ben's new car. Ellen enjoyed the trip. She had never seen so many orange trees in her life. They were on each side of the road for miles, from Madison to Lakeland. The orange blossoms were in full bloom and she kept her back window down all the way to Lakeland. This was the first time Ellen, had ever stayed in a hotel. They were shocked at how clean and convenient everything was inside the hotel. Martha told Ellen about her stay in a hotel in New York when they had come from Ireland. "I'm telling you, Ellen, it was nothing like this. We had small cots to sleep on and they looked like Ma big wood biscuit mixing bowl. The cots sunk so badly in the middle it almost touched the floor. We had a bathroom but it was nothing like this. It was down the hall and so primitive. We had to share it with everyone else in the hotel." This hotel had a modern bathroom right there in the room. The bed was so pretty. It looked so comfortable.

Ellen could not wait to get into the bed. She sat on the side and bounced up and down. "I want to sleep on this side," Ellen said.

The next morning Ben picked them up in front of the hotel. They went to a restaurant and had a full breakfast. The food was delicious. Martha and Ellen decided life could not get any better than this. Ben talked about the new house throughout breakfast. By the time breakfast was finished, Martha could not wait to see the new house. Ben drove the car and carried them to the edge of town on a small hill where a long lane ran from the road to the house.

When Louisa saw the house, it literally, astounded her. The house had covered wires running from poles to the house. "Is it going to have electricity, Ben?" Martha asked.

"It sure is and it's going to have built in plumbing." Martha did not know exactly what he meant by "built in plumbing", but she let it go. The outside of the house was finished. It was a big white house with black shutters on each side of every window.

"Ben, this is the prettiest house I have ever seen," Martha said.

"It is all yours, my dear," Ben said. She threw her arms around Ben's neck and gave him a big hug.

"I love you so much, Ben Parker," she said.

"I love you too Martha Marlow," Ben said. The girls followed Ben into the house. It had a small foyer that opened up to a big open room. The room had shiny wood floors. "This is the living room." Ben said. They followed Ben into another room off the living room. This also was a large room and it had a big chandelier hanging from the center of the room. "This is the dining room." Ben said. He flipped a switch and the big chandelier lit up. Ellen could not take her eyes off it. The glass shimmered and glowed as the light shined through it. It was the prettiest thing she had ever seen.

Ben led the girls through four more rooms and one of them had its own built in bathroom. Just like the hotel. Ben said it was the master bedroom. He carried them through another room and said it was the game room and library. The kitchen was beautiful, with many cabinets built into the walls and long counters tops with cabinets built under all them of them. The kitchen had a built in electric stove and two sinks. It had a refrigerator and a freezer. Then Ben showed them the utility room. It had a washing machine with a ringer inside the room where Martha would wash their clothes. Martha could not imagine washing clothes inside the house and she would not need to scrub them on the rub board. This machine would do it for her. There was another bathroom in the hall. This house had everything a woman could possibly dream about having. Martha did not know most of it even existed until she saw it in her own house.

The construction workers were coming back tomorrow and Martha and Ben would meet with them at the house where Martha would tell them the colors she wanted on the walls and floors. Martha walked around the empty house and imagined herself living there. It was hard to grasp. Would she know how to keep a beautiful place like this up? If not then she would learn how. She did not know anyone who lived in a house this beautiful. She never thought, in a hundred years, that she ever would.

Ben took Martha and Ellen to a nice restaurant for dinner that night. It seemed strange to the girls to hear supper called dinner. They had always called the midday meal dinner and the night meal supper, but Ben called the midday meal lunch and the night meal dinner. Martha made a mental note to try to learn all these new things and try to get into Ben's mental world. She knew she could if she tried. She would start getting magazines and books and reading them.

Martha and Ellen had sat down in the hotel room when Ben dropped them off after dinner. They thought about colors for each room. They looked at colors that were in magazines in the room. Ben had given them some color samples that he had gotten from the paint store. "I don't care what colors you pick, Martha, as long as it is what you like." The girls sat up most of the night trying to decide on colors. Finally Martha decided that she wanted all the inside rooms to be painted the same color and the color would be a light beige.

"That settles it, Ellen, now we can go to bed." Martha said. Martha knew that beige would go with anything and she still had not decided on the colors for her rugs. She would need to look at the rugs in the store and then decide which she liked best.

Martha needed to pinch herself at intervals to be sure this was real and she was not dreaming. Just a year ago she was worried out of her mind about whether or not she could keep the plowed rows straight and the crops gathered before they spoiled in the fields. Now she was making decisions on the colors for a beautiful new home that was going to be hers. Ben had told Martha that when they were married she would never work again.

They spent most of the next day with the contractors. When they left the house, they went to a local furniture store. "This is where we will purchase all the furniture for the house," Ben said. "Do you mean that we can't bring any furniture from our house?" Martha asked in disappointment.

"Of course, you can bring your furniture but we are going to need lots more furniture to fill our big house up," Ben said.

The next day Ben brought Martha and Ellen to the furniture store. Ben made no decisions on the furniture. He supported the girls with their decisions as to what pieces of furniture would look good. Martha could not believe she would actually have a living room. She had seen them in homes before but her home had always had a bed in the front room. It was just necessary when their family was so big. Now that the family had dwindled down to Ellen and herself, she just never saw the need to take the bed down. Besides, if she had taken the bed down, all she would have in the front room is a few straight back chairs and the rocker her mother had brought from Ireland. The most fun of all for Martha was selecting a living room suit. The furniture would be delivered the furniture next week when the inside of the house was painted and the paint had time to dry.

Ben sang to Martha and Ellen most of the way back home. Sometimes they would sing along with him if they knew the song. Ben's voice, without even having music played for him, was so beautiful. Martha thought to herself. With a talent like that, it is no wonder he is so wealthy. However all Ben's money had not come from his singing. It is true that his voice brought in a good living but he had invested the money his parents left to him and had saved money on his own that he also invested wisely. It was true he was a very wealthy man. Ben never flaunted his money. He was known to help anyone he knew who were in need. He also firmly believed in tithing his ten percent to the church.

When Ben walked Martha and Ellen to the door of their house, he gave Martha a kiss and said. "I will be back next week. I will bring a truck so we can move your things to Lakeland and we will get married there. By next week they will have all the furniture in the house so all we have to do is add your furniture and our clothes."

On Monday, Martha was so happy she could hardly contain herself. By the end of the week, she would be Mrs. Ben Parker and living in a big new home that belong to her and her husband. Ellen was equally excited. She would have her own bedroom with a big closet for her clothes and she would live in a house with all the modern conveniences. She felt sure that living in a town the size of Lakeland, Florida she would soon find her own perfect beau.

Dear Eliza and all,

I do not know how to start this letter. My life is shattered and I do not think I can go on. I know how you felt now when Robert died. How did you survive it?

Two weeks ago, Ben brought Ellen and me home after visiting our new home in Lakeland. Ben had it built for us and we were getting married when the house was finished which was one week ago today.

A week ago, our pastor came to the house and called me to the door. He told me to sit down; he had something to tell me. I could not imagine what he was about to tell me. I thought they might be throwing me out of the church since I was dating Ben. That is not what it was. I wish it had been.

The preacher gave me a speech on how fragile life is and how this life is only a small part of our lives. He said Christians go on to a higher plain of life where they are at the right hand of God. I could not imagine why the sermon. I wanted him to go on and tell me why he was there and I told him so.

"Martha, Ben has died." I do not know much of what he said after that. Later I learned that Ben was attending a revival in Tallahassee at the First Baptist Church. He was singing a hymn for the church when he began having chest pain. He sat down and suddenly became very pale and could not get his breath. Ben died in the pulpit chair of a massive heart attack while the church filled with revival attendances looked on. There was a medical doctor in the congregation and he came up and worked with Ben for a long time but he could not bring him back.

I sorta drifted through the funeral. None of it seemed real. It was as if I was looking on and someone else was going through this horrible ordeal. When the funeral was over a well-dressed man came to me and said he wanted to see me in the pastor's office. I had no clue who he was or what he wanted. I just felt so defeated and I followed him wherever he was going. I knew he could not tell me anything more horrible that what I had just witnessed. He said his name was Lou Parker and he had a law practice in Ireland when he was young but had moved to the United States and to Tallahassee many years ago. He said he had been Ben's attorney for many years. I did not ask but Lou and Ben may be related. He said he had handled all Ben's financial affairs for years.

However, instead of hearing more bad news he told me that Ben had willed everything he owned to me. All his stocks, bonds, savings and the new house were now mine. Lou said he had also left his new automobile to me. Now I am a wealthy woman but I would so prefer to be poor again and have Ben back.

Ellen and I have moved into the new house in Lakeland and I am now taking driving lessons. I wish you could come and see the beautiful place where I live. I am going to continue to allow Lou to handle the money. He says the money grows rapidly every day.

I miss Ben so much. It seems impossible that he is no longer with me. Why do bad things happen to good people, Eliza?" Ben was such a good person. He had so much life left to live. I will always love him.

Write to me and let me know how all of you are doing. Write my new address down here in Lakeland. It is in the return address on the envelope.

Love Always,
Martha

Eliza had Laura sit down right then and write Martha back. "We have to write her back right now. Look what she has gone through," Ma said. Rittie had heard Laura read the letter and she interjected, "But look where she is now. I'd sure like to be in her shoes." Rittie was always telling the family that she was going to marry a rich man, someday.

Chapter Eleven

Eliza's Family Continues to Grow

Within six months, Luke found a big farm. The landowner was searching for a sharecropper. Luke took the job and moved the family into the big house on the farm near Springhead Church out from Adel Georgia. Adel was the new county seat for the new county that had broken off from Berrien County. It was now Cook County.

Ma got the children in Springhead Baptist Church near where they lived. Everyone went to church every Sunday. Two gorgeous girls attended Springhead Church. They were the Simmons sisters and they were the ages of Luke and Russell. They lived in the area and had attended Springhead Baptist Church all their lives. The boys were interested in the girls. That was enough to keep them in church with no arguments. Soon Luke and Russell ask Ethel and Maude out on a date.

A fair was coming to the town of Nashville. Russell and Luke ask Maude and Ethel to go with them on Saturday. Maude was excited about going to the fair. "I want Russell to win me a teddy bear," She said to Ethel. Ethel was a quiet and proper girl. "I would not ask a boy to spend money on me for nothing." She said to Maude, "Well if they are taking us to a fair isn't that what it is all about? Playing games and winning prizes," Maude said.

"Yes, but I still would not expect him to spend his money trying to get me a prize," Ethel said. Maude thought Ethel was old fashion. Times had changed but Maude thought Ethel still lived like the old people. Not her though, she would move up with the modern women.

On Saturday, the girls were ready and waiting on their front porch when the boys arrived. The boys had borrowed a car from a friend. The girls enjoyed the ride from Adel to Nashville in the car. When they arrived at the fair all the lights were lit and loud music was playing. It was fun just to walk around and look at everything. At a ring toss the man was standing in the booth yelling, "Walk right up, Walk up and toss the ring and win your girl any of these stuffed animals."

"That is it, Russell, that is the one I want. I want that white teddy bear with the black eyes. Come on, Russell toss the ring and see if you can win it for me," Maude said while Ethel cowered in the back, embarrassed by her sister. Russell reached in his pocket and brought out the nickel that it would cost to throw the ring at the peg. The first toss Russell threw, he rung the peg, head on. Maude walked away happy as she could be, while clutching her teddy bear close to her.

Russell asked Maude to marry him six months later. They decided to go to Moultrie to the Justice of the Peace and say their vows. Maude was a beautiful girl with fair skin and golden blond hair. She had attended school in Berrien County before it had turned Cook County. She had a good business head. Russell knew he could go as far as he wanted with her by his side.

Ed had been looking around for a farm that may be for sale and within the price, the boys could afford. Russell, Noah, and Eppse had saved a little money. Of course, Luke could not venture out. He still had the family depending on him. He could not afford to save any money when there were so many mouths depending on him. Luke was a good leader for the family. He leased enough land to make a decent living for the family near Ed and his Grandparents in Berrien County. They grew cotton, tobacco, peanuts, and tomatoes for the market. Luke had become an expert on growing tomatoes. Every merchant wanted Luke's tomatoes. They were always redder, bigger and tastier than any one else.

When Russell married Maude he moved her in the house with the family. Maude fit right in with the family. She was a wonderful cook and it took a load off Ma. Maude and Russell would soon have a little boy and then a little girl. The family enjoyed having babies around the house again.

Laura had recently gotten married. She had met a man at church. His name was John Hires. John owned a place between Morvin and Barney, Georgia. He moved Laura there. It took some getting use to for Laura since it was a big old house. She did not know what to do with all the room. She decided to close off the rooms she did not need. However before the closed room could enjoy the quiet Laura was pregnant. She had a son. Joseph was the love of John's life. He carried Joseph with him every place he went. Not long after Laura and John had gotten into having children, Laura was pregnant with her second child. This one also was a boy and again the apple of his daddy's eye. When Laura got pregnant with their third child, John prayed this one would be a boy too. What more could a man want than three, sons? Sure enough little Johnny was born on a cold February night. John looked up to the Heavens and said a prayer of thanks to God for sending him little Johnny.

John was an easy going, good-natured man. Nevertheless, he treasured his family. He wanted no one to treat his family ill, in any way.

Joseph had a dog. He loved the dog and wanted the dog to go in the car, with him, every time his dad took him places. Joseph had named his dog Fido. He had taught Fido tricks, how to speak and shake hands. He was so proud of Fido. "Watch him, Dad," Joseph said. "Roll over Fido." Fido fell to the floor and immediately rolled over. "He listens to everything I tell him," Joseph said.

Johnny was not a year old but it had turned winter again. One January morning Joseph walked out the door with Fido's breakfast just in time to see the neighbor aim a gun and shoot Fido dead. Joseph started screaming and running to his dog that was almost in the yard by now. John heard his son screaming and ran out the door to see what was wrong. He saw the neighbor walking back to his house with his gun and his son squatted by his dead dog weeping his heart out. John yelled at the neighbor, "Why did you shoot my son's dog?" The man ignored John and walked on into the house. John ran to his house and stood outside the neighbor's door yelling at him. "Why don't you come out and answer me. I want to know why you killed my son's dog. Did he do anything to you? I do not think he did. He has always been a good dog. Why would you want to kill him?" The neighbor would not open the door. Finally, John said in frustration, "Maybe I will go get my gun and shoot you." When the man still did not come out the door, John turned and walked back home. When he arrived at home, Joseph was weeping for his lost dog in his mother's arms. John took him from his mother and tried to comfort him. There was no comforting Joseph. His favorite friend in the entire world was dead and he was never coming back.

Joseph was still sobbing when Laura and John heard a car stop in front of the house. John opened the door and saw the sheriff's car sitting beside the road in front of his house. The deputy sheriff of Brooks County, known as a low life, had a habitual drinking problem. The county residence knew that he stayed in office by buying votes. The deputy sheriff was leaning on the hood of his car with a long gun aimed at John's front door. "Come on out John Hires. You are under arrest. You are going to jail." The deputy sheriff said in loud slurred words. "What am I under arrest for?" John yelled back. "Your neighbor filed a law suit against you because you killed his dog." The deputy sheriff yelled. "I have not killed his dog. He killed my son's dog." John said to him. "Don't you talk back to me? You better git yourself out here before I come up there and git you." John turned and he was saying, "Let me get my coat." Laura heard a loud gun shot. She ran to the door and John was lying on the doorsteps dying from a bullet through his chest. "Laura was holding Johnny in one arm and trying to get John up with the other arm. She watched as the drunken deputy sheriff staggered to his car door, opened it and drove away. By the time Laura got help, John was dead.

Laura and the three little boys had to go back home to the family. Laura would never get over the catastrophe of her murdered husband. There was a trial and the deputy sheriff would go to prison, where he served many years for John's murder. He told the courts when John turned and started back into the house he thought he was going to flee. Laura could understand how he would have thought such a lame brained thing as drunk as he was. However, that would not bring John back. Now Laura would raise their three little boys alone.

The neighbor admitted in court that he had gotten the deputy sheriff and had told him that John had threatened his life because he was angry with him for killing his dog. He said he killed the dog because he thought it was he, who was coming into the chicken pens at night and eating his eggs. Later it was, proven. Fido was not eating the eggs at all. A possum was coming into his chicken pens at night.

By now, Russell had moved to his own place in Colquitt County Georgia where Ed had helped him to find a good farm. He and Maude had settled in and Russell had everything just the way he wanted it except a storage shed. Russell and Maude went to Ma's house where most of the family still lived. Russell wanted them to come and see their new home and the farm. Everyone loaded on Russell's new truck and headed back to the new house.

Ma was amazed and proud of her son's new home and the land he had purchased. However, Ma enjoyed being with her two grandchildren the most. She loved Rosie and Horace. It was hard when Maude and Russell moved them away. This was the first time she had seen them since they had moved.

Russell told Ma and Luke he needed a place to put his farm equipment out of the weather. He knew there was a sawmill on the Berlin road between Rock Hill and Berlin. He asked Luke if he knew anything about it. "Do you know if they sell to the public?" Russell asked. "I don't know," Luke, said. It will pay you just to stop by there." They would be going right by the sawmill on the way back to their house. They all loaded on the truck for the trip home. When they reached the sawmill Russell stopped and ask to speak to the owner. A sophisticated fellow who was a little on the heavy side soon came to meet Russell. Russell asked him about the lumber he needed.

While the two men discussed the lumber Rittie was getting off the truck and working her way closer to the sawmill owner. She had noticed he was not wearing a wedding band. When the two men were finished talking she ask the man when he was going to deliver the lumber. "I will deliver it in two days, if that is alright with Mr. Browning," Clint Hollingsworth said to Rittie.

"In two days will be fine with my brother, so we will see you in two days; Right?" Rittie said. Clint looked at Russell. Russell shook his head yes. When they were back on their way home, Rittie stuck her head around and at the truck window, she yelled. "Ma, I'm going back with Maude and Russell." "What is this child up to this time?" Ma asked. "She probably wants to be there when the sawmill owner comes," Russell said.

True to her word, Rittie refused to stay home. She was going back with her brother and she was going to be there when the lumber arrived. Mittie had given her some jewelry and some lipstick. On the day the lumber was to be, delivered, she got out of bed early. She got her bath, fussed and messed with her hair for an hour. Then she put on the prettiest dress she owned and put the bright red lipstick on. When she walked out Maude almost fainted. She considered herself a modern girl but "be dogged if I would dress up like that." She told Russell. "I guess she thinks the sawmill man is rich and single and that is what she wants," Russell said.

It turned out that Rittie was right. He was rich and single and before he dumped, the lumber and left Russell's house that day she let him know she was interested. Apparently so was he. They were married less than a year later. Rittie stuck to her word about having children also. She was only pregnant twice but the first pregnancy was twins. She and Clint would only raise the three girls. Clint would later go into politics and he went to Washington DC and collected funds for the city of Berlin to get their own water and sewer system, bringing Berlin into the modern world with other cities. They would live in a new house Clint had built near Berlin just for them. It had all the modern conveniences. Everyone loved going to their house to sit on the commode and run the hot water. Before they grew old, they would travel extensively in their recreational vehicle.

Ellen was a late bloomer. She just sat back and let the perfect man come along. Finally he did. Ellen married Royal Pridgeon. He owned a grocery store in Berlin, Georgia. She was pregnant one time. She had twin daughters. However before the girls were grown Royal died but he had left her with her own home and a good living. Ellen was one of Eliza's only daughters who took a job, other than farming, outside the home. Ellen had a tic. She would blink her eyes and rub her mouth often. She always stayed close to her family. She would later marry Henry Calvender, with whom she would grow old.

General was the only professional, out of all Ma's children. He learned to barber by putting his brothers in a chair every two weeks and practicing on them. Some times, they fussed about their awful haircuts but General would not let them get out of their biweekly haircut. When he thought he was good enough at cutting hair he had a small barber shop built in Berlin and started cutting hair for a living. He had married Iella Lasseter. She was a real beauty. She was actually one of the prettiest girls in the family now. She had long dark black hair and olive skin. She had big beautiful Spanish eyes that stole General's heart completely. General knew he was a lucky fellow since she could have chosen any one she wanted because of her looks and gorgeous figure. General followed his father's example. He and Iella would have eight children. However, he would need every one of them since he saved his money from the barbershop until he earned enough to buy a large farm outside of Berlin.

Orval was the thin one in the family. He would never need to worry about the Browning belly so well know within the family. He married a pretty girl whose family lived in Thomasville Georgia. They lived in Berlin and had four girls. Orval and Ella Mae had a grandbaby that they adored. However, she only saw her grandparents occasionally since she lived with her parents in Pavo, Georgia and they lived in Berlin. Orval did not have a car so either they caught a ride to visit her in Pavo or they had to wait until their oldest daughter brought the baby to see them. It was one of those rare occasions on a Sunday afternoon.

Orval and Ella Mae's daughter and her husband, brought the pretty little, six-month-old girl in and ask for a quilt "so that we can make a pallet on the floor for her." Ella Mae quickly ran and grabbed the quilt. She placed it on the floor for the baby. Everyone was sitting in the front room talking when Ella Mae could not stand it any longer. She wanted to hold her grandbaby. She got up from her chair and talking to the baby, she reached to take her off the pallet. Her son-in-law yelled at her and told her not to pick the baby up. He told Ella Mae that if she held the baby it would spoil her. He got angry, grabbed the baby, and walked out the door. His wife was right behind him and they got in their car and left. Ella Mae was shattered. As she reached over to pick the quilt up, she was saying. "Why would he think,..." and her words froze. Her three teenage daughters and Orval ran to her when they realized she was falling. They carried her to the couch. Soon they realized Ella Mae was very sick. They carried her to the car and rushed her to the hospital where the doctors pronounced her dead from a massive stroke.

Orval tried to raise the girls alone but found it to difficult for him. The two youngest daughters chose to live at a girl's home in Thomasville, Georgia where their mother's sisters andtheir grandmother lived. Their lives turned out very well; however, they never got over watching as their mother died, right before their eyes at such young age.

Noah was next to take a wife. She was very petite and pretty. She was barely four feet nine inches tall but she had a beautiful figure for her petite body. The first time Noah saw Austell Higgs, he knew she was the girl for him. He would cherish her, the rest of his life. They would go through much heartbreak in the earlier part of their marriage. They had several fully developed little babies that did not make it past birth. Austell was a true champion. She always bounced back from the heartbreak and carried her life in a positive way.

They raised three perfectly healthy and wonderful children who cherished their parents as much as their parents had cherished the three of them. Everyday they thanked God for these three little blessings.

Noah and Austell bought the grocery from Ellen Pridgen when Royce died. They ran the grocery store together until they retired. After that, Noah drove a school bus for years. He thoroughly enjoyed the children on his school route.

Rittie and Clint planned a trip to Lakeland, Florida to visit with Martha and Ellen. Rittie told the family about the trip. Mae asked Rittie if she could take the trip with them. "It is fine with me if it is alright with Ma. Rittie got Ma's approval. Mae had proven to be one of Ma's brightest children. She had taken over all the letter writing when Laura left home. Mae had written many letters to Aunt Martha for Ma and had read many replies to Ma. She was excited about going to Aunt Martha's house. It was such a pretty place or so it sound in the letters she had read to Ma from Aunt Martha.

When Clint and Rittie arrived to pick Mae up on Friday afternoon, Mae was ready, had her bag packed, and was on the front porch waiting for them. "Ma they're here and I am leaving," Mae yelled as she ran down the front porch steps. She jumped in the back seat of Clint's new car. It smelled so good. The car smelled like new leather. Mae could not imagine how much money Clint must make to afford a car like this one. However, she was glad that he did.

The big new car really went fast. Mae was shocked at how fast they went down the road. Sometimes when she looked out the window and saw the trees and fields go by so fast it scared her. I know Ma would not allow Clint to drive this fast if she was in this car, she thought. What she knew was if Ma saw the car speeding down the road at sixty miles an hour she would make Rittie and her get out of the car and she would shake her gnarled little finger at Clint and tell him not to drive this fast. However, Mae knew she was not going to tell her brother-in-law to slow down so she just relaxed and enjoyed the ride.

Soon they arrived in Lakeland, Florida. Clint had the directions to Martha and Ellen's house in his hand. He would slow down and look at the directions then he would speed back up. Clint turned into a narrow little road leading up a small hill. When they reached the top of the hill, they saw it there. There was the big beautiful white house with the black shutters. It was as pretty as Mae had imagined. Martha and Ellen was out the door almost the minute Clint stopped the car. Everyone hugged necks and then they went inside where Ellen offered them something cold to drink. Mae took a Coca Cola and Clint and Rittie took ice tea. This was only the third time Mae had had Coca Cola to drink. She enjoyed it, especially since she knew when she left there; she would probably have no more. Coca Cola was a luxury the family could not afford.

After they finished their drinks, Martha carried them on a tour through the house. Mae was astounded that it was so large and had so many bedrooms. The family had only three bedrooms for as many of them. All four bedrooms had only one bed with matching furniture to go with it. Back home there was still two or three beds in every room of the house except the kitchen. Martha's house had a big dining room with a big fancy light handing over the table. The family back home ate at a table in the kitchen. The family home had just gotten electricity. However, all they had was a light bulb hanging from a long cord in the ceiling. Rittie was not as impressed with the house as Mae was. She also had all the modern conveniences' in her home even though her house was not nearly this large.

After a wonderful dinner of beefsteak, vegetables, and mashed potatoes, they all went to their assigned bedroom for the night. It seemed impossible that Mae could just use the toilet in the house and then flush it right down. Rittie was the only other person that she knew of that had a bathroom inside the house. Martha had two of them.

The next day everyone got in Martha's new car and went for a ride around Lakeland. Then Martha took them to Tarpon Springs to watch the sponge divers and to go to the beach. Mae wished she had a swimsuit. She had never owned one. As far as she knew, none of her sisters had one except Rittie and she had one of those new swim suits with no legs and half of her back showing. Rittie would never wear it around Ma since she knew she would not approve.

Mae was wading out in the clear water. The sand felt so good to her feet and the sun felt good shining down on her. She swished her feet about in the water and stirred the sand up. Then she watched as it settled back to the bottom again. Suddenly she realized she had been in the water for a while and her family might be ready to leave. She turned around facing the beach. She did not see her family but she saw a young man standing at the edge of the water staring at her. She did not know how long he had been standing there and it gave her chill bumps thinking about it. Who was he and why did he think he had the right to stand there and stare at her? Mae had always had plenty of confidence. She walked out of the water and right up to the strange young man who had been staring at her. He was handsome but he had not right to stare at her especially when she was holding her skirt tail up a wee bit. "Who do you think you are, standing there staring at me in the water?" she said to the stranger.

"I am so sorry if I have offended you. My name is Roy Nellis and I work here." The young man said to Mae. "Well, just because you work her gives you no rights to stare at me." Mae told him. "I am sorry, but you were beautiful out there. I only wish I had a camera." Roy told Mae. "Would you have actually taken a picture of me out there with my skirt pulled up to my knees?" Mae asked.

"Yes, I would have," Roy, said. Mae had to give him credit. He was certainly a brave one.

"Well, I am glad you did not have a camera," Mae said as she started walking toward the car. Roy turned and walked right beside her. "Where are you going?" he asked.

"I am going to find my family. They are near here, somewhere. I can not see them but I know they are there, somewhere because I still see the car." Mae said.

"I will help you find them." Roy said, as he stayed right by Mae's side.

"You said you work here, what do you do?" Mae asked. "I am a sponge diver here." Roy said. *That is why he stays so slim and tanned, I suppose. Mae thought to herself.*

They walked around looking for Martha, Ellen, Clint, and Rittie. They talked non-stop the whole time about where they lived and what Mae was doing here in Florida. Finally, Mae spotted her family. They were on the other side of the building at the water's edge watching the sponge divers come in. They were on a boat and it was loaded down with sponges. Mae had never seen a sponge until now. They were strange looking things. Roy told her they were alive when they cut them off from their roots. She looked the sponges over well. "People use these things to take baths with?" she asked Roy.

"Yes, as well as many other things," Roy said.

"If you are working why are you not with them on the boat?" Mae asked.

"My boat came in earlier today. Our boat was the first to leave this morning. When we fill the boat with sponges, we come in. Sometimes we have to empty the boat and go right back out but since the weather clouds look like bad weather may be coming in, we didn't have to return to the waters today." "But you are not wearing those rubber black suits that they are wearing," Mae said. She figured Roy would look handsome in that black suit.

"I live right over there. Trust me; the last thing you want to wear is that suit when you are out of the water."

"It is not comfortable?" Mae asked.

"No it is not comfortable, in or out of the water." Roy said.

Mae introduced the family to her new friend. It was time to load up and go to a nice restaurant that Martha had picked out for them for dinner. As they were walking to the car with Roy right by Mae's side, he asked if they minded if he went with them to dinner. Martha said it was all right with her. Mae did not say anything. Roy looked at Mae and said. "Do you mind if I go along?"

"No," Mae said. "Since you have a car full I will just follow you in by buddy's car."

"Would you like to ride with me Mae?" Roy boldly asked.

Mae looked at Rittie, "Go on, ride with the boy, he won't bite you."

Roy and Mae followed the family to a restaurant near by. It was a fancy restaurant. It had the same lights that Martha had in her dining room, hanging from the ceiling all over the big restaurant. After they were seated and each one was handed a very big menu. Mae took one look at it and had no idea what to order. Beef Burgundy, Lamb chops, (surely they do not eat lamb, Mae thought.), scalloped Tomatoes and Artichoke Hearts, (What is Artichoke?) Sautéed Black fin Crabmeat, Cream of Oyster Spinach Soup. Mae was not usually one for menacing words. She looked across the table to the one that she felt had more of a chance than anyone else did, to give her some answers. "Clint what is all this stuff. I have never heard of it. Is this real live lamb they are talking about on this line?" Mae said as she held her menu up for Clint to see.

"Yes, Mae its real lamb but now he's cooked."

"You mean people eat those pretty little animals that sit in the pictures with Jesus," Mae asked Clint.

"Yes, lamb is a delicious meat." Clint said. "Are you sure it is not a sin to eat one?" Mae asked. "Why do you think the Sheppard's were guarding all those sheep?" "I always thought he was looking over them so they would not be hurt or something."

"Well what the family had the sheep and lambs for was food for their dinner table."

"Well I will eat none of it. I personally don't believe God intended us to eat them," Roy sat quietly in his seat but it was hard for him to contain himself listening to this pretty, little country girl go on. Finally, Mae saw something that she recognized, Southern Fried Chicken. "There is what I want. I will take the Southern Fried Chicken."

Upon finishing their dinner, Roy demanded that he pay for his and Mae's dinner. Mae liked him already but she hoped this would not make her indebted to him. As they were walking out of the restaurant Roy, ask Mae for her address and ask if he could write to her. Mae saw no harm in giving Roy her address so she gave it to him.

Roy watched the car as long as he could see it. When it had faded out of sight, he drove his friend's car back to the beach. There was a telephone booth outside on a post and in a covered box. It had a telephone book inside the box also. Roy knew that Mae had said she was visiting with her aunt Martha Marlow. He opened the box, got the phone book out, and went down the list. There it was. Mae's aunt had a telephone. He waited until he thought they had gotten home and then he picked up the phone. An operator came on the line and asked for the number he wanted to call. He called out Martha's phone number. Within a few minutes, he heard a woman's voice say hello. When the bell started ringing, it scared Mae out of her wits. She did not know where the ringing was coming from and thought it might be a fire alarm coming from town. By the time, she found the source of the ringing Martha was standing there holding a black banana shaped thing and she was talking to it. Mae stood watching her in amazement. She had heard of telephones but she had never seen one. This had to be a telephone. Suddenly Martha handed the phone to Mae and said, "It is for you." Mae took the phone but she did not know what to do with it. Martha showed her how to hold the phone and showed her which end the listening came out of and the end that you talked into. Martha had told her to say "Hello", She was not sure she had the ends placed right but she said, "Heelooo."

The voice on the other end said, "Mae this is Roy. I forgot to say goodnight when we left the restaurant. So I'm calling to say good night to you."

"How did you know my aunt had a telephone?" I didn't know she had one until it just rang," Mae told him.

"I knew your aunt lives in Lakeland and you had told me what her name is so I called the telephone operator and told her the information you gave me. The next thing I heard was your aunt answering the phone," Roy told Mae. "Telephones do wonderful things. I just can't imagine how they do that since I am in another town from you." Mae said.

"All I know is that our voices travel down the telephone lines from one place to another," Roy said.

"Well, good night." Mae said. "What are your plans for tomorrow?" Roy asked. "I don't know so far as I know we will be leaving tomorrow for home." Mae told him. "Is your family still up?" Roy asked. "Yes they are still up, why do you want to know?" Mae asked. "Will you ask them what the plans are for tomorrow?" Roy said.

"Why do you want to know what their plans are?" Mae asked.

"Just ask them please," Roy said. Mae laid the phone down on the phone table and walked into the living room where everyone had gathered. "What are the plans for tomorrow?" She asked as she looked at Clint and Rittie. Martha was sitting on the sofa with Ellen and before Clint and Ritte had time to say anything, she said. "I was hoping that y'all would go with Ellen and me the First Baptist Church in Lakeland for Sunday services. Then we could go out to that restaurant I was telling you about and have dinner before y'all leave." Martha said as she looked at Ritte and Clint.

"It suits me," Rittie said. "It is fine with me, if we leave soon after dinner we can make it back to Berlin before dark," Clint said. "So it is settled. We will go to church at eleven a.m. and then out to dinner when church is over." Mae said. Rittie looked at Mae with a confuse look. "Yes, Mae that is how we will do it, why do you ask?".

"I will tell you latter," Mae said as she left the room. Mae picked up the phone. "Roy, they said we are going to church at eleven a.m. and when church is over we are going out to dinner."

"What church are you going to?" Roy asked. "We are going to First Baptist in Lakeland, my aunt said." "Good, then I will see you tomorrow morning at eleven a.m." Roy told Mae.

"You go to First Baptist in Lakeland too?" Mae asked.

"No, but I'll be there tomorrow morning when you and your family arrive."

Mae and Roy talked for a long time on the telephone before hanging up.

When Mae got in bed, she did not sleep. She kept thinking about the handsome sponge diver and what all this meant. The longer Mae talked to Roy the more comfortable she became with him. She did not know what Ma would say about coming to Florida and meeting a beau; if that is what this was suppose to come to.

The next morning Mae was out of bed early. She had slept very little last night. The sponge diver with the handsome tan body kept going through her mind. At least, she would have someone to think about while she was out in the fields next week. In addition, no one would have to know. She would keep it her own little secret. Mae put on her Sunday clothes and was ready to walk out the door well before the others. Martha drove her car again. Mae sat up front with her and Rittie and Clint rode in the back seat of the big new car. When they reached the church, Mae saw the car Roy had been driving last night parked in the parking lot in front of the church. By the time Mae got her car door open and stepped out of the car, Roy was standing there. He was well dressed in a suit, white shirt and a pretty tie that matched his suit. He looks extra special good, Mae thought to herself. She wanted to tell him but she did not want to appear forward. "How beautiful you look this morning. I like your dress,." Roy said. Now is the time to tell him about what I thought about how he looked this morning. She tried but just could not make the words come out. They all walked in church together with Roy right by Mae's side.

The preacher's sermon was about love and commitment. "Your first love should be for our God and Savior Jesus Christ, your next love should be for your family, and lastly your third love should be for your job. Moreover, along with love you need commitment. If you love The Lord and Savior then you are going to be committed to him. If you love your family you are going to be committed to them and if you love you job you will be committed to it also and if you are not committed to your job, your job will suffer and eventually you and your family will suffer to. Now, if you are not committed to God, then you really do not love him. If you are not committed to your family you probably do not love them and eventually they to will suffer. Roy held Mae's hand throughout the sermon and every time the preacher said the word "Love", Roy squeezed her hand.

The sermon finally ended and the song leader came forward for the invitational hymn, some of the congregation came forwarded and committed their lives to the Lord. That caused the service to drag on for a while longer. Mae was hungry and she was wishing the service would end. Roy was hungry too but he wanted the service to drag on as long as possible. He really liked this beautiful girl and when she left today, she would be far away from him and he did not know he would see her again. He made up his mind that he would find a way to visit her. Mae was the girl of his dreams and he could not let her get away. She was the girl of his dreams. She was beautiful and had a positive attitude about herself and the things around her.

Church was finally over. They all went back to their cars and as the family was getting into Martha's big car, Roy said. "Is it alright if I follow you to dinner?" Clint shook his head yes, as well as did the women.

When they arrived at the restaurant, the greeter told them that she did not have a table ready for all of them to sit. She said, I can sit three of you at this table and the other two can sit in this booth near the table, if that is alright with you." Roy did not wait for anyone else to answer, he said. "That will be fine. Mae and I will sit at the booth." Everyone seemed pleased with that arrangement.

Roy proudly helped Mae into the booth and instead of sitting on the opposite side like Mae thought he would he sat down beside her in the booth. Mae thought this was going to look a little strange but as they started talking together, she forgot about if everyone was staring at them in their strange sitting arrangement. What was more, she did not even care if anyone was starring at them. She and Roy were in their own little world and the rest of the world could think what they wanted. Suddenly she realized she did not really give a rip if all of them were staring. She never took her eyes off Roy and he talked on and on to her about fishing, sponging, and his endurances that he did every day to stay in shape for his diving job. He told Mae that he was an only child and his mother and father had recently died. "I would like to follow the preacher's advice and apply it to my own life," he told Mae.

"What do you mean, follow the preacher's advice?"

"I would like to get God in my life and be totally committed to Him. Then I would like to have a family of my own whom I could spoil with my love and I would be totally committed to them. I would love to get a job that I loved so much it would be number three in my life. Roy said to Mae.

"You don't love your job?" Mae asked Roy.

"No I do not even like my job. It is fun but it is a dead end job. When we cut all the sponges out, my job will be gone. Sponge diving is fun but it is not reliable enough to have a family. The pay is not enough to support a family and there is no climbing to the top in sponge diving. Sponge diving is all you will ever do. There is no climbing the ladder in sponge diving."

Mae's heart went out to him. He seemed to be a happy person but she could tell that he was worried about his future. "Why don't you sit down and think about what you would like to do most and then just go for it?" Mae said.

"That was his little Mae. She always thought positive. If she were in his position, he knew she would do just that. In addition, there is no telling how far she would go. Roy thought. He had to have her in his life. "Maybe the starting place is to do just as you said and get God in your life and let him lead you in what you want to do."

When it was time to leave the restaurant Roy held back. Mae could tell that he wanted her to stay but that was out of the question. She had to get back to the farm and go to the fields wherever and whenever they needed her. Roy gave Mae a tight hug just before she got in the car. She knew all the others saw it. She prepared her statement for them. "Yes, he gave me a hug so what is wrong with that?" However, no one in the car said a word. It was if no one had ever seen the hug.

When Mae returned home, she told Ma about Roy. She left out the hug. Ma listened but did not seem impressed. That bothered Mae. If one of her brothers had told Ma something this important in their life, Ma would have been happy for them and would have told them so. Mae had tenacity; she would never let Ma know she had disappointed her.

Mae told Mary Jane and Mattie Lee about Roy too. They clung onto every word. "How do you feel about him?" Mary Jane asked. "I think I am in love with him. If he feels the same as I do, I will get a letter from him in a few days," Mae said.

"I bet you will never hear from him again," Mattie Lee said.

"Okay, let's put a bet on it," Mary Jane said to Mattie Lee. "If she gets a letter in a few days you have to give me that tube of lipstick you have and if she does not get a letter I will give you my high heel shoes that you like."

"It's a deal," Mattie Lee said as she reached to shake hands with her sister.

Day 3 passed and there was no letter from Roy. "Okay, Mary Jane, give me the high heel shoes," Mattie Lee said.

"Mattie Lee, we need to wait at least a week," Mary Jane said. She did not want to loose her new high heel shoes. "That is not what the bet was." Mattie Lee said. "So, we agreed on a few days and just three days is not nearly enough. We will give it a week," Mary Jane said. Mattie Lee went away grumbling.

Mary Jane sent a special prayer to God when she said her prayers that night. "Lord you know how much I love those brown high heel shoes. Please do not let Mattie Lee win my shoes. Please let Mae get a letter from her feller tomorrow."

The mailbox was almost a mile away from the house. Usually the boys collected the mail as they came in from the field in the evening. Today, the three girls would walk to the mailbox. All three of them had a stake in what did or did not come in the mail today.

Mattie Lee raced to the mailbox first. She opened the box and Mae and Mary Jane heard her say "Darn." Mae's eyes lit up and she started in a run herself. She took the letter from Mae. The return address was indeed Roy. Mae crushed the letter to her chest and looking up to the heavens said, thank you Lord. Mary Jane silently did the same.

> *Dear Mae,*
>
> *I told you I would write to you and I am keeping my promise. Not because I do not want to be a liar but I am writing because I love you and I want you to know it. I have thought of nothing but you ever since you left.*
>
> *If you are not coming back to your aunts, I have to go there. Do you think it would be OK if I came there to see you? I hope you told your family about me and they approve of me. Let me know if I can come and visit you.*
>
> *I will be waiting for your answer. If you say I can come I will pack my clothes and be on the train the same day I get your letter.*
>
> *XOXOXOXO*
> *I Love You,*
> *Roy*

Look girls, he signed it with hugs and kisses. Mary Jane grabbed the letter. Mae did not have to worry about Mary Jane reading her letter since she never learned to read and write. "Where?" Mary Jane asked.

"Here, see these X's and O's," Mae said.

"Yes," Mary Jane said. "Those mean hugs and kisses." Mae said.

"Mattie Lee, hand the lipstick over." Mary Jane said. Begrudgingly Mattie Lee got her lipstick and handed it to Mary Jane. "You can use it any time you want to," Mary Jane told her as she took her lipstick away.

Mae took the letter into the kitchen where Ma was cooking. "Ma, I got a letter from Roy and I want to read it to you." Ma stopped and turned around in front of the wood burning stove where she was cooking dinner. Mae read the entire letter. Ma never said a word. "Ma what do you think about what he said?" Mae asked. "Mae, you are only eighteen years old. Don't you think that is young for having a feller?" Ma said.

"Rittie and Ellen had a feller when they were only eighteen." Mae said. Ma did not say anything else. Mae knew why she did not want her to have a feller. If he asked her to marry, him and she accepted there would go Ma's letter writer. Mattie Lee could read and write. She could start writing and reading for Ma. Mae let it drop. It would probably take some getting use to for Ma.

Mae sat down in the porch swing and wrote Roy back that afternoon.

> *Dear Roy,*
>
> *I got your letter and yes, you can come here to visit me. Ma knows you are coming. Come whenever you want to but for me the sooner the better.*
>
> *I have missed you too. Are you still going out on the sponge boats everyday?" I think that would be an exciting job. I would love to do it but I guess they do not take women sponge divers. I love the water and wish I could go to the beach every day.*
>
> *Write me back and let me know when you are coming.*
>
> > *XOXO*
> > *Love,*
> > *Mae*

Cotton-picking time had come. Luke announced to the family at the supper table "The first thing Monday morning we will all be going to the cotton patch. All the cotton is ready now and we have to pick in a hurry before the late summer rains come and damage it in the field." Everyone suddenly started hurting in his or her back. Mae especially hated to hear the cotton-picking news. "Suppose Roy comes and I am in the cotton patch all dirty and sweaty," she said to Luke.

"Roy can get a bag and pick cotton too," he said. Anyone would have thought that would have been said in gist but Mae knew he was serious. Luke was always trying to find extra help for harvesting the crops. He often complained about how hard it was to find help and especially good help. Mae knew Luke would put poor Roy right in the cotton patch with all the others if he comes. Roy had probably never lived on a farm and did not know one thing about picking cotton.

"Luke please don't ask Roy to pick cotton if he comes," Mae pleaded with Luke. "If he comes here and he looks like he is strong enough to carry a bag of cotton on his back he's going to the cotton patch with the rest of us." Mae knew she was going to be embarrassed to death but there was no arguing with Luke. He was the head of the household since Pa and Robert had died. Ma had long since told them they were to mind Luke just as they minded her. Ma would often remind the girls how thankful they needed to be for Luke. By now, all the brothers were married and had houses and families of their own but Luke had devoted his life to helping Ma get the rest of the children raised. He still saw Ethel and they dated when Luke had time but he would not marry until he was twenty-eight years old.

World War I was in full swing. Ma had horrors that they would draft her boys into the military. She worried day and night about having to loose one of them to the war. She knew it was probably a good cause for the war but she had a horror of loosing her boys that way. Times were getting rougher and rougher at home, as the war went on. She did not like Woodrow Wilson at all. Before he became president, there was no draft. He had brought it about. Many of her friends at church were loosing sons to the war. She shook everyday when the boys walked in with the mail. So far, none of them had even heard from the government. She hoped it would stay that way. All the girls felt the difference that Ma treasured the boys as compared to them. They felt that the fear of war was the reason.

Roy got Mae's letter and he did not wait to write her back. He packed his clothes in a duffel bag and caught the next train to Nashville, Georgia. He hitchhiked through the country roads until he found Mae's house. He went up the steps to the front door and knocked on the screen door. Ma came to the door. "You must be Roy Nellis," she said to him. You can come in but Mae is not here. She is picking cotton in the backfield. I will tell you how to find her if you want me to. You can come in and wait for them to come in if you want to. They will be home late this evening," Ma told Roy. "I think I will try to find her if you don't mind," Roy said. Ma told him the direction to the field where they were picking cotton.

Roy had never lived on a farm and had never realized how big a farm is. He walked past fields of bushy short plants. He did not know what it was so he pulled up one of them to look at it closer. It had peanuts growing all over the roots. He never knew that peanuts grew underground. Then he had to walk through a big cornfield. The sharp blades on the corn stalks cut into his skin, if he was not careful to hold them out of the way, as he walked. Finally, he came to the cotton field. There were several people leaning over the cotton bushes and pulling cotton out of bust open brown holders. They did not see him at first so he let the procedure for collecting the cotton soak into his head as he watched them. They pulled the cotton out of the bolls until they got a handful and then they reached back and stuck it into a Crocker sack. They had attached a strap to the bag on each side and over their necks. They were pulling the sack along with them with the straps secured over their shoulders. Roy looked at the empty rows of cotton and the twice as many unpicked rows that were waiting for them. *He could not imagine how they walked all day long stooped over. They must have a giant size backache by the end of the day*, he thought.

Roy walked right up to where Mae was picking. She stood up, dirty, sweaty, tired and the most beautiful girl he had ever seen. Roy was smiling at her but Roy could tell by the look on her face that she was embarrassed. Roy held each of her hands in his and suddenly started laughing. Soon Mae was laughing too. "You are so beautiful," he said to her. He wanted to take her in his arms and hold her but not here, not now with all her family there. Mae went to the shade tree with Roy right beside her to get a drink of water. She was so glad that he was here. She did not realize just how much she had missed him until she saw him standing there beside her. Mae asked about, his train ride, and how he found her house. He told her all about it. Luke had been patient but now he wanted Mae to get back to work. "Hey, young fellow, there is an extra cotton sack if you want to pitch in and help us." This pleased Roy since Mae's older brother was apparently excepting him. He was happy to get the sack. Mae showed him how to make the strap from an old bed sheet that they had brought for that purpose. She helped him to get the strap around his neck and adjusted it to fit. Roy did not take another row. He helped Mae pick her row. The two of them were finished with Mae's rows well before any of the others. They emptied out their cotton sack onto the big burlap cotton sheet lying on the ground. It had more cotton pilled on it from this morning's work. "I think this sheet if full. We might as well tie it up and lay out another one. Mae showed Roy how to take the diagonal corner and tie it to the opposite corner and then take the two diagonal corners and tie them tight together. "You have to tie it tight or it will come apart when they start loading it onto the truck.

When they were finished, Roy said, "This cotton is not going any place except where they want it to."

"Well, that will be to the gin where they take the seeds out and make bales out of it. Then Luke will sell it for what ever the going price is."

Roy slept in the pack house with some corn they had kept from the spring crop for feeding the livestock. Mae gave him a quilt and a pillow. He told her that he slept as comfortable there as he had in the old bed in his apartment.

Before he knew it, Luke had him up to his ears in farm work. Roy enjoyed farm work. It gave him a big break from sponge diving. He had almost been burned out with the sponge diving and this was about as far removed from sponge diving as he would ever get.

Roy asked Ma if he could marry Mae. "Yes you can marry her but she needs to stay near home for a while since she is so young." Roy took that to mean Ma did not want Mae going back to Florida to live. That did not worry Roy. He would find them a little cabin somewhere near the farm.

"I have already asked your mother, gotten her approval and now I will ask you," Roy said to Mae as he dropped to one knee. He took Mae's hand in both his and said. "Will you marry me?"

Mae threw her arms around his neck and said, "Yes, Yes, Yes, I will marry you."

Luke planned a hoe down at the house in celebration of the wedding of Mae and Roy. He found a fiddle player and a banjo player. He liked Roy's work on the farm and was happy to keep him there.

Luke killed a pig, cleaned him and had the boys dig a cook pit in the ground. Luke brought in several wet burlap bags. On the evening before the hoe down Luke built a fire in the pit. He burned the fire until he had no flame but lots of hot coals. He had seasoned the pig with plenty of salt and had wrapped him tight in the burlap sacks. Luke laid the whole pig on the hot coals and carefully covered him good with the dirt from the hole. An unplanned party went on most of the night as the hog cooked. The delicious smells from the cooking pig permeated the air. The girls wanted to check on the cooking pig but Luke instructed them they could not disturb the cooking pig. "He has to cook just like he is until tomorrow. You can not make even a little hole in the dirt covering him."

The musicians arrived the next day about two o'clock. The music started in the back yard beside the still cooking pig. By now, most of the coals had died and the cooked pig stayed in the hole to stay warm until dinnertime. Ma and the girls had boiled dozens of ears of corn, prepared big pots of peas, butterbeans, creamed corn, potato salad, and fried okra. Mae made gallons of sweet tea. The boys would go to Adel for ice just before serving time.

The music went on until late in the evening while the guests were arriving. Some were sitting in kitchen chairs in the back yard talking, some were dancing on the ground, but all of them were having a good time.

Mattie Lee got a glimpse of a young man who was talking with her brothers. He was handsome and had a head full of dark hair. Mattie Lee did not remember ever seeing that much hair on any man's head. She sure wanted to know who he was. It seemed that he already knew her brothers.

Finally, it was dinnertime. Everyone gathered while Luke very carefully removed the dirt from the pit. The burlap sacks holding the pig were warm. They had to wait a few minutes while the burlap cooled enough that they could handle it safely. Soon it had cooled down. Orval took one end of the burlap-covered pig and Luke took the other end. They had already put the big kitchen table in the back yard. Orval and Luke carefully pulled the cooked pig out of the hole and placed him in the middle of the big dinner table. Luke took the burlap sacks off the pig and exposed the most beautifully roasted pig any of them had ever seen. The meat was so tender it almost fell off the bone. Luke had cooked the pig to perfection. The girls brought the many pots and big bowl of food from the kitchen to the table and placed it around the roasted pig. "All you need to do is just decide what part of the pork you want and pull it off with your hands," Luke told the crowd. Noah had gone to Adel and brought plenty of ice from the icehouse there. Dozens of glasses of sweet cold iced tea was poured and placed for the guest. Ma had made dozens of her wonderful biscuits to go with the meal. They were the last to come out of the kitchen. After dinner, Ma brought out a big bowl of, everyone's favorite—banana pudding.

Mittie and her family and Eddie and his family were there. This is the first time the whole family had been together in several months. Mae spotted Rittie and Clint on the dance ground doing one of those fast jazzy dances where Rittie twisted her rear end and threw her arms around. She wondered if Ma was going to say anything to her. Ma had decided that this was a celebration and, since it was short of taking her clothes off, she would not say anything to Rittie.

Mattie Lee had gotten her plate of food and was sitting on the bench that went with the table. Of course, now it sat on the ground along with the kitchen chairs. She did not have enough hands to collect her tea so she set her plate on the bench while she ran back to get her tea. When she returned to the bench her plate of food was gone. She looked under the bench. Her food was gone. Who would have taken my food, she thought to herself as she looked around the crowd. Standing at the opposite end of the bench was the same good-looking boy with all the hair that she had seen earlier talking to her brothers. He had a fork full of food and held it to his mouth. The plate he was holding, Mattie Lee could tell was her own plate. He looked at Mattie Lee and gave her a guilty grin. "Are you eating my plate of food?" she asked.

"Well, I don't know that it is your plate. It was filled with delicious looking food and sitting on the end of this bench when I found it," he said.

"That is my food you crook. Give it back to me." Mattie Lee said. The young man handed her the plate of food as he said. "Oh, I am sorry; I thought someone had prepared it just for me." They were laughing together as Mattie Lee took her plate back.

"You fix your own plate, Buster," Mattie Lee said to him.

"It is not Buster, it is Lancy." He said to Mattie Lee. How do you know my brothers?" Well, let me think, the first time I met them was when I needed more tobacco plants than my beds produced. I heard they had more than they needed so I came and bought some from Luke for my field," Lancy told her.

"Why have I never seen you?" Mattie Lee asked. "It is probably because I never came to your house, until today. I always caught your brothers in the field."

"Go and get your food." Mattie Lee said to him. Lancy lumbered off to the table. Mattie Lee thought he looked as good going as he did coming.

Suddenly Noah and Austell sat down on the bench with their food. "Don't sit close to me," Mattie Lee said to them. "What's wrong, do you have something catching?" Noah said.

"No, see that boy getting his food at the table," Mattie Lee said.

"Yes, that is Lancy Hiers," Noah said.

"Do you mean that you know him too?" she asked.

"Yes, I've known Lancy for a long time," Noah said.

"Well thanks a lot for introducing him to me," Mattie Lee said.

"You're too young to meet a boy," Noah said.

"Mind your own business. Just make room for him here beside me when he comes back with his plate."

Mattie Lee and Lancy spent the rest of the evening together. Lancy ask Ma if he could come and visit Mattie Lee at the house. "It is alright for you to come here to visit her but you know she is my baby and she is too young to be going out on dates." Mattie was standing beside Lancy when Ma gave him her little speech. Mattie Lee wished she could have melted and ran through the cracks in the floor. She was not a baby. She was sixteen years old now.

Lancy started coming once a week and swinging with Mattie Lee in the swing on the front porch. The more comfortable he became with Ma the more often he started coming. "Mattie Lee, if I ask your mother for your hand and she says yes, will you marry me?" "Yes, I will but I can bet you that she won't say yes," Mattie Lee said.

"Well it won't hurt to ask her," Lancy said. He talked to Ma every chance he got. He felt like he had her confidence by now. Anyway, he knew she liked him. "Mrs. Browning, I know she is your baby and that makes her special but I love Mattie Lee and I want to marry her. I promise you that if you say yes, I will always take good care of her." Ma only stared at Lancy. His knees began to shake. Suddenly all his confidence drained from him and he so wished he had never ask her.

"Okay, Lancy, but I am going to hold you to the taking good care of her." Ma said to Lancy.

"Oh, I will Mrs. Browning. I promise you I will take extra good care of her," Lancy said as he wiped the sweat from his forehead.

Mae and Roy had settled down in a little place of their own. Both of them came to the farm to work every day. Mae was grateful on the days there was only plowing to be done. She could stay home on those days, and catch her letter writing up and decorate her little house.

Soon Mae was pregnant. Roy was so excited and he hoped it would be a boy. Roy did not mind the farming, except for the plowing. He hated that part of farm work. He was soon to learn plowing was the major part of farming. He hated pushing the plow down into the dirt while attempting to plow a straight row. He hated the sight of the old mule's rear end. If the mule could get some manners and not let off gas, so often, maybe it would not be so bad. He knew there was no way to teach the mule manners. He had decided they were the dumbest animals in the entire world.

When Mae went into labor, Roy ran for Ma. Ma shooed Roy out of the room and got her hot water and towels ready. When the baby came, Ma let Roy come into the room. When Roy saw the baby was a boy he grabbed Ma and gave her a big hug.

"It is your wife you need to be hugging. She's the one who did all the work," Ma told him as she hugged him back.

"I wish you and Mae would name him Robert after his grandpa and uncle," Ma told Roy.

"Then Robert it will be," Roy said as he took the beautiful little boy all wrapped in his blanket. "Welcome to this world Robert," Roy said as he looked into his baby's face." Roy hoped Robert would choose another wage-earning career than farming when he was all grown up.

Mattie Lee and Lancy did not want a big shindig at their wedding. They quietly went to the justice of the peace in Moultrie and said their vows with only Ma present. Ma had to go so that she could sign for Mattie Lee since she was only sixteen.

Lancy lived in the old home place of his family. His father was dead but his mother still lived there. A big unpainted house, it sat high off the ground. A long back porch ran down to the kitchen that was unattached to the house. "Why did they build the kitchen separate from the house, Lancy?" Mattie Lee asked. "Back when they built this house all houses were built this way. It is to keep the rest of the house from burning if the kitchen catches on fire."

Mattie Lee loved Lancy's mother and soon, they were good friends. Within a year, they had their first child and he too was a boy. Lancy kept his word. He took good care of Mattie Lee. She did not have to work in the fields any longer. Lancy always grew Mattie Lee a big garden. She kept the garden harvested and she canned vegetables so that not a bean or pea ever went to waste. Every time she wanted to visit with her family, Lancy always carried her. She loved her family. Since she was would always remain the youngest, the family still pampered her and so did her husband.

Mattie Lee leaving home created a big void for Mary Jane. The two of them were very close and were not only sisters but best friends too. They missed each other terribly. Mattie Lee prayed that Mary Jane would soon find herself a feller. She felt so sorry for her sister. At least, I do not have to work so hard on the farm any longer. Mary Jane will still work as hard as we always have.

Luke and Ethel had been dating all these years. He still, had not asked her to marry him. However, she was willing to wait on him since she loved him madly. She knew, eventually he would ask her. Maude was concerned about it. She knew Luke loved her sister. It was easy to see when they were together. Luke had reached the age of twenty-eight. He decided that he would ask Ethel to marry him even though he would still need to live at home. There were others still depending on him. Luke felt it was unfair to Ethel to keep her in limbo and he really loved her. He did not want her to give up on him. All the family was happy when Luke and Ethel got married. Everyone loved Ethel.

Finally, Mary Jane met someone. Hal stopped at the Browning house because his car was running hot. He needed to get water from their well to put in the radiator on his car. He lived in Tifton Georgia, where he went to college. He was on his way home to Moultrie for the summer break. Hal was smitten with Mary Jane and he asked her out on a date. Mary Jane was now eighteen and she accepted his offer. He came the next Saturday and the two of them went to the movie theater in Adel. Mary Jane had never been to a movie before and she loved it. She could not wait to see Mattie Lee again to tell her all about the movie. She would write a letter if she could but she could not read and write. "Ma, why could I not learn to read and write like the others. I went to school as much as they did?" Mary Jane asked Ma.

"I don't know child. Maybe you can still learn to read and write." Ma said. Mary Jane knew that was not going to happen. Laura, Mae, and Mattie Lee had tried many times to teach her but she just could not grasp reading and writing. However, one week later Mary Jane would need to find herself a writer because she had gotten a letter from Hal. She ran down the road to Mae's house. "Mae, I got this letter from Hal. Will you read it to me?" she asked so excited she could hardly contain herself. Mattie Lee took the letter and opened it up.

> *Dear Mary Jane,,*
>
> *My car is all right now but I am glad that it broke near your house. I am so happy that I met you. I think you are an interesting and neat girl. I would like to get to know you better.*
>
> *I had a good time at the movie with you. I hope that you did too.*
>
> *I have to leave for school next Wednesday and I would love to stop by and see you on my way back, if that is all right with you.*
>
> *I will wait for your letter and if it is all right with you, I will see you then.*
>
>

Yours Truly,
Hal
>

Oh, Mae, you have to write him right back. Have you got time?" By now, Mae had had her second little boy. He also was a beauty and she named him James. "Let me finish feeding the baby and when I get him down, I will write it for you."

Mary Jane waited until little James had been fed and was now nicely sleeping in his crib. Mary Jane had already found the paper and a pencil.

> *Dear Hal,*
>
> *I was happy to hear from you. I am glad your car is fixed and I hope you will not have any more problems with it.*
>
> *I will be home next Wednesday and it will be good to see you again. You are welcome here any time you want to come.*
>
> *See you next Wednesday.*
>
>

Yours Truly,
Mary Jane Browning
>

Hal was true to his word. He showed up to see Mary Jane before lunchtime. Ma was cooking for the field hands. Mary Jane had to get out of the swing with Hal long enough to help Ma get the food on the table. Hal stood in the kitchen door and talked to Ma and Mary Jane while they worked. "You might as well have lunch with us," Ma said to Hal. Mary Jane set an extra plate on the table. The family came in from the field dirty and sweaty but very hungry. They went to the back porch pored the wash pan full of water and threw the water on their faces and washed their hands. They came and sat at their usual places. Mary Jane made a place by her for Hal to sit. After the meal was finished, Hal said. "Mrs. Browning that was the best meal I have ever had. Thank you very much for allowing me to join y'all."

"You are welcome but I bet your mother cooks wonderful meals too." Ma said to him. "Not really, well maybe she could cook if she had time but she works with my father in their real estate company and she is not at home most of the time. We eat hurried up food, most of the time."

"Do you have brothers and sisters?" Mae asked. "No, I am the only child. I think they wanted more children but it never happened."

After dinner, Hal helped Mary Jane clean the kitchen up. Mary Jane insisted he sit and talk to her while she did it but he would not hear that. "I will help you. I do most of the dishes at home alone, when I am there. The brothers heard Hal. Luke had this boy pegged and he had made his mind made up about him. He would have to tell Mary Jane when the boy left.

Soon after lunch was finished and the kitchen was clean, Hal told Mary Jane it was time for him to go. He needed to get in his dorm before six p.m. and he still had to drive to Tifton.

"I would like to write you letters from school if you don't mind. I will be graduating in six months but it is boring there and it is fun to get letters. Mary Jane was too embarrassed to tell him that she could not read or write. "I will be happy to get your letters and I promise to answer them back as soon as I get them."

Now that John had died, Laura and the three little boys had moved back home. Laura was usually very busy. She kept the boys clean and polished. She read them stories and worked with them with their numbers and letters. She was truly a good mother but she too had to go to work in the fields when Luke needed her. Sometimes Mary Jane could catch her not too busy and she would answer her letter from Hal, but most of the time Mary Jane had to run down to Mae's house for her letter to be written. Sometimes it was not easy for Mary Jane to answer the letter on time as she had told him she would. Most days she had to go to the field herself and work all day. Nevertheless, she did her best to answer Hal's letter soon after it came.

Mattie Lee was pregnant with her second baby. She prayed it would be a girl. She still had enough girlhood in her that she wanted a little girl so she could dress her up in little frilly dresses that she had sewn herself just for her baby girl. When Mattie Lee had the baby, it was the baby girl, which she had hoped she would have.

She named her Ayleen. Ayleen was the true dream baby. She was a good and happy baby. Mattie Lee played with her at every free moment. She made the little dresses that she had planned before her birth. She made little caps to match the dresses. Ayleen looked so precious all dressed up in the new clothes. Mattie Lee cherished her and she was the apple of her dad's eye.

Mae was so happy. She had, in her mind, the perfect family. She loved her husband and their two little boys. She like Laura, was determined that her children would go places when they grew up. She knew, in order to do that they would need to be well educated. She did not have storybooks to read to them so she read them the Bible. Robert hung on to every word Mae read. Little James was still too young to pay attention, more than a few minutes at a time. When Roy came in from the field that evening Mae had prepared fried salt mullet fish for him for dinner. Fried fish permeated the air as he walked into the house. Roy stopped in his tracks. "Is it Friday, Mae?" he asked.

"Yes, Roy it is Friday." Roy knew they always had fish on Friday night. He had no clue what day it was. Time just rolled on and he rolled with it. Time really did not mean that much to him any longer. He had not realized that about himself. He ate dinner with his family but he was deep in thought as to how miserable he really was. He wanted so much, to move his family to Florida and start sponge diving again. He could never do that. He had promised Ma that he would never move Mae away from her family. He wished he had never made that promise to her.

"Roy when you go to town tomorrow to get the groceries, please try to find a children's story book for Robert. I read to him from the Bible because that is all I have and he loves it. I know he would really love something for his own age." The men of the family always took the truck to town every Saturday for purchasing supplies. The women could not go to town, since they might buy things that were not necessary. Mae thought a storybook for Robert was a necessity. Roy did not argue with her since he felt the same way about Robert needing books for his inquisitive little mind.

On Saturday morning, the truck with the high wood side bodies on the back pulled in front of the house with the other men family members who were going to town. Mae watched as Roy went to the truck to join them. Luke, Eppse and Noah were already in the front of the truck. There was no room for Roy so he climbed over the high wood body and jumped into the back of the truck. Luke put the truck in gear and they rode off. Mae had intended to remind Roy one more time not to forget Robert's book but she had forgotten it. She ran out the door but it was too late. The truck was gone.

Mae thought she would take the boys and walk down to Ma. However, right now she had to clean the breakfast dishes and put them away. After that, it was time to feed little James and give him his morning bath. She watched Robert as she bathed the baby. He had pulled the Bible off the table and sat on the floor where he placed the Bible carefully across his little legs. He was looking at the words and turning each page so carefully. She wondered what he would grow up to be if he had a chance.

It was already lunchtime and Mae still did not have time to go to Ma's house. She prepared some lunch for Robert and breast-fed James again. Mae looked at the clock. It is too late now to go anyway. The men will be back from town any minute and I will need to be here to put our groceries away.

Mae waited for the men to come back from town. She wished they would hurry since she still wanted to go to Ma's before dark. They were running late. She decided she would take the baby and Robert and walk down to Ma's house.

As Mae walked in the door, Ma met her. "Mae what do you reckon has happened? The men should be back from town by now. I am worried about them."

"I don't know why they are taking so long, Ma. But I guess we will just have to wait until they do come home,." Mae said.

Laura and the boys were not home. The three boys other grandparents had come and gotten them to spend two weeks at their house near Hahira, Georgia.

"Mae, I was going to your house this afternoon. I got a letter from Hal. Will you read it for me?" Mary Jane asks, "Yes, get it and I will read it for you." Mary Jane got the letter for Mae.

> *Dear Mary Jane,*
>
> *I am afraid I have bad news. I got a draft letter last week and they are calling me into the army. I only have two weeks left until I graduate and they have said that I can stay until I graduate from school but then I have to go immediately to the draft office.*
>
> *I do not know where I might, be stationed, but I hope you will wait for me until I am out. I will try to see you before I leave but I do not know if they will give me that much time or not.*
>
> *If I do not see you before I leave for the military, I will write you and let you know where I am going and when I will be back.*

I enjoy being with you and cannot wait until we are together again. There is probably no need for you to answer this letter until I write you again since your letter might not make it before I am gone.

Love,
Hal

Mary Jane started to cry. "Don't cry, Mary Jane. He said he will write you back soon or see you one," Mae said to her sister.

Still weeping Mary Jane said, "I just hate to see him go into the service. With the war still going, he might never come back home." "You can not think that way. You need to stay positive for him," Mae said. Wiping her eyes Mary Jane said, "I will try to stay strong. Thank you for reading me the letter, Mae," she said.

It had gotten dark and the men still were not home. Ethel, Austell, Mary Jane, Mae, and Ma walked to the front porch and sat down to wait for them.

Finally, they saw car lights in the distance. Ma held her breath praying that it would be her sons. The truck pulled into the yard. It was they. Ma felt a burden lift off her.

Eppse, Noah and Luke got out of the truck. They did not go to the back of the truck to get the groceries as they normally did. Ma met them on the doorsteps. "Why are you boys so late?" Ma asked, as the three men appeared to hold back and keep a distance from the girls.

Austell asked, "Where are the groceries?" Before they had a chance to answer Mae yelled, "Where is Roy?"

Appearing scared, Luke said, "That is the problem. We haven't been to the grocery store."

Again, Mae said, "Where is Roy?"

"Mae, when we got to town this morning and we all got out of the cab of the truck, Roy was missing from the back of the truck," Luke said to her.

"I walked back there to help him get down but he wasn't in the bed of the truck. We thought he must have been in a hurry and had quickly jumped out of the truck and he was already in the store. We went into the store but he was not there. We walked all over town looking for him but we could not find him." Finally when we could not find him anywhere we went to the sheriff's office and told him. He told us to get in the sheriff's car and we traced our route back and forth from here to town several times. The sheriff thought he might have fallen out of the truck on the way to town. We searched the ditches and the edges of the woods to see if he had been hurt and had tried to get off the road. None of us ever saw any sign of him." "The sheriff put his name on a missing person list, for what ever good that will do." By now, Mae was wringing her hands and weeping loudly. Robert started to cry with his mother. Luke tried to answer every question Mae asked. Nothing comforted her. She sat on the front porch at Ma's house all night waiting for Roy to show up at the doorsteps. She knew something terrible had happened but she also knew he would come home.

When morning came and Roy still had not shown up, Mae decided to go back to her house and see if maybe he had gotten by her and gone home. She did not say anything to the family nor did she disturb Robert and James from their sleep. She simply got up from the swing where she had sat all night. She sprinted to the house to see if her husband was there. She walked in the door and all through the house. Roy was not there. She could tell that no one had been home since she left yesterday. With her shoulders slumped and her heart aching she walked back to Ma's. After breakfast, Mae got Mary Jane to go with her. They carried Robert and James with them. She wanted to walk the road all the way to town and see if she could see any sign of Roy possibly falling from the truck.

Their walk revealed nothing. They had slowly walked for miles, almost to Berlin and then back again. At the end of the day, Robert and James were, worn out. So were their mother and Aunt Mary Jane.

After they arrived back home Mae sat down and had another, good cry. What was she going to do? She could not continue to live in the little house since there was no money to pay the rent. She could not buy groceries since Roy had carried the grocery money with him yesterday. Now he and the money were gone. Mae and her boys would need to return to the family home.

Luke was now short one worker. This was going to be bad. He was already short of help and now with Roy missing he would need to try to find hired help. Where would he find extra help? Help was almost impossible to find. Every family used all their own members to work their farm. Luke voiced his concerns to Ma. Ma prayed about it but until he found someone, the females in the house would all start pushing the plow, and doing anything else it would take, to keep the farm going. The girls were not good at plowing since they were not strong enough to push the plow into the dirt. They made shallow furrows. This bothered Luke but he knew they were doing the best they could.

One day as the sun was setting in the western sky and the family was leaving the field, tired, hungry, and thirsty, they saw a strange man coming down the road. Mae's heart speeded up and her gait picked up. Maybe it is Roy. She thought. However, as the man got closer Mae realized it was not

Roy. "Hello Ma'm, My name is Robert Burgess and I am looking for work. Do you know where I might find work?"

"You can probably find work with my brother. He is coming behind me. His name is Luke and he is looking for help."

Mae left the strange man standing and went into the house. The stranger waited for Luke. When the group arrived from the field and was crossing the road to the house, Robert picked out the one he thought was Luke. He was the oldest male and that is who Robert thought he would be. "Sir, my name is Robert Burgess and I am looking for work. You wouldn't need any help, would you?" Robert said. "Where do you live son," Luke asked.

My family lives at Pavo, Georgia but I just sorta roam about and work where I am needed."

"I can use you," Luke said. Luke invited Robert to dinner with the family that night.

Robert slept in the corncrib that night and the next day Luke found him to be a good worker. Luke did not know how he had been so lucky yesterday. Robert's words, "I just sorta roam about," worried Luke. He hoped he stayed content on the Browning farm.

Luke came home from the mailbox that evening. There was a letter to Mary Jane from Hal. She got Mae to read it to her right away.

> *Dear Mary Jane,*
>
> *I am far away from where I was when I wrote you last. I am in Amsterdam, Holland now. The Germans are really giving us a fit. They know they are about to loose the war and they are having one last hurrah. They are fighting all over Europe. They are not fighting to win; they are just fighting now. It is almost as if they want to see how many people they can kill before they loose the war. However, I am safe since I have a desk job inside a strong building.*
>
> *I will write more next time. I miss you. Do not know when I will leave here but I will see you as soon as I can.*
>
> *Love,*
> *Hal*

As Mae read the letter aloud to Mary Jane, the family was standing or sitting near by. Most of them heard the letter. Noah thought to himself, what a pansy, working in an office. Luke thought, *it is for sure he will never be a farmer.*

The next day the men of the family got their heads together and made a big decision. They had noticed Robert looking at Mary Jane. "I don't think it would be hard to get Mary Jane interested in Robert if it were not for that Hal writing her. If Robert married Mary Jane then we would not have to worry about his roaming." They made a pack. One of them would go to the mailbox everyday and if a letter came from Hal they would tear it up and never tell Mary Jane about it.

Robert continued to showed no interest in Mary Jane but she showed not interest in him. After two weeks, Mary Jane was concerned that she had not gotten a letter from Hal. Mary Jane worried that Hal may be deceased, killed in the war. She prayed every night for his safety. Never the less the weeks rolled on and she still did not hear from the love of her live.

Luke was going to Moultrie to get fertilizer for the farm. Mae had heard of a fortuneteller in Moultrie. "Luke, can I go with you to Moultrie?" "If you want to ride in the back of the truck but there is not enough room for you to ride in the cab," He said. Mae climbed over the rails and jumped into the truck bed. When Luke arrived in Moultrie at the feed and seed store, she went inside with him. She asked the storeowner if he knew about the fortuneteller she had heard about. The man directed her to the fortuneteller's house. Mae knocked on the door. A dark haired, dark skinned woman came to the door. She had a pointed nose and deep-set eyes. "Ma'm, my name is Mae Nellis and I need to talk to you about my missing husband," Mae told the woman.

"Come in. Do you have a dollar?" The woman asked. "Yes," Mae said as she handed her a dollar bill. The room she had led Mae to was half dark with only small rays of sunshine coming through cracks in the heavy dark curtains. She ordered Mae to sit in a chair facing a short small table. She sat on the opposite side of the table. "You need me to tell you what happened to your missing husband?" "You said." "Yes," Mae said to her. The woman had a book that looked like a bible but it did not appear to have scripture written in it. The woman picked the book up from the small table. She closed her eyes and held the book. Then she turned it over and held it, still with her eyes closed. Then she told Mae to hold her hand. Mae reached out, and took the woman's hand. The woman again closed her eyes. Total silence surrounded them. With her eyes still closed, she said. "I see a long dirt road. I see your husband jumping from something onto this road and running through some woods." Mae started to cry. The woman quickly opened her eyes. "You are crying?" She asked. "Yes, my husband was riding on the back of a truck." "Do not cry, your husband is fine. He climbed up the side of the high body on the truck and jumped while the truck was still in route. He did not hurt himself. He only wanted to get away. He ran through the woods to another road where he hitched a ride down south to a small town in Florida. He is there now and he is doing fine." Still weeping, Mae asked, "Why did he do it?"

"He was very unhappy with farming. He wanted to go back to the work he did before the two of you were married. He wanted to take you and your boys with him but he had made a promise to your mother that he would never take you away from home."

"He saw the easiest way out, was to do it the way he did," Mae wished she had a way to go to Tarpon Springs, Florida. How could he walk out on his little boys? Mae thought.

After six months without a letter from Hal, Mary Jane had given up on hearing from him. It broke her heart but she had to accept the fact that Hal was, killed in the war. Now the war was over but it did not matter to Mary Jane any longer. Her love was gone and he would never return.

Robert continued to pursue Mary Jane. Mary Jane was now twenty-one years old. All her family was married and had families of their own except her and Eppse. Mary Jane thought about Robert. She wondered if she could ever learn to love him. She knew she did not want to die an unmarried woman with no children. Up until now, she had gone out of her way to avoid Robert.

It was cotton-picking time and Mary Jane ended up with her row of cotton right beside of Robert's row. She started to take her cotton sack and go to the last row to get away from him. Then the thought of her situation swept over her. She decided she would keep the row beside Robert. If Mary Jane got behind with her row, Robert would switch to her row and catch her up with him. Mary Jane allowed him to talk to her. Something she had not allowed in the past. By the end of the day, Mary Jane had made up her mind that she would try to be friends with Robert. Within a month Robert, ask her to marry him. The boys were delighted when Mary Jane accepted his proposal.

However, as soon as Robert was married to Mary Jane he wanted to leave the farm and go back to his family in Pavo, Georgia where his father owned an automobile repair business next to the grocery store that they owned and his mother ran. Mary Jane did not want to go away but now she was married and it was her place to follow her husband wherever he wanted her to go.

There were soon to be drastic changes in the family. Russell had sold his farm near Berlin and had bought a farm near the Little River. Eppse still held onto the money he had earned. He bought a small house near Russell and Maude. Eppse and Ma would move there and Ma would have to tell Mae in tears that she would have to leave since the house was small. Eppse owned it and he did not want children there. Mae had no choice but to gather her children and the paper sacks holding their clothes and start walking. She had no one to carry her and she had no place to go. She and the two little boys walked to Berlin. When she arrived in Berlin, her feet were killing her, her back hurt and she was worried sick. She saw a bench and she sat the sacks and the two little boys on the bench and then sat down herself. It was getting close to sundown. Mae did not have a penny and she knew the boys were hungry. She had no way to feed them or even put them to bed tonight. She was so worried that she burst into tears. Mae sat on the bench with tears flowing and her face in her hands. The grief poured from her through the tears.

Suddenly a voice jolted her to reality. "Why are you crying? Can I help you some way?"

She looked up and into the eyes of an old man with a caring face and a big heart. "I am so worried. I do not have a way to feed my children or give them a bed tonight." She told the old man with tears flowing down her face.

"What were you planning to do tonight?" he asked.

"I plan to sleep right here on this bench with my two boys but I still do not know what I will give them to eat," Mae said.

"My name is Charlie Mercer and I live right down the road and I have plenty of room and plenty of food in the kitchen. If you want to come to my house for the night you will be welcome," Charlie said. Mae suddenly felt the big burden lift from her shoulders. She gathered her bags and her children and followed Charlie Mercer to his house. Charlie was right, he had a nice house, and the kitchen was full of food. Mae went straight to the kitchen and prepared the two little boys a nice hot meal to eat. Both little boys ate eagerly and so did she.

Mae gave the boys a bath and then put them to bed. She sat down on the front porch where Charlie was rocking in his favorite chair. "I want to thank you for giving us a place to stay tonight and for the hot meal," Mae said to him.

"I want to thank you for cooking the meal. It was really good," Charlie said. Mae learned that Charlie had come to America from Russia when he was just a boy. His dad had told him so much about Russia as he grew up and his memories of the country when he was a boy caused him to miss his native land. He called it the *Old Country*. He really enjoyed talking about his memories of Russia and comparing the two countries. Mae enjoyed listening and learning about his native country. Charlie had also served in the war. He had medals that he had earned for several different events that he had been involved in while he was a military man.

The next day when Mae started repacking her brown paper bags Charlie said, "You and the boys are welcome to stay here as long as you want to. Nobody lives here but I and I have all this room going to waste."

Therefore, Mae stayed on another day. She had her own bedroom and the boys had a bedroom for themselves but Mae preferred the boys to sleep in the room with her. She had never slept away from them. Charlie brought out a cot and Mae helped him to put it up in her bedroom. "Now Robert can sleep on the cot and that will give you more room." Mae thanked him but she doubted Robert would sleep on the cot. It had affected him when his father disappeared. Mae felt that he always worried that he might loose her too some day.

Luke moved Ethel and their little girl to another house near Barney, Ga. It felt good to have his own home with only his own family depending on him. One day Luke was cleaning out the foliage near the yard to provide more yards for his growing family when a car came, speeding down the lane to his house. Luke propped the ax on a tree and started walking toward the car. He realized it was Lancy. He did not attempt to get out of his car. Luke walked up to the car and found Lancy sitting behind the steering wheel weeping his heart out. "What is wrong, Lancy?" Luke asked.

"My baby has just died," he said between sobs. "Do you know where I can find Mary Jane and Mae? Mrs. Browning is already there but Mattie Lee keeps calling for her sisters."

Mary Jane is in Pavo. I will go to Pavo and bring her back to your house."

"Mae is living in Berlin just on the other side of General's Barber Shop," Luke told him. "I will stop and pick her up," Lancy said as he was driving off. Luke ran into the house and told Ethel what had happened but he did not know the details. "I have to run to Pavo and get Mary Jane and take her to Mattie Lee. I won't be gone long and I will find out what happened before I come back," Luke told Ethel.

When Luke arrived at Mary Jane's house in Pavo, he was shocked at what he found. He found Mary Jane weeping her heart out with two baby girls at her feet. "What is wrong, Mary Jane?"

"Robert came here drunk with his drunken friend a little while ago. The old drunk man that he brought in fell on my babies. I don't know if they are hurt or not." Luke squatted down and looked the little girls over.

"They seem alright to me," he said to her. Mary Jane was still crying.

"This is the first time I have seen him since soon after the baby was born. I ran them out of the house and told Robert not to come back until he was sober. He does nothing but stay drunk and run around with women." Luke felt so sorry for her and now he has to tell her the terrible news about her sister.

"Mary Jane, Lancy just came to my house. He said that Aylene is dead and Mattie Lee needs you."

Mary Jane's weeping became intense. She could not believe it. "What happened, Luke?"

"I don't know what happened, yet. I have come to take you there now." It was almost as if Mary Jane was relieved that she was going to leave her home. She grabbed some clothes and put them in paper bags.

On their way out of town, Mary Jane asked Luke to go by the grocery store so that she could tell her mother-in-law where she was going. "She will worry about us if she found us missing and did not know where we are," she told Luke.

"Have you told her about what her son is doing?" Luke asked her. "I don't have to tell her, she already knows. She told me soon after I married Robert that he had a wild streak and that his dad was joining him. She told me that her husband had started taking Robert to honky-tonks and giving him liqueur to drink when he was just a boy."

"She said she had tried to get Jim Bob to stop and that he was ruining Robert but he would not listen."

When Mary Jane and Luke arrived at Mattie Lee's house, there were cars everywhere. Mary Jane knew something horrible had happened to Aylean for this many people to be, gathered here already. Luke said that Lancy said she had died this morning. They got out of the car and went inside the house. People were standing around with handkerchiefs to their eyes. Mary Jane went into the bedroom where she found Mattie Lee lying in bed sobbing the same sad sobs she had done when she was a little girl. Ma and Mae were at her side. They were trying to comfort Mattie Lee but it was hopeless. Ma and Mae were also crying. Mary Jane reached over, and hugged her sister. She whispered, I love you in her ear. Mattie Lee realized it was Mary Jane and she sprung up from the bed and grabbed her sister. She held on to Mary Jane as if somehow she might bring her baby back. Mary Jane sat on the side of the bed and held her sister while she rocked back and forth with her on the bed. After about five minutes, Mattie Lee dried her eyes, blew her nose, and looked at Mary Jane.

"Ayleen was scalded to death. She was playing near the fireplace and Lancy had hung a pot of water over the fire to heat so that he could shave. My baby somehow knocked the water over while she was sitting in the sunken hearth. The boiling water spilled out covering her in the boiling water. When I got the little thing and picked her up out of the water the meat started coming off her bones at her back, back side and legs." In a desperate scream, she said; "We rushed her to the hospital in Moultrie but I knew she wouldn't make it. The doctor pronounced her dead when we arrived there."

"Oh, Mary Jane it was the worse thing I have ever seen. You could see her little bones where the cooked meat fell away from them." Aylene had never learned to crawl but she scooted around on her butt. It was hard to realize that the baby could have gotten that close to the fire and boiling water without her face and hand having suffered a burned, from the heat that radiated outward. Her face had no signs of a burn at all. Only where the water had touched her skin showed the horrible burns. No one knows how she did it. Maybe she had gotten the broom, knocked the boiling water over and then went to investigate and accidentally fell into the water. Although Aylene, advanced for her age, was only a year old. It seemed unlikely that a one year old could hold a broom to do something like that. As to what really happened, no one would ever really know. Mattie Lee never accepted the death of her daughter. Her death would haunt Mattie Lee the rest of her life. She felt very responsible for the accident. If she had not left her in the room alone only for the two minutes she was away, it never would have happened.

When the funeral was over and everyone, except Mary Jane, had left, Mattie Lee wept in her sister's arms again. Mary Jane tried to reassure her. "Mattie Lee, God needed a special Angel and he chose Aylene. She is in a wonderful place now." Mattie Lee listened but she still could not except that the Angel had to be her only little daughter.

Mary Jane was in no hurry to leave. Her sister needed her and even with the death of Aylean the Hiers household was a much happier and peaceful place than her own. Lancy had told Mary Jane he would take her home anytime she wanted to go but she was welcome to stay with them as long as she wanted. Lancy was grateful that Mary Jane was there. Mattie Lee did not need to be alone now and he had to go to the fields and work. Mattie Lee begged Mary Jane not to go back, "You and the girls can stay with us. Luke told me about how Robert is treating you. You don't need to go back into that."

Mary Jane and the children settled in quiet well. Mary Jane wanted Mattie Lee to talk about the death of her baby and not hold it inside her. Mary Jane only gave her support but allowed her to vent her feeling as much as she needed.

Six months later Robert showed up at the door. "Are you ready to come home, Mary Jane?" he asked.

"No, I will just stay here until Mattie Lee gets over the loss of her baby. Then I will come home."

"And how long do you think that will take?"

"I don't know but she is getting better every day."

"Will you walk with me outside so we can talk?" Robert asked Mary Jane.

Mary Jane gave a quick look at Lancy and then walked out with Robert. Lancy knew the look she had given him, was meant to keep an eye on them. Lancy was one of the most respectable, loving and honest men in the world. Those he cared for were not going to be in any danger on his watch.

"Honey, I am so sorry about my friend falling over the children. I did not know he was that drunk or I would have never carried him into the house. I love you very much and I need you to come home. I miss you and the girls. If you will not come back with me today, I do not know what I will do. If I did not love you and my girls, so much I would not be here today. However, I do and I need you home. I promise, what happened that day, will never happen again. I will straighten up and we will start going to church the way you want to. I want you home."

"Just let me stay a little longer until Mattie Lee gets back to her old self," Mary Jane said.

"She may never get any better, hell, she lost a child. I know I need you more at home than she needs you here."

Mary Jane could tell that Robert was about to get angry. She did not want him to cause a scene here after all that Mattie Lee and Lancy had gone through. She decided she must go back with him.

Mattie Lee was disappointed when Mary Jane told her she was going back with Robert. The two little girls started to cry. They did not want to go back either.

"Mattie Lee, he promised me that he is going to straighten up and start doing right by us," Mary Jane told her sister.

"Maybe so but I don't believe a word of it."

"Well, I think I should try for the kid's sake," Mary Jane said.

Mae decided after almost a year Roy was never coming back. She went to Moultrie and filed for divorce on terms of abandonment. When her divorce was final, she decided that Charlie had been too good to her and her boys for her to abandon him.

Mae and Charlie were married in a quiet little ceremony at the justice of the peace office in Moultrie. Mae knew she had done the right thing. Charlie was good to her and the boys. The boys loved him.

Charlie and Mae immediately began building a family of their own. Their first baby was a little girl. Mae was so proud of her. She was a beautiful baby with a full head of blond hair.

Mattie Lee was right. Nothing changed about Robert except he became worse in all his bad ways. Soon after Mary Jane went back, home she was pregnant again and he left her again. If his parents did not have a grocery store and allowed Mary Jane to get food for the children there, she would have had no way to feed the children or herself. She found out that Robert went to Mattie Lee's to get her to come back to him it was only because his mother had made him feel so bad and almost forced him to get his family back. She felt like he might settle down, some if his family was back. She worried that he may be killed while driving drunk or ruin his health because of the drinking and his rough life style.

When Mary Jane had the third child, it was a baby boy. When Robert got word that, the baby was born and he was a boy he showed back up again. However, the baby boy was not healthy. He was tiny and he vomited often. This disgusted Robert, so he left again. Nevertheless, before he left, Mary Jane was pregnant again.

Again, he stayed gone until the next baby was born. Then he showed up again only to stay a short while, until Mary Jane was pregnant again. This was the forth child and Mary Jane was devastated. She knew by now that Robert was never going to settle down. She could see through to his thinking. He did not want the responsibility of a family. He knew his family would be, fed since his parents had no choice other than to let the children starve. However, Mary Jane could tell that his parents were getting tired of feeding her family.

Mary Jane went to her neighbor and had her to write a letter to her sister.

> *Dear Mattie Lee,*
>
> *You were right. Robert has not gotten better. He has only gotten worse. I do not think I can take it any longer. Will you send Lancy to get the children and me? I promise I will not come back to him if you will.*
> *I hope to hear from you soon.*
>
> *I Love You,*
> *Mary Jane*

When Mattie Lee got Mary Jane's letter she immediately sent Lancy to get Mary Jane. Mary Jane loaded her children and all their belongings onto Lancy's truck. This time she left no clothes behind. Again, Mary Jane asked Lancy to go by the grocery store and he did. Mrs. Burgess wept as Mary Jane and the children rode away.

When they arrived at Lancy's house Mattie Lee met them at the door. Grinning Mattie Lee said, "I hate to say it but I told you so."

"You were right. He had not changed one bit except to get worse."

"You are not going back this time," Mattie Lee said. "I don't want to go back this time," Mary Jane said.

This pregnancy was not going well for Mary Jane. She felt tired and sick all the time. Mattie Lee talked Mary Jane into going to the doctor. Finally,

Mary Jane decided Mattie Lee was right. She really did need to go to the doctor.

The next day Lancy and Mattie Lee carried Mary Jane to the doctor. Their oldest son would baby-sit, all the older children. He was a teenager now. Mary Jane would take the baby with her.

On the way to Moultrie Mattie Lee said, "I hope we can get you in to see Doctor Josh Parker. They say he is the best doctor in Moultrie. They were lucky. Lancy carried them to Dr. Josh's office and they got right in. Dr. Parker checked Mary Jane over good. When he was all finished, he ordered her to go into his office. "Mary Jane, I have bad news and good news for you. You have gestational diabetes." "What is that?" Mary Jane asked Dr. Parker. "It happens to many pregnant women, and it is when your body does not use sugar right and it builds up in your tissue and blood stream. It can be very bad if it is not treated but it can be treated and controlled, well if you go by my orders. That is the good news. Now you have to listen to me and do just as I say. You cannot eat anything with sugar in it. You have to control the amount of food that you eat and you can only eat fresh cooked, or raw, fruits and vegetables. You can eat any kind of meat except fried meat or fat pork. Broil, bake, or boil all your meat. Do you understand what you are supposed to eat?"

"Yes, I think I do." Mary Jane told the doctor. Dr. Josh Parker requested Mary Jane repeat her diet to him. When she had repeated it correctly, Dr. Parker told her that she could go but he wanted her back in one month for another check.

Lancy told all the children to load into the wagon. He carried them all to the watermelon patch and let them pick out the perfect watermelons to carry home and eat. Within an hour, the children were up to the elbow in watermelon. They ate the first one Lancy cut. With watermelon dripping from their faces, arms and elbows, they used the second one for a watermelon fight. When they were too tired to throw another piece, Mattie Lee directed the children to the washtubs, filled with water and waiting on the long back porch. "You have to have a bath before you can come inside." Mattie Lee said to them. Her back yard was, covered with little pieces of red watermelon. She looked out over her yard and said, "It would not surprise me if we get up in the morning and little watermelon bushes are growing all over the back yard."

The country was going into a big depression. Wall Street collapsed and people lost all their money in banks that went bankrupt. Of course, none of this bothered any of the family since they did not know what Wall Street was and had never had any money in a bank. They still mostly lived off the land and only went to town to buy staples once a month. However, when they did go to town they found that the depression was going to affect them after all. They found many of the staples they needed was now, rationed and they would be issued stamps for buying the product. The stamps were the way the government would control how much each person, was allowed to purchase of any one time. Mary Jane's baby was on carnation milk, since her mother's milk had dried up. Mary Jane was issued only a few stamps per month for the baby's milk. She would need to start adding regular cows milk from Lancy's milking cows to the carnation to make it stretch further.

The family did not know about it but one of their own was suffering from the fall of Wall Street. Poor Martha (Eliza's oldest sister) lost every dime she had. Her stocks and bonds went away and all the money she had in the bank was lost when her bank also went bankrupt. Now she and Ellen (Martha's younger sister) would grow a garden for their food all over again. They would go back to the old days. The only thing that would be different was the big house. Since Ben had paid cash for it, as he had it built, it was free and clear of debt. Martha and Ellen would be able to live out their days there. Martha was thankful that Ben had bought enough land for some cows and a garden. They would not go hungry.

Mary Jane and Mattie Lee would need to go to the grocery store more often now that food was, rationed on the amount they could buy each time they went. Mattie Lee's oldest son was now a teenager. He had been driving on the farm since he was nine years old. The day he turned sixteen years old, he wanted his dad to drive him to get his driver's license. Charles passed the written test and the driving test with no problems. Mattie Lee was happy Charles had his license. Now she could go anytime she wanted without waiting for Lancy to drive her.

"Charles, you can take your mother and Aunt Mary Jane to town today. I will stay with the kids since I need to replace the wash pan board on the back porch." A wide board ran from one post to another on the back porch. The board was, used for holding the water bucket and dipper and a wash pan for washing hands before meals. Lancy always kept the water bucket filled with fresh water that he drew from the well. When one wanted a drink of water, he just brought the dipper out of the bucket by its long handle. The person had a drink and threw out any water left over, before returning the dipper. They replaced the dipper in the bucket with the curled handle tip hooked over the bucket rim. He kept Mattie Lee a fresh bucket of water in the kitchen also that she used for cooking.

Every few years the board needed replacing. Since it stayed wet most of the time, the wood would rot. Lancy always had wide boards available for this since he had changed the board many times before. He was born in this house and had never lived any place else.

Mattie Lee and Mary Jane had left with Charles to go to the grocery store in Berlin. Lancy was working on the bench on the back porch. The children were playing in the yard while Lancy watched. Suddenly the children disappeared from the back yard. Lancy went through the house to see if he might have missed them coming inside. They were not there. He went out the front door and found a car parked in his front yard closer to the road than to the house. A man was loading Mary Jane's children into the coup car. Lancy ran as fast as he could and caught the car door just as the car moved off. He ran as fast as he could while pulling the door open. He jumped into the back seat. The man driving the car was Robert. He did not stop the car. Lancy did not say a word. Finally, Robert slowed down and said. "These are my children and I am taking them."

"That is fine, but you need to know that wherever they go I go too." Robert stopped the car and ordered Lancy to get out. "I will get out when you allow the children to get out first," Lancy said. Robert knew there was no need for a confrontation since Lancy was much bigger and stronger than he was. After sitting on the side of the road for fifteen minutes trying to persuade Lancy to get out of the car, Robert finally gave up and carried them back to the house. Lancy put each child out of the car and last he got out. Robert left with spinning tires and dust flying.

When Robert returned home his mother asked, "Where are Mary Jane and the children?"

"Mom, when I went through Berlin I saw Mary Jane and her sister getting out of a car and the children were not with them. I went to Lancy's house, thinking that the children were there alone. I was going to get them and then stop in Berlin on my way back and get Mary Jane." "I repeat, where is Mary Jane and the children?" his mother asks.

"Lancy would not let me have them. I had them all loaded in the car and then he jumped in and would not get out until I let the children go. I had no choice but to let them go."

"Why did you not get Mary Jane and then go and get the children?" his mother asked.

"I figured if I already had the children she would be forced to come with me. Mom, I do not think she is going to be willing to come back to me. I do not know why you keep fussing at me about it. They are doing fine right where they are."

"Robert, I am going to say it one more time. It is because they are your responsibility, not Lancy Hiers responsibility."

"Do you think you can bring children into this world and then push them on someone else to raise?"

"Lancy Hiers must not mind or he would have let me have the children."

"It was because Mary Jane was not with them. He did not know you intended to pick their mother up in Berlin." His mother said to him. "I don't see why I can't just bring the kids back anyway. They are the ones you keep fussing about." "No, you will never do that. Do you think that at my age I can start raising babies all over again? You go back there and get those children and their mother, and don't come back here until you have them." Robert left but he was not anxious to get his family back. He decided he would keep on partying and having a good time and he would go later to get them. He would just need to remember to stay away from Mom until he had gotten them back. He just could not understand how his mom could think he needed the responsibility of a bunch of children anyway. He was still a young man. He still had lots of living to do. His mom had turned on him. She had always been on his side. He did not know why she had turned so the opposite now.

When Mary Jane and Mattie Lee returned home from the grocery store, Lancy told them about the incident that had happened while they were gone. Mary Jane's heart sank. "Thank you so much Lancy. What would have happened to my children if he had taken them away? He sure was not going to care for them." Mary Jane shook as she thought about it. She knew if he had gotten the children he would have taken them to his mother and if she had refused to take them, he would have taken them out somewhere and killed them. That is the kind of heart he had and Mary Jane knew it.

It was time for Mary Jane to go back to see Dr. Josh. She had no money and she knew with times this hard, Lancy did not have the money to pay it again either. She never mentioned the appointment as it came and went. It was getting more difficult for Lancy to afford to feed them all. There had been a drought and many of his crops failed that year. Lancy or Mattie Lee never complained but Mary Jane could see the strain on them. If only she could get a job. She knew nobody would hire her now with her advanced pregnancy. If she were lucky enough to find a job that would mean Mattie Lee would be stuck with babysitting her three children and, how would she get too and from a job? It was hopeless. There was no way out.

Mary Jane was worried. If she did not return to the doctor and her blood sugar was still too high, would it affect the baby. She did not know what to do. She decided that if Robert showed back up she would go with him.

She did not have to wait long. Within another month, Robert was again at Lancy's front door. "What do you want?" Lancy ask. "I want to talk to my wife." Robert answered. Mary Jane heard him at the door and she walked closer to the door. "I will talk to him, Lancy," she said.

"Mom wants you and the children to come home," he said.

"Is that why you came? Because, your mother wants us to come home," Mary Jane answered.

"She said I could not go to her house anymore until you and the children are back." Mary Jane had to give him credit. He was too stupid to lie about it.

"I will go back with you but it is not for you. I will be going back for your mother," Mary Jane told him. Mattie Lee wept the entire time that Mary Jane was packing her brown paper bags. "He's just going to put you through more hell. Please do not go back with him. If you don't want to stay here you can stay with Ma and Eppse."

Mary Jane knew better than that, since Ma had already told her the same thing she had told Mae. "You can't live here because this is Eppse's house and he does not want children living here."

"I will be alright Mattie Lee. I will figure a way out when he starts again," Mary Jane reassured Mattie Lee.

For a while, Robert was kind to Mary Jane. She told him about what Dr. Parker had told her and he carried her straight to a doctor in Barwick. She still had the gestational diabetes but it was in control, since she had only eaten the foods that Dr. Parker had told her she could have. When it was time for the baby to arrive, Robert carried Mary Jane to the doctor and he placed her in the hospital for the delivery. This would be the only child Mary Jane would have in a hospital. It was good that she had this baby girl in the hospital since it was a long labor and the baby weighed almost ten pounds. Ten pounds was a big baby for five feet, 110-pound Mary Jane.

Robert started staying out until past midnight almost every night before the baby was born. Now it was every night and some nights he did not come home at all. However, he would be there long enough to get Mary Jane pregnant one more time.

Immediately after Mary Jane told him she thought she was pregnant again he left. This time he did not return. Mary Jane was feeding the children from the store that Robert's parents owned. When Mary Jane was three months pregnant, Robert's mother said to her. "Mary you are going to have to put these children in an orphanage. Robert spread the word before he left town that he was never coming back. We can not continue to feed them and you are not going to be able to do it alone."

Mary Jane was devastated. She knew parents were loosing their children at an alarming rate because the government said they were not able to care for them right. Would Mrs. Burgess call the government? Had she already called the government? Mary Jane sneaked into a phone booth, at the edge of town that evening. Mary Jane called Rittie. She knew that Clint had a big truck. "Rittie will you get Clint to come and move me somewhere."

"Where do you want to move?" Rittie ask.

"I don't know. I don't have anyplace to move but I have to get away from here as soon as possible." Mary Jane told her sister. "Why, what is wrong?" Rittie ask. "I think they are going to take my children." Mary Jane said as she broke down in a flood of tears. "I have to get them out of here and hide them some place." Rittie told her she would have the truck there before daylight the next morning. The next morning while it was still dark Mary Jane and her children loaded all their belongings onto it and left. Clint knew of an old house in the country near where many of the family members lived now and he arranged for Mary Jane to move into it.

Now, Mary Jane was on her own, with four little children, all under seven years old and three months pregnant with the fifth one. She immediately went to work for the man who owned the house. She picked cotton, chopped peanuts, and did anything else the man needed her to do. He let her have the house free and he paid her for working for him. She would raise her children on her own.

Chapter Twelve

Sons Go to War

When Joseph (John and Laura Hires son) was older and with the help of his father's parents, he bought a farm of his own. Now Laura would finish raising her boys in a place of their own. Laura loved each of her boys with great affection. A second world war had broken out and America stayed out of it until Japan commenced a surprise attack on Pear Harbor in Hawaii. One of the first to go to war was Laura's second son. This was devastating to Laura. She worried and prayed the full three years that he was away at war. Tim made it through with no problems much to Laura's relief. As soon as Tim returned from war, he took a wife. Laura loved her daughter-in-law and felt that she finally had the daughter that she had always wanted, but never had.

Horace would also go away to the war. Russell and Maude also worried and prayed every day for their son's safe return. Horace would return without injury, when the war was over. He was so happy to see his family again but more than anything, he was so excited to be back to Betty Jo. Horace and Betty Jo had been dating for a year before he had to go off to war. Betty Jo was a beautiful girl and she was devoted to Horace. Every day she would mark off another day closer to the date her Horace would return to her. Horace felt the same about her and he had so much love to give. Horace had five little cousins whose father had deserted them and they lived on the same road going to town. Horace enjoyed buying candy for them. He would throw the covered candy from his car window as he went past their house. He enjoyed watching the children scurrying to get the candy. The children could not wait for their grown up cousin to come riding by in his new car.

Horace threw the candy from his car window and gave them a big wave as he drove by. He was on his way to see Betty Jo. She was ready and waiting when he arrived. "Let's go to the movie and see *Gone with the Wind*," Betty Jo said to Horace. The movie had come out about six years before but Betty Jo never had a chance to see it. Everyone said it was a very good movie but it was a long movie.

"That suits me," Horace said. He had never seen the movie but he had also heard many people talking about. Betty Jo told her parents she would be late getting home and told them about the movie they were going to see.

The movie was very good, however, Betty Jo cried through most of it. When they were out of the movie, Horace asked Betty Jo if she would ride with him to a beautiful meadow that he had come upon several days before. She agreed but it was curious to her since Horace had never even parked as most other couples did, "to watch the moon," when all they did was actually smooch. That was not Horace. He was a man with high standards and high morals. He respected Betty Jo much more than that.

Horace drove into the beautiful green meadow. There was a small pond in the distance and the water glittered in the moon light. They got out of the car and walked down by the water. Horace pulled something from his pocket. He took Betty Jo in his arms and gave her a special hug. "I want to ask you something, sweetheart." On one knee he said, "Will you please marry me?"

"I will be happy to marry you sir," Betty Jo said as she trembled inside with excitement. Horace placed the beautiful engagement ring on her finger. Then she threw her arms and gave him a passionate kiss. Every ounce of love that she felt for Horace flowed out to him from that kiss.

They slowly walked back to the car while they discussed when their wedding day would be. They decided it would be one year from that day. Betty Jo wanted to have a nice wedding and it would take a year to get it all planned and ready by their wedding day.

Everyone in the family on both, his side and her side, was so excited that Horace had asked Betty Jo to marry him. They were a beautiful couple and they both had the same elegant charm about them.

Betty Jo started right away planning her wedding. She had a wonderful mother who was so happy for her daughter and was happy to help her plan her wedding. Luckily, Betty Jo's father was a very successful farmer and could afford his daughter's wedding.

It was tobacco-gathering time and Horace would help his dad, brother, and sisters with the tobacco. It felt good to be back on the farm again and not shooting at people that he did not know. It also felt good not to be dodging bullets aimed at him. Sometimes at night when he was sleeping, he would relive one of the awful situations he had been in, in the war.

He was in Germany and it was very cold and snowing. Horace and his battalion had orders to take over a barn at the top of a small hill. The enemy was using it for a hide out. They could pick the American Solders off at their leisure from the top of the hill while hiding in the barn. Horace and his twenty men huddled together in a tight circle. They decided the strategy they would use to climb the hill and take the barn. Five of the military men would go far to the right; five of them would go far to the left. Ten men would stay directly in the center. They would wait for the snow to come down in thick flurries. The right and left group would move in as close as possible. The ten men in the center would bury themselves under the snow. While the snow came down in thick sheets, they would scurry along under the snow until they reached the building. They held hand grenades and they would toss the grenades in the building while those on the left and right fired rapid fire at the enemy. It was a slow go getting up the hill without being, seen by the enemy.

Horace raised his hand out of the snow and the five men on the left and right, now much closer to the building began firing rounds into the back and front of the building. Horace scooted around and close to the opened front door. He tossed a grenade inside the building. The Germans were firing at random from the building. The soldiers would need to be careful where they threw the hand grenade. They did not need the grenades bouncing back and onto them. All ten men managed to get a grenade inside the building. Some of them gravely escaped death when they walked up to the building and actually poked the grenade inside a hole in the building. The men knew it was they or the Germans. One side would need to die if the other one lived. Horace had no indention of allowing them to be the ones to live.

Soon no gunfire came from the building. The Americans stayed very still and waited for another twenty minutes. It remained quiet within the building. Horace had his rapid-fire riffle ready and aimed as he jumped around the building and stood in the open door. Men were lying about on the floor. He walked through the building and saw or heard no one. He was confident they had gotten all of them. All his men gathered in the barn and celebrated their victory.

Now they would inch on up the hill. There was always a battle waiting on the other side. Horace did not remember the last time he was warm. His toes felt like small ice cycles in his shoes. His body shivered until it was too tired to shiver any longer. This was war and every man involved was going through the same thing as he was. They could not allow the cold to take over their minds. They needed to focus entirely on the war they were fighting. If they did not, they would surly die. Horace would never write home about the conditions they lived in.

Now Horace was home and safe. In one year, he would be married to his sweetheart. The war was behind him and if he could get rid of the dreadful dreams he could wipe his hands clean of the war and all that went with it.

Horace had not felt well since he had returned from the war. He felt tired and worn out all the time. He would not tell Maude and Russell about it. They were so grateful he was home and would never have to face war again. Horace did not them to start worrying about his health. They had had enough worrying for a while.

He pushed himself everyday just to get out of bed and make it through the day. When he helped in tobacco, by the end of the day he was so tired he was unable to eat. He just got a bath and went to bed. This concerned Maude. She knew how much Horace had once, loved to eat and especially her cooking. He had mentioned it in most of the letters he had written home.

"Russell, I am worried about Horace. He seems tired most of the time and he looks pale to me," Maude told her husband. Russell had not noticed but he would talk to Horace tomorrow.

"Son, how are you feeling?" Russell asked him the next day. "Dad, I don't feel really great, but I think I am alright," Horace said. "Why don't you go to the doctor and let him check you out to be sure nothing is wrong?" Russell asked. "If I don't start feeling better soon I will go to the doctor." Horace told his dad. Russell told Maude what Horace had said. Maude knew she would keep a close eye on her son.

After another week had passed and Horace still showed not signs of real energy Maude said. "Horace, I think it's time you go to the doctor."

"I'm alright, Mom, I think I'm still tired from the war."

"Please go Horace; if there is nothing wrong that will be great, but if there is, maybe the doctor can help you get your energy back."

"Okay, Mom, if you really want me to." Horace said. "I really want you to go." Maude said to her son.

Maude got up early the next morning and got breakfast on the table. Everyone would go to work after breakfast except Maude and Horace. They went to Moultrie to find the doctor that everyone was still talking about. His name was Dr. Josh Parker and everyone who had been to him, raved about his knowledge and abilities. Maude told Horace about his aunt Mary Jane going to him while she was pregnant and he found exactly what was wrong with her and just what to do about it. She told Horace that Ellen Ellen went on to have a healthy baby after he had told her what to do to keep herself and her baby healthy. Everyone who knew Dr. Josh Parker said he was the best doctor that Moultrie had ever had.

When Maude and Horace walked into Dr. Parker's waiting room the receptionist behind the desk greeted them. "I want Dr. Parker to take a look at my son. He has just returned from the war and he is weak and tired." The receptionist was telling them that she would be happy to make an appointment to see Dr. Parker tomorrow but today he was booked solid. Josh Parker had heard Maude when she said her son had just returned from war. He stepped into the cubical where his receptionist sat and said, "Sir, I will be happy to see you now."

Horace stood there not really knowing what to do. "Come with me, Sergeant." Josh said. Horace followed the doctor down the hall and into a small room with an examining table there. Dr. Parker told Horace to take his shirt off and get on the table. When Dr. Josh Parker saw the color of Horace's skin under his shirt and pulled his eyelids down a cold chill went down his spine. "Please God; don't let it be what I think it is," Josh said in a silent prayer to God. Not only was Josh a good doctor but he was a good Christian. He knew that in the end, life and death was totally up to the Lord above.

Dr. Parker drew blood from Horace's arm and told him he wanted him to go over to the hospital, "just until the blood test comes back." Josh did not want to scare Horace and his mother. If Horace's illness were what he suspected, he would have to find a way to tell them but not now. He would pray while he waited for the blood test to come back. Horace walked out of Dr. Parker's office confused. "I wonder why he wants me to go over to the hospital to wait for the blood test." This scared Maude. "I do not know but what ever he says to do it what we will do," she said to her son.

They walked into the hospital waiting room and sat down in one of the many chairs there. They had been sitting there about fifteen minutes when a woman came up to them. She was wearing a hospital badge. "Can I help you?" She asked politely. "My son's doctor sent us up here to wait for a blood test," Maude said. The woman looked at Horace and asked if his name was, Horace Browning?"

"Yes, it is," Horace answered. "You need to come with me. Doctor Josh Parker wants you to be admitted to the hospital," she said to him. Horace got up and followed the woman as if he had been expecting this. Maude sat in the chair until she could gather her wits. "I will be there in a few minutes, Son," she said. When she felt like her knees would carry her Maude walked to a phone booth she saw in the lobby. She pulled a dime out and dialed Rittie's telephone number. Rittie answered to phone. "Rittie, will you and Clint go out to the house and tell Russell that the doctor has put Horace in the hospital."

"Yes, we will go. What is wrong with Horace?" Rittie asked.

"I don't know yet, the doctor is running blood test and we have to wait until they are back."

The nurse gave Horace a hospital gown. She helped him to get it on, and then she put him to bed. The nurse inserted a small catheter into his arm and soon Dr. Parker stood in the doorway of his room "Are you comfortable?" he asked Horace.

"Yes, but why did I need to come into the hospital to wait for a blood test?" Horace asked. "I am sorry. I guess I did not make myself clear. I want you in the hospital so that I can make you feel better. The nurse is coming in with a bottle of blood for you. When you receive it you are going to feel much better," the doctor said.

When Dr. Josh got the results from the blood test the next day, it showed Horace had a hemoglobin Level of six. His worse fears were coming true. However, he would still wait on more blood tests that would tell him more.

By sundown, that day Russell and the kids were at Horace's bedside. He had a sister only a few years younger than he was. She was worried about her brother. He had always seemed so strong and healthy to her. He was her hero. To see him lying in a hospital bed took its toll on her. She stayed outside his room most of the night weeping and praying for her brother. The laboratory staff drew more blood from Horace that night.

When Horace awoke the next morning, he felt like a new man. Now he could get up and go home. He had not felt this good since he had gotten home from the war. However, when Dr. Josh came on his morning rounds he put a damper on Horace's hopes. "No, you can't go home. We will wait till the new blood test come back and then maybe we will talk about it."

"Doctor Josh, I feel better than I have felt in a very long time," Horace said to him. "That is because you had the blood. They are going to give you some more today and you'll feel even better."

"Why do I need the blood?" Horace asked.

"You need blood because your oxygen carrying blood cells are low. We just to build them back up again."

"Why are they low?" Horace asked. "We will know why as soon as the blood they took from your arm is back today. I want you to rest today, in bed. No getting out of bed to watch pretty nurses in the halls," Horace laughed and agreed that he would stay in bed.

By lunchtime, the results of Horace's blood test were back. It confirmed what Dr. Josh feared the most. Horace had Leukemia, cancer of the blood. It was almost like a death sentence. No one survived more than a year. He would have to tell Horace and his family. Josh loved medicine but this part of his job he hated. Josh prayed all the way to the hospital from his office that the Lord would give him the right words to say so that his patient and family would understand what he was telling them and he could do it in a way that would not cause terror in their minds.

Doctor Josh walked into Horace's room. Horace was lying in bed and he had the bottle of blood still dripping into his vein. A big grin came across Horace's face as he saw the doctor walk into the room.

"You are right, Doc. I am feeling better every minute," Horace said to him.

"Good, I knew you would, and you are looking better too," the doctor said.

"Horace, we got the blood results back from the lab."

"Good, now can I go home?"

"Well, not right now. I think we need to give you more blood and maybe some medicine in your IV so that you will feel, really fine, when you do go home. The test shows that you have Leukemia. I know you have probably never heard of it before but it means sick blood. We have to treat your blood and see if we can kill this Leukemia.

Josh was careful not to use the word cancer right away. Horace agreed with the doctor. He had never heard the word Leukemia and did not know anyone could get sick blood. However, the way he felt now he knew that what ever it was he could beat it before it beat him. Maude, Russell and Rosie sat at the bedside while Dr. Josh was talking to Horace. Maude had a sick feeling in the bottom of her stomach. She did not know what this condition was but she knew it was serious.

When Dr. Josh walked out of the room, Maude followed him. "What is Leukemia, Dr. Josh?"
"Mrs. Maude, it is not good. It is cancer of the blood. We can give him chemotherapy but there is only one drug used for this kind of cancer. It works on some people, and for some, it does not work. We will start the chemotherapy as soon as it comes in from Atlanta. That is the closest place where the drug is available. We will give him the entire amount of the drug, if his body can take it. The chemotherapy drug has bad side effects. He will get very sick and will probably loose his hair. But since that is the only treatment that we have available to us now, in 1945 we will give it to him and then we will pray that if it is the Lord's will that the drug will kill Horace's cancer."
Maude backed up to the wall and wept. Dr. Josh held her in his arms for a long time. When she was finished crying she thanked Dr. Josh, went into the rest room, wiped her face off and went back into Horace's room. Dr. Josh had not told Maude that the survival rate on patients like Horace was only about three percent.

The days rolled on and Horace stayed in the hospital. The chemotherapy drug started on Horace's third day in the hospital. Just as Dr. Josh had said,

Horace became violently ill. He vomited so much that the pounds was falling off. They gave him medicine to control the nausea but it did little. Soon Horace's hair began falling out in wads on his pillow. He was too sick to care much about his hair.

The family had gotten word of Horace's illness to Betty Jo. She came straight to the hospital even though she lived twenty-five miles away. She stayed by his bedside day and night until her mother came to the hospital and talked her into going home long enough to get a good night sleep. She went home for her mother, but within three days, she was back at the hospital.

Horace was in and out of the hospital for a year. Betty Jo would attend Horace's funeral on their wedding day. No one knew how Horace's death had affected Dr. Josh Parker. Horace was only a few years younger than he was. He had grown so close to Horace and his family, but besides that, he had wanted to save him. He knew if there had been more drugs available, he probably could have save him. Dr. Josh decided from Horace's death that one day he was going into medical research. If Washington had medical people there that were dedicated, there would be more than one drug to treat this deadly disease.

The whole family was distraught with Horace's illness and death. He was a grandson who Ma loved dearly and he was his aunts and uncles precious little boy. He had always been so sweet, considerate, and caring all the years he was growing up and when he became an adult, it never went away.

All the funeral cars lined up and following behind the hearse to the cemetery. The funeral possession was almost a mile long. Suddenly a car coming in the opposite direction at a high rate of speed started weaving from one side of the road to the other. The funeral procession cars started pulling off the road as far as they could go. The ditches were deep on each side of the paved road. The racing car would barely miss one car then swing to the other side of the road. He would swing from that side to the opposite side barely missing another car. He barely missed approximately ten cars. Finally, when he swerved a sharp right again, he could not straighten the car and it started rolling. It was a new car and it rolled several times then came to rest in the upright position. The car was cross ways in the ditch and the front of the car was facing the highway. Some of the men in the funeral possession ran to the car to see if they could help the driver. His car trunk had opened during the crash and automobile batteries were, strewn all over the ditch. The man still sat under the steering wheel. "Can we help you?" one of the men asked.

"Yes, help me out of this damn car. I think I have broken my leg." Two of the men helped him out of the car. They sat him on the grass where he wanted to sit. After about five minutes he cursed some more and told them to put him back in his car. They did as he asked. He reached over on the seat and got a piece of paper and a pencil. He wrote something on the paper and handed it to one of the men. "Call my wife please," he said as he handed him the paper. The man took the paper and started to walk off. Suddenly everyone started yelling, "Watch out, he has a gun." The man carrying the paper looked back at him and started running toward him. He did not make it in time. The man opened his shirt, placed the gun over his heart and pulled the trigger.

Later the family heard that the man sold car batteries for a living. He had a mental illness and was in a state of depression. Not only did he want to take his own life but also he had tried to take many other lives with him. Everyone felt that Horace was watching over them that day and the man did not achieve what he had wanted.

Chapter Thirteen

Martha is Getting Old

Martha still lives in the great big beautiful house. However, she is getting old now and without money, it is a struggle to keep the place up. Ellen is doing most of the gardening now. There is little time left over for yard work. It grieved Martha to see the beautiful place looking run down. She longed to get into her yard and do as she had in the past. Work her flowerbeds, keep the grass cut and, trim the hedges. She had to admit to herself that she was no longer able to do it.

Martha was sitting inside her living room looking out the big window and thinking about Ben and what might have been if he had lived. She still missed him as she had when he first died. Suddenly she saw a group of people coming up the little road leading to her house. The doorbell rang. Martha went to the door. When she opened it, she found a large group of boy scouts standing straight and tall in their brown uniforms on her little front porch. Some of them had so many badges that the front of their shirts was almost covered. Their Scout Master was there with them. "Ma'm, we would like to do some yard cleaning for you if you don't mind," one of the boy scouts said to Martha. Martha reached over and gathered most of them in her arms. "You will never know how much I will appreciate it." She said to them. They all scurried off to get their hoes and rakes that they had left down the lane. Martha watched as they got started. They were all hard workers and Martha knew each one of them would go far in life.

When the boy scouts were finished with Martha's yard the place looked new all over again. Martha was overjoyed. The boy scouts told her they would be back every two weeks to do her yard work again. Martha thanked God for the blessing the boy scouts had provided her.

The next day Martha felt like getting out in her yard now that she could walk safely. She had sat down in the swing that was hanging from a big oak tree at the side of her front yard. Ben had hung the swing before the house was finished. At least she had had a chance to swing in the swing with Ben before he died. The swing would always have special meaning for her. Martha's mind was deep in thought about the time she and Ben had shared the swing when someone beside her said. "Martha, is that you?" Martha was jolted to reality. She looked up and there stood an older beautiful, well-dressed woman. Martha did not recognize her.

"My name is Hannah. I was on the ship with my two children that brought your mother, father, you, and your baby sister to America. Do you remember that trip?" she asked Martha. Martha jumped out of the swing and threw her arms around Hannah's neck.

"Heavens yes, I remember that trip and I also remember you." Martha was astonished. Hannah was at least ten years older than she was but she looked so young. Martha was now seventy years old. "Hannah, you look so good. How did you keep your youth all these years?"

"Oh, Martha," Hannah said with a chuckle, "I am not young any longer. I just turned eighty years old."

"But you still look so young," Martha said.

"Well, I have had plastic surgery a time or two but that doesn't take away the years," Hannah said.

"I am so glad you came. How did you find me?" Martha said. "It wasn't easy, I found out you lived here through someone I hired to look for you when I couldn't find any of you in Madison. He got me here to Lakeland and when I arrived here, I stopped in town and got the directions to your house. I have to say, everyone in town knows you," Martha noticed that Hannah was in a big beautiful black car. She had a driver who stood just outside the car door. He was wearing a black suit and a white cap. "May I stay with you a few days, Martha?" Martha hugged her again.

"I will be happy to keep you as long as you will stay," Martha said to her. Hannah walked back toward her car. "Jim, you can go now to your hotel and I will call you the day I am ready for you to come and get me." The man tipped his hat at Hannah and said, "Yes, Ma'm." He drove away in the beautiful car.

Martha introduced Hannah to her little sister, Ellen. Of course, Ellen was not little any more. She was now fifty years old herself. Martha caught

Hannah up on all her family. Then she told Hannah about Ben. The two women wept together at Martha's loss. Martha told Hannah that she still thinks of him every day and sometimes she feels that he is by her side. Hannah knew Martha loved him with all her heart. Martha told her about the massive amounts of money that Ben had left her and how it had all disappeared over night with the great depression and the fall of Wall Street. "That is enough about me. Tell me about your life in New York."

Hannah's mind drifted back as she thought about her life in New York. She could not believe the trial and triumphs had had since she moved there with her mother. Molly had been a wonderful mother. She had taken Hannah and her children into her apartment to live when they arrived in New York from Ireland. Molly had a big apartment with four bedrooms. "I do not know why I chose such a big apartment when I came here. I guess my instincts were that some day I might need the extra room. Now, I know why I had the instincts."

Hannah settled in at her mom's home. The children settled in quiet happily. They loved their Grammy and let her know it. Molly enjoyed spending time with the children. Molly had money of her own when she went to New York to live and when her parents died, she inherited their money and property expanding her worth by millions. Molly invested her money wisely and it kept growing. She spent her time watching Broadway Shows, frequenting art and history museums and shopping. Molly loved all three and they kept her quiet busy.

When her grandchildren came, Molly started taking them to children shows on Broadway and taught them to love for the arts. Hannah enrolled the two children in private schools where they would be prepared for Yale or Harvard when they graduated high school. Hannah and Molly spent most of their time supporting the children in projects and events they encountered in school.

However before the children were ready to start Yale or Harvard the Great Depression hit and just like Martha, over night all Molly's money was gone. Molly went to Wall Street but the door was, locked and a sign on the door read. "Sorry but we cease to exist at this time. Please pray for these difficult times." She caught a cab and went to each bank where she had money. Every bank was, closed and people were standing outside yelling angry words and holding signs. There was nothing, Molly could do to get her money back. Molly was old now and the strain of loosing all her money was too much for her. She died peacefully in her sleep one night. She was so happy to join her Nate again.

Since Hannah had been in New York, she had fought the banks in Ireland. The bank had finally released one hundred thousand dollars of her money to her but they were refusing to release almost a million dollars. The bank had sent a letter explaining the reason they were holding the money. Hannah did not understand a word of it. She hired a lawyer to help her. It had been nearly thirty years and so far, Hannah had not received a dime of her money. Her lawyer said he was still working on it but after all these years Hannah had given up hope on ever receiving a dime of the money.

Molly refused to allow Hannah to touch a dime of the one hundred thousand dollars she had. "You need to save it for the children's education," Molly told her. Hannah was angry at banks since the Irish banks kept her money. She had hidden her money in the house. When the banks failed, she was so thankful that she had. Now that they had no money except the hidden money, Hannah would need to pull it out so that they could have a living.

As the months began to pass and Hannah watched the money dwindle, she realized she would need to use the money that she had left to create some means of an income for her family.

People were only buying necessities for their homes and family. The only business Hannah had known was the millinery business her mother had owned in Ireland. She had spent enough time in the store that she knew the functioning of the millinery business. However, the millinery business was the last thing New York needed. People could do without hats.

Hannah watched as New York City continued to grow even though there was a depression going on. The city continued to grow daily with new immigrants. Hannah knew these people would need places to live.

Hannah knew nothing about real estate and construction. She went to the city library and read every book she could get her hands on related to or remotely related to the two subjects. She spent hours studying these books.

Finally, she felt that she was ready to put what she had learned to the test. She could not see into the future and the last thing she could afford to do was throw, what money she had left, away.

When Hannah counted her money, much to her dismay, she found she only had a little more than twenty five thousand dollars left. She did not know how she could possibly take twenty five thousand dollars and turn it into all the money she would need to educate the children and support them.

As Hannah walked to the library each day, she passed a small run down house. The little house looked so out of place in the neighborhood of large commercial buildings that had sprang up around it. She knew no one would ever want to live in the house again. She started thinking of ways she might change that little house into something someone would want in this time of depression and despair. She was able to purchase the house for ten thousand dollars. Now she only had fifteen thousand dollars left.

As Hannah sat in her favorite chair by the window, she looked out onto the city streets of New York City. She watched as women scurried by in a hurry to get to their factory jobs. Now that so many of the men were off to war their wives, daughters and mothers had taken over the jobs they had left behind.

Suddenly it occurred to Hannah, "Where are all these mothers leaving their children while they are at work all day, every day.

The next morning Hannah was also walking the street. She would start a conversation with a woman while they walked hurriedly along. "Do you have a good baby sitter for your children while you are at work?" Hannah asked. "No, I have to leave them alone and I worry about them all day." Hannah would let the mother walk ahead for a few steps and then she would walk beside another woman. "Do you have children?" "Yes," the woman said. "I had to drag them out of bed at five o'clock, so that I can get them to their grandmother's house thirty miles away, before I leave for work. My children are tired all the time."

One mother Hannah talked to started weeping and said she had to send her children three hundred miles away to her mother. "I see them only occasionally anymore. I miss my children."

Hannah went back to the apartment her mother had bought and she now owned. She knew what she would do with the little house. She hired a carpenter. Hannah carried the carpenter through the little house. She told him about each change she would make inside the house and the added room she wanted. When she was finished, the carpenter handed her a list of the supplies she would need to do the job. He told Hannah that he would do the job for two thousand dollars and that price would include erecting a fence around the house enclosing the yard. Hannah took the supply list to the local lumber company and the local hardware store. Together the goods Hannah would need to renovate the little house and turn it into a day nursery for children, came to almost five thousand dollars. This money included, enlarging the house, installing plumbing and electricity. She arranged with the two companies to deliver the supplies.

Hannah was present everyday while the work continued on her nursery school. She could not imagine why someone else had not thought about housing children while their mothers worked. However, she knew mothers did not work in the past. It was only since the war that women had started taking, out of the home, jobs.

Hannah saw that every aspect of the building evolved around the children. A place where they could take quiet naps. A large dining room where they would have nutritious meals at tables and seating for their size. She included a large playroom, with lots of room, to prevent injury. Nice equipped grounds for playing safely outside. She furnished the grounds and house with everything children could possibly ever want or need. The playroom had many toys for all ages and the playground had everything children would enjoy. She chose one room for nothing but cribs for the little babies. She painted all the rooms in different colors of pastel. She painted the outside baby blue and with pink shutters and trim. Hannah named the house "Happy time House." Hannah had the entire property enclosed with a white picket fence. She planted daffodils, sunflowers, and periwinkles.

When the mothers passed everyday after they had realized what the pretty house was going to be, they stopped and gave Hannah a hug for coming up with it. Before it was finished, Hannah had already enrolled 48 children. Hannah advertised for help to staff the nursery in the paper and hand hundreds of response. She chose six of the best qualified to staff the place.

When the nursery was up and running with a good profit, Hannah started advertising the business for sale. She had gotten a call from a man who wanted a tour of the building that afternoon. Hannah met him at the nursery at three o'clock. But when Hannah took one look at the man she knew she was not going to sell to him. He was a pudgy man with a red face and held a cigar in his mouth. Somehow, in her gut Hannah knew this man would never be kind to children. "I'll give you whatever you want for the place. It is a good investment; I could never build one on my own. Only a mother could have built this," he said to Hannah. "Sorry but I can not sell it to you. Maybe someday I will help you to build one of your own." Hannah said. From that, Hannah learned a lesson so she stopped her ad in the newspaper and changed it to read. For Sale: Children's Day Nursery. "Must love children, and buy the nursery because you do. This property is not for sale to buyers, looking for an investment." The day after the new add ran, she had another request to look at the building. When she met with him at the little house and began to open the door, he said. "Oh you don't have to show it to me. I just want to buy it for the property. I will tear down the house when I get it."

"It is not for sale," Hannah said.

"You listed this property for sale in the paper. What do you mean it is not for sale?" he said to Hannah.

"It is not for sale to tear down. This property is a needed property and that is why it is here. It is not going to be torn down."

"Miss I will give you a million dollars for this property."

"Sorry, like I said it is not for sale." The wealthy man pleaded with Hannah to change her mind but she held steadfast and the man finally gave up in disgust and left. She did not change her ad again. Hannah would screen everyone, who wanted the nursery and if the person did not fit her expected profile, she would not allow him or her to buy. It was just that simple.

The next week Hannah had another possible client who wanted to see the property. He was a well-dressed man and appeared well read on the running of a nursery. "I am interested in buying your nursery." Hannah carried him through the house from one room to another. He seemed impressed at the children. "They all appear happy and having fun. I like the staff you have chosen; they seem to really have the children at heart," he said to Hannah. "Will you take one hundred thousand dollars for the business?" the man asked.

Hannah thought she would ask eighty thousand for it but now that he had said the price he was willing to pay, she said. "Yes but before we start the paper work I have to ask you why you want a children's nursery, Hannah said.

"I own the pants factory down the street and most of my employees are women. Many of them have small children and since you have opened up this nursery, it has taken a load off many of my employees. They are now happier, healthier, and seem to enjoy coming to work much more. I think all their children are here. They talk about the nursery all the time and about how much happier their children are since they started staying here. I want to buy the nursery so that I can see that it stays here and is always run right for my employees." Hannah started to laugh. "Did you know that your factory and the other factories here in town are the reasons that I built this nursery?" You will be the perfect owner for "Happy Time House." The paper work was finished and the new owner gave Hannah the one hundred thousand dollars and Hannah handed him the key to the business.

Since Hannah was down to only five thousand dollars in her little wood box where she kept her money, she knew she would need to work fast to find another property that she could afford and still have money left over to fix it up with.

Everyday Hannah walked the streets of New York City. One day she spotted an empty building. It was in desperate need of repair. Weeds and foliage were grown up so high on the property that it was hard to see from the street. She walked through the weeds until she could get a good look at the building. *Uhmmmm,* she thought to herself. I could probably, get this property for a steal but is it even worth fixing up? The building looked like it might have been an old boarding house at one time. It was in a good location for just about anything. It was on main street and downtown where everyone always congregated, to do their business, go to work, go to a restaurant, or just to meet up with each other. Hannah thought about what she could do with the property.

Hannah remembered last month when she went to her doctor he had another doctor working with him. Hannah congratulated her doctor on having a helper. "He is a great doctor having just graduated from Harvard Medical School. He does not need to be here but he is having a hard time finding a place to set up his own office. A new group of doctors has just entered the work force here and they are all having problems finding a place of their own to set up practice. Before Hannah realized what she was doing, she picked up the phone and dialed her doctor. "Dr. Richards, tell your colleague not to worry about finding himself a nice office to practice in. I think I have just found him one. Of course he won't be able to move in right away, but give me a few months and I think I will have just what he wants." Dr. Richards was very busy when Hannah called and he had no clue what she was talking about but he said he would tell him.

Hannah had to go to the courthouse to find who owned the property. After looking through large ledger books and many, many papers, she finally found him. He was an old man who lived alone in her own apartment complex. She found the number of his apartment and went to pay him a visit. She rang the doorbell. No one answered the door. She rang a second time. Still there was no answer. Then she used the doorknocker and gave a few hard hits. Finally, the old man came to the door with his cane. "Sir, my name is Hannah Gooding and I am interested in the property that you own at the corner of fifth and Laurence Street. Is that property for sale?" Hannah asked.

"No," the old man replied.

"Why would you not want to sell it? It is going to ruin just sitting there."

"I can't sell it," the old man said.

"Why can't you sell it?" Hannah asked.

"The property is buried up to its neck in past due taxes," the old man said. "If I pay the taxes on it will you sell it to me then?" she asked.

"No," the old man said.

"Why would you not sell it to me?" Hannah asked.

"There are more taxes owed on the place, than it is worth." "Will you give me permission to go to the court house and see how much is owed in taxes on it?" Hannah asked.

"I don't care what you do," the cranky old man said.

"I will come back to see you tomorrow." Hannah said as she walked down the stairs.

Early the next morning Hannah was at the courthouse. She was early and had to wait until the doors opened. She was the first to walk into the building when the doors opened. She started searching again for the property. When Hannah, found the property tract, she carried the big ledger to the clerk and asked how much in back taxes the old man owed on the property. She opened another ledger and thumbed through it. "There have been no taxes paid on that place in eleven years."

"How much money would it take to get the taxes up to date?" Hannah asked.

"It would take twenty four thousand dollars and ninety two cents to catch it up to date." Hannah took some money from her pocket and started counting out money. "You are aware of the state of the property, I hope," the clerk said to Hannah.

"Yes, I am aware if it's condition," she said as she handed her the twenty four thousand dollars and ninety-two cents.

"Okay, here is the deed. You now own the property."

"What do you mean?" Hannah asked. "If you pay back taxes on a place for this many years, the property then belongs to you." The owner had been warned year after year that it would be sold for the taxes on the place, if he didn't pay up." "He didn't pay them, you did and now the property is yours."

This concerned Hannah. She knew the place was worth far more than twenty-four thousand dollars. Hannah returned to the owner's apartment. She remembered this time that the old man was almost deaf. When she finally got him to the door, she handed him the receipt for the taxes she had paid.

"Now, your taxes are paid and you can sell the building. May I buy it?" Hannah asked.

"No, you can not buy it but you can have it," he said.

"What do you mean, I can have it?" Hannah asked.

"Just what I said, you have paid the taxes on it and now it is yours."

"Mr. Levi, I can't just take the property. It is worth much more than twenty four thousand dollars," Hannah told him. "It may be worth more than that to you but it's not worth a damn thing to me. My wife and I ran a boarding house in that house. There was a time when we loved the house but when that deranged boarder murdered my dear wife in that house, it became useless to me. I moved out and I have never been back. I do not want any money from that house. It is blood money."

Almost as if Mr. Levi wanted to talk about it, he said. "I would tell you all about it but you are not interested in hearing it." Hannah had a deep feeling that this is what had made Mr. Levi so bitter. He had probably never talked about his wife's death since it happened.

"Of course, I am interested. I want to hear what happened that day," Hannah told him.

"It was about twenty years ago. At that time, my wife and I had four boarders, all men. My Mattie loved cooking big meals for the boarders. We always kept as many boarders as we had rooms. These four men had been with us three or four years."

"One day an officer came to the door. My wife answered the door and the officer told her that one block down the street a man had tied up three dogs. He said the man had a big cleaver and he was cutting the live dogs into little threads. He said a woman walked by and saw what he was doing and she was attempting to release the third dog that was waiting for his turn with the hacker. One looker said the poor dog saw what was happening to the other dogs and knew it would soon be his turn. They said the dog had terror in his eyes as he pulled and bucked trying to get loose from the rope. They said as she tried to untie the dog the crazed man turned the machete on her and before anyone could get to her, the man had ripped her to threads. A group of men surrounded the man and took the machete away from him. Then they carried him to the jail where the police place him and booked him with murder. During the night, the man got out of the jail somehow. They never knew how, since there were no signs of his escape. Everyone thinks the jailer that night opened the cell and let him go. The next day is when the police came and told my wife that they thought he was one of her boarders and if he was, he might try to come back to the house. They told her to be on the watch out for him. After three days and one of the four men still did not show up at the boarding house, we assumed the police was right and he must have been the man who did the horrible crime and then escaped jail. Anyhow, he escaped and the police hunted him for weeks. They never found him."

"The other three man did not know anything about the forth boarder. No one knew if he had family. Occasionally we heard little noises under the house. I thought it was squirrels or badgers playing under there. About a year later, my wife was outside weeding the flowerbeds at the side of the house. She wanted a special rake that she didn't have to do her yard work. I went to the hardware store to get the rake. When I got back home, she was not in the flowerbed. I assumed she had gone inside for a drink. I took the rake to the place she was working and started raking the grass. I worked for about an hour and she still had not returned to her flowerbed. I went inside to look for her. She was not in the house. I walked around the house. I could not find her any place. I went to the neighbors on each side and in front of the house and all the rest of the houses in the neighborhood where she visited occasionally. No one had seen her. Then I thought she must have needed something else and had gone to the store. I waited until almost dark on the front porch but she still did not return.

I went to the police department and told them my wife was missing but they would not do anything until she had been missing for twenty-four hours. I went back home and sat on the porch all night watching for her to arrive. When the twenty-four hours were up, I went back to the police department. They started helping me to look for her. We walked the streets and they sent wire messages to all the other police departments in New York and the surrounding states.

A month later, I still had not found her. The police were telling me that she had gotten tired of the marriage and had just walked away. I knew my Mattie better that they did and I knew she would never do a thing like that. Mattie was happy and so was I. We had a good marriage. Nevertheless, what could have happened to her? It was as if she had just walked off the face of the earth."

"By now I and the boarders were eating food from cans. None of us knew how to cook. One night while we were in the kitchen opening up the cans of food for supper that night one of the men complained about the smell of a dead rat. I assumed a rat had gotten between the walls and had died. There was nothing we could do short of taking down the walls. Soon the odor got so bad we could not eat in the kitchen at all. We searched every place that we could see for the dead rat but none of us could find it. All the time the odor was getting worse. One day a big burly police officer showed up at the door and said that the neighbors were complaining about a bad odor coming from my house. I told him that we had been hunting for the dead rat for days but so far had not found it. He told me he did not think it was a dead rat. He said it smelled to him like a dead body. Chills went down my back and I shook. This could not be my missing wife. I reminded the police about my missing wife."

"The officer went into the house and to the kitchen where the odor was worse. He had a tool in his hand and he began to rip off the walls. Nothing was there. He went out the back door and looked under the house. He saw nothing. The boarders and I had looked under the house for the odor many time but we saw nothing. The police officer scooted under the house on his belly to the kitchen area. What is this? He yelled back at me. What is what? I answered. It looks like a wooden hatch buried down here. I got on my knees and scooted under the house. There was a strange looking little square wood door buried in the dirt there. The officer took his tool and pulled at the small wood hatch. Suddenly it popped open. As he started to lower himself down into the cave, he quickly jumped out and scooted back. There is a tramp down there. He has set up living quarters in a cave he had dug under the house. He pulled his revolver out of its holster and told me to go to the police department and bring back help. He kept his pistol aimed at the cave but he had replaced the hatch door to its original place. He wanted the man to stay in the cave until back up arrived."

"When I arrived at the police department, and told them what was happening, four more police sprinted to my house. By the time, I got to the house all five police officers were under the house. They surrounded the little hatch door. The first officer snatched the door off and with five guns aimed directly in the hole he ordered the man to come out. It took a while but soon the tramp climbed out of the hole. One officer pushed himself from under the house backwards while holding his gun on the man while the others surrounded him. When they got him out from under the house, four of the officers placed handcuffs on him and led him away to the jail. The first officer stayed behind to examine the cave. It was obvious by now that the horrid smell was coming from there. I was right on the officer's heels, crawling back to the cave, when the officer yelled. "Do not come any closer. Stay where you are." I thought he had found another man in the hole and I hurried. However, he was talking to me. His head popped out of the cave and he said, "You do not want to see what is down there."

"Is it my wife?" I asked.

"I am afraid it is sir," the officer said.

"My worse fears had come true. I knew the tramp was the hacker who had killed the dogs and woman down town. In addition, he was the same man my dear Mattie had cooked so many meals."

"The officer never allowed me to look inside the cave. I guess I could have looked even if he did not want me to but deep down I did not want to see my Mattie in the condition she was probably, in. The officer told me what he thought had happened. It ended my world. I did not want to live any longer after that. I could never walk into that house again after he told me what went on right under my nose in the cave. The officer imagined he had dug the cave when he had escaped jail. He stayed hid out there and that is why they could never find him. He said when he knew no one was home he would go into the back door, since he had a key to both doors, and got food and water from the kitchen. He said when I left and went to the hardware store to get the rake and Mattie was right beside the house working in the flower bed, the evil man had the urge to kill again. He said he imagined when she had her back turned to the house while she weeded the border plants he grabbed her left ankle. He yanked her under the house and into the cave. He said the deranged man first tied Mattie up and taped her mouth closed. He cut Mattie's little finger off, and held the site with his filthy hands until the bleeding stopped. Then he cut off the next finger and did the same thing to keep it from bleeding and causing her death. He kept on doing this until all of Mattie's fingers were gone and then he started on her toes. He repeated the routine until all her toes were gone. Then he chopped off her hand, holding it until it stopped bleeding. Then he chopped off the other hand. He kept Mattie alive by holding back

211

the blood each time he dismembered her. He finally cut both arms and both legs off. Then he cut off each breast still keeping her alive. She did not die until he gorged out her female organs. Mattie had died the most horrendous death of any human being that any of the law officers had ever seen. The law sent that awful man away to a mental institution. The officer said that when he was mentally able he would stand trial for Mattie's death. However, he will never become mentally sane. He will die in the mental institution probably of old age. During all these years, he will eat three hot meals every day that are, laid before him and at night, he will climb into a clean bed to sleep."

"No missy, you can have that house with my best wishes. I want no money for it and I sure was not going to pay any tax money on it. You take it and go with my blessings." Mr. Levy had a very different expression on his face that he had had before he told her the story of his Mattie. Somehow, Hannah felt that this is exactly what he needed. He had probably told his story for the first time and his face looked as if a load lifted from him. He was not an angry old man any longer. Hannah was so glad she had taken the time to listen to him. Hannah knew she would always keep a close check on Mr. Levy.

Hannah did the same with this house, which she had done with the children's nursery. She hired the same carpenter. They went through the house and she told him exactly what she wanted. He would need to take all the walls out only leaving the support beams. All the rotted wood on the outside would need replacing. Hannah wanted big white columns on each end of the front porch and some white, oriental wood placed at the outside ceiling of the front porch. The carpenter told her everything she would need. Hannah knew she wanted six rooms in the house along with two restrooms. She wanted hand-washing sinks in every room except the waiting room. The outside of the house would be painted white with pretty, indigo blue shutters. All the walls inside would be painted white. Hannah carried her list to the building and hardware store. They tallied up her list and gave her a price of twenty five thousand dollars. She paid for the supplies and told them she would call for delivery on the supplies, as she needed them.

Hannah hired a landscaper for the lawns. He charged her only two thousand dollars to dig out all the overgrown foliage do a complete make over on the lawns and put in a paved parking lot. She paid the man and allowed him to decide when he would do each project. She did not want him to do something that the carpenter would mess up getting supplies to the house.

Hannah told the carpenter that she wanted it finished as soon as possible. The carpenter worked from the break of day until it was too dark to see what he was doing. With in three months he had the house finished. Now all he had to do was section off the rooms where Hannah wanted them and finished painting the inside. Hannah showed him where she wanted each room, the rest rooms and the lobby. Within another month, Hannah had her finished building. It was everything she had hoped it would be. It was very stately and beautiful. She paid a visit to her doctor's office. "Dr. Lance I need to speak to your helper," she said.

"What helper?" Dr. Lance said to her.

"The new doctor who was working here when I was here for a visit six months ago," Hannah told him.

"Oh, he is not here any longer. He found a place where he could set up his own practice and he left three months ago," Dr. Lance told her.

"Oh no, I have the perfect place for him to have his practice," Hannah said to the doctor.

"Well you can go and talk to him. He is upstairs over the drug store at the corner of Fifth and Main Street. He still might be interested. I hear the place he has is pretty run down." Hannah thanked the doctor and ran out the door.

She found the drug store and went inside but she saw no stairs going anywhere inside the drug store. She asked the pharmacist about the doctor. "Yes his office is upstairs," he said.

"Can you tell me how you get up there?" Hannah asked.

"Oh I'm sorry, you need to go outside and around the corner and you will see the metal stairs leading up to his office." Hannah thanked him and walked out the drug store and around the building. There it was. She saw some metal stairs coming out of the mess and clutter along with the overgrown weeds and leading to the upstairs where there was a door at the top. She waded through the trash and weeds and climbed the stairs. The door was partially open and it held a sign that said "The office of Dr. Browning." She pushed the door open and stood in a dark dirty room with a few straight chairs were sitting about.

"Hello is anyone there," Hannah said in a moderated tone. Suddenly the same doctor she had seen at Dr. Lance's office walked from the back and into the waiting room. "Yes, I am here. Can I help you?" He asked. Hannah walked right up to him and stuck her hand out to him.

"Yes" she said. "I am Hannah O'Malley and I have built you a building for your practice." The doctor was thoroughly confused. "How did you know I wanted an office?"

"On my last appointment with Dr. Lance, I saw you working with him. I congratulated him on having a helper. He told me that you had recently graduated for Harvard Medical school and wanted to set up your own practice but could not find a suitable place."

"I called Dr. Lance and told him to tell you not to worry about finding a building for your practice that I had found you the perfect one, but I guess he didn't tell you."

Willie Cordell

"No Dr. Lance is a busy doctor and he has stress forgetfulness."

"Dr. Owens, I have you the perfect place to set up your business," Hannah said to him. "Well I don't know. I have built a business here. I know this office is not in the best condition but I attract the poor in the city because of the run down conditions. Sometimes I get paid and sometimes I don't," he said.

"Did you buy this upstairs business?" Hannah asked.

"No I just pay rent every month to the pharmacist. He owns the building." Hannah saw there were no patients in his office. She took his hand.

"Come on with me. You have to see what I have built for you." Reluctantly, the doctor followed Hannah down the stairs. They talked about medicine and the importance of a nice looking place to work and for the patients comfort.

When they reached Hannah's new building, Dr. Browning said, "Wow, this place is beautiful." Hannah led him on a tour through the examination rooms, the lobby, and restrooms. He was overjoyed with the sinks in each examination room. "Maybe some day all American doctors will get the message that they need to wash their hands between each patient to prevent spreading germs. The Spanish doctors have known that and have practiced it you many years. However, most American doctors still pay it no attention.

"How much are you asking for these luxury quarters?" "Well you know it is business property and I want a fair price," Hannah said. "How much do you think it is worth?" Hannah asked.

"I would be happy to pay two hundred thousand dollars for this building," The doctor said to her.

"Then it is yours," Hannah said to the young doctor. "I will need to go to the bank and take out a loan so it may be tomorrow before I know I can get it," he said.

"Take all the time you need." She handed him her address and phone number.

The next morning at eleven o'clock, Doctor Owens called Hannah on the telephone. "I have your money. Can you meet me at the new office in thirty minutes?"

"I will be there in thirty minutes." Soon Hannah had her two hundred thousand dollars in her hands. Now she had retrieved the money that she had when she arrived in New York as well another hundred thousand.

Hannah decided her next project would be a high-rise in the city and would be an apartment building with 1800 square feet in each apartment. The apartments would each have three roomy bedrooms, two baths, a kitchen, and a living/dining room in each apartment.

Hannah's projects were getting more complicated. She had been at the two building sites almost every day when the work was going forward. However, this project was going to be too big for her to devote that much time to it.

After all, she still had two teenagers in school. She talked to Mr. Owens. "I would like you, to hire a crew to work with you on my next project since it will take a long time to finish."

"Where is the building located that you are looking at?" Mr. Owens asked. "I do not have it yet but give me a few days and I will come up with something." After Hannah walked away, Mr. Owens shook his head and said only a woman would get the cart ahead of the horse. He thought it would have made more sense to find the building first, see if she could purchase it and if so, then call him to talk about the building.

However, this time Hannah would not be buying a building. She had passed a large grassy slope of land near downtown. She assumed that no one had built on it since it was not level land. It sloped enough at the rear of the land that building on it would require building the land up at the rear to the level of the front of the land. Nevertheless, she knew leveling the property, could be done. She would just use dirt and have it packed. That was simple enough. Of course, first, she would need a sound foundation, but that, would be completed, when the extra dirt was moved in and packed securely.

Mr. Owens almost fainted when Hannah carried him to the lot that she wanted to buy. He had never taken on a project this large. He was not sure how much help he would need for the project. Hannah did. She had studied her books well and had learned a lot. She told him the different tradesmen he would need to hire but she left the number of carpenters he would need up to him. Mr. Owens gathered his crew of carpenters, plumbers, electricians, architects, landscapers, bricklayers, concrete layers, and drafters. He hired a land moving company with several big trucks to transfer the dirt. Everyone he involved with the building was very grateful. In these hard times, most of them had been having trouble feeding their families and jobs were hard to come by. Mr. Owens knew most all the men he hired. He knew they were good and capable men. He also knew he could depend on them. If they said, they would be at the job site at six in the morning he could count on them being there.

Hannah discovered from the courthouse that the land belonged to a bank in town. Apparently, the bank held the mortgage for the client who later could not make the payments and it fell into foreclosure. The bank was anxious to get rid of the land since they had held it for five years already. They gave her the property for fifty thousand dollars Hannah drew a rough draft as to the way she wanted the apartments and she told him she wanted him to make each one 1800 square feet each. She wanted the building to be six stories tall and approximately one hundred square yards around the outside of the building. "It is going to be a really big building." Mr. Owens said. "Yes and I want it build very sturdy and safe for people to live in for hundreds of years."

"I can do that for you, Ma'm. Mr. Owens told her.

Mr. Owens wasted no time getting his men to work. His crew of nine men was clearing land, moving trees, and putting in drainage ditches. Within two days, the land was cleared, and ready for the dirt to be, moved in. Truck after truckload of dirt, was hauled in and dumped where Mr. Owens had ordered it. Now Mr. Owens ordered the men to spread the dirt out over the low places at the rear of the property. All the workers had shovels, hoes, rakes and some of them used only their hands. Mr. Owens brought a bulky looking heavy machine and he ran the big heavy rollers over the land repeatedly. Sometimes the man had to apply more dirt and he would continue the process of packing the dirt. In less than a week, they were ready to build the foundation.

This time Mr. Owens would go to the supply stores and get what he needed. Hannah had relieved herself of that duty. Now that the initial building process was well under way, Hannah stayed home and cared for her children. She knew she could trust Mr. Owens by now.

Occasionally Hannah and the children would drive by the housing complex to see how it was coming along. Hannah was pleased to see it was moving along very well. She felt very good about the progress.

Six months later Mr. Owens called Hannah. "We have your apartment building finished. Come and see what you think. When Hannah saw her new building, she was breathless. It was truly a very big building, but it still had a home look to it. It was white with the same white columns she had placed at the doctor's office and it had black shingles on each side of every window. The landscaping was stunningly beautiful. It had a brick walkway walking to the front door and the back of the house had a huge brick patio with a beautiful white pergola. Comfortable lawn chairs and tables were, arranged on the patio. It had a black wrought iron fence going all the way around the house on the property line.

Within another three months, families who could afford the $30,000 that Hannah was charging for them bought all seventy apartments. After paying all the expenses for the property and paying the contractor, landscapers, and brick mason, Hannah and cleared more than half a million dollars.

Mr. Owens kept his crew together since he knew Hannah would have another one ready for them to start when this one was finished and she did. She wanted to build a bank. She found the perfect site down town. An old general store was there. The older individuals who owned it were more than happy to sell it to Hannah for the hefty price she offered them for it.

Within a year, a big beautiful thirty-story high-rise sat where once the mom and pop grocery had sat. Hannah sold it to the biggest banking company in New York City. They made the bank they had been in a branch and they moved all their belongings and most of the money to the big high rise. The banker loved it and paid her three million dollars for it.

Now Hannah was on her way to totally independence. No more money worries for her. Her kids could go to Harvard, Yale, or any place they wanted to. Their grades through high school were good enough that they had their choice. Hannah loved saying to the children, "Remember this, when the going gets tough, the tough get going."

Now the children were all grown up and had families of their own. Grandma doted on her granddaughter and grandson. Both her children had chosen to go to Harvard. Her daughter was a pediatric doctor and her son was a corporate lawyer. They each had married wonderful young adults. Hannah loved them as if they were her own.

Hannah kept her construction projects going and sometimes she had as many as three projects going at the same time. As long as she had Mr. Owens, she did not have a thing to worry about. She would find the site and decide what she wanted there and that was about all she did anymore. Mr. Owens was a fine and capable man and he had built himself an empire as well as becoming the contractor everyone tried to get. Hannah kept him too busy for that. Moreover, he was happy about it.

Hannah enjoyed the building business. After turning most of the business over to her contractor, she had more time to look for interesting building sites. Before the big beautiful bank was finished, Hannah had several banks vying for the new building. She was able to ask top price for the building with the many banks making increased offers in hopes of securing the building for themselves. She repeated her procedure for acquiring new sites for buildings and then decided the business that needed to be on the site. She built everything from auto dealerships to more high rises where she placed department stores and financial firms.

By the time the children were in college, Hannah had more money than they would ever need for their tuition fees, books, and food at the school cafeteria. Any other money they would need they would need to earn through a part-time job. They were both good, considerate children and she intended to keep it that way.

When Hannah's son graduated from Law School, she built him the biggest high rise in New York City. Of course, she put him on a payment plan and he would pay all the money back. When her daughter graduated from medical school Hannah built her office similar to the one she had built before. However, Lisa added her own touches to this building. She also would pay her mother back with set payments every month.

Martha and Ellen enjoyed hearing about Hannah's life. She had had an interesting life. Hannah did not tell them how she had fought for women's suffrage and the rights of women throughout the years. She felt that Martha and Ellen might think it a little radical.

Hannah stayed a week with Martha and Ellen. She called her driver to pick her up the following Thursday morning. As she was leaving, she slipped something in Martha's apron pocket.

She hugged Martha and Ellen good by and told them at any time they felt they could come to visit her, "Please call me and I will send a driver or plane tickets for you." Martha thanked her but deep down she doubted they would ever be able to make the trip.

As the sisters walked, back inside the house Martha slipped her hand in her pocked and pulled the folded paper out that she found there. When Martha finished counting it, she discovered that Hannah had left them five thousand dollars. Now Martha could pay the taxes on the house. Martha sent a thank you note to Hannah. She told her how good it was now that the burden of her back due taxes was behind her.

When Hannah returned home, she had a strange request waiting for her. Mr. Owens called her on the telephone. "Miss. Hannah, do you remember the new building we developed for the car dealership owner?"

"Yes, I remember him...let me think, his name was Mr. Bennett, if I recall correctly," Hannah said.

"Yes he is the one. He had been calling almost daily since you have been gone. He wants us to build him a house and he wants it built near Savannah, Georgia."

"Did you tell him we only build commercial buildings?"

"I have Miss. Hannah, but he refuses to accept that. He says this is going to be a special house and no one but you can build it."

"Sorry but we do not build single-family dwellings. I guess you will have to try somehow to convince him." Hannah could tell that Mr. Owens was frustrated as he walked away.

Hannah took her bags to her bedroom and started unpacking. She lovingly pulled out her black dress. She loved this dress. She thought of the happy memories the dress gave to her as she held it close to her chest. She had danced the night away with her dear husband while they had vacationed in Hawaii one summer. Oh!...if I could only bring back those days! However, that was then, this is now, and I have to live in the present, Hannah thought as she put the dress away. She was happy that she could still wear it after all these years. Just as she turned back to the suitcase, the phone rang again. Hannah picked up the phone from the table by the bed. "Miss. Hannah, this is Buck Bennett. I am the one for whom you built the car dealership. Do you remember me?"

"Yes, Mr. Bennett, I remember you."

"Well, I have a favor to ask of you."

"Mr. Bennett, if it is about building a single family dwelling, I'm sorry but I can't help you."

"Please don't turn me down until you have heard the whole story." Mr. Bennett pleaded.

"Mr. Bennett, you can tell me the whole story but I am afraid my answer is still going to be no." Hannah could hear the excitement in Buck Bennett's voice as he heard her answer. "I want the house to have 3000 square feet of living space and I want it built to your design. I want it to look like a mansion. There is no dollar restriction. I want my house to have the best of everything, inside and out."

"You must have a very large family, Mr. Bennett," Hannah told him.

"Not really. It is only my wife and me and our two children. We only want this house for a sort of get away place. I own another dealership in Savannah, Georgia and this will give us a place to stay when the family is here. Mind you, they are not here often but they will enjoy it when they are here. I want a swimming pool and tennis court in the back yard." Hannah couldn't put her finger on it but something did not seem right about the way Mr. Bennett kept going to extreme with trying to explain who and when someone would be staying in the house. To Hannah it was trivial about whom, and when they would stay in the house but Mr. Bennett seemed to, over explains, that particular part of it.

Hannah and Mr. Owens decided they would drive to Savannah on Thursday to see the property where Mr. Bennett wanted his new house. They would meet Mr. Bennett at the boardwalk down by the battery.

Mr. Bennett walked the boardwalk and chewed his cigar in anticipation of Hannah and Mr. Owens arrival. He would still need to convince them to take the job. He stepped into a phone booth on the boardwalk and picked up the phone. He placed his dime into the slot and dialed a local number. "Hello Darling, They're on their way."

"Oh, I'm so glad. I hope they will agree to sign a contract and build our house."

"How are things going at the office?" Mr. Bennett asked.

"It's going fine except just lonely without you here. I miss you."

"Sweetie you just saw me fifteen minutes ago."

"I know, but I am always lonely without you."

Mr. Bennett saw Hannah and Mr. Owens walking toward him on the boardwalk. He hung up the phone and started toward them. "Thank you for coming," Mr. Bennett said to Hannah as he shook her hand and then Mr. Owens hand. "We can go to the building site in my car, if you'll just follow me." Hannah and Mr. Owens turned around and followed Mr. Bennett down the street to his big new shinny car.

"This is a pretty car." Mr. Owens said.

"It is the latest version of the new Chevrolet. It has a new feature this year. It has power everything. Man, this is the car of the future." Mr. Bennett said as he opened the rear door and looked at Hannah. Hannah stepped into the back and sat down. Mr. Owens opened the front passenger door and got into the car. Mr. Bennett wedged his heavy body in the driver's seat. Mr. Owens felt uncomfortable with the seating arrangement. However, neither he nor Hannah had a choice. Hannah always rode in the front seat. Hannah did not mind sitting in the back seat. Apparently, everyone always thought she preferred the front seat but she never really had.

They chatted about the new house and Mr. Bennett asked Hannah if she had made up her mind yet. "Let's wait and see the building site, then we will discuss it. I can tell you now that you're going to like it. The new house will sit in the middle of three hundred acres and I own all three hundred acres."

After riding twenty-five miles, Hannah asked, "How far away from Savannah is this property?"

"It's only fifty miles. I am building in Bullock County. I want to get away from the hustle and bustle of the city."

"You wanted to get fifty miles away?" Hannah asked.

"Yes, sometimes you just need privacy with peace and quite. Hannah thought about what he had said and thought to herself, why would you need fifty miles away for peace and quite.

However, when they finally arrived she had no doubt that he was serious about his privacy, peace and quite. They had traveled for miles and miles on a paved road, then they turned down a dirt road where they traveled many more miles before they turned into a narrow trail that went two or three miles deep into the woods. Hannah could not believe what she was actually seeing. Finally, Mr. Bennett stopped at a clearing. "Here is where I want my mansion."

Hannah got out of the car and walked around the plot. "Why on earth would anyone want to build a mansion, or even a log cabin, way out here?" she asked.

"Remember, I told you I wanted privacy, peace and quite."

"Mr. Bennett it will be extremely expensive to build anything way out here."

"I don't care how much it cost. I have the money and this house is very important to me."

"You are probably right about the three million dollars even though I know you said it in jest."

"I did not say it in jest. I imagined it would cost at least three million." Mr. Bennett said.

"But Mr. Bennett, you'll never get that much money out of the house with it way out here," Hannah said.

"Don't worry about that. I never intend to sell it."

"Now, will you build my house?" Mr. Bennett asked.

"I will build it but before we can even start on it you will need to build a road to the building site. We'll never get building equipment down that narrow little lane," Hannah told him.

"I will have the road built by Monday."

"Never happen, it's Thursday you know," Mr. Owens said.

"I promise you there will be a road back here on Monday," Mr. Bennett said.

When Hannah and Mr. Owens returned to New York City Hannah told Mr. Owens he could go ahead and start making plans to build the house. "However you can take your time since it will take weeks for Mr. Bennett to get the road built."

On Monday morning, Mr. Owens arrived at his office. He was carrying a stack of papers and a cup of hot coffee. While he struggled to unlock the door with his key and hold everything together, the office phone started ringing. He finally, managed to get the door unlocked. Mr. Owens rushed to his desk. He put the papers and cup of coffee there and while answering the phone he accidentally spilled the coffee all over the desk. He grabbed the phone and yelled into it, "Hello."

"Sorry, do you want me to hang up and call back later?" Mr. Owens caught the voice, and while he watched, the coffee slowly as it creeps over his important papers. He said, "No, Mr. Bennett, I am just having a difficult morning. Sorry I yelled. I did not mean to do that." For some reason Mr. Owens did not like Buck Bennett. He could not put a finger on it but something about the man put a sour taste in his mouth. Happy and cheerfully Mr. Bennett announced, "The road is ready."

"What road?" Mr. Owens asked.

"What do you mean? The road to my building site for my new house, of course."

"You have the road widened already?" Mr. Owens asked.

"Yes, it is now twenty feet wide. Do you suppose that is wide enough?"

"Yes, twenty feet is plenty wide enough. How did you get it finished so soon?" Mr. Owens asked.

"I took three crews with equipment out there. I had one crew start at the entrance to the lane and a second crew started half way to the house. The third crew started at the building site. They had big lights shinning at night and the three crews worked around the clock until it was finished yesterday evening."

"That must have cost a mint," Mr. Owens said.

"I promised Miss. Hannah I would have it ready by Monday morning and when I make a promise I always keep it."

"Now are you guys going to be as prompt on building my house as I have been on building your road?" Mr. Bennett asked.

"Yes, we will start on your house this week but I do not promise to be as fast as your road builders were." When Mr. Owens told Hannah about the phone call, she almost fainted. "That is impossible. How on earth did he do it?" "He said he hired several different road crews."

Hannah caught the next plane leaving New York for Savannah. She hired a cab to transport her during the time she would be in Savannah. She first went to Mr. Bennett's new dealership. Hannah had all the legal papers needed for the contract Mr. Bennett would need to sign. When she walked into the beautiful building Hannah was lead to Mr. Bennett's office by a beautiful, buxom woman wearing lots of jewelry and makeup. She appeared to be twenty-five years old with a warm personality.

"Mr. Bennett, I think this is the nice lady you have been expecting."

Mr. Bennett jumped to his feet and twisted around his desk. "Yes, Yes, Yes Mrs. Hannah. Welcome to my office." "I hope the papers you are holding are my contract and the plans to the new house."

"Yes but you need to read over them before you sign them. Maybe I will leave them here with you while I go for a bite of lunch and I will come back and you can sign them if you want to."

"What do you mean, if I want to, of course I want to sign them?"

"You will still need to read them." Hannah said as she walked out the door.

Buck Bennett and the beautiful young lady took the papers to a quiet conference room and laid them out on the table. "Here it is, darling; here are the plans for your house." Kelly Keen walked to the end of the table where her lover was standing. She looked in awe at the plans for her new home. The plan had three stories, with the bottom floor showing as a very large basement. The plan was exactly what Kelly had wanted. When Buck looked at the price on the contract, it showed three million and twenty five thousand dollars. He did not read any more of the contract. Kelly gave him a big hug and told him how much she loved him and how good it would be to make love to him in their own, beautiful home. He signed it and had it ready and waiting for Hannah when she returned.

After lunch Hannah, ask her driver to drive her around the beautiful old city. It was a delight seeing all the old buildings and houses with the picket fences. The owners were all, probably, wealthy plantation owners in the early years. Hannah thought.

When Hannah returned to Buck Bennett's Automobile Dealership she was met again by the beautiful, well-jeweled young lady. This time she was even more gracious with her southern accent. She led Hannah to her boss. "Did you read the contract?" Hannah asked Mr. Bennett.

"Sure did, read every line and already got it signed."

"You signed it?" Hannah asked. "Yes I did, all it needs now is your signature, and it's ready to go."

"Mr. Bennett we need to sign the contract before a notary public. The contract has to be notarized to make it legal," Hannah said.

"Oh, I'm sorry, I didn't know that. However, don't worry I have a notary right here at my business. I will get him to notarize it,." Hannah was not happy with his business practices but she allowed him to get his own notary. The notary asked Mr. Bennett to take a pen and go back over his name without touching the paper while he watched. Hannah signed her name and the notary notarized the contract.

Hannah caught her plane on time and arrived in New York City by three p.m. She called Mr. Owens and told him the contract is, signed and he could plan to start work on Wednesday. She told him she had contracted for apartments where the carpenters would stay while they were there and she had rented him a house so that he could take his family if he liked. Hannah had also arranged for rented automobiles for him and all his workers while they were in Savannah. "You and the crew can fly home every weekend if you like or you can choose to work week ends too and finish the job that much sooner, if you like.

Mr. Owens met with his workers. He told them about the plans for building a big house in the woods fifty miles out of Savannah, Georgia. Faces in the crowd appeared to drop. However, when Mr. Owens told them the amount of money they would earn to do the job the frowning faces suddenly turned to big smiles. "We will make the same amount of money if we drag the job out and fly home every weekend or we can hurry it up and work seven days a week on the project. One way or the other we will get paid the same thing."

The group in unison said, "Let's work seven days a week."

Mr. Owens spent most of the remainder of the week getting his heavy equipment to the site by train. Some of the men helped him with the transfer while the others left to find their apartments. Hannah had told them that she had gotten their apartments in Statesboro, Georgia. Statesboro was a small town but it was large enough that one could find about anything they needed there and the building site was only ten miles from Statesboro. The carpenters picked up their rented cars in Savannah and drove to the small town where they located their apartments Hannah had leased for them.

The carpenters were on the site Wednesday morning cleaning and clearing foliage from the building site. By Monday all the heavy equipment and the entire crew was on the job. They had no problems getting the equipment they needed over the new road.

The entire crew worked harder than they had ever worked. They knew they were making good money and the sooner they got the house finished the quicker they could move on to something else where they would earn more money. Of course, they would be paid by the hour when they went back to work for Mr. Owens in New York. This was the first time they earned a lump of money for their work.

Almost six months to the day after they started the job, they were finished. Hannah sent in a landscaping company to landscape the grounds around the house. When it was all finished with a swimming pool in back and a bowling alley in the basement Hannah flew from New York to Savannah to look at the finished house. It was truly beautiful inside, and outside. It fact, with all the places Hannah had built this was by far the most beautiful. Mr. Bennett was so proud of his new house. He also thought it was the prettiest home he had ever seen. Now all he would need to do is close the road off coming to the house and make it into a lane again. He did not want anyone to notice it was there. He would replant the trees they had taken down while clearing the land to build the road.

No one was happier about the new house than Kelly Keen was. She moved in the day the builders left. "Darling, now that I have such a big house to take care of I might need to quit my job," she said to Buck.

"Do you think I can stay at the company all day without you being there?" Kelly walked to the chair where he was sitting. She sat on his lap and played with his face with her fingertips.

"Maybe you need to stay home too," she said.

"I think I will be doing lots of that from here on out."

After two weeks, Buck Bennett had to leave for New York again. "I'm sorry darling, but I need to check on my business there and I have to make a showing at home. I will be back in a few days. I can't stay away from you very long."

Buck Bennett's dealership had carried a car for him to Heathrow airport. He reached under the floor mat and got the key, slipped it in the ignition, turned the car on and drove directly to his home. He walked in the door and yelled, "I'm home." His two children age six and eight came running to the door. They grabbed their dad in a big bear hug. Each little girl was saying together, "Papa I love you." Margie came from the kitchen taking her apron off. She went into her husband's arms. Now, she felt complete again. "You have been gone longer this time and I have missed you terribly." She said. "I know Love, I missed you too. I tried to get home several times but something always came up that demanded my attention and I was not able to get away until now."

Margie planned a picnic for the next day. She packed a picnic basket with all Buck's favorite foods. She drove several miles to find his favorite wine but she loved him so much she wanted everything to be just right.

The girls hopped out of bed early the next morning. They had their straw hats and were ready to go on the picnic. Margie chose a place down by the river where there was also a beautiful meadow. The girls brought their butterfly nets and fishing polls. Buck Bennett helped the girls catch butterflies and fish in the river. "Oh Papa, look, I have a big one." Little Mandy said as she held up her small fish. Her dad gave her a hug and told her how proud he was of her. Mom spread a party tablecloth on the grass. She sliced the cheeses and fresh fruits she had brought. She poured punch for the girls and a stemmed glass of wine for herself and her husband.

When the family arrived home late that afternoon Margie had dreams of getting the kids to bed early and having a private quiet evening with her husband. "I have to run to the company for a little while," Buck said as he started back out the door. 'Oh Buck, I had wonderful romantic plans for us tonight," Margie told him. "Sorry, but I need to go. I will be back as soon as possible."

"Please hurry back. I miss you and I would love to spend some alone time with you."

"I will, see you soon," Buck Bennett said to his wife and he was out the door. When he arrived at his automobile dealership all his employees were just leaving. "Hey, you come and we go," one of his sales representatives said to him.

"How are things going?" Buck asked his business manager as he walked out the door. "Couldn't be better Mr. Bennett, we've already doubled what we made all of last year."

"That sounds good," Buck said as his manager walked on toward his car. Suddenly he turned and said, "Oh, Mr. Bennett---You had a caller who must have called a dozen times today trying to find you." Thank God, he had enough sense not to give out my house phone, Buck thought to himself. However, Buck knew who it was and he was certain that his manager also knew who it probably was. They covered for each other like that. Buck locked the door when everyone was out of the building. He went to a desk and picked up the phone. "Hello Darling, have you missed me?" Buck Bennett said into the phone.

"Where have you been? I have been trying to get you all day long," Kelly said into the phone.

"I spent the day with my family, Kelly. You knew I had to do that."

"You could have gotten away long enough to call me."

"Let's not argue since we don't have that much time to talk. What were you trying to get me for?" Buck asked.

"I just wanted to tell you that I love you and I miss you. The house is not the same without you." Kelly set out on a spree of all her and the business activities throughout the last two days. Buck knew she was doing it just to hold him on the phone. He felt pulled. He truly loved Kelly but he also loved his wife. His wife would be devastated if she knew about Kelly. Kelly was extremely jealous of his wife.

"You didn't sleep with her last night, did you?"

"Kelly lets not discuss that, I love you. Isn't that what is important?"

"No, I want you back here. You need to leave there tomorrow."

"I can't do that, I have to spend some time here at the business before I leave."

"Why didn't you spend today there, if you needed to spend time at the business?"

"Kelly I went with my children on a picnic. They fished and caught butterflies. They enjoyed that and they needed my time with them."

"Was she there too?" Kelly asked.

"I need to get off the phone. We have been on here more than an hour," Buck said.

"Let me tell you this and then you can go." Kelly said. She began another long uninteresting conversation. She went on and on, leaving Buck to answer only yes or no but no room to get a sentence in.

When Buck returned home three hours later he found his wife curled up in a chair fast asleep. There were candles in candleholders about the room providing a warm glow over the room. Margie was wearing a beautiful gown and negligee. One pretty little puffed high heel house shoe had fallen onto the floor the other one was half on her foot. Buck felt a tinge of guilt build inside him. Buck carefully picked his wife up and carried her to bed. As he was placing her on the bed, she opened her eyes sleepily and smiled up at him. He had never felt so much love for Margie as he felt at that moment. What have I done to myself and what have I done to her? Buck thought to himself as he walked quietly from the bedroom.

On Wednesday, Buck tried to spend some time with Margie, but before the day was half over, one of the sales representatives from the business called him on the telephone. "Mr. Bennett you need to call your Savannah Business. They say it is urgent." The news frightened Buck and before he had time to think about it he picked up the phone and dialed the business.

"I need to speak to my manager, please." Buck said to the secretary who answered the phone. "Hello." The manager said in the phone. "This is Buck Bennett, what did you need me for?" "I don't need you Mr. Bennett. Why do you ask?" Suddenly it hit Buck. It was Kelly and her conniving way to talk to him. Marge stood right beside him, looking into his face. She was also worried that something was wrong. "I'm sorry Don, I must have misunderstood," Buck said, in hopes that he could get off the phone before Kelly found out he was on the phone line. "Buck you should have talked to someone else. Maybe something has happened and word has not gotten to the manager yet. "I don't think so, Marge. He would know if anything was wrong." Buck hung up the phone relieved that it was going to be that simple. However, his confidence did not last. As Buck, Margie and the two girls were having dinner together the telephone rang. Margie was nearest to the phone and she said, "I will get it." as she got up from the table. Margie promptly returned to the table. "It is a girl and she is demanding to speak with you. I tried to tell her you were having dinner but she requested that I get you anyway."

Buck got up from the table with three things going through his mind, please don't follow me to the phone and what can I say to her to keep her from calling back and how the hell did she get this number? Luckily, Marge did not follow him to the phone. "Why in hell are you calling me here and who gave you this number?"

"Hold on a minute darling, this is your sweetheart, remember."

"Kelly you can not call me on this number any more. Do you understand?"

"Either you will come home to me, tomorrow or I will call every hour on the hour." Buck had to do some quick thinking. He knew he had no choice since Kelly would keep her promise if he did not go back to Savannah tomorrow. "Okay, I will see you tomorrow." Buck said as he hung up the phone. "You were right Love, it was an emergency from the bookkeeping department, and Don didn't know about it. I am afraid I will have to go back to Savannah tomorrow to get it straightened out."

"Oh Darling, I so hoped you would stay the entire two weeks, like you promised us."

"I wish I could too but this is important. It is in reference to a possible law suite against us. We would win if it should go to court but I need to try and get it straightened out before it comes to that."

Margie believed her husband and she felt so sorry for him. His plans were ruined.

Early the next morning, Margie stood at the front door with her daughters saying good-by, to her husband while she reassured her children, "It is not Papa's fault. He has to go back to Savannah to take care of some business. He wants to stay as much as we want him to stay."

All the way back to Savannah on the plane, Buck thought about the mess he had gotten himself, into. He turned his options over in his mind. Maybe, he could get rid of Kelly. He knew the only possible way to do that was to hire a hit man. He had lots of guts but not enough to kill someone. Divorcing Marge was out of the question. He still loved her and more than anything, divorcing Marge would mean divorcing the children too. He would never let that happen. Buck had made up his mind when he got to Savannah. He was going to put into action some kind of plan to break it off with Kelly.

When he arrived at the business, Kelly was waiting. Apparently, she had decided not to try to hide their relationship any longer. When Buck walked in the door, Kelly threw herself onto him. She tried to kiss him in front of several employees. All of them knew he was a married man. How embarrassing! He tried to push her away without being conspicuous, but she kept coming back. The gossip started immediately.

That night at the new house, Buck tried to keep himself busy and away from Kelly. She took off all her clothes and put on a little white apron with a ruffle around it and a bib at the top surrounded with ruffles. Buck was in the garage working at the workbench. In her high heel shoes and apron, she appeared in the doorway holding a glass of his favorite wine with some French bon-bons. "I have been saving these until you got home, Darling." She sat on the top step of the descending short stairwell. She put a bon-bon in her mouth leaving half of it protruding from her mouth. She slowly inched closer to him while he continued working. He tried to pay no attention to her. She was wearing the perfume that always made him wild. Soon she was in his face and trying to force half of the bon-bon she was still holding in her mouth, into his mouth. Before Buck realized it, he was joining her in her little game. Slowly things got back to the place they had been before he left for New York. Kelly was on top of the world and she tried in every way to make Buck feel the same way. Buck knew he still loved her but he also knew it was a dangerous love and he knew that Kelly would go to any extreme to keep him. No matter what happened, the one thing that Buck could not allow. He could not allow his wife to find out about Kelly. It would not just break her heart, it would shatter her heart into millions of pieces, and that was something he could not live with.

Buck found himself a prisoner in Kelly's world. She was always with him. "Do you remember when you said, with a house the size of this one you might need to stay home to care for it? I think that is a good idea. I think you would enjoy staying here. You can clean, decorate, swim or just do nothing if you feel like it," Buck told Kelly.

"No, Darling, I can keep the house and work at the business also. You need me there." Kelly said to him. Kelly never tried to hide her affection for Buck in front of any of the staff at work. The staff knew Buck felt uncomfortable about it but that only made the gossip more interesting. There was an unsaid rule. If a call came in from New York and it was not from the business there, the staff was not to talk to the caller. Only Buck or Don would take the call. The only problem with that was that Kelly did not know the rule. Don threatened the secretaries with their jobs if they put any calls through to Kelly unless it was cleared by Don or Buck first. Kelly worked in bookkeeping and her job did not include answering the phone.

Buck put on a big front. He showed Kelly more attention than ever. He had to keep her confidence up for fear that she might pick up the phone and call Margie herself since he had the phone number now. When Buck was alone in the house for the brief moments that he was he franticly looked for his home phone number in New York. He was sure she had it so secure by now that Scotland Yard would not find it. This worry was causing entirely too much stress on him. He would need to figure out a way to get rid of that worry.

The next morning, Buck got out of bed very early. He quietly got his shower, got dressed, and was out the door before Kelly woke up. He hurried the fifty miles to Savannah and to the business. He let himself in and went straight to the phone. He heard the phone ringing on the other end. It seemed that no one was home. Maybe Marge had carried the girls to school. Suddenly, a sleepy voice said, "Hello," "Oh, I was so afraid you weren't home." "Buck it is seven o'clock in the morning." "We were still sleeping. Is anything wrong?" Marge asked. "Yes, darling, there is something wrong." "You know I told you about the lawsuit someone is trying to file against us."

"Yes, I remember."

"Well, these people who are trying to file the law suite are real rednecks. I do not think they have a conscious. They are threatening everything. Somehow, they got your phone number and now they are threatening to start calling you and "giving you hell too. I do not want you exposed to this by these hoodlums. I want you to change our telephone number as soon as possible. Do not even call the new number to me on the phone. Write me a letter and place it in there. We cannot allow these people to start calling you. They will frighten you and the girls and they will enjoy doing it."

Margie did as Buck had told her. She went to the phone company the next day and had her number changed. She sent the new number in a letter where she also told him how proud she was of him trying to protect her and

the girls and how much she appreciated him. That was his Margie. She was
never a pessimist and always an optimist. She was so innocent. She trusted
and believed everyone. Something Kelly would never be capable of doing.

Thank God, that stress was over. Buck would never tell his colleague
anything about the number change. He just let it go. However, he had the
assurance that if Miss Kelly attempted to call his wife because she got angry
with him it would not work. That brought Buck great comfort. No one would
ever know his wife's new number. Not even the managers of his businesses.

Buck missed his family and although he loved Kelly and enjoyed being
with her he would much rather be with his wife and children. His mother
had a saying that she used to tell them when she thought they were making an
unwise decision. "Son you make your bed hard and you must lie in it." Buck
knew he had made his bed hard but sometimes lying in it was very hard.

Life dragged on. He had excellent managers at both his businesses and
his businesses were always doing very well. He was rarely, needed at either
business. Every chance he got he ran home to New York but it was for no
more that a day or two. Kelly saw to that.

It did not matter to Margie. Just as long as she could see him enough
to know that, he was healthy and happy. However, Margie began getting
concerned when Buck showed signs of depression. She tried to talk to him
about it but he told her he was only tired and needed some rest. She tried
to talk him into the four of them going on a vacation together and leaving
everything behind for a week. Oh, how he would love to do that but he
knew it was very impossible. Kelly would track them down and show up if
possible.

Buck went to elaborate parties with Kelly. He never felt comfortable at
parties like that. There would be many young men there much younger than
he and a much more suitable match for Kelly than he was, but she would not
even dance with them even though they asked her repeatedly. "No, thank
you, I am taken, and she would hold to Bucks arm the entire night.

Buck had a light bulb moment one day. Maybe he could solve his
relationship with Kelly in a different way. "Don, I want you to find the
most handsome young bachelor in this town and I want you to offer him an
astronomical salary to work for Buck Bennett Chevrolet. Do you think you
can do that?"

"I can try but why on earth do you want to do that Mr. Bennett." "Just
find him and then I will tell you why." Buck Bennett said to him. Don was
at a total loss. Where would he find a prosperous handsome young man and
how would he hire him out from under his employer? Don went home that
evening and told his wife of his assignment. "Do you think you have some
friends who might be able to help us?"

"I don't know but I will see what I can do," Don's wife told him.

It took her a week to come up with someone but Don's wife thought she had the perfect one for Buck. "Don, he is young, handsome and he is a wealthy lawyer." When Don told Buck what his wife had found, Buck leaped with joy. "You have to find out what he is making in his law practice now and what ever it is we have to go over that amount. You can tell him that we need our own full time lawyer here at the business. We will section him off an area for his desk in the bookkeeping department. He can work closely with the bookkeepers."

"Oh, I get you now. You are trying to find Kelly a man, right?"

"Right," Buck said. "Well, good luck."

Buck carried the new hire around the business introducing him to the staff. He saved the bookkeeping department until last. Buck walked into the bookkeeping department with a big smile on his face. "Ladies, I would like you to meet your new coworker. Brad is an attorney and he will be working strictly for our company from now on. Please make him welcome and Ms. Kelly if you will show him around so he can get a feel of the place, I will leave him with you.

"What do we need with a lawyer?" Kelly asked in a not very pleasant tone. "Ms. Kelly we are growing every day and all large companies need a good lawyer."

"Well, I don't see why." Kelly said as she grudgingly got up from her desk. Any of the other girls sitting there would have been more than happy to do the tour with the fine looking lawyer but not Kelly. Buck took Brad with him every place he went. Sometimes Kelly was along and it irked her to sit in the back seat while this haughty lawyer sat up front with her lover. Buck asked Kelly if they could have a company party at the house.

"And let everyone know where we live. I thought we did not want any of them to know where we lived," Kelly said.

"Yes, that was the plan until you ruined it by showing romantic affection to me in front of them all. Now they know we are together so it doesn't matter any more." Against her wishes, Kelly finally agreed to the company party. She had to have a house cleaner come in and clean the house and she wanted professional food chefs preparing food and serving it at the party. Buck went out and found people who were suitable for her desires.

Food and alcoholic drinks flowed at the party. Buck kept watching Kelly. The more she drank the more she opened up to Brad. Buck hoped this was the beginning of something good. When the party was over and everyone was gone, it was obvious that Kelly was a little tipsy.

"I don't like your lawyer friend, Buck. I wish you would fire him."

"Why do you not like him and why do you want him gone?"

"He is a, nobody; did you know he still lives in an apartment?"

"Kelly he is a single man, why would he want the responsibility of a house to keep up all by himself?"

One day, Buck and Brad were having lunch together, Buck said. "Brad, how long have you been out of law school?"

"Only six months," Brad said.

"Are you paying back student loans?" Buck asked.

"Am I ever, I have bushel baskets of them."

"How would you like those student loans to go away so you could have all the money you earn to have a good life?"

"Mr. Bennett, there is nothing I would like better."

"I have a plan. I am going to tell it to you and if you don't like the idea just say so and we won't discuss it again." Brad sat across the table from his boss. He could not imagine what he was about to say.

"How do you feel about Miss. Kelly Keen? I think she is a little younger than you, but do you like her?"

"Yes, Mr. Bennett, I like Kelly very much but she won't give me the time of day. I have tried to talk to her just as friends and she will not even do that. I think she really doesn't like me."

"Tell you what Brad, I will give you three months to see if you can make her come around and start dating you and if you can do that I will pay off all your college debt and it will be above and beyond your salary at the company. You will never have to pay me back. There was total quietness for a while.

"Mr. Bennett you are telling me that if I can get a date with Kelly Keen that you will pay my college debt back for me."

"That's what I am telling you." No one but God knew the joy and happiness that was going through Brad at that time. He would do anything to get that damn debt paid off. It would take him at least fifteen years to pay it off the way it was going now.

"Mr. Bennett, you have a deal. How long do I need to date her?

Well, you will get the money if you are able to get her interested in you enough that she will go on one date but I would be happy if you dated her at least six months. Maybe the two of you would fall in love and we would get to hear wedding bells." Brad had a feeling that is what Mr. Bennett wanted most but he did not know if he could make that happen.

The days went by. Mr. Bennett did not talk to Brad again about their little deal. Everyday, Kelly came home and just as the day, before she complained about the lawyer "trying to be friendly and I don't even like him." Buck said nothing. He pretended not to notice when she complained. Life went on in the household as it had before. However, it got harder and harder to go to

New York even for a short visit with his family. Margie wrote several times a week and always told him how much she missed him and loved him.

One day Kelly came home and said, "I guess I am going to have to go to dinner with that damn lawyer just to get him off my back."

"That sounds fun."

"I can't believe you don't care that I go out with another man."

"Kelly this life is short. We never know when our number is coming up to go to the big house up there. We had all better live life to the most before that day comes."

That is when Kelly started dating Brad. Finally, she did not complain about it anymore and soon she was looking forward to their dates. Buck was counting the days until he would have his family back. Things were defiantly looking up.

When they had been dating six months Brad ask Buck if they could have lunch together today. "Yes, we will meet at the club down town if you like," Buck, said to him.

When they arrived at the club and had ordered their food Brad said, "Mr. Bennett, I have been dating Kelly for six months. I love her very much and I believe she loves me the same but she is not going to marry me. She is a money grabber and she is going to be with whoever had the biggest bank roll."

"Love does not matter to her that much, it's just the money. She is the money hungriest girl I have ever seen. She tells me that she would always rather have a "sugar daddy.""

"I am sorry Brad. I have your tuition money here to pay off your student loans and I appreciate what you have done for me." "I just ask one more thing, that you hang in there and see if maybe someday she might change her mind."

Two years from the few days the family had had the picnic by the river, Buck was sitting at his desk in his office. An employee walked by and saw him with his head on his desk. That was unusual for Mr. Bennett. He never took naps at his desk. She walked into his office and spoke to him. He did not answer. She went down the hall and got Don. "He has his head on his desk and I can't wake him up." Don hurried in. He pulled Buck up to a sitting position. His face was snow white and around his mouth was blue. They immediately called for an ambulance. Don and Brad followed behind the ambulance. When Buck arrived at the hospital and the doctor checked him over, he came to the waiting room and told his friends that Mr. Bennett had expired. "It could have been a sudden heart attack or it could have been a brain stem stroke, but there was nothing we could do for him. He arrived here with no heartbeat and no respirations and we were unable to get it started again. When Don and Brad arrived back at the business, everyone seemed saddened. They had already heard that Mr. Bennett did not make it. In a cheerful tone, Kelly announced that she was going home to make arrangements. As she walked out the door, the staff looked at each other. "Make arrangements, doesn't she know he has a wife and a family."

Don called the New York business and somehow got the phone number to Buck's house. "Mrs. Bennett, I am so sorry but Mr. Bennett has just passed away. We found him slumped over at his desk. When we could not wake him, we call an ambulance. They carried him to the hospital and he was, pronounced dead on arrival. They said it could have been a stroke or a heart attack and either of them would have been fatal the minute it hit. I don't think Mr. Bennett suffered any pain." Margie wept openly on the phone. My love, my life is gone, she kept repeating.

"Do you want us to fly his body back to New York to a funeral home there?"

"Yes," she said through sobs. "Send my love home to me."

It was a sad time for Margie and the children. They had missed so much time with their dad. They would always remember the picnic and the fun time they had with Papa.

Kelly was back at the big house, happily deciding now that Buck was no longer there how she would rearrange the furniture and pictures the way she had really wanted them in the beginning. However, she felt that Buck wanted them placed where they were and she did not want to disappoint him.

After the worse of the grieving process was over for Margie and the girls, Margie knew they needed to get a lawyer and go through Buck's financial situation. The funeral had been expensive. She hoped there would be enough funds to pay for it. The lawyer she hired met her at her house. She told him all she knew about any assets he may have.
The lawyer told her that he would check into all of it and get back with her in a few days.

The lawyer returned four day later. Margie asked him in and offered him a cup of tea. Margie shooed the children to their bedrooms because, "Mama and the lawyer are going to have an adult conversation." Margie knew all of this would be too confusing for them to hear especially if their father was far into debt and they had no money to live on. Margie had always been as careful with the money as she could be. She never spent frivolously and did not ask for or expect fine things.

"Mrs. Bennett, I need to tell you that you are a very wealthy woman. You will never spend all the money in a lifetime that your husband has left for you." Margie started to cry again.

"He was always a good provider but we never went to extremes on anything. We saved where we could." She said. The lawyer went over both the businesses and their estimated values and the many banking and savings account that held masses of money.

"Now this is a strange one or it was to me. Maybe you can shed some light on this one for me." Did you know your husband just built a three million dollar house in the woods fifty miles from Savannah Georgia? I did some research on it and found the house was, built two years ago. I checked with the builder and he said Mr. Bennett was building it so that you and the children would have a place to stay when you come to Savannah and that I was going to be a "get away house." Did you know about this house?"

"No, I never heard my husband mention building a house in Georgia."

"Would you like to go to Savannah tomorrow with me and check it out?"

"I sure would. Is the house finished or are they still building it?"

"I think it is finished." "Anyway we will see tomorrow."

The next day Margie left the children at home with a caretaker and she and the lawyer flew to Savannah. They learned where the house was located and that they would need to rent a car to go to it. It seemed like such a long trip to get there. "Why would my husband build a house, this far out?"

"Beats me." The lawyer said. When they finally arrived up the narrow little lane and back into the woods both of them were in awe. There was a great big mansion stretching up from the land. It looked completely out of place in the middle of all the woods. Both of them got out of the car and began walking around the place. Suddenly the front door opened wide and a fancy dressed young lady was standing there.

"What, may I ask, are you doing on my land?"

"Is this your land?" Margie asked.

"Yes it is and I will appreciate it if you will please leave." Margie and the lawyer got back into the car and drove away. They went to the courthouse in Savannah. The lawyer searched the deed, found that the property was solely the property of Buck Bennett, and the property was, paid in full. They explained what had happened that morning and how the lady was apparently occupying the house and had ordered them off the property.

"Maybe when you go back tomorrow you may need to take a deputy with you. No one should be in that house. We have no records of renters or a sale on the property.

They did as the court clerk had recommended. They had a deputy sheriff escort them there the next day. The lady came to the door and tried to pull the same thing she had yesterday but this time it didn't work. The deputy sheriff pushed his way through the door and told the lady to sit in a chair and answer only when she was spoken to and if she did not do as she was ordered he would handcuff her and she would be taken to jail.

"But you don't understand. This is my house. He built it for me," she said.

"Who built it for you?"

"Buck Bennett loved me and he built it for me." Margie's knees became weak. She sat down in the chair behind her to keep herself from falling.

"Mr. Bennett built this house for you and put your name on the deed, did he." "Yes, he said he did. It is right there at the courthouse. You can go and look for yourself," she said. The attorney stepped forward; he pushed a paper at her. "We did go to the court house and here is the deed. Do you see your name on it anyplace?" She took the deed and looked at it.

"That lying crook, I slept with that old fat slob and he promised me this house and everything that's in it and I intend to get it. I'll go through the courts if I have to."

"I guess that is what you will have to do since we are taking over the house now and you need to get out."
The lawyer said.

"I can't go now, I was going to take a swim in the pool, and then I wanted to lie out and get some sun."

"Sorry to bust up your plans, but you are out of here. Do you want us to get your things and throw them out in the yard or are you going to do it the right way. Either way I want everything that is yours out of this house in thirty minutes and we will wait right her and watch while you do it."

Margie went to the Salvation Army and asked them to go to the house and pick up all the furnishings and distribute to the poor. She had a locksmith come to the house and change all the locks on every door. She locked the doors and walked away. She never intended to allow the big mansion to enter her mind again. The house would sit empty for the next fifty years. The woods consumed even the lane to the house, soon again. Some young people who discovered the big empty house hide deep in the woods started rumors that the house was haunted. Fifty years later the stately house still stands and on occasion young adults, who visit it, always manage to hear or see something each time they enter the house. They always fall over each other trying to get out of the haunted house. Margie never looked back.

Mr. Owens found out the house that he and Hannah had built, was in fact, for Buck Bennett's concubine. In addition, apparently the stress of hiding the girl friend and the expensive house from his wife for two years had become so stressful for Mr. Bennett that he had a fatal heart attack. He felt that Hannah deserved to know. Her main reason for helping Mr. Bennett with his new house was the idea that his two little daughters would get to enjoy the house too. Mr. Owens decided not to tell Hannah on the telephone. He decided it would be more proper to visit her and tell her.

When he went up to the door of her apartment, he rang the doorbell. No one came to the door. He knocked on the door and still no response. Mr. Owens had seen Hannah's car in the carport before he came up to her apartment. Maybe one of the children came and picked her up for a ride or shopping. Mr. Owens had Hannah's, daughter's phone number. He called her, "No I haven't heard from Mom in two days. I will be right over." Mr. Owens waited until Hannah's daughter arrived. She placed her key in the lock and opened the door. Hannah was in bed in her bedroom. She was wearing her pretty nightclothes. She was wearing perfect makeup as though she was going on a trip. Her arms folded over her chest causes her to appear very peaceful. She lay very quiet and still. "Mom, Mom, you sleeping?" Hannah's daughter said as she laid her head on her mother's chest. Tears weld in her eyes. "Mom you are not with us. Are you? You are now with my dad, your wonderful husband Jake, the only love of your life, whom you lost so many years ago."

And she was right. Hannah felt tired last night so instead of going to bed at ten p.m. she went to bed an hour early at nine. She had bought one of those new television sets that had just come on the market. She usually watched the evening news from her bed and then she turned the television set off and went to sleep. But tonight she would miss the news. She soon drifted off to a wonderful sleep and some time during the night, she dreamed she was walking through a very large field of beautiful pink roses. There were rows of roses as far as she could see all around her and none of the roses had thorns. She was amazed at so many roses and the wonderful aroma that drifted from them. She had never felt so peaceful and whole. She heard a slight rustling of the roses behind her. She turned to look and coming toward her was Jake. His arms were out stretched to her. She ran through the roses to Jake and into his arms. Jake kissed her the way he had done in their marriage. "Thank you Hannah for waiting all these years for me. I have been waiting for you." They chatted as they walked through the roses when suddenly they appeared at a snow-white path. It was not a winding pathway but straight and it went on as far as the eye could see. "Jake I am so happy to be with you again," Hannah said. "Honey, we will never be separated again. We will never be sick or have any worries again. I want you to meet my mother and father. They are here and my mother is anxious to see you again." Hannah saw a beautiful woman coming toward them on the path ahead. Hannah had perfect eyesight again and she soon saw that it was Molly. Hannah ran to her mother and into her arms. Her mother was so beautiful.

"Hannah, life for us will go on like this forever. We will never become tired, hungry, sleepy or restless. The peace that you are feeling now will always be there and we will all be together and never be separated again." Hannah thought of her children but she was not sad. She would be waiting until the day that they and their families would join them in Heaven.

At the reading of Hannah's will, she had left several million dollars to her builder Mr. Owens. He had stood by her and together they had built a fortune. She left several million dollars for control by the city for feeding the homeless and the will read, "I would like one thousand dollars a month sent to my dear friends in Lakeland Florida, Martha and Ellen Marlow. They lost their finances during the depression and I began sending them one thousand dollars every month so that they could resume their accustomed life style. Hannah had written their address on the will and said she wanted the money to continue going to them every month for as long as each of them lived. All the rest of her massive fortune she left, to her children and grandchildren.

Chapter Fourteen

Martha Visits Eliza

By 1952, Ma and Eppsie lived in Berlin, Georgia, and all her children lived within a twenty-five radius of her. Ma was eighty-five years old and getting feeble. Arthritis had taken a toll on her little body. However, Ma never was officially, diagnosed with anything except Pellagra, which is a B vitamin deficiency.

All the children visited her often. She still gave them advice as she had done when they were little. They were grown and with families of their own but they still wanted her advice before making any major decisions on their own.

Ma missed her sisters who now lived in Lakeland. She would love to see them but she was not able to go to their house and since, by now, Martha was ninety-five years old and Ma was sure she was disabled. One day she was talking to Rittie about missing her sisters. Rittie went home and told Clint to try to get a telephone call through to her aunts for Ma. Clint dialed Martha's number in Lakeland, Florida. On the first ring, Martha answered the phone. "Aunt Martha, this is Clint and Rittie wants to talk to you." He handed the phone to Rittie.

"Martha this is Rittie. How are you doing?"

"Oh Rittie, it is so good to hear from you. I am doing well considering my age." Martha laughed and Rittie laughed with her. "I really have nothing wrong with me except this old arthritis. It limits me but I do quiet well anyway." "How is Ellen?" "She is doing just fine; you know she's still just a kid." Ellen was fifteen years younger than Martha was.

Martha do you suppose if I sent Clint to pick you and Ellen up you could come and visit Ma? She talks about you all the time and said yesterday that she would sure love to see you. She is not able to go there but if you and Ellen can make the trip, I can send Clint for you to come for a visit."

"Honey you won't need to send Clint to pick us up. Ellen drives everywhere. We were talking yesterday about planning a trip to Georgia."

"You tell your mother that we will see her next week." Rittie told Martha the directions to Eliza's house in Berlin.

When Rittie told Ma about her conversation with Martha, she was ecstatic with joy. She had not seen her sister in so many years that it was hard for her to remember when it was. Eliza spent the rest of the week telling Eppse what to do in the house to get it ready for her sister's visit.

The days rolled by slowly for Eliza. She prayed that she would be feeling good while her sister's were visiting her. She had her bad days and her good days. Some days she felt really awful and some days she enjoyed spending the day with Ellen's grandchildren who lived just two doors down. They were little and on Eliza's good days, she enjoyed them all around her. Eliza would patch up, boo-boos, make peanut butter, and jelly sandwiches. On Sunday, Eliza was happy that she felt well enough to go to her church at the First Baptist Church in Berlin. She had so much to be grateful for and she enjoyed going to church and showing her gratitude to Christ. She still had all her children; they were all healthy and happy with families of their own. Eliza marveled at the fact that she had only lost one child and she had lost him when he was a young adult. However, Robert Jr. death still grieved her. She had raised every child she had had. She had never miscarried the way her mother had in the bad weather on the wagon train trip. She still grieved each time she thought about her brother and sisters' succumbing while they were still only children. However, Eliza knew she had lots to be thankful for especially when she thought about her two-step children who she had finished raising when their mother died. They had been her salvation when Pa and then Robert Jr. died. She could not imagine what she would have done if it had not been for Ed and Mittie. She had always felt the same toward them as she had the ones she had birthed.

Next week finally came and Eliza sat in front of her fireplace waiting for her sisters. "Eppse, do you want something to eat?"

"No Ma; I ain't hungry yet." Mattie Lee had come this morning and cooked a pot of chicken and dumplings and a pot for fresh butter beans for them to eat when Martha and Ellen arrived. The children who lived near by would come every day and bring food or cook food there for the three sisters and Eppse. All Eliza's children were excited that Ma was going to spend some time with her sisters.

Soon a big black car pulled into Ma's yard and stopped. Eliza started out the door but Eppse grabbed her arm. "Don't fall Ma." He said as he helped her down the steps. The three sisters were so happy. They were hugging and giggling as if the were teenagers again.

They spent the evening reminiscing. "Eliza, you don't remember any of the boat trip from Ireland, do you?" Martha asked.

"Sometimes I think I can remember some things but then I don't know if I am really remembering or if it is what I had heard long ago." Eliza said to her sister. "I wish you had been old enough to remember it. It was really a journey. Did you know that while we were on the boat and on the way to America there was a very big storm and the lightning blew out a big hole in the upper deck?"

"No, I never heard about that," Eliza said.

"It happened, and the boat tipped on its side and you, Ma and I were thrown through a hole in the middle deck where everyone was housed. We ended up in a big old wooden box used for storing the sails to the boat, located in the bottom hull of the boat. I remember well about being in the box but I never knew how we got inside it with the lid closed." Martha said. "How did we get in the box?" "You'll never believe what I found out about it years later after Ma had died. I don't think she ever knew what had actually happened after we had fallen into the box."

Ellen and Eliza said simultaneously, "What happened and how did you find out about it?" Pa told me not long before he died." Martha said. "I already knew that the lightning hit the upper deck and blew a big hole in it. Then the boat tipped on its side and as it tipped on its side, a little hatch covered with a piece of heavy metal became dislodged from the floor where we were sitting and we fell into the hole. At the same time that the hole appeared in the floor the big box below tipped on its side too and the heavy hinged lid popped opened. That is when we fell into the box. When the boat popped upright again, the metal lid closed over the hole again and the heavy lid to the box closed with us inside the big heavy box. Ma and I tried many times to open the door on the box but we could not budge it. We yelled and screamed but no one heard us."

"Finally, after what seemed like a week the big box lid was removed and there stood Pa. I remember Ma fussing at him for not getting us out sooner but we were so grateful to get out of there her grumbling soon turned to happiness." Martha said. "But, you said something happened after that. What did Pa tell you?" Eliza asked. "He told me that while we were down there in the box the whole middle deck was flooded with about four feet of water. He said people died by the dozens including little children and pregnant women. He told me he thought we had been washed into the ocean since he could not find us anywhere. He said he waded through the water and pulled many people out who would have died if he had not but many of the ones he pulled out of the water was already dead. He said he saw a little girl floating on the water and she was dead. He thought it was you, Eliza and he could not get to you. He said that when it was all over the ship captain sent them all down to clear the water and clean the floors. Pa said with every step he made he looked for one of us but when it was all over none of us was accounted for. Assuming that we had been washed into the ocean, he lay down in the spot where we had originally had our little spot on the ship and prayed to die. He said since his family was all dead he could not go on and was sure he could eventually will himself to die." "He said suddenly he heard a tapping sound that would not go away. The sound he was hearing were we beating on the box trying to get someone's attention. Anyway, that is when Pa rescued us. We never knew about all the death and carnage that took place on the ship while we were in the box. Pa said he never wanted Ma to know about it and so far as I know she never did."

Eliza sat in awe at what she had just heard. She remembered the talk about them being in the box but this is the first time she actually knew what had happened. She looked up to the heavens and said "One more thing for me to be grateful to you for, Lord."

The three girls went to the kitchen and set the big pots waiting on the stove, on the table. Eliza had made them a hoecake of cornbread to go with their chicken and rice and fresh butterbeans with ham hocks. The food was extra good and they kept on chatting while they ate.

This dinner carried Martha back to the first dinner she had prepared for Ben. It was such a lovely memory. She could not wait to tell Eliza about her life with Ben. Eliza knew all about their meeting and early times together but she was gone long before Ben had built the new house. Eliza knew Ben had died but she did not know the details. However, Martha would save that until tomorrow.

The next morning the girls got out of bed and hugged each other all over again. Then they sat down in front of the fireplace to continue their catching up. "Eliza, I know you don't remember the friend that we met on the ship either but she has stayed in touch with me the last several years," Martha said.

"I don't remember her but I remember you and Ma talking about her. She had two children didn't she?" Eliza asked.

"Yes and one thing we did not know about her when we were on the boat together was that she was a very wealthy woman."

"Somehow I had thought that everyone on that boat were indigent, just like us. I did not know that anyone could come to America on that ship," Martha said.

"We saw her ride away from the battery in New York in a pretty carriage. The pretty lady that had come for her must have been her mother."

"Did you talk to her about why she came to America without her husband and who the woman was that picked her up?" Eliza asked.

"Yes and it was a terrible thing that happened to her husband but that was the reason she came to America on that ship instead of a nice big ship that she could have easily afforded. Her husband and his mother burned to death in a house fire and Molly, that was her name, was devastated. She wanted to get to her mother as fast as she could. She had no family left in Ireland to support her through her tragedy. The free ship was the only one leaving for America for several days. Molly took it to avoid staying there in her grief alone. She still says even living through all the horror on that ship she doesn't regret her trip to America on it."

"Anyway, she had plenty of money on her but she had left much, much more money in the bank in Ireland. The bank never sent her the money she had stored in their bank. Somehow, her money was buried in bureaucracy with the government of Ireland and she never could retrieve it. For that reason, Hannah had a bad taste for banks. After she arrived in America, she refused to place her money in a bank. She put it in a sock and hid it under the foot of her mattress. She really did not need it anyway since her mother was so wealthy and would not have allowed her to pay for anything, anyway."

"When the depression hit and the banks collapsed Molly lost every dime of her money. Hannah thinks that the grief of being broke with no hopes of regaining her money may have caused her death. She said it was an awful time for her. She watched her mother die of grief. Now, Hannah had nothing but the $100,000 in the sock under her mattress. Since she still had the children to finish rearing, she was grateful she had not put her money in the bank. If she had, Hannah says she does not know what would have happened to them."

"Well so far as I see it, she was lucky from the beginning for never having to want for nothing," Ellen said. "But Ellen, she was not that kind of person. You would have never known Molly had anything. She was a loving giving person." Martha told Ellen. "Hannah was a wise and caring person. At the time after her mother's death, she sat in her Mother's apartment, now her own apartment, and watched the poor women going to work at the factories. World War II was in full force and her heart went out to those poor mothers who had left their children at home alone. The mothers and grandmothers forced to work just to keep food on the table. It took two women working to bring in the same salary that one man would earn doing the exact same thing. Therefore, there was no extended family available to keep the children. Hannah took what money she had and built a day nursery near the factory where all the women worked. Hannah then went to the owners of the factories and talked them into paying for the day care for the children of his workers. Reluctantly, they all agreed. Hannah saw happy mothers as they rushed passed her apartment now carrying or holding the hands of their children."

"Hannah walked the streets to see what could make life better for New York City citizens. When she found a need, she searched out a site, bought it, and hired the carpenter who had built the nursery to build the building. Her buildings were very well built and safe. She saw to that."

"She kept repeating her procedure over and over until before she realized it she was a very wealthy woman. She sent her children to the best universities where they got their degree in law and health."

"Just after the depression was getting over Hannah hired her driver to bring her for a visit to our house. Ellen and I never told you but we also lost everything we had during the depression when the banks failed. They would not let us get enough of our own money to buy some groceries. It caught us completely by surprise. We still had all the money Ben left us and we had a good living just on the money's interest. However, we had lost it all. One night we went to bed wealthy and secure. The next morning we woke up and had nothing. Not even enough for food. We had to go back to living as we did on the farm after Pa died. We planted a big garden and we ate off the land. When we had sold enough vegetables to buy an old milk cow and a pig we fenced off an area out back and put them there. We bought chickens and we were back to living off the land. Unlike most of the city folk living around us we knew just how to do it all, but they had never lived a farm life and some of them almost starved and some are still having a hard time."

When Hannah saw how we were living now and she knew how we had lived before the depression it really bothered her. I think it bothered her more than it did us. Anyway, when she left to go back to New York, she slipped a bill in my apron pocket. When I looked at it was five thousand dollars. I am telling you Eliza, you will never know how good that money came in. They were about to put a lien on our house for back taxes. We had just not had enough money to pay them for years. I took the five thousand dollars to the courthouse and pushed every dime that I owed at them. I made them give me a paper saying my house was free and clear of taxes. One month later Hannah I began getting a check from her for one thousand dollars every month. That is the kind of woman she was, she would take the shirt off her back and give it to someone if she thought they needed

Because of the thousand dollars that she sent to us each month, we were able to get the house back in shape. Ben would be proud of it now and, we were able to regain our life style that we had before the banks took our money. "I got a phone call the other day. He said he was an attorney and he represented Hannah. He said she had quietly passed away in her sleep. He said her will read about the thousand dollars that she had been sending to me and my sister and he wanted to let me know that at her request the money would continue to come as long as Ellen and I live."

"We traded in our old dilapidated car for a new one and repaired everything in the house that had gone neglected while we had no money. I am telling you Eliza, life is good for Ellen and me. I have one, regret, and that is that Ben was never there to share it with us. I would have been happy to live off the land for the rest of my life without a penny to my name if I could have shared my life with him," Martha said as tears trickled down her cheeks.

Eliza knew Martha would never get over Ben. Eliza remembered the picture Ben took of her family. It was the only picture ever taken of her family together. She loved him for that. Eliza took the picture out often and looked at it. Eliza pulled the picture out of her picture box and the three girls looked at it together.

Martha and Ellen stayed four days and then it was time to go home. It was a sad parting. They all knew they would probably never see each other again. They were thankful that they had this time together.

Only two months after Martha, Ellen and Eliza's visit together, Rittie got a phone call from Ellen. She called to tell Rittie that Martha had died. She said that Martha had been having problems with lightheadedness. She said she had taken her to the doctor but they could not find anything wrong with her. However, twenty-four hours later she had a fatal stroke. "The doctor said she never suffered. He said Martha died immediately as soon as the stroke hit her." Ellen told Rittie. Rittie dreaded having to tell Ma about her sister. Clint drove Rittie to Ma's house and he knew how hard this was going to be on Ma. He decided to wait in the car. "Ma, I got a phone call this morning from Ellen," Rittie said to Eliza.

"She told you that Martha had died, didn't she," Ma said. "How did you know, Ma?" Rittie asked. "Last night in my dream I saw Ben coming down a long narrow lane with big trees on each side and canopied over the top of the lane. Then I saw Martha coming from the other end of the lane toward him. They met in the middle and drifted away together." "I knew the dream meant something. I just did not know what it was. I know Martha is completely happy now. She and Ben are back together again. Good for her." That was all Ma had to say about it and she did not shed a tear. Rittie went back to the car and got into the front seat. "Clint you are not going to believe this."

When she told him what Ma had said, he said. "I guess that answers the question how did you get out of there so fast."

It seemed that Martha's death was only the beginning of the losses in the family. Noah notified all his brothers and sisters. Ma seemed to be sick. She was not able to get out of bed. Eliza's children started a vigil. They took turns staying with her. Someone was with her both day and night. Ma continued to get weaker and soon she too was gone. Ma's children wept openly. This was a terrible tragedy for them. How would they live without their Ma? She had always been there. She had always been their rock. Rittie could only think about what Ma had said about Martha being with Ben. She discussed it with her siblings. This seemed to give them comfort.

Ma was now with her own Ma, and father, Louisa and Reason Marlow. She was again with Martha while they held hands and chatted away. James who had died from the sugar disease and all the girls who had succumbed with Ma to the yellow fever were there. Everyone was together again except for Ellen, she would join the family much later and what a story she had to tell the family when she arrived.

Ellen gets a Life

Sometimes Ellen had a repeated dream that she was standing with a very powerful handsome man who loved her with all his heart. Every decision made in their lives he allowed her to make it. She dreamed it was a big challenge but she somehow always ended up making exactly the right choice. She was always disappointed when she woke up from her dream.

Ellen needed to go to the grocery store. She grabbed her shawl and threw it over her shoulders. She walked out into the warm autumn air, got into her car, and drove down the lane to the main road. While she shopped in the grocery store, she came upon pickled beets. Ellen loved pickled beets. She felt guilty but she picked them up and placed them in her basket. Martha had never liked pickled beets so they never bought them.

Ellen felt that if she could overcome her quilt feeling when she made a choice that she knew Martha, Ma or Pa would not approve of she would feel much better. However, in every phase of her life some little incident would always creep in. Ellen had decided that she would plant a fall garden. Fall gardens always did well in Florida. She intended to limit her vegetables to only a few since she could not handle the big garden that she once grew. When she pulled her seeds out of the storage house, she found all Martha's favorite vegetables. Some of them were her favorite also but she wished she had some lettuce and radishes to plant. Martha did not like lettuce or radishes so they never planted them. Ellen decided tomorrow she would go to the hardware store and buy some lettuce and radish seeds.

That afternoon Ellen planted one row of green beans, one row of tomatoes, and one row of red potatoes. When she finished she brushed her hands off and said to herself, Lots of work for an old woman. She still had her health. She took no medicine and had no medical complaints. She really felt herself lucky. Sometime, however, she wished she could hurry and get old so that she could die and join the rest of her family. As she looked back over her life, she really could not see any reason why she was born. She had sorta drifted through life. She had never been married or had a boyfriend. She could not imagine what it felt like to kiss a male. Ellen went to bed that night with those thoughts still on her mind. She dreamed she was having a suitor visit her. She was so excited. She could not believe that she might get a boy friend after all. She scrubbed the floors so that they would be spotlessly clean for her suitor. While she was scrubbing, the doorbell rang. She begrudgingly stopped scrubbing the floors and answered the door. There was a well dress man standing there and he said he wanted to come in and read the Bible with her. "I don't have time now. I am preparing for a visitor", and she closed the door in his face. After she had finished the floors, she started dusting all the furniture. Suddenly the doorbell rang again. She went back to the door and it was the mail carrier. Ellen looked at him annoyingly. "I am sorry to disturb you Ma'm but, I have a letter that you need to sign for." Ellen grabbed the paper he was holding and signed her name rapidly, took the letter and closed the door. Finally, Ellen dreamed she had the house all clean and perfect then she move to the kitchen and began preparing a gourmet meal for her suitor. She had gotten her meal completed and her suitor still had not come. She sat in the chair and waited some more. Suddenly it came to her mind. "Ellen you are too selective. Suppose one of the two men who came to your door today was your suitor. You kept your mind so narrow that you never even thought about that. Ellen woke up but this time she wanted to wake up. She sat up in the bed. The dream had seemed so real. Maybe I have never opened my eyes to the possibility of meeting someone. Maybe there have been available suitors out there but my mindset always telling me that I was not worthy, never allowed me to open my mind to the possibility.

Ellen decided that morning that she was going to start getting out more. It would be no fun and eating alone in a restaurant certainly was no fun but she was determined to start some place. When Ellen thought about her dream, it was as if God was saying to her. You made yourself the way you are. No one pushed you in the direction you went. You chose that direction. It was there for you all the time if you had just opened your eyes.

Ellen got dressed and went to the local hospital. "I would like to volunteer if you need someone." They welcomed her with opened arms. She decided she would work three days a week. Ellen enjoyed her new job. She carried pretty plants and mixed arrangements to the patients who had received them from loved ones. She rolled a book cart down the halls finding patients who wanted to choose a book to read. It was fun talking to the patients and Ellen met many new friends.

The pink ladies would meet every Thursday evening for dinner at a place they had previously chosen. Everyone laughed and talked the night away. Ellen had never felt so much a part of something not even with Martha or Ma

Ellen made a point to meet her neighbors. They were not close neighbors on either side or in back, since Ellen's land covered so many acres. Her neighbors had lived in their houses since soon after she and Martha had moved in theirs. However, Ellen never saw any of her neighbors, and knew nothing about them. Ellen found, they were very nice and fun people. Ellen and her neighbors started sharing apple pies, chicken potpies, and cakes of all kinds. Ellen loved cooking and according to all the neighbors, her food was superior to all the other.

Ellen soon realized she was turning into a social butterfly. Who in a hundred years would have considered her a social butterfly? She sure wished she could tell Martha, Eliza, and Ma. Now Ellen stayed busy most of the time and it felt so good. She had more friends now than she had had in her total lifetime.

It was early on Sunday Morning. Ellen was getting dressed for church and Sunday school. There was a knock on the door. This person had not used the doorbell just the titanium knocker there. "Ellen, can I come in?" "My name is Lou Parker and I need to talk to you." Ellen was never afraid. She never thought about an invader. However, how could this well-dressed man standing outside her front door, know her name and why would he want to talk to her? Ellen cracked the door a bit. "What did you say your name is?"

"I am Lou Parker, I am the lawyer that handled Ben's and then Martha's money. There is never a day goes by that I don't think of you two and regret what happened." This really peeked Ellen's curiosity. Ellen opened the door and allowed the stranger to come in. She remembered the name Lou during the time Martha and Ben were planning their wedding but she could not put it all together.

Ellen, I know that you are dressed and ready to go to Sunday school. However, if you will stay here with me for one hour and hear me out then I will go to church with you.

Ellen went to the kitchen and poured Lou and herself a cup of fresh coffee from her new electric pot. She brought it back to the living room and sat Lou's cup on the coffee table in front of him. She went to her favorite chair and sat down, placing her coffee on the side table by her chair.

"What is so important that you have to tell me?" Ellen asked.

"Do you remember when all the banks closed and Wall Street failed?" Lou asked.

"Yes, I remember it well."

"Well Martha would not have lost all her money if I had been on duty when all of it started happening. I had been called to Ireland to try to retrieve a lady's money that had been held up there in red tape. What it amounted to was the city had all intentions of stealing her money? It took me a month but I finally got her money back. They had known that her husband had suddenly burned to death in a fire. All his wife could think was to get out of Ireland and back to her mother in New York. They thought they could keep the money tangled in some kind of bureaucracy for a while and concern about the money would slowly fade away and they would divide all her money among themselves. I got the money for her but apparently she left in her will that if the money should ever be retrieved it was to go to this household and to whom ever is living in it at the time. I have researched it and found out you are living here alone. "It isn't relevant but I would like to know how you knew the lady?" Tears started spilling from Ellen's eyes. She told Lou the full story of how Hannah and her two children had come over to the United States from Ireland and how her mother, father, and Martha had made friends with them. Ma and Pa could not read or write so she was the one who read all the documents for them the night of their arrival. However if she had had her money she would have been much better off then. All her mothers' fortune got lost in the depression too. It caused her mother to go to an early grave. Hannah had a little money under her mattress and that is how she got started. She helped Mom and Dad decide where was best for them to settle when they landed in New York. She came to see us several months before Martha died. She started giving us money then and she never stopped. She is dead now but her estate sends me one thousand dollars every month. However, I can tell you now, she did not need the money. She died a very wealthy woman and she started in New York from scratch in the building business.

"Martha and I had a few slim years that we did not know how we would survive but we grew vegetables, raised livestock, and mostly ate off the land those few years. Ellen told Lou.

I have your check here for thirty six million dollars. The money is to be given directly to you. I also finally earned all my money back so since it was my fault that you lost your money I am giving you another check for three million, five hundred and seventy dollars," Lou said. Ellen looked stunned and sat quietly for a few minutes. "Are you telling me that you are giving me all your money?" Ellen asked. "No, I have plenty more, I only refunded the money that you and Martha probably lost when the market crashed, and I was not there to do anything about it."

"Lou what in nations name will I do with all that money?" "For one thing you can start living. You can go places you have never been, eat fine foods and buy anything you want without worrying about the price tag. Ellen thought about what Lou had said. All of it sound fun and she would love to do it but not alone.

Suddenly the dream came back into head. Keep an open mind. Do not be too selective.

"Lou, are you married?" "No, like my brother I wasn't interested until I got much older. Now it is too difficult to find someone. "I don't want to be too brazen and bold but I will take the money if you come with it." Ellen said. Lou sat there looking thoroughly confused. His face turned white. Ellen thought he was going to faint. Ellen knew she had scared him to death.

"Just think about it, if you don't stay with me I don't take a dime of the money. I want to do all the things you talked about but I don't want to do them alone."

"You have never had any children and neither have I so who will go with either of us on long trips, fancy restaurants, picnicking, shopping till we both drop. I don't have anyone and unless you have children someplace you don't either," Ellen said.

Lou started laughing and said in a "How could you say that" sorta way. "No I don't have children, Ellen. "So, do you want to marry me or not?"

"What about love, Ellen?" Lou said.

"Oh we can fall in love later; we'll be planning our trips and thinking of nice things to buy for now."

"It all sounds nice except for one thing. I am Catholic and we believe in marriage before consummation of a marriage." Geeez, Ellen had not thought about that. She has thought they would each have their own bedroom. "How do you feel about sleeping in different rooms?" Ellen asked.

"Positively not. We will sleep in the same bed in the same room," Lou said.

"Would you sleep with me?" Ellen asked. Somehow, that old thought of her not being good enough sprang into her head again.

"Of course, I would sleep with you. I would be more than happy to sleep with you." Lou said in a surprised tone.

"Lou, I have never even kissed a boy and I don't know how all of that works. Why would you want to sleep with me when I'm certainly not the prettiest girl on the block and I am totally ignorant about such things as that?" Lou walked over to the chair, took her hand, and said "Ellen you are the girl men cherish. I will not go into the why part since I know you would not understand. You just trust me."

Does all this mean we need to go to the court house tomorrow and get married?" That is what it means my Love." Ellen's heart soared when Lou called her Love. No one had ever called her a sweet name before.

Lou had been having serious thoughts of retiring. This day had cleared that thought up. He would defiantly retire as of today. In his wildest dreams, he would never have suspected to walk into a marriage proposal. In fact, he had had many proposals over the years. Some of the girls looked like beauty queens and some looked like cherub little angels but never had it entered his mind to except their proposal. Some of them he had dated but saw or heard nothing that interest him.

He had thought that some day he might marry, if the perfect girl came along. Well Ellen was precious but she did not look like a beauty queen nor did she look like a cherub angel. When she blurted out her proposal to him, he knew immediately she was the perfect girl. He could not figure out why. He had never really liked forward women. However, Ellen was not a forward woman. Ellen was Ellen and there would never be another like her.

Lou and Ellen did not make it to church. They had far too much on their minds right now to hear a word the preacher would say. "Lou, do you like turnip greens?"

"Yes, Ellen I do like turnip greens." "I am glad," she said.

"Why?" Lou asked.

"Because I really love them," she said. "Even if I didn't like them you could still eat them," Lou said.

"Really?" Ellen asked. "Of course you could still eat them, but I like them so you don't have a worry there."

Ellen, I need to ask you a question and if you don't like the idea, just say so and I won't bring it up again."

"What is the question?" Ellen asked.

"Do you mind if we hire a full time maid. That way we can go when we get ready without making prior arrangements for the house and I want you to spend the rest of your life with me and not in the kitchen."

"Oh, Lou but I cook so well," Ellen, said to him. "You can tell the maid how you like it cooked." Ellen thought about it for a bit. "Lou, I will make a deal with you."

"Ok, what is the deal?" Lou asked. "I will have a full time maid if I can continue to grow a little garden." Lou pulled Ellen out of her chair and gave her a tender hug. "It doesn't take much to make you happy, Darling."

Lou and Ellen went out to dinner that night. Since it was, Sunday night there was not many restaurants to choose. They settled on a fish house. Ellen had her fish fried and Lou had his fish broiled.

When they returned home, Ellen made a fresh pot of coffee and they sat on the sofa and talked about their lives in the past. They had so much catching up to do. Lou had known Ellen slightly but Ellen never remembered seeing Lou before. They discussed how strange this marriage was going to be. Lou said, "If the Moslem religion can do it we can too."

"How do they marry?" Ellen asked Lou. "Their mate is selected by their parents. The boy is usually told whom he is marrying but the girl does not know until their wedding day. She is allowed to peek through a small hole in the door and take a quick look at him."

"If she doesn't like the way he looks and doesn't want to marry him, well that would be sad, since she has to marry him anyway." "They are married in separate rooms. The boy says his vows in one room with all the men and the girl says her vows in another room with the all the women. They are allowed to be together after the reception is over." Lou and Ellen decided together, if their friends question their short relationship before their wedding they would just tell them they have turned Moslem.

Suddenly, Lou looked at his watch and he said, "Would you believe it is five o'clock in the morning." They had sat on the couch and talked all night. They felt so comfortable with each other already.

"I will go to my room and take a nap and you can use Martha's room. We won't sleep long since we need to get married in the morning." Lou agreed with Ellen. Ellen was too excited to sleep but she knew she needed to look her best and that was not going to happen if she had puffy red eyes. Ellen slipped out of her clothes and slipped her gown on while she repeated, "I have to go to sleep," over, and over. Ellen knew she could will herself to sleep if she tried hard enough. She was in bed and asleep almost as fast as her head hit the pillow. It did not happen for Lou that easily. He stayed awake until he heard the big wall clock strike seven strikes. He knew Ellen was still asleep and he would allow her to sleep until she woke up.

Lou got out of bed and got a shower. He dressed in what would be his wedding clothes. Then he went to the kitchen and made a pot of coffee. Soon Ellen slowly came out of her room. "Are you awake?" Lou asked Ellen.

"How could anyone sleep with that delicious smelling coffee aroma floating around?"

"I am sorry if I woke you with the coffee brewing."

"No, Lou, we have to get going. We have to go to the courthouse and then find out what we are supposed to do."

"You are right sweetheart. We need to get going."

That fuzzy little feeling came over Ellen again. *Sweetheart, he called me sweetheart.* She loved it.

When they arrived at the courthouse and walked to the information desk to question where they were suppose to go to get their marriage license, they were in for a big surprise. First, they found they would need to fill out papers and apply for the marriage license. It would need to stay posted in the courthouse for five days before they could be married. "This is necessary in case one of you is already married."

"Neither of us has ever been married before," Lou said.

"Sorry, I don't make the rules; I just have to see that they are enforced," the woman told them. Then, to make matters even worse, they found they would each need to go to the health department and have blood drawn for testing in a lab. They would be checking their blood for syphilis, and other sexually transmitted diseases. The lab test would need to be in the courthouse before they could apply for their marriage license. Lou and Ellen tried to persuade them to exempt them since neither of them had a disease of any kind.

"Sorry, we don't make the rules; we just have to enforce them."

Lou and Ellen rushed out the courthouse and drove directly to the health department. They signed in and sat down in one of the well-worn straight back chairs in the waiting room. Soon a nurse called their names. They followed the nurse who took them to a back office. After she had taken blood from each of them she said, "You can come back in five days and pick up your results."

"We cannot pick it up until five days from now?" Ellen asked.

"That's right," the nurse said, "five days." Lou and Ellen walked out of the health department with slumped shoulders.

"I could just cry." Ellen said.

"We are looking at ten days away before we can be married. Since we must wait, let's make the time useful," Lou said.

"How can we make it useful?" Ellen asked.

"Why not have a big wedding now that we have the time to do it."

Ellen thought about it a few minutes. "Hey, that's a good idea. How did you think of it?" she asked Lou.

"Because Miss. Ellen Marrow, I am so proud of you and I would like to announce to the world that I am taking you for my wife."

Lou kept the guest bedroom and Ellen stayed in her bedroom. They had no idea how to go about planning a wedding. They checked out the phone book and apparently, Lakeland, Florida did not have a wedding planner so Lou pulled out his New York phone book and they selected one there. Soon they had hired a wedding planner. She immediately flew to Lakeland Florida. Lou told the wedding planner she had no limitations on cost. "Just put us a wedding together that will be the wedding of the century."

The wedding planner assured him that she could do that. All she needed from them were the names and addresses of the wedding attendees. They decided they would not hold a limit of people they would invite to their wedding. They decided "the more the merrier."

Ellen started her list and Lou started his. They worked hard on the list all day and well into the night. After two days, they had the list ready and Ellen handed it to the wedding planner. The wedding planner gave Ellen and Lou a copy of their wedding announcement.

You are invited to the wedding of Lou Parker and Ellen Marlow. The wedding will take place at Lakeland First Baptist Church on June 22, 1936 at 3:00 in the afternoon. The couple will, be honored at a dinner at the Lakeland Country Club on June 21 at 6:00 in the evening. Following the wedding, a champagne, and caviar reception will, be held at the ballroom of the Astor Hotel. Reservations for out of town guests will be made at the Astor Hotel.

There was no RSVP placed on the invitation. Lou told Jenifer, the wedding planner, to leave the RSVP off since they were pressed for time. He told her to plan for everyone who received an invitation to attend. All left over food, would go to the homeless. The invitations were well on the way to their destination now and Lou thought how surprised and happy all his colleagues would be when they received their invitation. "Lou Parker is getting married!" The last one I would have thought would do it. Lou could just hear them now. Lou had always been a serious, conservative, and skilled lawyer. He took on the jobs that no one else wanted because they found the job too difficult. To Lou, the hard cases were a challenge to him. He was always studying and taxing his brain to learn more. He had taken on some of the most famous lawyers in Philadelphia and won the case as well as their respect. Ellen knew all her friends and family were going to be surprised, excited, and happy for them. Friends Ellen invited included all her family in Georgia. She hoped that, at least, some of them could come. She also invited friends back in Madison that she had not seen in years. Some of them she had grown up with and they had attended the same schools. She also invited all her friends at the Concord Baptist Church, some cousins still in Madison and she invited all her friends in the First Baptist Church in Lakeland--Ellen had a very long list of names. Lou's list was even longer. Two days later, Jenifer told them their invitations were in the mail. Lou's list included people from all over America and some from Ireland.

Lou arranged for housing the out of town guests coming for the wedding at the downtown Astor Hotel.

The next day, filled with fittings for the wedding gown and Lou's tuxedo. Ellen chose her favorite colors for the wedding party. The girls would wear a beautiful pale pink and the men would wear purple tuxedos. All the flowers for the wedding would be pink roses and lavender baby's breath. The wedding planner would select the wedding party from the First Baptist Church and a little boy and girl for the flower girl and ring boy. The wedding party included eighteen not including the bride, groom, and preacher.

Jenifer had hired eight different dressmakers. Each dressmaker was provided with, the same material and the same pattern, sized for each bridesmaid. Each girl would meet with her dressmaker and the dresses would need to be ready in five days. The dresses were to be made of soft fine velvet.

Jenifer had ordered Ellen's wedding gown from a company in New York and when it came, it fit Ellen to perfection. She was stunning in the long closefitting white satin wedding gown with its long flowing train and cultured pearl bodice.

Lou said to Ellen the next morning, "Honey, we have forgotten the most important thing."

Ellen's heart dropped. "What have we forgotten?"

"You are taken and no longer available. We have to get an engagement ring on your finger."

"Well, that shows how much I know about marriage. I would never have thought about a ring."

The two of them drove down town and to the nicest jewelry store in town. When they walked out Ellen had a three-carat solitary diamond ring on her finger. They decided to pick their matching gold wedding bands since they were already there.

Ellen could not keep her eyes off her ring. She had never seen many engagement rings but this was the mother of them all. They had picked it out together. Of course, the first thought that came to Ellen's mind that the perfect three-carat diamond ring cost absolutely too much money. However, before she started to argue, she remembered she had over thirty-nine million dollars and Lou had millions of his own as well as assets that amounted to more than fifty million dollars. Lou wanted to do it the right way. While they were still in the jewelry store Lou took Ellen's diamond ring, kneeled to one knee and asked, "Ellen will you marry me?"

"Yes, Yes, Yes, I will marry you." Ellen said bubbling over with joy. Lou placed the ring on her left ring finger. Now their intentions were set in diamond and gold.

Ellen hired a housekeeper who was happy to stay full time in the house and keep it up. Ellen set Maggie, the house cleaner, up a checking account at the bank for house money and salaries for herself and the maintenance man.

Lou hired a landscape company to re-landscape the grounds and the landscape man said he would find him a maintenance man to keep the yards up. Lou told the landscaper that he needed the maintenance man full time. The yard maintenance man whose name was Joe would also help Maggie in the house if she needed any thing heavy put a way. The landscaper said he would come every three months to see that everything was going all right. Ellen knew the landscaper. He and his family went to First Baptist with her.

Jenifer had selected the songs for the wedding and the boy-girl team was already practicing together. She had gone to the country club and talked to the head chef. She decided he was well qualified to head up her menu. Jenifer had checked out the ballroom at the Astor Hotel. The hotel manager told her she could decorate it any way she wanted. She had the entire ceiling draped in pink satin for a tent top effect. She had purple velvet covers for all the chairs. Jenifer covered the tables with pink linen table clothes with pink napkins tied with little purple bows. Jenifer would fill the room with big purple vases holding dozens of big round pink roses.

It was the day before the big sit down dinner at the country club. Jenifer spent most her day there. There were large arrangements of pink roses with lavender baby's breath placed in oblong gold containers lined in the center of the table and extending to each end of every table. There were forty tables decorated the same as those at the hotel waiting for the reception.

While Jenifer was busy getting the wedding together, Ben and Ellen were planning their honeymoon. They discussed it for hours offering up all their options. Finally, they settled on a trip to Hawaii first. They would spend a full week there, and then they would fly to Europe, starting in Germany they would rent a car and travel all over Europe at their own pace. They intended to spend more time in Ireland than any of the other countries. Ellen wanted to see where her mom, dad, Martha and Eliza had come from and see if she might find relatives who stilled lived there. This pleased Lou since he had spent some much time in Ireland as a very young lawyer, just out of law school. They would rest a week in London after they had finished touring Europe, then they would fly to Turkey and Egypt.

If they followed their plan they would not be back home for six months. They did not care about the time. So long as they were having a good time, they could stay a year if they liked.

Guests started arriving on Thursday evening. They knew where the hotel was located since Jenifer had sent directions, with the invitations, to all three places the guest would need to be. Jenifer was the perfect wedding planner. She forgot nothing and although she had worked almost day and night, each aspect of the wedding and events was perfect.

Jenifer had hired a receptionist for greeting the wedding guest at the hotel. She was young and very energetic and showed deep concern for her guests. Nell showed them around the facility and led them to their room. She gave each of them a card with her phone number and told them, "if you need, anything, any time, please, send me a message and I will be right there." Lou arranged for each out of town guest flying into the Tampa Air Port to receive a rental car until the day after the wedding. Ben had reserved almost every room in the Astor Hotel in Lakeland.

Everything was ready for the wedding. The maid had been hired and was already in the house working. The landscapers were still working in the yards but they were already shaping up to be gorgeous. The maintenance man already worked for the landscaper so he was busy in the yards also. Lou had a meeting with the hired help and explained to each of them what their job included. He explained that two accounts had been set up at the bank. The bank would control one account. That one would be their salaries, and the bank would send their paychecks every Friday. Mattie would control the second account. She would use this account for running the household and purchasing needed supplies.

Lou had gone to the power company and had paid a year in advance for their electricity. He had done the same with the phone company and the garbage service.

The couple had their bags packed with plenty of clothes for all seasons. Jenifer had gone with Ellen one day and assisted her with a new wardrobe. Ellen loved her new clothes. She had never owned things this expensive in her life. She remembered growing up, Pa would put pasteboard in the soles of their shoes to cover the holes until there was enough money to buy new shoes. Now she felt so blessed that it brought tears to her eyes.

The guests started arriving. They were coming by the dozens and then hundreds. What fun it was meeting again some of the people Ellen had not seen most of them since they were kids going to school together. There were so many of Ellen's friends from Concord Baptist Church in attendance. Some of the Browning family was able to go. This really thrilled Ellen. The large lobby/sitting rooms at the Astor Hotel soon filled with guests for the wedding. Lou was able to spend some time with his best friends whom he had grown up with and they remained friends still today. He had many working partners and colleagues there too as well and most all his family.

Jenifer had suggested that Ellen wear the stunning mint green chiffon dress she had purchased, for the wedding rehearsal dinner on Friday night. She would wear black diamond earrings and a black diamond solitary pendent on a gold chain around her neck. Jenifer applied Ellen's makeup just right. Instead of her being sixty-two years old, she looked more like forty-two years old. Lou could not stop looking at her when she walked out ready to go to the wedding dinner. He had to steal a kiss even though they had an audience. However, Lou was a charmer himself, standing there beside her in his deep green wool suit with the mint green, and dark green diagonal stripped necktie. Jenifer refused to settle for a mint green tie that was not the exact green as Ellen's dress. The professional photographers were there and took their pictures as they were coming down the steps of their beautiful home on the way to the country club for the wedding dinner.

The wedding dinner consisted of six courses. There were small crystal goblets of fresh cold tomato juice, then thin chicken bisque soup followed by a beautiful crystal bowl of salad containing soft leaf lettuce, spinach, cucumbers, tiny red tomatoes, yellow bell peppers, radishes, sliced grapes, mandarin orange slices, cantaloupe, and nuts. A dressing made of raspberries, cold-pressed olive oil, and spices served as the dressing.

Dozens of waiters and servers appeared and placed big warm white china plates with grilled prawns arranged around the edges of the big plate in front of each guest. Chefs wearing white high-topped hats and white suits appeared pushing small butcher blocks followed the waiters and servers. The guest received a portion of prime rib. They had their choice of thickness and rare or medium meat. The center of each plate covered with meat that looked delicious and smelled even better. Following the chefs were pretty girls dressed in pink and wearing white aprons pouring au jus over the meat. Then they put a small crystal bowl of horseradish by each guest plate. The guests, and Ellen and Lou, were in for a big surprise for the entertainment for tonight. Waiting back stage was everyone's favorite entertainers, Benny Goodman and his band, and Tommy Dorsey and his band. The entertainers danced on to the stage and began to sing and engage in the hilarious humor, with most of it centered on the bride and groom. The guests went wild when they appeared unexpectedly. The guest had phonograph records of their music and knew all about the entertainers, but none of them had ever seen them in real life. The two famous bands with their star singers provided the group with three hours of delightful entertainment. Then when they were finished, they sat down with the group and had their dinner while talking directly with the guests.

The entertainers continued with their acts and music while the entire six-course meal was completed. Then, the guests were allowed to pick their favorite off the dessert cart and as many different ones as they wanted.

Drinks, of every kind imaginable, were available throughout the evening. The waiters serving drinks made sure that a glass was never empty. After the dinner and through the desserts, most of the guests were drinking coffee. Some were enjoying coffee with their dessert, and some were drinking coffee because they had imbibed too much champagne.

Every guest went away that evening saying it had been the most fun dinner party ever attended. The wedding guests arrived at their plush hotel rooms and they were ready for the comfortable beds. The guests had Sunday morning free. Some of them rode to the beach and waded in the beautiful gulf waters. Others chose to sleep in and some of them went to the church of their choice. Many old friends gathered and had a miniature reunion.

Ellen and Lou were back at home. Jenifer had decided to spend the night at the Marlow household Saturday night so that she could see that the bride and groom were dressed to perfection. There had been no rehearsal. Jenifer said that if she had done her job well there would be no need for a rehearsal. She had talked extensively to each person in the wedding party as a group and she had talked to them extensively individually. She had faith in her group and saw no need for a rehearsal. In the past, she might have a rehearsal if she knew her wedding party did not understand her directions. However, luckily she did not do many of those wedding.

Jenifer had arranged for two limousines to arrive promptly at 2:45 p.m. Ellen would get dressed in her dressing room and Lou would get dressed in his bedroom. Jenifer would bring Lou out to his waiting limousine first. After Lou was gone, Jenifer would bring Ellen out to her waiting limousine. Neither, the bride or groom would see each other before the wedding.

Neither, the bride or groom had seen the church, since the decorations were finished for the wedding

The church doors opened promptly at 2:30 p.m. The wedding guests began pouring in. Soon the church filled and extra chairs placed at the back of the church. They opened the balcony and it, also filled. The piano player sat at the piano playing hymns, selected by the bride and groom. Since it was a Baptist church, all songs had to be sacred songs. However, that was all right with Ellen and Lou since they both loved gospel songs.

Promptly at 3:00 p.m., they locked the church doors. The piano player lowered her tone and the minister walked out from the back of the church carrying his bible. Followed by him were Lou and his best man. Lou was handsome in his coal black tuxedo, white shirt, and black silk tie with white stripes. The pastor welcomed everyone to this wonderful occasion. A beautiful young girl and her partner stood from the choir. It was difficult to see the two because of all the beautiful roses that filled the choir. Their beautiful voices rang out as they sang "He Arose" and "Wherever Thou Goest," people started rubbing their arms afterward. The couple's beautiful words and voices caused goose bumps to spread over everyone's skin. Some of the guests dabbed away tears.

When the singers were finished, there was total quiet for approximately three minutes. Then in a very loud tone, the piano started belting out "Here Comes the Bride." The front doors of the church were opened and starting down one isle were the first bride's maids. On the opposite aisle was the first groomsmen followed by the second two, then the third pair and last was the forth pair. When they had taken their places at the front of the church, they were stunning in their beautiful mint green chiffon dresses with each carrying a pretty cascade of pink roses with purple streamers. The eight groomsmen could never been more handsome in their deep purple tuxedoes and their pink rose boutonnières on their lapel. With the wedding party stationed at the front of the church, a little boy of about three years old and wearing his deep purple tuxedo and pink rose boutonnière came down the aisle holding the gold ring on a beautiful pink silk pillow. Following the ring bearer was the little flower girl, also about three years old. She was wearing her pretty mint green chiffon dress designed to look exactly like the big girls. She was carrying a white basket of pink rose petals in her little gloved hands and she strewed them slowly on the floor as she walked along.

When Ellen walked from the side room in the vestibule where she had been waiting, she was in total awe at the beautiful church. Every available space filled with beautiful roses with sprigs of lavender babies' breath stuck in here and there. Roses were placed down each side of the church and filled the front of the church. She had never seen a more beautiful sight in all her life. All the roses were in different sized big gold pots that looked exactly alike. There were gold candelabras holding twelve pink candles one each side of the podium and one in the center that held sixteen. The glow from the candles put out a fabulous glow about the wedding party. Ellen had chosen to walk alone down the aisle to her husband. When Lou saw Ellen walking, down the aisle in her beautiful white silk gown with islets and pearls placed on the bodice, it astounded him. She was the most gorgeous woman in all the world and she would soon be his. Her headband held beautiful pink roses and began the long train that flowed behind her while her maid of honor kept it in place as she walked.

Suddenly it struck Ellen. She had been so in awe of everything she had not even seen her soon-to-be husband. She caught his eye. He was so very handsome. She wanted to kiss him right then, and there. She was the happiest girl in the whole world.

The vows went off without a hitch. They seemed to last, nearly an hour to the sweating couple, but in actuality, it only lasted fifteen minutes. There were pictures made and more pictures made. Finally, it was time to cut the wedding cake. Everyone drove to the Astor Hotel in his or her cars. This time Ellen and Lou was able to ride in the same limousine to the reception. They held each other tight all the way to the hotel. It would have been nice if they could just skip this part but since that would be impossible, they would go.

The reception was even prettier than the church. The recreation hall decorations started from the front entrance of the hotel and down the hall. The reception hall looked more like a swanky place in Las Vegas. The Glenn Miller band played live throughout the party. Two wedding cakes towering almost to the ceiling looked much to pretty to cut. One was the high wedding cake with all the ornaments, and the other was for Lou-- it was made of chocolate and mint with whole fruit placed like a work of art around it. There were cute little crackers and caviar by the bowl full. There were every fresh fruit and fresh vegetable cut in bite sized pieces with different kinds of dips. There were large ham and cheese trays with fresh baked sourdough rolls. There were roasts of top grade beef still turning on the spit. The chef would shave off all that you wanted, and serve your meat at the level of doneness that you wanted. Champagne flowed like water. People became happier and happier.

Lou whispered in Ellen's ear, "Do you think they will miss us if we slip away?"

"I don't know but I am going to ask Jenifer if that would be proper."

Ellen finally found Jenifer and said, "Jenifer--Lou and I are ready to go. Do you think that would be rude on our part?"

"No, it would not but I will announce that the bride and groom are on their way to your honeymoon, so be ready for rice throwing."

Jenifer took the loud speaker from the band and announced that the bride and groom will be departing now. Everyone grabbed a little net bag of rice and raced to the front door. The bride and groom were sprayed with rice as they tried to get out the door. They ran to Lou's hidden car, so as not to have shoe polish and tin cans all over it. They quietly slipped away. Jenifer had reserved them a room at the Imperial Hotel in Lakeland for the night. Their flights would leave tomorrow.

With the help of the maid Jenifer had packed their luggage. If they were missing something or needed something in addition, they would buy it along the way. Jenifer told them she would see that everything was cleaned and the all the wedding party got their gifts. They had bought the cultured pearls that the girls were wearing for their gift and a gold key chain for the men in the wedding. Jenifer told them that she enjoyed doing the wedding for them and she thought it turned out superb. They agreed with her and they each gave her fifty thousand dollars each. She thanked them and told them that the money was far too much but they insisted she keep it all.

After they told each other how handsome they looked, they took the formal clothes off. Their bodies had never felt so good to get out of those heavy, scratchy clothes. They each put on a robe, built a fire in the fireplace and just relaxed in front of the fire until they had almost fallen asleep. It was after midnight when they finally got into the comfortable bed. Lou placed his arm around Ellen's neck. Ellen snuggled up to his warm body and both of them were asleep almost as soon as their head hit the pillow.

Tomorrow they would fly off to Hawaii. Ellen was so excited. She had read about Hawaii and had studied about it in school but never in her wildest dream would she have thought she would be going there someday.

Their trip to Hawaii was everything that Ellen had thought it would be. They stayed in Honolulu and rented a car for sightseeing. They walked the streets and ate at exotic restaurants. They watched the Hula dancers in their grass skirts as their bodies swayed and their arms and hands flowed out the words of the song that was playing.

They boarded a small plane and flew to the big island of Hawaii. They rented a car, and went to the Kilauea Mountain and watched as the volcano erupted and poured bright red lava down the mountainside. They drove to a new farm at the other end of the island and watched as the cowboys rounded up the cattle. They stopped at Kona and watched as the natives picked coffee beans. They bought some of the coffee beans to bring with them.

The miles and miles of charcoal looking large black chunks of lava reminded Ellen of what hell must look like. As far as she could see, there was nothing but large black rocks, piled high onto each other.

The week flew by and before they realized it they had to leave Hawaii, but Lou promised Ellen that they would return another time and do it all over again.

The next morning they boarded their plane for Germany. They did not intend to spend too much time in Germany since Ellen and Lou were so anxious to get to Ireland and visits places Ellen's parents must have been. Lou wanted to look up some old friends he had met while he was there working on law cases he had handled.

Germany was immaculately clean. Not like America with paper and trash along the roadways. There was no trash or debris anywhere. The mountains all covered with plush green grass and little gardens covered the landscape. It was all beautiful. There were charming old castles and beautiful clean rivers. Ellen thought that Germany must be the healthiest place on earth to live.

Then they were off to France. They climbed part way up the Eifel Tower, sat on the benches along the streets and fed the hungry birds. They visited art and history museums. It was fun, but the most fun of all in Paris for Ellen was the shopping. Paris had clothing stores with everything you could think up in fashion wear and Ellen helped herself to much of it. She bought beautiful gold jewelry. Ladies had just begun wearing pants and she even bought herself some of those too. She was glad Martha was not here to see them. She would surely pooh-pooh women wearing pants.

They had been married almost a month now. Tomorrow would be their one-month anniversary. They would fly to Ireland tomorrow and find the perfect place to celebrate this special day.

When they arrived in Dublin, Ireland the next day, they rented a car. Getting around there would not be difficult for Lou since he knew Ireland very well. They found an upscale hotel that also had a nice restaurant inside the hotel. Lou suggested they rent a suite since they might be there some time. Ellen agreed and even though their suite had a kitchen, she did not intend to use it. Ellen thought to herself, "Funny how a country girl can get use to this city life so fast." What troubled her the most was that she did not even miss home or her past country life at all. In fact, she was having so much fun and was so happy she had not even thought about it.

Lou was the perfect husband for Ellen and she loved him so much. When they stepped into the elevator and the door closed, Lou always tried to steal a kiss. "What if the door opens?" Ellen would say.

"We will just greet the new guest and go on kissing." Lou would say. Ellen wanted to be modest but she loved Lou more than her modesty. She soon found herself helping him with their kiss every elevator ride. All the way up and all the way down. *If the door opens, so let it open*, she thought, *the kiss was much more important than that door.*

Ellen and Lou rested in their suite in the afternoon. In the evening, they got up and dressed for formal dining. They each looked lavishing as they walked out of the hotel suite. They walked downstairs to the front desk and Lou inquired about a very upscale restaurant where they could celebrate their anniversary.

"You can go across the street to the O' Riley Beef House. It is about as upscale as a restaurant can get. It is one of the oldest restaurants in Dublin and still the most popular with the locals. However, you will need a reservation to be seated," the hotel clerk said.

"Well that rules that one out. Where could you suggest next?" Lou asked.

"Tell you what, just give me a minute and I will see if I can get them to seat you without a reservation." Ellen and Lou looked at pamphlets while they waited. Soon the clerk returned. "I got your seats and I got good ones for you. Your table sits near the entertainers. The maître d' said you can come on now," the clerk said.

"Thank you very much," Lou said as he slipped a fifty-dollar bill in the clerk's hand.

"Thank you sir, thank you very much," the clerk said as they were still walking out the door.

"We have a friend there. If we run into another little problem we'll find him," Lou said to Ellen. They held hands and walked down to the red light. They crossed the street and walked back down to the restaurant. As they opened, the door to the restaurant a young man dressed well greeted them, "You are Mr. and Mrs. Parker?" he asked. Stunned, Lou said, "Yes we are the Parkers. How did you know our name?"

"The hotel clerk told me your name. We were waiting for you...just follow me sir and madam," he said. The waiter seated them at a table for four and only about twenty feet from the stage. As they came in they noted several people waiting for seating, but this table was the only empty table in the restaurant. They thought that was a little strange but dismissed it from their minds. A waiter immediately appeared at the table with stemmed glasses of water. Another was waiting there to get their drink order. Ellen had never drunk any kind of alcoholic drink in her life and did not know what the names were. Florida sweet ice tea was out of the question. They had no idea what ice tea was. Lou saw the confusion on her face and said, "My wife will have a glass of water with lemon and a small glass of champagne and I will have a martini, please. After the waiter left the table Ellen said what is champagne, Lou?"

"It is only a light bubbly wine and there won't be enough for you to even know you drank it."

"OK, Ellen said, but when the small stemmed glass of champagne came to the table and Ellen tasted it, she thought it tasted sort of like horse pee with a fizzle. She did not tell Lou that she did not like it but she knew that little tiny glass would last her the whole meal. She was glad she had the water.

Another waiter appeared at the table. He wanted to get their salad order. Again, Lou ordered for Ellen. She sure was glad he knew all this fancy stuff. Ellen knew all about potato salad and lettuce and tomato salad but that was about her limit in the salad line.

By the time they had finished their salad, Ellen told Lou she would learn how to make a Caesar salad since that one was so good. Another waiter appeared at their tableside to get their entrée for dinner. Ellen knew what that meant since she had seen it on other menus at other restaurants they had eaten. She started reading down the list of meats to choose. There was roasted duck with other fancy names; there was escargot, chicken cordon blue and some others she could not even pronounce. She decided she would have the chicken cordon blue, what ever that was. She knew for sure it was made from chicken and she knew chicken meat well. Lou wanted steak and the waiter rolled out a small chopping block with all these different cuts of raw steaks for him to select the one he wanted. Lou especially liked that. He chose the one he wanted and the waited rolled the butcher block back to the kitchen.

Suddenly the stage began to fill with young men with music instruments. They began to play the instruments. The music was beautiful and relaxing and every sip of the champagne that Ellen took improved the music. Soon the music stopped and the lead singer stated that he had an announcement to make. The room was as quiet as a church mouse. "We are proud to have a couple here tonight celebrating their anniversary with us. We would like to tell you that we appreciate you choosing our restaurant to celebrate your anniversary. Mr. and Mrs. Lou Parker, will you please stand?"

Lou and Ellen stood and every one clapped. "Now, what makes this anniversary so special is the length of time that you have been together as one." He was assuming by their age that it had been many years. "See, every married couple can grow older together. Sometimes it just takes work but I will bet you this couple will tell you that it is all worth it. Give them another big hand everyone for hanging in there."

Everyone clapped and there were a yelp or two. As Lou and Ellen was sitting back in their chairs the MC said, "How many years of married bliss have you two spent together."

"Thirty days," Lou said in a low tone. Everyone was still clapping and no one heard it except the MC. He was not sure but he thought he heard thirty days. One way or the other he decided fast to let it go. He decided that night that he would never do that again.

When Lou and Ellen finished with their dinner and got up to leave, everyone gave them another hand of applause. As they went past some couples, they said "congratulations on your anniversary." They walked out the door and had difficulty getting to the hotel across the street since they were laughing so hard. They both wondered how many years most of them thought they had been married. Apparently, they were already so comfortable with each other no one doubted that it had not been at least their fiftieth anniversary.

"Let them think what they will." They said together.

Lou and Ellen spent the next day in the courthouse looking through archival records. They were looking up the name Marlow and anything to do with that family. They started looking in the early eighteen hundreds. Every book they picked up and every page in it showed the Marlow's did not own land. They spent the entire day looking in every old book they found having anything to do with families whose name started with a M. Unfortunately, they were unsuccessful. Ellen was about to think she was very confused. *I am sure daddy and Martha said this is the part of Ireland they came from*, she thought. However, they could find no records of a Marlow paying taxes of owning property.

They went back the next day and started all over again covering as many years as they could. The court clerk worked for a while with them but she too was unsuccessful.

On the third day, they spent the day walking around the city. Ellen thought, maybe she would see something that might jog her memory on something they might have said about places or things. Near the end of the day, they rounded a corner and there was a big church. It was a Catholic church. Ellen clearly remembered her father talk about going to church at a cathedral and she knew that her father had been a Catholic when he was growing up. "When the doors open to this church tomorrow morning we will be here," Lou said.

266

That night they had dinner brought to their room since they were tired from all the walking. The hotel restaurant sent their food up to their room on a little rolling table all dressed with a tablecloth, fine china, and crystal with silver pots. One long stemmed pink rose sat in the middle of the table in a pretty crystal bud vase. They looked at each other at the same time. "It's as if they knew, about the pink roses," Ellen said. "Yes, but I think that was just coincidence."

"However, it makes it even nicer," Lou said.

The next morning the Parkers got up early, had their showers, and went down to the hotel restaurant for breakfast. They had a light breakfast and were out the door in thirty-five minutes.

They walked from the hotel to the cathedral. They found the entrance door to the cathedral closed. However, it was not, locked. Lou slowly turned the large metal handle, opened the door and they walked in. It felt cold, damp inside, and a little spooky to Ellen. There were beautiful stained glass windows high on the walls but the walls seemed to be made of mortar and dirt. It was obvious that this building was very old.

Suddenly a woman dressed in habit appeared in the big room. Sister Sarah asked if she could help them. "Yes, I am Lou Parker and this is my wife Ellen. We are here from America. My wife and I are looking for any records we can find on my wife's family who emigrated from here to America some time in the middle to later part of the eighteenth century. We think this is the church where they were members."

"Exactly, what kind of records are you looking for Mr. Parker?" Sister Sarah asked.

"Any records that we can find on the Marlow family would be good. We went to the municipal building and apparently, the family never owned land. We could not find any records on them there," Lou said.

"Do you know they came to church here?" Sister Sarah asked. "I am almost positive that I heard my father talk about this church while he was still alive," Ellen said.

"Follow me," Sister Sarah said to Ellen and Lou. They followed her across the big room filled with pews and to a corner room. The room was small and dark. Sister Sarah put on a small light. "I hope you can see well enough in here. We do not allow bright lights since they may desecrate the historical vital records. Taking care of these records is of utmost importance. Please handle them with care and turn pages slowly and carefully. What did you say the family name is?" she asked.

"Marlow is the family name," Ellen said. "My dad's name was Reason Marlow. The nun turned swiftly and looked at Ellen.

"Marlow you said?" she asked.

"Yes Ma'm, my father was Reason and my mother was Louisa."

The nun gave Ellen a strange look and walked to the door without showing them where to begin looking. "If you need me I will be in my office across the sanctuary at the far end of the building. Ellen and Lou were so please that they had finally found some place to look for records on the family. They never noticed the nun's strange behavior.

Each of them being mindful of the fragility of the old records began thumbing through the rows and rows of thousands of folders. They were looking for the letter M. When they found that letter of folders then they would have a starting place. Some of the records were so old and faded it was difficult to read in the dark room. It took a long time to finally find the records started with the letter M. "Maaco, Maalo, Maasio, Lou called out the names as he started at the beginning of the rows of the names beginning with the letter M. Ellen had started at the end of the five rows of records whose names began with the letter M. It was as though they needed to study the name to make out each name. This was going to take time. When Ellen complained about the amount of time they would need to spend here at the church.

Lou said, "It does not matter how long it takes. If we do not get through all the names today we will come back tomorrow."

"Well I am going to think positive and think that we will find it today and soon," Ellen said. "That's my girl," Lou said.

It was lunchtime and Ellen and Lou were famished. "Let's go to the closest place and have a bite," Lou said.

"That sounds like a winner," Ellen said. They walked across the large sanctuary and to the office where the sister said she worked.

Her desk was against the wall and she faced the door. Sister Sarah was sitting at her desk and she appeared in deep thought. The door was open and she did not hear them as they approached her office. Lou gave a light tap on the doorframe. She appeared startled and looked up immediately. "May I help you?" she asked.

"I'm sorry, we didn't mean to startle you," Lou said. "We wanted to tell you that we are still looking for the Marlow records but we are going to take a break and get some food. Would you like us to bring you back something for lunch?"

"No, thank you, I usually fast throughout the day and have an early dinner. Did you say you are coming back?" she asked.

"Yes, Ma'm," Ellen said.

"I will be leaving here at four this afternoon and you will need to be out before I leave, and you will not be able to return tomorrow," Sister Sarah said. "That is bad news for us. Why cannot we return tomorrow if we do not find the record today? There are so many records and the lighting is so poor that it is taking much more time to look at the records than if we had good lighting."

Ellen challenged her. "I am sorry but I cannot do anything about the lighting," Sister Sarah said. You can go now," she added and stood up from her desk chair. She appeared annoyed. Ellen and Lou walked to the front entrance of the sanctuary, opened the door, and walked out into the fresh air.

"The sister appeared annoyed at us. Why do you suppose she was so abrupt with us?" Ellen asked Lou.

"I do not know, but it was evident that she is annoyed about something. However if couldn't have anything to do with us," Lou said.

They found a nice little pub where they could eat on the sidewalk. They ordered their food. "We're not going to hurry with our food even if we never find the records," Ellen said.

Lou did not say anything in return. He knew it took Ellen forever to eat her meal. Something as important as finding records on her family was not going to come in the way of her eating her food the way she always had. Ellen loved her food and she proved it each time she slowly chewed and swallowed each bite carefully.

Finally, they were finished with their lunch and hurriedly returned to the church. This time they found the entrance door locked. "Why do you suppose she locked it?" Ellen asked Lou.

"Because she didn't want us coming back inside, I suppose," Lou said. The locked door irritated Lou. She could have just told them not to come back. Why would she want to do a thing like this? Lou thought as he knocked harder and louder on the door. He knew the sister was still inside, since she had already told them that she never ate lunch and she would be there until four this afternoon. Lou's knocks became louder and louder. Ellen thought, a rat at the further end of this church could hear this knocking. Lou was determined. He was not going to give up.

Sister Sarah was in her office and on her knees praying. "Lord please forgive me for what I am about to do." She got to her feet and walked to the entrance door. Slowly she opened the door.

"Sister Sarah, we don't want to be a nuisance but you did tell us that we could come back this afternoon." Sister Sarah only looked at them and said, "Follow me to my office." Ellen and Lou walked behind Sister Sarah as she slowly walked to her office.

As they walked into Sister Sarah's office she pulled out a chair and motioned for them to sit in the two chairs sitting there. They sat down with blank thoughts running through their heads. What this could possibly be about befuddled both of them.

Sister Sarah looked at Ellen and said, "Your family records are in the archive room. Your family was faithful to come to church for many years but when the potato famine hit it affected almost every family in Ireland in a very bad way. Your family did not come to church after that except on rare occasions. However if you find those records they only tell about the parents when they first took communion with the church and then when each child was old enough to take communion. All the children did take communion when they were of age. Therefore, if you find that record it will not give you much information. However, there is a record on one member of your family in the Father's office. The Father is on vacation and will return tomorrow. I have the key to the sealed box that holds the record that I am referring. The record, is sealed because it is never to be seen by anyone ever again."

Then there was dead silence in the room. Sister Sarah only looked at them with a disturbed look on her face. The silence got louder and louder until Ellen thought she would explode. Lou suddenly dropped a pencil on the floor. "I am sorry; I didn't mean to do that," Lou said as he picked up the pencil. Ellen would never believe dropping the pencil was an accident. However one way or the other, it worked.

Sister Sarah said. "For me to let you observe this file is strictly forbidden and I will need to pray for forgiveness for the rest of my life. I know the Father would never approve of even telling you about the record but I feel that you have a right to know since you are a direct descendent. I am going to give you the record and you may look at it here in the church until three p.m. I will then take it from you, put it away, and pray no one ever discovers that the file has been disturbed." Sister Sarah walked out of the room and soon returned with a file folder in her hand.

As she handed the file to Ellen she said, "Please promise me that you will not disturb it in any way."

"I promise," Ellen said as she took the file from Sister Sarah. She felt as if she was going through an out of body experience. What was she going to find in these records? Did she really want to know?"

"You may go through the file right here in my office. I will occupy another until you are finished and remember you must be finished by three p.m." Lou looked at his wristwatch. Two o'clock--they had one hour to be finished with the file. Ellen opened the file up and laid it on the Sister's desk.

"Lou, you read it first and then tell me if I want to hear it or not." Lou sat down with the records on the desk in front of him. He was expecting many papers but the file only contained two pages. What could possibly be so important if it takes only two pages to tell it? Lou wondered. Ellen backed away and was standing near the wall. Lou read on while Ellen watched the expression on his face. Lou's expressions were showing surprise and another expression Ellen had never seen on his face before. "What, What does it say, Lou?" She could not stand it any longer.

"Baby, it appears that your father helped a friend to steal a forty-pound gold cross from this church. It says they sold the gold cross to some pirates. The gold cross-had great historical significance since it was place here four hundred years before they took it. Here is a short history of the man who placed the cross in the hidden place here in the church. It says that the boy had once been from royalty in Scotland with all the money that goes with royalty, but he, was kidnapped, by pirates, and sold in this country as a slave while, he was only a boy. Apparently, his owner came to this church and brought him along too, no doubt to prevent him from escaping. The boy seems to have fallen in love with the church and it's doctoring. It says he ran away from his kidnapper when he was older and returned to his homeland whose people were still idol worshipers. Lou began to read aloud. He went to school, got his education, got a good job, and earned much money. He still had money that his Royal family had left to him. However, something was never right again. He longed to return to Ireland where, he had been a slave to a wealthy planter. He missed the church and he wanted to return and spread the word of the heavenly God that he had learned existed. He did return to Ireland and spent the rest of his days spreading the word of the Lord. When he was old, he wanted to give something permanent to the church that would remain there forever. He had the beautiful heavy pure gold cross-made and he placed it in the floor construction of the father's side of the confessional booth. Since no one but the father is allowed to enter that side of the confession booth, he thought it would be safe there. Everyone in the church knew about the cross but no one knew where it he had hidden it, except the father of the church. The gold cross was never located. It says that your father took all the blame and he was the one caught during the commission of the crime. The church refused to file charges against the boy who had grown up in this church. But the Father did disband him from Catholicism for the crime. However, the police were unhappy about that there were no charges filed against the criminal and they deported him from Ireland for the remainder of his life. The papers said not much else.

"Look Lou, see if you can find the friend. Maybe if we could find him we could find out the rest of the story. There are no other names on these papers, only your father's name. Ben looked at his watched. It was three forty p.m. They had twenty minutes left. "Do you suppose we can go to the Archives and find the Mallory file? Maybe it will tell about a friend or give an address of something that may be helpful. The two of them sprinted to the Archives. They began a desperate attempt to locate the one file. Suddenly Ellen yelled, "I have it. I have found the Malory file." Lou ran to her. They opened up the file and this one had many pages to it. Their address listed at the top of the page would be of great help. They wrote the address down and scanned through the names of each member who has begun communion. They noticed that Reason Marlow's name had been, scratched out. Two other boys, about the same age as Reason took communion the first time Reason had taken it for the first time. Their names were not marked out. Lou jotted the names down—the names made it sound as though they could be twins. One was Timmy, one was Tommy, and their ages were the same. Now they would try to find the records of the twins since they may know something about the gold cross.

Still looking to find anything else that might be useful in the file, they heard footprints coming. "I'm sorry but it is three p.m. You must leave now."

Ellen ran to Sister Sarah, threw her arms around the sister's neck, and gave her a big hug. "Sister Sarah, I pray you never hear a thing about this day and you won't need to pray every day because you are already an angel. You will never know how much I appreciate what you have done for us. God bless you in a big way."

"God go with you." Sister Sarah said

Lou and Ellen left the church confused and ecstatic. *Why would her father want to steal anything? Especially, something as important, and valuable, as the gold cross? He was not the dad she had always known. She could never imagine him doing a thing like that. Was it supposed to be a boy's prank? Did he get angry at the church about something and was attempting to get revenge. That did not sound like her father either.*

It was too late to start looking for the address in their hand. "We will start again, early in the morning and see what we can find," Lou said.

They returned to the hotel and got dressed to go out to dinner. They chose a unique little bistro near the hotel. It was bright and well decorated inside. It felt good to sit in these surroundings after being in the dark drab conditions they had spent the day. Lou had his martini with the olive and Ellen had her horse pee with a fizzle just as they had before. Ellen pretended to enjoy her drink. She did not want to disappoint Lou by telling him what she thought it tasted like and she sure did not want to try another drink. If this one was supposed to taste "really good", she shuttered to think what the other drinks must taste like.

Ellen had a fitful sleep that night. She dreamed three men with guns were chasing her. They were in a covered wagon and she was on foot. They would almost catch her and she would wake up in a start. She would fall asleep again and the same dream would come again. Finally, at five a.m. she got out of bed and sat down in an upholstered chair in the hotel room. She thought about going to the mini kitchen in her suite and making herself a cup of coffee but she did not want to disturb Lou. He was sleeping soundly.

Ellen thumbed through a magazine on the table but that did not interest her. Her mind was wandering all over. *What was she going to find out about her father?* The words kept turning repeatedly in her head. *I have to get my mind off this,* Ellen thought to herself. *Whatever it is, dad survived it and so will I.* Ellen attempted to redirect her mind to other things. *When we get home, I am going to get a dog. I will not get a big dog, just a little lap dog. I wonder if Lou would agree with me. We have never discussed dogs before. I hope Jenifer got all the thank you notes sent. I wonder when this fancy old hotel was developed. It is all modern now but I bet it is at least a hundred years old. I cannot wrap my mind around the fact that I am in the country where my father grew up. If the church was willing to dismiss the crime it looks like the cops should not have been involved. There I go again, I was not going to think about that now.*

Finally, at seven a.m. Lou woke up. When he saw his wife sitting wide-awake in the chair, he was startled. "What is wrong darling? Are you sick?" he asked.

"No, I just could not sleep," Ellen said.

"How long have you been up?" Lou asked.

"I fell asleep when we went to bed and had a nightmare. It frightened me and I woke up but when I went back to sleep I continued dreaming the same scary dream. Finally, I gave up on sleep and got up. I have been up since around two o'clock this morning," Ellen told him.

"Oh my goodness, you are going to feel rough today. Are you sure you want to go out looking for addresses today?" Lou asked.

"I will feel fine today, and yes I do want to go looking for addresses today," Ellen said.

"There is no rush on what we are doing. We have no dead line to meet. If you need to stay here and rest today we can always do it tomorrow," Lou said. He knew if she did not sleep at all last night and her defenses were probably low. Lou did not want Ellen getting sick. He wanted her to stay healthy and happy for many years to come. He loved her and could not bear to see her sick. "Why do you suppose you kept having the bad dream?" Lou asked. "I don't know but I hope I never have it again." Ellen said. "Are you worried about something?" Lou asked. Ellen did not answer right away. It was as though she was thinking about the question he had asked. "Yes Lou, I am." "Why would you worry about something that happened so long ago?" Lou asked. "I guess I don't want to know about it, if my father was a bad and deceitful person. In our eyes, our dad was a hero and someone always to be, honored. It is like I don't want to ruin that, I guess." Ellen said. "Darling we don't know for sure your father did anything. You know she said "he and a friend". Maybe your dad had nothing to do with it but agreed to take the blame. We do not know what happened but, hopefully, by night we will. However, there is no need to worry over spilled milk. Let's wait until we know what happened and then you can decide if it is worth worrying over." Lou said. "You are right and I won't worry any more." Ellen said as she dabbed at a tear on her cheek.

They had the same light breakfast in the hotel restaurant that they had yesterday. Ellen especially enjoyed the coffee. She had thought about coffee since she got out of bed at five o'clock this morning.

They walked out into the bright sunshine. Lou pulled his sunglasses from his shirt pocket. We will need to drive today since Sister Sarah said it was about ten miles out." They slowly walked to the parked car they had rented.

It took a while to get out of the city and onto the road, which they thought was the right one. They did not see a street sign but Lou felt sure it was the right road. As they drove out of the city, Ellen saw a street sign. "This is it, Lou, this is the right road. I saw it on that sign on the right side of the road back there." Ellen said.

When they had driven about ten miles, Lou saw a big farmhouse ahead on the right side of the road. "I'll bet that is the house up there." Lou said as he pointed ahead.

Soon they were sitting in the front of the big white farmhouse with the big front porch. Lou and Ellen got out of the car and walked up the steps and onto the front porch. Lou knocked on the door. They heard footsteps inside and shortly the door opened. A large man stood at the opposite side of the screen door. He was wearing over alls. It is so much like it would be in the country at home. Ellen thought. "Can I help you mate?" The man asked. "Yes, we are looking for the family of Reason Marlow. I understand his family use to live in this house." Lou said. "I am Reason Marlow's great nephew and the Marlow family still lives here." The large, tall man said. "I am Ellen Marlow Parker and this is my husband, Lou." Ellen said as she motioned with her hand toward Lou. I am the daughter of Reason Marlow. We are here from America. I wanted to try and find some family of my father's while we are here."

Gerald told Ellen and Lou to have a chair in what appeared to be the living room. It was clean and neat but the furniture told the tale of time. It was nice furniture but well worn. The rug on the floor told the same. "Your grandfather, grandmother and all their children are no longer alive. They have been gone for many years. Only their descendents like me are left." They talked about Gerald's family and then came back to Reason Marlow. "Did you ever hear anything about why my father left Ireland and went to

America, Gerald?" Ellen asked. Gerald looked a little rattled. It was easy to see, this subject made, at least, this family member uncomfortable.

"I don't really know. That is something the rest of the family would not discuss. All I know is that he got into trouble and had to leave the country," Gerald said. "Do you know who his friends were at the time this happened?" Ellen said. "Yes, I know that he was good friends of Tommy and Timmy. Timmy was killed by a kicking horse and he died," Gerald said. "What was Tommy's and Timmy's last name, Gerald?" "I can't remember what their last names were. All I ever knew was Timmy and Tommy and every one use to talk about Timmy getting killed by a kicking horse."

"Do you know anyplace we could go where someone may know them?" Ellen asked.

"Tommy and Timmy's family use to live about three more miles down the road. When the potato famine hit the owner of the land and the house they occupied burned the house down. Times were bad back then and people were starving. The English noblemen made a law banning any landowner from allowing the down trodden from starving to death on their land. Since the land owners were also in bad shape because they no longer had an income either, they attempted to put the families out. However, the families had no place to go, and they refused to leave so the landowner burned down the house to get them off his land."

"Timmy and Tommy's family moved in with Reason and his family. Soon after that, the three teen-age boys, Timmy, Tommy, and Reason, left home and went to town to find work. I do not know what happened after that except after moving to town is when the horse killed Timmy".

"We need some kind of hint, as to where we could start looking, but they could be anyplace in Ireland." Ellen said. "Someone has built the house back three miles down the road. You could go there and see if they know anything about them," Gerald said. "That is an excellent idea," Lou said.

Ellen and Lou thanked Gerald for all his help and left to find the house three miles down the road.

As they drove up to the house, they could tell it was a newer house but not nearly as large as the big older farm houses in the area. Lou walked up the steps and knocked on the front door. An older woman, wearing an apron, came to the door. Lou told her who he was and why he was there. "You have found the right house." The woman said. "Does Tommy live here?" Lou asked. "He doesn't live here, but I am Tommy's sister, and I can tell you where he lives." She gave Lou directions to Tommy's house. He lived two towns away.

When Lou told Ellen about his find, she was elated. Lou cranked the car and they started on the one hundred and four miles trip to Belfast Ireland where Tommy lived. "I think the thing that surprises me the most is that Tommy is still living. He must be very old." Ellen said. "You are right. If your father was still living, how old would he be now?" Lou asked. "Well, let's see. Pa was born in 1851 and it is now 1940 so that would make him ninety-one years old.

The two hour, ten minute drives seemed more like four hours and twenty minutes. They were both so anxious to get there.

They finally made it. Now finding the right address would not be as easy as coming from city to city had been. Lou stopped at a filling station and bought a city map. He sat in the car with the map unfolded on the steering wheel. Lou soon found the right road. It was not inside the city but about four miles out of the city.

Lou and Ellen drove the four miles out to locate the house. They stopped at a house. They were not sure but they thought this one might be the house where Tommy lived. They were wrong; however, the homeowner gave them the exact directions to Tommy's house.

When they drove up to the house, Ellen felt frozen. She was not sure she wanted to talk to Tommy. "Come on Darling, you have come this far, you might as well get answers that will always haunt you if you don't." Slowly Ellen got out of the car while Lou held the door open for her. Together, they walked up to the house. It was a nice house and very large. It was not an elaborate house but it was nice enough. Lou rang the doorbell. No one answered the door. He rang the doorbell again. Still no one came to the door. Ellen would never let Lou know but she was feeling relieved.

Just as they were walking away from the door, the door opened. It was an old man with a full head of white hair, who looked well kept and seemed to move about freely. "Can I help you?" He asked as they turned back to the door. "We are looking for Tommy Mallory," Lou said. "You have found him, that's me. I am Tom Mallory. What can I do for you?" "Did you once know a man named Reason Marlow?" Tom opened the screen door.

"Yes, I know Reason Marlow. He is the dearest friend I have ever had. Why do you want to know?" Tom asked. "My name is Lou Parker and this is my wife, Ellen Marlow Parker." Tom looked at Ellen. His eyes enlarged as he glared at her. "Oh my God, you must be Reason's daughter. You look so much like him." Tom said. "Yes sir, I am Reason Marlow's daughter." Tom grabbed her hand and gave it a good shake, and then he gathered her in his arms and hugged her. Tom seemed, totally overjoyed. He shook, Lou's hand, and then asked them, to come inside the house. "Have a seat and let me get you some tea." Before they could answer, Tom had left the room.

He returned with three cups of hot tea on a tray. He offered Lou and Ellen a cup. They took a cup of the tea and thanked him. He took the last cup and set the tray on a table in the center of the room. He pulled a chair from across the room and sat down near Lou and Ellen. "Please tell me about my dear friend and your dad?" Tom said. "Dad is no longer with us; he died about twenty years ago." Ellen said. Tom's chin started to tremble. Tears rolled down his face. "What happened? Why did he die so young?" Tom asked.

"He got pneumonia and never got over it. Lots of people died that year of pneumonia," Ellen said.

With his chin, still trembling Tom said, "He was the best man who ever lived."

"Why do you say that, Tom?" Ellen asked.

"Ellen, let me tell you about your father." "Reason was a year older than me and Timmy. Timmy was my twin brother. We lived near each other while were growing up and we were together all the time. The potato famine hit and everyone fell on hard times. The three of us were just teenagers but we decided it was time for us to leave home and fin for ourselves so that our parents would have fewer mouths to feed. We went to the city and found jobs. The jobs did not pay much but it fed us. Timmy and I got married to two girls who were sisters. We lived in little shacks and barely got by. Reason was a little smarter than we were. He waited another year before he got married but his job did not pay much either so all of us were struggling. Timmy and his wife had five children. They were like doorsteps. They had one baby, right behind the other, until there were five. I had three children and Reason and your mother had two but they were ten years apart. All of us were struggling but Reason and your mom were in better shape than Timmy and me. While your dad was out on the fishing boat, owned by his boss, a horse kicked Timmy in the head and he died.

When your dad came in from the fishing trip, we were all walking around like the 'walking dead'. I did not know what to do. I was grieving for my dead brother and I knew we were in real trouble. Timmy and his wife was living day to day on what little they could scrape up to feed all the children and my wife and I weren't doing much better. Now it was only me left to feed both families. People in Ireland still had not gotten over the potato famine and some were still dying on the streets. I could see that for my brother's family."

"When your dad discovered what had happened he jumped right in to help me. Not with emotional support, which he did that too, but with a solution for Timmy's family also. He held down his full time job and worked on a solution to our hardship just as if it was his own. In the mean time, I had to take on a second job so I was working day and night just to feed all of us. My wife and I moved Timmy's wife and family into our little shanty that was already crowded. After they moved in, it was like sleeping in layers with eight children and three adults in our little shanty. I did not have any time left, after working the two jobs, to think about a solution to the problem, let along getting out and working on a solution for our situation. However, your dad did. He worked every day toward a solution to my dilemma. With me, so stressed out and not having enough food to eat I lost twenty-seven pounds in three months. Reason was afraid I was going to die."

"He came up with the idea of moving my family to a big farm house in the country where I could farm with help from all the children and I would be able to raise the children, have plenty of food, and not need to work twenty hours a day the way I was doing then. The only problem was there was no money to buy a farm. He tried for two weeks to find someone who would loan us the money but everyone turned us down."

"Finally in desperation Reason came up with an idea. He knew there was a gold cross buried in the church we went to when we were growing up. He discussed how we could steal the cross and sell it to pirates. It would bring enough money to pay cash for a farm and have enough money left over to live until I started turning out produce for sale."

"No one knew your father better than I knew him. He would never take a thing that did not belong to him. He had a heart so big that he would take away from himself to give to someone who he thought needed it worse. He loved God and believed in the Bible. He hated sin and never condoned it. However, he was so desperate for me and my family that he suggested stealing the gold cross from the church so that I could buy the farm. I knew he was right when he said, "Tommy if we don't do it, you are surely going to die and probably your family and Timmy's family too.""

"Well, we did steal the cross. I climbed through the window and dug it up from the floor of the church. I handed it out the window to Reason. After we had gotten the cross to the pirates and received the money. I remembered I could not cover the hole up properly since I needed more dirt and rocks to do it. It was so late and I was suppose to be at work an hour before then, Reason decided he would go back early the next morning and put more dirt and rocks in the hole. I tried to get him to go back then and do it but he said he would go to work early and carry a bucket with dirt and rocks with him."

"While he was stomping down the dirt on the floor of the church early the next morning, the Priest walked in on him. He told the Father that he was doing it for someone else but he would never tell him who. Since he was, doing it for someone else, who was not even a relative of his, the Priest dropped it and refused to file charges. Nevertheless, the police were, called, and they refused to allow Reason to get by with it without any punishment. They expelled him from Ireland for the rest of his life. He had one night to get this business in order since he would never return to Ireland."

Again, Tommy's chin began to tremble. "I loved your father more than anyone will ever know.

"I took the money and came here as far away from Dublin as I could go. I bought a farm, not the one Reason had picked out for me. I wanted to get as far away from the memories as I could. I raised my children and Timmy's children right here on the farm and sent all of them to school. Now they are doctors, accountants, lawyers and other professionals. They are all smart children and used their heads well. However, I paid a big price for it. I missed my friend everyday and I still miss him. I was disgraced in Belfast since one of the policemen let the news out about what had happened. I have carried the guilt of allowing my best friend to carry all the blame for it all of my life. I have worked hard all my life but I never enjoyed living it."

"Mr. Tom, may I tell you that you did not need to worry about my dad. He had a very good life. He never had much money but he was a happy man. He was totally at peace with himself. I believe he trusted that God had forgiven him and understood that he had done what he did for very good reasons. Do you know what? If I had been in my dad's shoes, I would have done the same as he. I am so proud of him. You are right. He was a good and noble man. I do not think I have ever loved him more than I do at this very minute. Please do not hold yourself responsible. My father had a good and blessed life and he was as happy as any man could be. Ellen said to Tom, "Reason had a good life?"

"Yes, Mr. Tom. My father had a very good and fulfilling life. He loved my mother and they were very close. The night that my father died, my sister and I observed him praying at his bedside. He said, "Lord, please--forgive me for what I did. I am sorry but I had to help my friend. Let me join my precious Louisa in Heaven, I pray. He climbed into bed and went to sleep. He never woke up. My sister and I wondered what he was talking about but we never had a chance to ask him. Now I know, and I am sure my sister knows too since she is there with Ma and Pa."

Ellen could see as Tom held his shoulders up. He gave a sign of relief as if he had been waiting over seventy years to hear what she had just told him.

When it was time for Ellen and Lou to leave, Tom walked them to the door. He hugged Ellen again. He kept telling her, how happy he was that she came to see him. Ellen knew he was sincere. His face appeared as if a heavy weight had lifted from his shoulders.

Since it was so late in the day when Ellen and Lou left Tom's house, they decided to get a room in Doblin for the night and drive back to Bellfast in the morning. They found a unique old bed and breakfast on a cobble stone street and decided it would be the perfect place to stay.

After they checked into the Bed and Breakfast, they went back to the car and pretended to get their clothes. Of course, they had no clothes. They were all back at the hotel suite in Belfast. They felt like teen-agers trying to sneak by the little old woman with sweaters rolled up and tucked under their arms, appearing as bags. They knew she could not see very well and she would never know they really had no clothes.

After they had rested, a while in the beautiful old room that she had assigned to them, they went out to find a restaurant for dinner. They found the perfect authentic Irish pub. Lou and Ellen ordered from the menu. It was for sure, because both of their meals had potatoes on the plate. "Lou, they sure aren't having a potato famine here any longer. Every meal on this menu has a potato dish of some kind on it." Lou laughed and agreed with her.

The food was very good but Ellen refused to try their Irish beer. She was glad that they did not serve champagne.

While they ate their dinner, they discussed the day's events. "Lou today has been one of the most important days in my life. I am so happy that we came to Ireland. I feel like I know my dad better now than I ever did."

"He was a man of conviction and stature, that is for sure," Lou said. "It is a shame that he and Tommy didn't stay in touch. Tommy worried all these years, about something that your dad never looked back on, with regret," Lou said.

"You are right." Ellen said.

Tonight they would have to sleep in the buff. Ellen was not happy about that but it did not bother Lou too much.

The next morning, Ellen said, "We are finished here. I really like Ireland but I think we need to leave tomorrow and fly to London for that week of rest that we had planned.

"You are right. We will leave tomorrow but we have one more thing to do before we leave," Lou said.

"What do we still need to do?" Ellen asked.

"I will tell you in the morning."

"Why do I have to wait till morning to hear about it?"

"Let's just say, it will be a surprise," Lou said.

It felt good to be back with their belongings. Ellen would have a gown to sleep in tonight. Ellen hated to admit it but she was really, tired. She knew that Lou was just as tired as she was. However, he would never complain.

While they were having breakfast in the hotel, restaurant Ellen said. "We're going to miss this restaurant. No other restaurant can make breakfast as good as it is here."

"London has really good food, but you are right about this place for breakfast."

This morning as they walked out of the hotel, a gust of wind blew past them so hard that Ellen almost lost her footing. Lou grabbed for her and held her tight until they reached the car. He was always a gentleman. He never allowed Ellen to open a door. That was his job and he loved it.

Lou drove away from the hotel and into town. He drove into a bank parking lot and stopped the car. Lou asked Ellen to wait in the car. Soon he returned to the car and they drove away only to stop at another bank one block away. He stopped again, and again, asked Ellen to wait in the car. Ellen was completely confused. What, on earth was he doing? They had bought thousands and thousands of dollars worth of traveler's checks before they left home. She was sure they had brought enough money to make the entire vacation and still have plenty of money left over. She knew they had been careful about their spending. Why could he possibly need two banks?

When he returned to the car, he was holding a large white envelope. Lou handed the envelope to Ellen. Ellen looked inside, and there was a thousand dollar bill then another and another and another until she could not count it any longer. "Lou, what on earth are you going to do with all this money?"

"Ellen we are going back to the church."

"So what are you going to do with the money?"

"We are going to find Sister Sarah and we are going to give this money to her. I do not know what the price of gold is right now and I don't have time to find the answer but we are going to pay for that cross. We will leave it up to Sister Sarah to tell where the money came from. She can say a stranger gave a donation or she can tell them that the daughter of the young man who took the cross gave it to the church. Anything she wants to tell them is all right. We just want to right a wrong that happened a long time ago. We know why the wrong happened and it took an admirable man to do what he did. If anyone of us had been in Reason's place, we would have done the same thing. As hard as it probably was for him to do what he did, it seemed to him that the buried cross was not worth the wasting of so many lives. I know I would have done the same thing."

Ellen had never loved Lou so much than in this moment. She was so happy that God had sent her a man who was so much like her own father.

When they reached the church Lou got out of the car, opened the door for Ellen and they walked up to the church together. The entrance door closed, but not locked. Lou eased the door open and in a low voice said, "Sister Sarah?" As they were walking to her office, Sister Sarah rounded the corner coming toward them. Lou and Ellen stopped and waited for her to come to them. They did not want to discuss the money where someone may overhear. Sister Sarah reached out her hand to shake hands with her.

"Did you find the information you were looking for?" she asked them. "Yes Ma'm, we did find what we were looking for and it brought us happiness, sadness, joy and admiration. You will never know how very much we appreciate your help. We can never thank you enough," Ellen told Sister Sarah. Lou stepped up and handed the envelope to Sister Sarah.

"This is a little something that we would like to donate to the church for your help and the loss of the cross."

Sister Sarah said, "I will tell the Father it is donated money. Thank you. The church always needs money. It will help us to do many good things.

Ellen hugged Sister Sarah, and Lou shook her hand again and they left. As they walked away Sister Sarah said, "God go with you my children."

Ellen and Lou really loved Sister Sarah. They secretly hoped she would keep some of the money, but Ellen knew she would not.

The Father was out of town on a business trip today. Sister Sarah went into her office and locked the door. She took the money out of the envelope and started counting it. After she was finally finished counting she could not believe the amount. She counted it again. Lou and Ellen had donated one million dollars to the church. She grabbed the money and ran to the entrance door. She needed to stop them. She could not keep all this money. How would she ever explain it?

"God give me the answer", she said as she realized Lou and Ellen were long gone. Almost as if, her guardieing angle whispered in her ear. "It's all in American money. Just tell them it was a wealthy American who dropped by and donated it."

Yes, that would do. That is what she would say. Sister Sarah skipped all the way back to her office. "Hey, I've still got a spring in my step," she said.

What Happened to
Eliza's Children?

Life went on for the family after Ma died. They had to go on. They had families of their own depending on them. It was hard but they knew, it was the way, Ma would want it.

Ed, Nancy, and Mittie (later called Sis), and Bill Edwards had their children, raised them and lived out their lives in Berrien and Cook County Georgia.

Eliza's daughter Ellen, whom Ma had named after her sister, had twin girls. Before they were grown, her husband died. She remarried after the girls were grown. She had a massive stroke in her sixties and died three days after the stroke. She was one of the only daughters who worked a factory job. She finished raising her daughters on her own.

Mae was third to the youngest and she would be next to go. She and Charlie had kept their home together and had raised Mae's two sons and were raising their own six children. Mae got pregnant again and had a perfect pregnancy. When she went into labor, Charlie carried her to the hospital in Moultrie for her delivery. Soon after she was, admitted to the hospital, she began having extremely high blood pressure. The doctor diagnosed her problem as Toxemia and soon it advanced to Eclampsia. Mae went into a coma and never came out of it. She and the baby died while her six little children stood at her bedside over the next several days. They watched as their mother slowly slipped away. She remained in the deep coma until her death. Their mother's dying was a trauma that they would need a long time to overcome. Their grieving dad continued to raise his children however it was a long difficult road—but he made it just the same.

Laura managed to raise her three boys alone. When she was young, she developed a goiter in her anterior neck. She looked perfectly normal to all the grandchildren of Ma, with the large baseball sized ball handing from her neck, since they had never seen her without the goiter. In the twenty's the US doctors realized that American citizens were getting these goiters at an alarming rate. They did research and discovered US soil was extremely low in the nutrient Iodine. They realized this was the cause for the goiters. Several pediatricians gathered to discuss a solution to this problem. They decided that if the salt companies placed the Iodine in their salt and since all citizens used salt on their food, they would get the Iodine they needed. This plan worked and now although the problem of hypothyroidism, in Americans, has decreased greatly, America still has her fair share of the Iodine deficiency problems resulting in hypothyroidism.

Laura had her goiter removed when she was in her sixties. She was still the same good, caring and God loving, person that she had always been but to her nieces and nephews she did not look like herself anymore. To her sons nothing about her had changed. Laura could, have been called the world's best mother. She loved her boys with the whole of her life. She loved her grandchildren as well and they all returned that love to her. In her older days, she lived out her life with one of her three sons. She died quietly one night in her sleep. Her sons knew she was in the arms of their dad, her dear husband John again. However, life without their mother would never be the same again.

Russell would be the next to go home to the waiting family already there. He died in 1968 from a sudden heart attack. Russell had never been sick and did not believe in sickness. He was always a "get at it and get it done" person. When he lost Horace many years before, he never got over it but it made him even more determined to succeed. When he died, he left a very successful farm with hundreds of acres of land and a beautiful home where he and Maude had raised their children. At Russell's funeral, Eliza's grandchildren decided to start having a reunion for all of Ma's living children. The grandkids worked hard and had the first reunion that year. Maude would join her husband many years later and she stayed a very active member of the family almost to the end.

After forty years, it is still a full three-day affair at a 4-H club camp serving as the meeting place. A full slate of officers, selected each year will plan the reunion for the next year. There is a planned program on Saturday night and hired cooks prepare all the food. Most of Ma's children were able to enjoy their reunion for many years before any other siblings died. Only Laura, Mae, Ellen and Russell missed it since they had died before the reunions started.

Orval was next to go to his heavenly home. He developed cancer of the bone. The doctors removed his leg but the cancer returned. He gave a brave fight but in the end, he was ready to join the family also. He was ready to be with his love, Ella Mae who was waiting there for him.

Luke and Ethel had six children and Ethel was pregnant with the seventh. It had not been an easy pregnancy. Ethel's feet swelled and she did not feel well. Luke carried her to the doctor. He gave her vitamins and sent her home. Ethel made it to full term with her baby but soon after she went into labor, she started having seizures and then she died.

Luke never got over the loss of his wife and baby. He vowed to raise his children alone and he did. He never remarried. When he was in his seventies, he died of a sudden heart attack. He too would join the family in heaven and be with his loving wife Ethel and Ma again.

Rittie stayed feisty all her life. She lived to an old age and still wore her pierced earrings and other jewelry. She never gained weight like most of her sisters. She and Clint raised their daughters. Some of their raising was on the road while their parents lived full time in a recreational vehicle (RV). All the other cousins envied them but their daughters did not like the life style very much. Clint and Rittie died only months apart. They finished out their lives in their loved RV while it stayed parked in their daughter's yard. Everyday Clint went out to get the daily newspaper from the front yard. Rittie got her snuffbox, spit can and settled in her favorite chair in their newly built den. She sat with Clint while he read the paper and she dipped her snuff.

General had also had a very successful life. He also died of a heart attack at an old age. He kept his barbershop until close to his death. He still managed his farm up to his death. He had lost his oldest son long before his own death. Remer was a young man with three small daughters when he suddenly succumbed to a fatal heart attack. He was the first grandchild to die at an early age of a heart problem that would also affect many other cousins before they grew old. Some of them survived it and some of them did not. General and Iella had lost another young son. He was probably the most successful grandchild that Ma had. He was a very loving and caring person. He and his wife Sue had been married many years and remained childless. They each wanted a child. Finally, they found that they would finally be parents. They were over the moon with excitement. However when the baby was only six months old Albert found that he had a fatal spinal cancer. He fought with all his heart but in the end, the cancer took his life. His death was a devastating blow to the whole family since he was such a major part of the family and the reunion.

Mary Jane would be the next to go. She raised her five children on her own. Her last child was grown up, and left home for the Air Force. Six months later Mary Jane found a little white firm spot on the side of her tongue. She would not mention it for three more months. Finally, she told her daughter about the little spot. Her daughter carried her to the doctor and that was the beginning of her nine-year battle with cancer. She lost her entire tongue and all her left jawbone. She never lost her will to live or her faith. Her doctor, who was also a medical professor for the Medical College of Georgia had grown very close to her over those nine years. He sliced tiny slivers from her removed tongue and kept researching drugs that might kill the cancer cells until he had no tongue tissue left. He was never able to discover a drug that would destroy the cancer that Mary Jane had. Doctor Zeigler told Mary Jane's children that her whole purpose for life was getting her five children raised. He said when the youngest one was inducted into the military, leaving her with no children to raise, she lost her purpose for living. He said she was, totally focused on raising the five children that she loved.

Eppse would follow Mary Jane only a few years later. He lived out his life with Ma. After her death, he wandered around Berlin as if he were lost. His younger brother Noah kept an eye on him. He never married. He died in the house that he and Ma had shared for so many years in Berlin, Georgia.

Mattie Lee was the last born and next to the last of Ma's children to expire. She had had the five children and raised four of them after Eileen's fatal accident before she was a year old. Mattie Lee and Lancy had two boys then waited almost fourteen years and had two more boys. She would also die of cancer. She had been the joy of the family and loved having all the family together. Mattie and Lancy would live out the last days of their lives sharing the same nursing home room. Lancy would follow her in death soon after her death.

Last, to go was Noah. He had given up the grocery store when he got older and drove the school bus for the Colquitt County school system. He grew close to his students and enjoyed driving the school bus. He was the only one of Ma's children who lived long enough to suffer with Alzheimer's disease. He spent the last few years of his life in a nursing home. Austell and the children saw that he had anything that he needed or wanted. As long as he was able, they carried him on outings. He enjoyed that. Austell lived many years after Noah expired and remained healthy up until about six months before she died. She was truly made of good stuff.

They spent days and days talking, laughing, and catching up on everything that had happened back on earth as well as in heaven. They enjoyed watching their living children down on earth going about their daily life. They knew they could put little thoughts in their children's heads during decision-making and lead them to the right choice. The family really enjoyed that. The children felt their presence and knew they were nudging them to continue making wise choices as they raised their own families.